AND COUNT

or h

The
Life List

Lori Nelson Spielman, a former speech pathologist and guidance counsellor, currently works as a homebound teacher for inner-city students. She enjoys sailing, running, and reading, though writing is her passion. She lives in Michigan with her husband and a very spoiled cat.

The
Life List

Lori Nelson Spielman

arrow books

Published by Arrow Books 2013

10

Copyright © Lori Nelson Spielman, 2013

Lori Nelson Spielman has asserted her right under the Copyright, Designs and Patents Act 1988 to be identified as the author of this work.

First published in Great Britain in 2013 by
Arrow Books
Random House, 20 Vauxhall Bridge Road,
London SW1V 2SA

www.randomhouse.co.uk

Addresses for companies within The Random House Group Limited can be found at:
www.randomhouse.co.uk/offices.htm

The Random House Group Limited Reg. No. 954009

A CIP catalogue record for this book
is available from the British Library

ISBN 9780099580157

The Random House Group Limited supports the Forest Stewardship Council® (FSC®), the leading international forest-certification organisation. Our books carrying the FSC label are printed on FSC®-certified paper. FSC is the only forest-certification scheme supported by the leading environmental organisations, including Greenpeace. Our paper procurement policy can be found at www.randomhouse.co.uk/environment

Book design by Karin Batten

Printed and bound by CPI Group (UK) Ltd, Croydon, CR0 4YY

For my parents, Frank and Joan Nelson

Who looks outside, dreams; who looks inside, awakes.

—CARL JUNG

The
Life List

CHAPTER ONE

Voices from the dining room echo up the walnut staircase, indistinct, buzzing, intrusive. With trembling hands I lock the door behind me. My world goes silent. I lean my head against the door and take a deep breath. The room still smells of her — Eau d'Hadrien perfume and goat's-milk soap. Her iron bed creaks when I crawl over it, a sound as reassuring as the tinkle of her garden chimes, or her silky voice when she'd tell me she loved me. I came to this bed when she shared it with my father, complaining of an ache in my belly or monsters under my bed. Each time Mom took me in, holding me close and stroking my hair, whispering, "There will be another sky, my love, just you wait." And then, as if by miracle, I'd wake the next morning to find ribbons of amber streaming through my lace curtains.

I kick off my new black pumps and rub my feet in relief. Scooting backward, I settle against the yellow paisley pillows. I'm going to keep this bed, I decide. No matter who else wants it, it's mine. But I'll miss this classy old brownstone. "She's as sturdy as Grandmama," Mom would say about her home. But to me, no house, no person, was ever as steady as Grandmama's daughter — my mother — Elizabeth Bohlinger.

Suddenly I have a thought. Blinking back tears, I bound from the bed. She hid it up here, I know she did. But where? I throw open her closet door. My hands grope blindly behind designer suits and dresses. I yank at a rack of silk blouses, and they part like theater curtains. There it is, nestled in her shoe rack like an infant in its crib. One bottle of Krug, sequestered to her closet for the past four months.

Once it's in my clutches, guilt infests me. This champagne belongs to Mom, not me. She splurged on the outrageous bottle on our way home from her first doctor's appointment, and promptly tucked it away so it wouldn't be confused with the regular bottles downstairs. It was a symbol of promise, she rationalized. At the end of her treatments, when she was given a clean bill of health, she and I would open the rare champagne as a celebration of life and miracles.

I finger the silver foil and bite my lip. I can't drink this. It was meant for a celebratory toast, not for a grieving daughter too weak to make it through a funeral luncheon.

Something else catches my eye, wedged between the spot where I found the champagne and a pair of suede loafers. I reach for it. It's a slim red book — a journal, I suspect — secured with a faded yellow ribbon. The leather cover is cracked and weathered. *To Brett,* she has written on a heart-shaped gift tag. *Save this for a day when you are feeling stronger. Today, raise a glass to us, my dear. What a duo we were. Love, Mom.*

I trace my finger over the handwriting, never as neat as one would expect from someone so beautiful. My throat aches. Despite her assurance of a happy ending, my mom knew the day would come when I would need rescuing. She's left me her champagne for today, and a sliver of her life, her inner thoughts and musings, for tomorrow.

But I can't wait until tomorrow. I stare down at the journal, desperate to read her words right now. Just one quick peek, that's all. When I tug the yellow ribbon, though, an image of my mom takes shape. She's shaking her head, gently chastising my impatience. I glance at her note, telling me to wait until I'm stronger, and I'm torn between my wishes and hers. Finally, I set the journal aside. "For you," I whisper, and tap the cover with a kiss, "I'll wait."

A moan rises from my chest, cracking the silence. I slap a hand over my mouth to catch it, but it's too late. I double over, clutching my ribs, and literally ache for my mother. How will I ever manage to stumble through this world without her? I have so much more daughter left in me.

I grab the champagne. Holding the bottle between my knees, I pop the cork. It shoots across the room, knocking over a bottle of Kytril from my mom's bedside table. Her antinauseants! I scramble to the bedside and gather the triangular tablets in my fists, remembering the first time I offered one to Mom. She'd just had her first chemo treatment and was full of false bravado for my sake. "I feel fine, really. I've had menstrual cramps that have given me more grief."

But that night, nausea hit her like a tsunami. She swallowed the white tablet, and later asked for another. I lay with her while the drug mercifully took effect and allowed sleep to come. I snuggled next to her, in this very bed, and stroked her hair and held her close, just as she'd done for me so many times. And then, raw with desperation, I closed my eyes and begged God to heal my mother.

He didn't listen.

The pills stream from my palm into the plastic prescription bottle. Leaving the lid loose, I position the bottle on the table's edge, close to her bed, so she can easily reach them. But no . . . my mom's gone. She will never take another pill.

I need the champagne. "Here's to you, Mom," I whisper, my voice cracking. "I was so proud to be your daughter. You knew that, right?"

In no time the room is spinning, but my pain is mercifully eased. I lower the champagne bottle to the floor and pull back the down comforter. The cool sheets smell faintly of lavender. It feels decadent to lie here, away from the crowd of strangers one floor below. I burrow deeper under the covers, indulging myself in just one more moment of silence before returning downstairs. Just one more minute . . .

A loud knock startles me from my stupor. I sit up. It takes a second before I realize where I am . . . shit, the luncheon! I bolt from the bed, stumbling over the champagne bottle as I lurch for the door.

"Ouch! Oh, damn!"

"You okay, Brett?" my sister-in-law Catherine asks from the open doorway. Before I can answer, she gasps and rushes into the room. She squats before the damp rug and lifts the bottle. "My God! You spilled a bottle of Clos du Mesnil 1995?"

"I drank a good bit of it first." I plop down beside her and dab the Oriental rug with the hem of my dress.

"Jesus, Brett. This bottle cost over seven hundred dollars."

"Uh-huh." I drag myself to my feet and squint at my watch, but the numbers are all blurry. "What time is it?"

She smooths down her black linen dress. "It's almost two. Lunch is being served." She tucks a stray curl behind my ear. Even though I tower over her by a good five inches, she still manages to make me feel like I'm her unkempt toddler. I half expect her to lick her fingers and pat down my cowlick. "You look downright gaunt, Brett," she says, repositioning my pearl necklace. "Your mother would be the first to say that despite your grief, you must take care of yourself."

But that's not true. My mom would tell me I look pretty, even though my makeup has been cried off. She'd insist that the humidity has enhanced my long auburn waves, not created a frizzy rat's nest, and that my puffy, red-rimmed eyes are still the soulful brown eyes of a poet.

I feel tears threaten and I turn away. Who's going to boost my confidence now that my mom's gone? I bend down to grab the empty bottle, but the floor wobbles and lurches. Oh, God! I'm on a sailboat in the middle of a cyclone. I grab hold of the bed frame like it's my lifeline and wait for the storm to pass.

Catherine cocks her head and studies me, tapping her bottom lip with her perfectly manicured nail. "Listen, sweetie, why don't you stay put. I'll bring you up a plate."

Stay put my ass! It's my mother's luncheon. I need to get downstairs. But the room is fuzzy and I can't find my shoes. I turn in circles. What was it I was looking for? I stagger to the door barefoot, and then I remember. "Okay, shoes. Come out come out wherever you are." I squat down and peer under the bed.

Catherine grabs me by the arm and pulls me up. "Brett, stop. You're drunk. I'll tuck you into bed and you can sleep it off."

"No!" I shake off her hold on me. "I can't miss this."

"But you can. Your mother wouldn't want you —"

"Ahh, there they are." I grab my new black heels and work to plant my feet into them. Jesus, my feet have grown two sizes in the last hour.

I barrel down the hallway as best I can, my feet half in, half out of my pumps. With both hands outstretched to steady me, I stagger from one wall to the other, like a pinball. Behind me, I hear Catherine. Her voice is stern but she's keeping it low, as if she's speaking through clenched teeth. "Brett! Stop right now!"

She's nuts if she thinks I'm going to skip the funeral luncheon. I have to honor my mother. My beautiful, loving mother . . .

I'm at the staircase now, still trying to push my swollen feet into these Barbie doll pumps. I'm halfway down the staircase when my ankle twists.

"Eeow!"

At once a sea of guests, all who've come to pay tribute to my mother, turn to watch me. I catch glimpses of horrified women raising their hands to their mouths, and men gasping as they rush to catch me.

I land in a heap in the foyer, my black dress hiked to midthigh, minus one shoe.

The sound of clattering dishes wakes me. I wipe the drool from the side of my mouth and sit up. My throbbing head feels thick and murky. I blink several times and look around. I'm at my mom's house. Good. She'll have an aspirin for me. I notice the living room is cast in shadows, and workers mill about, stacking plates and glasses into brown plastic bins. What's going on? It hits me like the crack of a baseball bat. My throat seizes up and I cover my mouth. All the pain, every scrap of anguish and sadness crashes in anew.

I've been told that a long battle with cancer is worse than a short one, but I'm not convinced that this holds true for the survivors. My mother's diagnosis and death came so quickly it seems almost surreal, like a nightmare I'll wake from with a cry of relief. Instead, too often I wake having forgotten the tragedy, and I'm forced to relive the loss over and over, like Bill Murray in *Groundhog Day*. Will it ever feel okay, not having that one person in my life who loves me unconditionally? Will I ever be able to think of my mother without my chest cramping?

As I rub my aching temples, short snippets of fuzzy snapshots come rushing in, re-creating my humiliating fiasco on the stairs. I want to die.

"Hey, sleepy girl." Shelley, my other sister-in-law, walks over to me carrying three-month-old Emma in her arms.

"Oh, God!" I moan and hang my head in my hands. "I am such an idiot."

"Why? You think you're the only person who's ever gotten tipsy? How's the ankle?"

I lift a bag of mostly melted ice from my ankle and turn my foot in circles. "It'll be fine." I shake my head. "It'll heal much sooner than my ego. How could I have done that to my mom?" I plop the bag of ice water on the floor and pull myself from the sofa. "On a scale of one to ten, Shel, how awful was I?"

She bats a hand at me. "I told everyone you were suffering from exhaustion. And they bought it. It was an easy story to pitch, since you looked like you hadn't slept in weeks." She peeks at her watch. "Listen, Jay and I are getting ready to go now, it's after seven."

From the foyer I spot Jay squatting in front of their three-year-old, stuffing little Trevor's arms into a bright yellow slicker that makes him look like a miniature fireman. His crystal blue eyes find mine and he squeals.

"Auntie Bwett!"

My heart trips and I secretly hope my nephew never learns to pronounce his *R's*. I walk over to him and tousle his hair. "How's my big boy?"

Jay clips the metal fastener at Trevor's collar and pulls himself up. "There she is." Aside from the telltale crow's-feet flanking his dimpled grin, my brother looks closer to twenty-six than his thirty-six years. He drapes an arm around me. "Have a nice nap?"

"I'm so sorry," I say, swiping a flake of mascara from under my eye.

He plants a kiss on my forehead. "No worries. We all know this is hardest on you."

What he means is, of the three Bohlinger children, I'm still single, the one with no family of my own. I counted on Mom the most. My brother feels sorry for me.

"We're all grieving," I say, pulling away.

"But you were her daughter," my oldest brother, Joad, says. He rounds the corner of the foyer, his wiry frame nearly hidden by a colossal floral spray. Unlike Jay, who brushes his thinning tresses straight back, Joad shaves his head smooth as an egg, which, along with his clear-framed eyeglasses, gives him an urban-artsy vibe. He turns sideways and pecks me on the cheek. "You two had a special bond. Jay and I couldn't have managed without you, especially near the end."

It's true. When our mother was diagnosed with ovarian cancer last spring, I convinced her we would fight it together. I'm the one who nursed her after surgery, the one who sat beside her at every chemo treatment, the one who insisted on a second, and then a third opinion. And when all the experts agreed her prognosis was grim, I'm the one who was with her the day she decided to stop the heinous treatments.

Jay squeezes my hand, his blue eyes bright with tears. "We're here for you. You know that, right?"

I nod and pull a Kleenex from my pocket.

Shelley breaks our silent grieving when she steps into the foyer, lugging Emma's car carrier. She turns to Jay. "Hon, could you grab that jade plant my parents sent?" She glances at Joad, then me. "You guys don't want it, do you?"

Joad nods at the botanical garden in his arms, in case she might have missed it. "Got mine."

"Take it," I say, baffled that anyone would care about a plant when our mother just died.

My siblings and their spouses shuffle from our mother's

brownstone into the misty September evening while I stand holding open the rosewood door, just as Mother used to do. Catherine is the last to pass, tucking an Hermès scarf into her suede jacket.

"See you tomorrow," she says, planting a Casino Pink kiss on my cheek.

I groan. As if deciding who'll get which plant isn't enough fun, at ten thirty tomorrow morning, all of Mother's assets will be doled out to her children like it's a Bohlinger awards ceremony. In a matter of hours I'll become president of Bohlinger Cosmetics and Catherine's boss — and I'm not the least bit confident I can handle either.

The night's stormy shell cracks, revealing a cloudless, blue-skied morning. A good omen, I decide. From the backseat of a Lincoln Town Car, I stare out at the frothy shoreline of Lake Michigan and mentally rehearse what I'll say. *Wow, I'm humbled. What an honor. I'll never replace Mother, but I'll try my damnedest to move the company forward.*

My head throbs, and again I curse myself for drinking that damn champagne. What was I thinking? I feel sick — and not just physically. How could I have done that to my mother? And how can I possibly expect my siblings to take me seriously now? I grab my compact from my purse and dab powder on my cheeks. I must appear competent and composed today — the way a CEO should. My brothers need to know that I can handle the business, even if I'm not always able to handle my alcohol. Will they be proud of their little sister, moving from advertising executive to president of a major company at age thirty-four? Despite yesterday's debacle, I think so. They have their own careers, and aside from their stock shares, they have little to do with the family business. And Shelley's a speech pathologist and a busy mommy. She doesn't give a whit who runs her mother-in-law's company.

It's Catherine I fear.

A graduate of Penn's prestigious Wharton School of Business and a member of the U.S. synchronized swim team swim during the Olympic Games of 1992, my sister-in-law has the brains, the tenacity, and the competitive edge to run three companies simultaneously.

For the past twelve years she's held the title of vice president of Bohlinger Cosmetics and been Mother's right hand. Without Catherine, Bohlinger Cosmetics would have remained a small-but-prosperous cottage industry. But Catherine came aboard and convinced Mother to expand her line. In early 2002, she got wind of a new episode Oprah Winfrey would be launching called "My Favorite Things." For twenty-one weeks straight, Catherine sent exquisitely wrapped packages of Bohlinger's organic soaps and lotions to Harpo Studios, along with photos and articles about the all-natural, ecofriendly company. Just as she was preparing her twenty-second shipment, Harpo Studios called. Oprah had chosen Bohlinger's Organic Black Tea and Grape Seed Facial Mask as one of her favorite things.

The episode aired and business exploded. Suddenly every spa and high-end department store demanded the Bohlinger line. Manufacturing quadrupled in the first six months. Three major companies offered outrageous sums to purchase the company outright, but Catherine convinced Mother not to sell. Instead, she opened shops in New York, LA, Dallas, and Miami, and two years later expanded to the overseas markets. Though I'd love to think my marketing prowess had something to do with it, the company became a multimillion-dollar enterprise largely because of Catherine Humphries-Bohlinger.

It's undeniable. Catherine is the queen bee, and as director of marketing I've been one of her loyal worker bees. But in a matter of minutes, our roles will be reversed. I'll become Catherine's boss — a thought that terrifies the bejesus out of me.

Last June, when my mother was in the throes of treatment and her presence at Bohlinger Cosmetics was a rarity, Catherine called me into her office.

"It's important that you learn the nuts and bolts of the operation, Brett," she said, perched behind her cherry desk with her hands folded in front of her. "As much as we'd like to deny it, our lives are going to change. You need to be prepared for your role."

She thought my mother would die! How could she assume the worst? But Catherine was a realist, and she was rarely wrong. A chill came over me.

"Naturally, all of your mother's shares will go to you, once she passes. You are, after all, her only daughter and the sole child in the business. You've also been her business partner longer than anyone else."

A lump rose in my throat. My mother used to boast that I was still in diapers when I joined the company. She'd hoist me into my baby backpack and off we'd go, pitching her soaps and lotions to local shops and farmer's markets.

"And as the majority shareholder," Catherine continued, "you're entitled to her position as CEO."

Something in her cool, measured tone made me wonder if she resented this. And who could blame her? The woman was brilliant. And me — I just happened to be Elizabeth's daughter.

"I'm going to help you prepare — not that you aren't already." She tapped open her computer calendar. "How about we start tomorrow, eight A.M. sharp." It wasn't a question, it was an order.

So each morning I'd pull up a chair next to Catherine's and listen as she explained overseas business transactions, international tax codes, and the company's day-to-day operations. She sent me to a weeklong seminar at Harvard Business School bringing me up to date on the latest management techniques, and enrolled me in online workshops on topics ranging from streamlining budgets to employee relations. Though many times I felt overwhelmed, I never once considered bowing out. I'll be honored to wear the crown that was once my mother's. I just hope my sister-in-law doesn't come to resent each time she's asked to help polish it.

Mother's driver drops me off at 200 E. Randolph Street and I gaze up at the granite-and-steel structure of Chicago's Aon Center. Office space in this place must be outrageous. Obviously, Mother's attorney is no slouch. I make my way to the thirty-second floor, and at precisely ten thirty Claire, an attractive redhead, leads me into Mr. Midar's office, where my brothers and their wives have already gathered at a rectangular mahogany table.

"Can I get you some coffee, Ms. Bohlinger?" she asks. "Or perhaps tea? Bottled water?"

"No, thank you." I find a seat beside Shelley and look around. Mr. Midar's office is an impressive concoction of old and new. The space itself reeks of modernity, all marble and glass, but he's softened it with Oriental rugs and several key pieces of antique furniture. The effect is soothing lucidity.

"Nice place," I say.

"Isn't it?" Catherine says from across the table. "I adore Stone architecture."

"Same here. And there's enough granite in this one to open a quarry."

She chuckles as if I'm a little tot who's just made a funny. "I meant Stone, as in Edward Durell Stone," she says. "He was the architect."

"Oh, right." Is there nothing this woman doesn't know? But rather than impressing me, Catherine's intelligence makes me feel ignorant, her strength makes me feel weak, and her competence makes me feel as useless as a pair of Spanx on Victoria Beckham. I love Catherine dearly, but it's a love that's tempered by intimidation — whether the result of my insecurity or Catherine's arrogance, I'm not sure. Mom once told me I had all of Catherine's intellect but only a smidgen of her self-confidence. Then she whispered, "And thank God for that." It was the only time I ever heard Mother speak ill of Catherine the Great, but that single, uncensored statement gives me enormous comfort.

"It was originally built for Standard Oil Company," she continues, as if I'm interested. "Back in '73, if I'm not mistaken."

Jay rolls his chair back, behind Catherine's line of vision, and mimes an exaggerated yawn. But Joad seems riveted by his wife's prater.

"Very good, dear. Third tallest building in Chicago," Joad says, looking at Catherine, as if for confirmation. Though my big bro is one of the city's most esteemed young architects, I sense that he, too, is a bit intimidated by the horsepower of the woman he married. "It's surpassed only by the Trump Tower and Willis Tower."

Catherine looks at me. "Willis Tower — you know, the former Sears Tower."

"The Sears Tower?" I ask, rubbing my chin in mock befuddlement. "Why would a department store need an entire tower?"

From across the table, Jay grins. But Catherine eyes me as if she's not entirely sure I'm joking before resuming her lesson. "This place has eighty-three floors aboveground and —"

The architecture trivia game ends when the door opens and a tall, disheveled man rushes into the room, a bit breathless. He looks to be about forty. He rakes a hand through his dark hair and straightens his tie. "Hey, everyone," he calls, moving to the table. "I'm Brad Midar. Sorry to have kept you waiting." He strides around the table and shakes each of our hands as we introduce ourselves. The intensity of his gaze is tempered by a slight overlap of his front teeth, lending him an authentic, boyish charm. I wonder if my siblings are thinking what I'm thinking. Why did Mother hire this young guy, a complete stranger, rather than Mr. Goldblatt, who's been our family attorney for years?

"I just came from a meeting across town," Midar says and finds his chair at the head of the table, kitty-corner from me. "I didn't expect it to run so late."

He drops a manila file folder on the table. I glance at Catherine, poised to take notes with her legal pad and pen, and cringe. Why didn't I think to take notes? How the hell am I going to run an entire company when I can't even remember my legal pad?

Mr. Midar clears his throat. "Let me begin by saying how sorry I am for your loss. I liked Elizabeth very much. We met just last May, right after she was diagnosed, but somehow I feel as if I knew her for years. I wasn't able to stay long at the luncheon yesterday, but I did attend her funeral. I like to think I was there as her friend, not as her lawyer."

I immediately like this busy attorney who found time to attend my mother's funeral — a woman he knew a scant sixteen weeks. I think of the lawyer in my life, my boyfriend Andrew, who knew my mother for four years, yet couldn't clear his schedule to attend yesterday's luncheon. I push back the ache in my chest. He was in the middle of a trial, after all. And he did break away for the funeral.

"Having said that," Mr. Midar continues, "I'm honored to be the executor of her estate. Shall we begin?"

An hour later, my mother's favorite charities are substantially more solvent, and Jay and Joad Bohlinger are worth enough money to spend the rest of their days in idle folly. How had Mother managed to accumulate such wealth?

"Brett Bohlinger is to collect her inheritance at a later date." Mr. Midar removes his reading glasses and looks over at me. "There's an asterisk here. I'll explain this in detail later."

"Okay," I say, literally scratching my head. Why wouldn't Mom give me my inheritance today? Maybe she'll explain in that little red journal she left me. And then it dawns on me. I'm getting the entire company, which today is worth millions. But God only knows how it'll fare under my leadership. A dull ache kicks at my temples.

"Next is your mother's home." He plants his reading glasses on his nose and finds his place on the document. "One Thirteen North Astor Street and all of its contents are to remain intact for twelve months. Neither the structure nor its contents are to be sold or leased during this time. My children may inhabit the home not longer than thirty consecutive days, and are welcome to utilize household items for their personal use."

"Seriously?" Joad says, staring at Mr. Midar. "We've got our own homes. There's no need to keep hers."

I feel my face burn and turn my attention to my cuticles. Obviously, my brother thinks I'm co-owner of the loft I share with Andrew. Even though I've lived there since Andrew bought it three years ago, and have more money invested in it than he does, I'm not on the title. Technically, it's his. And I'm okay with that, for the most part. Money's never been an issue for me, the way it's been with Andrew.

"Bro, it's Mom's will," Jay says in his usual good-natured tone. "We need to respect her wishes."

Joad shakes his head. "Well, it's nuts. Twelve months of outrageous taxes. Not to mention the maintenance on the old relic."

Joad inherited our father's emotional temperament — decisive, pragmatic, and devoid of sentimentality. His impassive nature can be helpful, like last week when we were making funeral arrangements. But today it feels disrespectful. Left to his own devices, Joad would probably plant a FOR SALE sign in Mom's yard and a dumpster in her driveway by day's end. Instead, we'll have time to sift through her belongings and thoughtfully say goodbye to pieces of her, one at a time. It's too traditional for Andrew's taste, but it's possible one of my brothers could even decide to keep her treasured property permanently.

The same year I left for Northwestern, Mom bought the tumbledown brownstone when it went into foreclosure. My father chided her, told her she was nuts to take on such an enormous project. But he was her ex-husband by then. Mother was free to make her own decisions. She saw something magical beyond the rotted ceilings and smelly carpets. It took years of hard work and self-denial, but eventually her vision and patience prevailed. Today the nineteenth-century building, located in Chicago's coveted Gold Coast neighborhood, is a showpiece. My mother, the daughter of a steelworker, used to tease that she was like Louise Jefferson, having "moved on up" from her hometown of Gary, Indiana. I wish my father had lived long enough to witness the spectacular transformation of the house — and the woman — I felt he'd always underestimated.

"Are you sure she was of sound mind when she made this will?" Joad asks.

I see something conspiratorial in the attorney's grin. "Oh, she was of sound mind, all right. Let me assure you, your mother knew exactly what she was doing. In fact, I've never seen such elaborate planning."

"Let's continue," Catherine says, ever the manager. "We'll deal with the house on our own time."

Mr. Midar clears his throat. "Okay, shall we move on to Bohlinger Cosmetics now?"

My head throbs and I feel four pairs of eyes on me. Yesterday's scene resurfaces and I'm frozen with panic. What kind of CEO gets drunk at her mother's funeral luncheon? I don't deserve this honor. But it's too late now. Like an actress nominated for an Academy Award, I try to make my face a picture of neutrality. Catherine sits with her pen poised, waiting to take down every last detail of the business offering. I'd better get used to it. Subordinate or not, the woman's going to keep watch on me for the rest of my career.

"All of my shares of Bohlinger Cosmetics, as well as the title of chief executive officer, will go to my daughter —"

Act naturally. Keep your eyes off Catherine.

"— in-law," I hear, as if I'm hallucinating. "Catherine Humphries-Bohlinger."

CHAPTER TWO

"What the hell?" I ask aloud. In a flash, I realize I've lost the damn Oscar, and to my horror I'm not the least bit gracious. In fact, I'm unabashedly pissed.

Midar looks at me over his tortoiseshell frames. "I'm sorry? Would you like me to repeat that?"

"Y-yes," I stammer, my eyes traveling from one family member to the next, hoping for a show of support. Jay's eyes are sympathetic, but Joad can't even look at me. He's doodling on his legal pad, his jaw twitching manically. And Catherine, well, she really could have been an actress, because the look of incredulity on her face is completely believable.

Mr. Midar leans nearer to me and speaks deliberately, as if I'm his infirm old grandmother. "Your mother's shares of Bohlinger Cosmetics will go to your sister-in-law, Catherine." He holds out the official document for me to see. "You'll each get a copy of this, but you're welcome to read mine now."

I scowl and wave him off, trying my damnedest to breathe. "No. Thank you," I manage. "Continue. Please. I'm sorry." I slouch into my chair and bite my lip to keep it from trembling. There must be a mistake. I . . . I've worked so hard. I wanted to make her proud. Did Catherine set me up? No, she'd never be that cruel.

"That about wraps up this part of the process," he tells us. "I do have one private matter to discuss with Brett." He looks at me. "Do you have time now, or shall we arrange to meet another day?"

I'm lost in a fog, struggling to make my way out. "Today's fine," someone says in a voice that sounds like mine.

"Okay, then." He scans the faces at the table. "Any questions before we adjourn?"

"We're all set," Joad says. He rises from his chair and searches for the door like a prisoner going for the break.

Catherine checks her phone for messages and Jay rushes to Midar, full of gratitude. He glances at me but quickly averts his eyes. My bro feels sheepish, no doubt. And I feel sick. The only one familiar to me is Shelley, with her unruly brown curls and soft gray eyes. She opens her arms and pulls me into a hug. Not even Shelley knows what to say to me.

In turns, my sibs shake Mr. Midar's hand while I sit silent in my chair like the naughty student who's been kept after class. As soon as they leave, Midar closes the door. When it shuts, it's so silent I can hear the swish of blood as it races past my temples. He returns to his seat at the head of the table, so that we form a right angle. His face is smooth and tan, and his brown eyes softly incongruent with his angular features.

"You doing all right?" he asks me, as if he actually wants an answer. We must be paying him by the hour.

"I'm fine," I tell him. *Poor, motherless, and humiliated, but fine. Just fine.*

"Your mother worried that today would be especially hard on you."

"Really?" I say with a bitter little cackle. "She thought it might upset me to be written out of her will?"

He pats my hand. "That's not entirely true."

"Her only daughter, and I get nothing. Nada. Not even a token piece of furniture. I'm her daughter, damn it."

I yank my hand from his and bury it on my lap. When I lower my gaze, it lands on my emerald ring, meanders up to my Rolex watch, and eventually falls on my Cartier Trinity bracelet. I look up and see something resembling disgust darken Mr. Midar's lovely face.

"I know what you're thinking. You think I'm selfish and spoiled. You think this is about money, or power." My throat tightens. "The thing is, yesterday all I wanted was her bed. That's it. I just wanted her old antique . . ." I rub the knot in my throat. "Bed . . . so I could curl up and feel her . . ."

To my horror, I begin to weep. Dainty at first, my whimpers turn into misshapen, blustery sobs. Midar races to his desk in search of tissues. He hands me one and pats my back while I fight to regain my composure. "I'm sorry," I croak. "This is all . . . very hard for me."

"I understand." The shadow that crosses his face makes me think he really might.

I dab my eyes on the tissue. *One deep breath. Now another.* "Okay," I say, teetering on the edge of composure. "You said you had some business to discuss."

He pulls a second manila file from a leather portfolio and places it on the table before me. "Elizabeth had something different in mind for you."

He opens the file and hands me a piece of yellowed notebook paper. I stare at it. The mosaic creases tell me it had once been wadded into a tight little ball. "What's this?"

"A life list," he tells me. "*Your* life list."

It takes several seconds before I recognize that this is, indeed, my handwriting. My flowery, fourteen-year-old handwriting. Apparently I'd written a life list, though I have no recollection of it. Beside certain goals, I spy my mother's handwritten commentary.

MY LIFE GOALS

*1. Have a baby, maybe two

~~2. Kiss Nick Nicol~~

~~3. Make the cheerleading squad~~ *Congratulations. Was that so important?*

~~4. Earn straight A's~~ *Perfection is overrated.*

~~5. Ski the Alps~~ *What fun we had!*

*6. Get a dog

~~7. Answer correctly when Sister Rose calls on me and I'm talking to Carrie~~

~~8. Go to Paris~~ *Ah, the memories we made!*

*9. Stay friends with Carrie Newsome <u>forever</u>!

~~10. Go to Northwestern~~ *I'm so proud of my Wildcat!*

~~11. Be super friendly and nice~~ *Way to go!*

*12. Help poor people

*13. Have a really cool house

*14. Buy a horse

~~15. Run with the bulls~~ *Don't even think about it.*

~~16. Learn French~~ *Très bien!*

*17. Fall in love

*18. Perform live, on a super big stage

*19. Have a good relationship with my dad

*20. Be an <u>awesome</u> teacher!

"Huh," I say, scanning the list. "Kiss Nick Nicol. Be a cheer-leader." I smile and slide the list back to him. "Cute. Where'd you get this?"

"Elizabeth. She kept it all these years."

I cock my head. "So . . . what? She's willed me my old life list? Is that it?"

Mr. Midar doesn't smile. "Well, sort of."

"What's going on?"

He scoots his chair closer to mine. "Okay, here's the deal. Elizabeth fished this list out of the trash years ago. Over the years, every time you accomplished one of your goals, she'd scratch it off." He points to LEARN FRENCH. "See?"

My mother had slashed a line through the goal and beside it written *Très bien!*

"But ten goals on the list haven't been accomplished yet."

"No kidding. These are nothing like the goals I have now."

He shakes his head. "Your mother thought these goals were valid, even today."

I scowl, stung to think she didn't know me better. "Well, she was wrong."

"And she'd like you to complete the list."

My mouth falls open. "You've got to be joking." I shake the list at him. "I wrote these twenty years ago! I'd love to honor my mother's wishes, but it's not going to happen with these goals!"

He holds out his hands like a traffic cop. "Whoa, I'm just the messenger."

I take a deep breath and nod. "I'm sorry." I sink back into my chair and rub my forehead. "What was she possibly thinking?"

Thumbing through the file, Mr. Midar removes a pale pink envelope. I recognize it at once. Her favorite Crane stationery. "Elizabeth wrote you a letter and she's asked me to read it aloud to you. Don't ask me why I can't just give it to you. She was insistent that I read it aloud." He gives me a smart-aleck grin. "You do read, don't you?"

I hide a smile. "Look, I don't have a clue what my mother was thinking. Before today I'd have said that if she asked you to read it aloud to me, there's a reason. But today all bets are off."

"I suspect that's still the case. She had her reasons."

My heart quickens at the sound of the tearing envelope. I force myself to sit back and fold my hands on my lap.

Midar positions his reading glasses on his nose and clears his throat.

"'Dear Brett,

"'Let me begin by saying how very sorry I am for everything you've had to endure these past four months. You were my spine, my soul, and I thank you. I didn't want to leave you yet. We had so much living and loving left, didn't we? But you are strong, you will endure, you will even thrive, though you don't believe me now. I know today you are sad. Let that sadness sit with you a bit.

"'I wish I were there to help you get through this time of sorrow. I'd grab you into my arms and squeeze you until your breath catches, just like it did when you were a little girl. Or maybe I'd take you to lunch. We'd find a cozy table at The Drake and I'd spend all afternoon listening to your fears and sorrows, rubbing your arm to let you know I feel your pain.'"

Midar's voice sounds a little thick. He looks over at me. "You okay?"

I nod, unable to speak. He clutches my arm and squeezes before he continues.

"'You must have been very confused today when your brothers received their inheritance, and you didn't. And I can only imagine how angry you were when the top job was given to Catherine. Trust me. I know what I'm doing, and everything I do is in your best interest.'"

Midar smiles at me. "Your mother loved you."

"I know," I whisper, covering my trembling chin.

"'One day almost twenty years ago, I was emptying your *Beverly Hills, 90210* wastebasket and I found this crumpled ball of paper. Of course, I was too nosy to let it go. You can imagine how delighted I was when I unfurled it and discovered you'd written a life list. I'm not sure why you chose to throw it away, because I thought it was lovely. I asked you about it later that night, do you remember?'"

"No," I say aloud.

"'You told me dreams were for fools. You said you didn't believe in dreams. I think it may have had something to do with your father. He was supposed to have picked you up that afternoon for an outing, but he never came.'"

Pain grips hold of my heart and twists, contorting it into a wretched knot of shame and anger. I bite my bottom lip and squeeze shut my eyes. How many times had Father stood me up? I've lost count. After the first dozen times, I should have learned. But I was too gullible. I believed in Charles Bohlinger. Like a mythical Santa Claus, my father would surely appear, if only I believed.

"'Your life goals touched me deeply. Some were funny, like number seven. Others were serious and compassionate, like number twelve: HELP POOR PEOPLE. You were always such a giver, Brett, such a sensitive, thoughtful spirit. It pains me now to see that so many of your life goals remain unfulfilled.'"

"I don't want these goals, Mother. I've changed."

"'Of course you've changed,'" Midar reads.

I snatch the letter from him. "Did she really say that?"

He points to the line. "Right here."

The hairs on my arms rise. "Weird. Keep going."

"'Of course you've changed, but darling, I fear you've abandoned your true aspirations. Do you even have any goals today?'"

"Of course I do," I say, racking my brain to come up with even one. "Before today, I hoped to run Bohlinger Cosmetics."

"'The business was never a fit for you.'"

Before I have time to grab the paper, Mr. Midar leans over, pointing to the sentence.

"Oh, my God. It's like she's listening to me."

"Maybe that's why she wanted me to read it aloud, so you two could have a bit of dialogue."

I blot my eyes with a Kleenex. "She always had a sixth sense. Whenever something bothered me, I never had to tell her. She'd tell me. And when I'd try to convince her otherwise, she'd look at me and say, 'Brett, you're forgetting, I made you. I'm the one person you can't fool.'"

"Nice," he says. "That kind of connection is priceless."

I see it again, that flash of pain in his eyes. "Have you lost a parent?"

"They're both alive. They live in Champaign."

But he doesn't say whether they're healthy. I leave it alone.

"'I regret letting you work for Bohlinger Cosmetics all these years —'"

"Mother! Thanks a lot!"

"'You were much too sensitive for that environment. You were a born teacher.'"

"Teaching? But I hated teaching!"

"'You never gave it a fair chance. You had a terrible experience that year at Meadowdale, remember?'"

I shake my head. "Oh, I remember all right. It was the longest year of my life."

"'And when you came to me, crying and frustrated and filled with angst, I welcomed you into the business, and found a spot for you in the marketing department. I'd have done anything to erase that pain and worry from your beautiful face. Aside from insisting you maintain your teaching certification over the years, I've let you abandon your true dream. I've allowed you to stay in a cozy, highly paid job that neither challenges nor excites you.'"

"I like my job," I say.

"'Fear of change makes us stagnant. Which leads me back to your life list. Please look at your goals as Brad continues reading.'"

He positions the list in front of us and I study it, more carefully this time.

"'Of the original twenty, I've placed an asterisk beside the ten remaining goals I want you to pursue. Let's begin with number one: HAVE A BABY, MAYBE TWO.'"

I groan. "This is insane!"

"'I fear you'll forever live with a shadow on your heart if children — or at least a child — are not part of your life. Though I know many childless women who are happy, I do not believe you're one of them. You were my girl who loved her baby dolls, who couldn't wait to be twelve so she could babysit. You were the girl who used to swaddle Toby the cat in your baby blanket and cry when he'd wriggle free and leap from the rocking chair. Remember, darling?'"

My laugh gets tangled in a sob. Mr. Midar hands me another tissue.

"I do love kids, but . . ." I cannot finish the thought. It would require me to blame Andrew, and that's just not fair. For some reason, the tears keep coming. I can't seem to stop them. Midar waits, until finally I point to the letter and wave him on.

"You sure?" he asks, his hand on my back.

I nod, the tissue pinched on my nose.

He looks skeptical, but he continues.

"'Let's skip number two. I hope you did, indeed, kiss Nick Nicol, and I hope it was delightful.'"

I smile. "It was."

Midar winks at me, and together we look at my list.

"'Let's move down to number six,'" he reads. "'GET A DOG. I think this is a grand idea! Go find your puppy, Brett!'"

"A dog? What makes you think I want a dog? I don't have time for a fish, let alone a dog." I look at Brad. "What happens if I don't complete these goals?"

He pulls out a stack of pink envelopes, bound together with a rubber band. "Your mother stipulated that each time you complete a life goal, you return to me and receive one of these envelopes. Upon completion of all ten goals, you get this." He holds out an envelope that reads FULFILLMENT.

"What's in the FULFILLMENT envelope?"

"Your inheritance."

"Of course," I say, rubbing my temples. I look him square in the face. "Do you have any idea what this means?"

He lifts his shoulders. "I'm guessing it'll mean some major life revisions."

"Revisions? Life as I know it has just been shredded! And I'm supposed to piece it back together in a way that some — some *kid* wanted it to be?"

"Look, if this is too much for you today, we can arrange to meet again."

I pull myself to my feet. "It is too much. I came here this morning expecting to walk out the CEO of Bohlinger Cosmetics. I was going to make my mother proud, take the business to new heights." My throat seizes up and I swallow hard. "Instead I'm supposed to get a horse? Unbelievable!" I blink to keep my tears at bay and extend my hand. "I'm sorry, Mr. Midar. I know this isn't your fault. But I just can't deal with this right now. I'll be in touch."

I'm nearly out the door when Midar rushes to me, waving the life list. "Keep this," he says, "in case you change your mind." He tucks the list in my hands. "The clock's ticking."

I cock my head. "What clock?"

He looks down at his Cole Haans, sheepish. "You must complete at least one goal by the end of this month. In one year from today — that'd be September thirteenth of next year — the entire list is to be completed."

CHAPTER THREE

hree hours after sauntering into the Aon Center, I stumble out, my emotions flashing and fading like a meteor shower. Shock. Despair. Fury. Grief. I throw open the door of the Town Car. "One Thirteen North Astor Street," I tell the driver.

That little red book. I need that little red book! I'm stronger today — much stronger — and I'm ready to read my mother's journal. Maybe she will explain herself, tell me why she's doing this to me. It's possible it's not a journal after all, but rather an old business ledger. Perhaps I'll learn that the business was in a financial free fall, and that's why she didn't leave it to me. Somehow, there must be an explanation.

When the driver pulls up to the curb, I yank open the iron gate and race up the concrete steps. Without bothering to take off my shoes, I sprint up the stairs and head straight to her bedroom.

My eyes survey the sun-drenched room. With the exception of

her lamp and jewelry box, the dresser is empty. I throw open the closet doors, but it's not there. I hurl open drawers, and then turn to her bedside tables. Where is it? I rifle through her secretary's desk, but find only embossed note cards, assorted pens, and stamps. Panic rises. Where the hell did I leave that book? I pulled it from the closet and put it . . . where? On the bed? Yes. Or did I? I flip back the comforter, praying it'll be nestled within the bed-sheets. It's not. My heart pounds. How could I have been so care-less? I turn circles, raking a hand through my hair. What in God's name did I do with that book? My memory is a blur. Was I so sloshed that I've forgotten even earlier events? Wait! Did I have it when I went tumbling down the stairs? I rush from the room and race back down the steps.

Two hours later, having searched beneath furniture cushions, through every drawer and closet and even the trash, I come to the horrifying conclusion that the book is nowhere to be found. When I call, nearly hysterical, my siblings haven't a clue what I'm talking about. I collapse on the sofa and hide my face in my hands. God help me, I've lost my promotion, my inheritance, and my mother's last gift to me. Can I sink any lower?

When the alarm clock buzzes Wednesday morning, I wake to a blissful oblivion of yesterday's nightmare. I stretch and throw my arm over the bedside table, blindly groping for the obnox-ious little beep. Silencing the alarm, I roll onto my back, grant-ing myself one more moment of shut-eye. But suddenly it all comes flooding back. My eyes fly open and a net of dread en-snares me.

My mother is dead.

Catherine is head of Bohlinger Cosmetics.

I'm expected to dismantle my life.

The weight of an elephant plops down on my chest and I

struggle to breathe. How can I possibly face my co-workers, or my new boss, now that they know my mother had no confidence in me?

My heart races and I prop myself up on my elbows. The drafty loft has the crisp feel of autumn and I blink several times, adjusting to the darkness. I can't do this. I cannot go back to work. Not yet. I collapse against the pillow and stare up at the exposed metal ducts in the ceiling.

But I have no choice. Yesterday, when I didn't show up for work after the meeting with Mr. Midar, my new boss called, insisting we meet first thing this morning. And as much as I wanted to tell Catherine — the woman my mother believed in — to go to hell, without an inheritance, I need my job.

I throw my legs over the side of the bed. Taking care not to wake Andrew, I peel my terry-cloth robe from its hook on the bedpost. It's then that I realize he's already gone. It's not even five A.M. and my incredibly disciplined boyfriend's already up and running. Literally. Clutching my robe, I pad barefoot across the oak floor and lumber down the cold metal stairs.

I take my coffee into the living room and curl up on the sofa with the *Tribune*. Another scandal in City Hall, more corrupt government officials, but nothing distracts me from the day ahead. Will my co-workers sympathize with me and tell me how unfair Mother's decision was? I turn to the crossword puzzle and scramble to find a pencil. Or did the office erupt in applause and high-fives when the news hit? I groan. I'll have to square my shoulders, hold my head high, and make everyone believe it was my idea that Catherine run the company.

Oh, Mother, why have you put me in this position?

A lump rises in my throat and I swallow it down with a gulp of coffee. I don't have time to grieve today, thanks to Catherine and her damn meeting. She thinks she's being coy, but I know exactly what she's up to. This morning she'll offer me a consolation prize — her old position as vice president. She'll make me second in command in exchange for her amnesty and my obedience. But she's delusional if she thinks I'll accept without some serious demands. Without an inheritance, I'm going to need one heck of a raise.

My pout softens into a smile when Andrew breezes through the door, damp with sweat from his morning run. Clad in navy shorts and a Chicago Cubs T-shirt, he studies his black runner's watch with furrowed brows.

I rise. "Good morning, sweetheart. How was your run?"

"Sluggish." He removes his ball cap and rakes a hand through his short blond hair. "You taking the morning off again?"

Runner's guilt punches me in the gut. "Yeah. I still don't have the energy."

He bends down to untie his laces. "It's been five days. Better not wait too long."

He turns in the direction of the laundry room while I retrieve his coffee. By the time I return, his lean body is sprawled on the sofa. He's wearing a fresh pair of warm-up pants and clean T-shirt, working the crossword puzzle I'd just started.

"Can I help?" I ask, coming up from behind and leaning in over his shoulder.

He gropes for his coffee cup without looking up from the puzzle. He writes *birr* in twelve down. I check to see the clue. Ethiopian currency. God, I'm impressed.

"Oh, fourteen across . . ." I say, excited for the opportunity to display that I, too, have a modicum of intellect. "Treasure State capital . . . that's Helena, I think."

"I know." He drums the pencil against his forehead, deep in thought.

When, exactly, did we stop doing the crossword puzzles together? Sharing the same pillow, we'd work the puzzle and sip our coffee. And every now and then, when I provided an especially hard answer, Andrew would kiss the top of my forehead and tell me he loved my brain.

I turn to leave, but stop midway to the staircase. "Andrew?"

"Hmm?"

"Will you be there for me, if I need you?"

Finally, he raises his head. "Come here." He pats the spot beside him on the sofa. I make my way to him and he drapes an arm around my shoulder.

"You still upset I missed the funeral luncheon?"

"No. I understand. That trial was important."

He tosses the pencil onto the coffee table and grins, exposing the adorable dimple in his left cheek. "I have to admit, when you say it like that, it sounds lame, even to me." With his eyes locked on mine, he turns serious. "But to answer your question, of course I'll be there for you. You never have to worry about that." He grazes his thumb over my cheek. "I'll be with you every step of the way, but you'll make one helluva CEO, with or without my guidance."

My heart speeds. When Andrew came home last night toting a bottle of Perrier-Jouët champagne to celebrate, I didn't have the heart — or the guts — to tell him I was not, and never will be, president of Bohlinger Cosmetics. The man who rarely gives compliments was practically gushing. Is it too much to want one more day to bask in his approval? Tonight, when I can soften the blow by telling him I'm the new vice president, I'll come clean.

He smooths my hair. "Tell me, boss lady, what's on the agenda today? Looking to hire any attorneys in the near future?"

What? He can't possibly think I'd go against my mother's wishes. I play it off as a joke, forcing a chuckle from my parched throat. "I don't think so. Actually, I'm meeting with Catherine this morning," I say, letting him think it was me who called the meeting. "We have some issues to discuss."

He nods. "Good move. Remember, she's working for you now. Let her know you're calling the shots."

I feel blood rush to my cheeks and pull myself from the sofa. "I better shower."

"I'm proud of you, Madame President."

I know I should tell him it's Catherine who deserves his pride, that it's Catherine he should be calling Madame President. And I will. I absolutely will.

Tonight.

Despite the clicking of my heels against the marble foyer, I manage to scurry across the lobby of the Chase Tower without being noticed. I ride the elevator to the forty-ninth floor and enter the posh headquarters of Bohlinger Cosmetics. Pushing through the double glass doors, I head straight for Catherine's office with my eyes downcast.

I poke my head into the corner office that was once my mother's and see Catherine behind the desk, perfectly groomed as always. She's on the phone but waves me in, lifting an index finger to let me know she'll be with me shortly. As she wraps up her call, I wander around the once familiar space, wondering what she's done with the paintings and sculptures Mother adored. In their place she's positioned her bookcase and several framed awards. All that remains of Mother's once sacrosanct office is the breathtaking cityscape and her nameplate. But upon closer inspection I see that it's not my mother's nameplate, after all. It's Catherine's! The same font and brass and marble now reads CATHERINE HUMPHRIES-BOHLINGER, PRESIDENT.

I seethe! Just how long had she known she was Mother's heir apparent?

"Okay, great. Get me the numbers when you have them. Yes. *Supashi-bo, Yoshi. Adiosu.*" She hangs up the phone and turns her attention to me. "Tokyo," she says, shaking her head. "The fourteen-hour time difference is a bitch. I have to be here before dawn to catch them. Lucky for me, they work late." She points across the desk to a pair of Louis Quinze chairs. "Have a seat."

I sink into the chair and run a hand over the cobalt-blue silk, trying to remember whether Catherine had these chairs in her old office. "Looks like you're all moved in," I say, unable to resist my inner snark. "You even managed to get your nameplate in . . . what? Twenty hours? Who knew it could be made so quickly."

She rises and comes around to my side of her desk, positioning the matching chair so that she's facing me. "Brett, this is a hard time for all of us."

"A hard time for all of us?" My vision blurs. "Are you serious? I just lost a mother and a business. You just inherited an absolute fortune and my family's company. And you, you set me up. You told me I'd be CEO. I worked my ass off, trying to learn the ropes!"

Looking as composed as if I'd just told her I liked her dress, she waits. My nostrils flare and I want to say more, but I don't dare. She's my sister-in-law after all — and my damn boss.

She leans in, her pale hands folded on her crossed leg. "I'm sorry," she says. "I truly am. I was as shocked as you were yesterday. I made an assumption last summer — a colossal mistake, to be sure. I fully expected you to receive your mother's shares, and took it upon myself to groom you, without first consulting Elizabeth. I didn't want her to think we'd given up on her." She covers my hand with hers. "Believe me, I had every intention of working for you for the rest of my career. And you know what? I would have been proud to do so." She squeezes my hand. "I respect you so much, Brett. I think you could have made it as CEO. I really do."

Could have? I scowl, unsure whether this is a compliment or an insult. "But that nameplate," I say. "If you had no idea, how come you already have the nameplate?"

She smiles. "Elizabeth. She'd ordered it for me before she died. She had it delivered and on my desk when I walked in yesterday."

I drop my head in shame. "That would be Mother."

"She was remarkable," Catherine says, her eyes glistening. "I'll never fill her shoes. I'll consider it a success if I can simply squeeze my toes in."

My heart softens. Obviously she, too, grieves the loss of Elizabeth Bohlinger. She and Mother formed a perfect partnership, Mother being the elegant face of the enterprise, and Catherine her tireless, behind-the-scenes assistant. And looking at her now in her cashmere dress and Ferragamo pumps, her smooth ivory skin and sleek chignon knotted at the nape of her neck, I can almost understand my mother's choice. Catherine looks every inch a CEO, a natural to be her successor. But still it hurts. Couldn't Mom see that with time, I could have developed into a Catherine?

"I'm sorry," I say. "I really am. It's not your fault that Mom didn't see me fit to run BC. You're going to be a huge success."

"Thanks," she whispers, rising from her chair. She squeezes my shoulder as she passes behind me to close the door. When she returns to her seat, she fixes her gaze on me, her eyes alarmingly intense.

"What I'm about to say is very difficult for me." She bites her bottom lip and her face flushes. "I want you to prepare yourself, Brett. This will be shocking."

I laugh nervously. "My God, Catherine, your hands are shaking! I've never seen you so anxious. What's going on?"

"I have one order from Elizabeth. She left a pink envelope in my desk drawer. There was a note inside. I can get it if you'd like to see it." She starts to rise but I grab her arm.

"No. The last thing I need is another note from Mom. Just tell me." My heart is galloping now.

"Your mother instructed me to . . . she wants me to . . ."

"What?" I nearly scream.

"You're fired, Brett."

CHAPTER FOUR

I have no memory of driving home. I only remember staggering into the loft, stumbling up the stairs, and falling into bed. For the next two days I repeat a cycle of sleeping, waking, and crying. By Friday morning, Andrew's compassion is waning. He sits on the edge of our bed, impeccable in his charcoal suit and crisp white shirt, and smooths my snarled hair.

"You've got to snap out of this, babe. You're overwhelmed with this promotion, so naturally you're avoiding it." I start to protest, but he silences me with an index finger. "I'm not saying you're incapable, I'm saying you're intimidated. But, hon, you can't afford to be away for days at a time. This isn't your old advertising job, where you could slack off from time to time."

"Slack off?" I feel my hackles rise. He thinks my old position as director of marketing was insignificant! And what's worse, I couldn't even keep that job. "You can't imagine what I'm going through. I think I deserve a couple of days to grieve."

"Hey, I'm on your side. I'm just trying to get you back in the game."

I rub my temples. "I know. I'm sorry. I'm just not myself these days." He rises but I grab hold of his coat sleeve. I need to tell Andrew the truth! My plan to come clean Wednesday night was thwarted when my mother fired me, and since then, I've been mustering the courage to explain.

"Stay home with me today. Please. We could —"

"Sorry, babe, I can't. My client load is insane." He wriggles from my grip and smooths his coat sleeve. "I'll try to get home early."

Tell him. Now.

"Wait!"

He stops midway to the door and looks at me over his shoulder.

My heart thrums in my chest. "I need to tell you something."

He turns and squints at me, as if his normally transparent girlfriend is suddenly out of focus. Finally, he returns to the edge of the bed and kisses the top of my head like I'm a featherbrained five-year-old. "Stop this nonsense. What you need is to get your gorgeous ass out of bed. You've got a company to run." He pats my cheek, and before I know it he's disappeared from the room.

I hear the door click shut and bury my face in my pillow. What the hell am I going to do? I'm not the CEO of Bohlinger Cosmetics. I'm not even a menial advertising exec. I'm an unemployed failure, and I'm terrified of what my status-conscious boyfriend will think of me when he finds out.

I wasn't surprised when Andrew told me he was from the wealthy Boston suburb of Duxbury. He had all the trappings of someone from old money — Italian shoes, Swiss watch, German car. But he was always evasive when I asked him about his childhood. He had one older sister. His father owned a small business. It frustrated me that he offered nothing more.

Three months and two bottles of wine later, Andrew finally spat out the truth. Red-faced and angry that I'd pressed him, he told me that his father was a mediocre cabinetmaker whose aspirations far exceeded his accomplishments. His mother worked behind the deli counter at the Duxbury Safeway.

Andrew wasn't a rich kid. But he was desperate to be perceived as one.

I felt a surge of warmth and respect for Andrew I hadn't felt before. He wasn't an entitled child. He was a self-made man who'd had to struggle and work for his success. I kissed his cheek and told him I was proud of him, that his working-class roots made me love him more. Instead of smiling, he shot me a look of contempt. I knew then that Andrew found nothing admirable about his modest beginnings, and that growing up among the affluent had left a scar.

At once, a wave of panic grips me.

The rich-little-poor-kid has spent his entire adult life accumulating markers of success, hoping to compensate for his humble roots. And I wonder, now, if I'm just one of them.

From the driveway, I stare up at Jay and Shelley's picture-perfect Cape Cod. Manicured shrubs line the brick sidewalk, and orange and yellow mums spill from white concrete urns. An uncharacteristic wave of jealousy comes over me. The proverbial bed they've chosen to lie in is sumptuous and cozy, while mine is lumpy and teeming with bedbugs.

Through the brick walkway, I gaze into their lush backyard and catch sight of my nephew running with a rubber ball. He looks up when my car door slams.

"Auntie Bwett!" he calls to me.

I rush to the backyard and scoop up Trevor, and we twirl until

I can't see straight. For the first time in three days, I can feel a genuine smile light my face.

"Who's the boy who makes me happy?" I ask, tickling his belly.

Before he can answer, Shelley steps from the brick patio, her hair heaped atop her head in an accidental ponytail. She's wearing what I suspect are a pair of Jay's jeans, rolled up at the ankles.

"Hey, sis," she calls. We were friends and college roommates before she married my brother, and we still get a silly kick out of calling each other sister.

"Hey, you're home today."

She traipses over to me in ragg wool slippers. "I quit my job."

I stare at her. "No you didn't."

She bends down to pull a weed. "Jay and I decided it'd be best for the kids if one of us stayed home. With your mother's inheritance we don't need the extra money."

Trevor wriggles from my grip and I lower him to his feet. "But you love your job. What about Jay? Why doesn't he quit?"

She stands up, holding a dead dandelion in her hand. "I'm the mommy. Makes more sense."

"So you're done. Just like that?"

"Yup. Lucky for me, the woman who filled in during my maternity leave was still available." She plucks dried fronds from the dandelion and tosses them at her feet. "They interviewed her yesterday and she started today. I didn't even need to train her. It all worked out perfectly."

I hear the catch in her voice, and I know it's not as perfect as she wants me to think it is. Shelley was a speech pathologist at Saint Francis Hospital. She worked in their rehab unit, teaching adults with traumatic brain injuries not only how to talk again, but how to reason and negotiate and socialize. She used to boast that it wasn't a job, it was her calling.

"I'm sorry, but I just can't picture you as a stay-at-home mom."

"It'll be great. Almost all the women in this neighborhood are stay-at-home moms. They gather every morning at the park, have playdates, take Mommy–toddler yoga classes. You wouldn't believe all the social stuff my kids missed out on when they were in day care." Her eyes find Trevor, running in circles with his arms outstretched like an airplane. "Maybe this speech pathologist can finally teach her own kid how to talk." She chuckles, but it hits the wrong chord. "Trevor still can't say his —" She stops midthought and looks at her watch. "Wait, aren't you supposed to be at work?"

"Nope. Catherine fired me."

"Oh, my God! I'll call the sitter."

Lucky for us, Megan Weatherby, the hypotenuse of our friendship triangle, has a hobby job as a realtor, with little ambition to actually sell houses. And lucky for Megan, she's practically engaged to Jimmy Northrup, Chicago Bears defensive end, rendering real estate commission optional. So when Shelley and I call her on our way to The Bourgeois Pig Café, she's already there, as if she'd anticipated this little crisis.

We've declared The Bourgeois Pig, in Lincoln Park, our favorite non-alcohol spot. It's cozy and funky, filled with books and antiques and threadbare rugs. And best of all, there's just enough background chatter to make us feel immune from eavesdroppers. Today the warm September sun beckons us outside, where Megan sits at a wrought-iron table wearing black leggings and a low-cut sweater that clings to the perfect mounds she insists are her real boobs. Her pale blue eyes are smudged with smoky gray shadow, and I'm guessing at least three coats of mascara. But with her blond hair captured in a silver barrette and a hint of pink blush on her ivory skin, she manages to maintain a smidgen of innocence, making her appear half call girl, half sorority girl — a look men seem to find irresistible.

Engrossed in her iPad, she doesn't notice us as we near her table. I grab Shelley's elbow and pull her to a stop.

"We can't interrupt her. Look, she's actually working."

Shelley shakes her head. "She's a poser." She pulls me nearer and nods at the computer screen. "Check it out. PerezHilton.com."

"Hey, y'all," Megan says, grabbing her sunglasses from the chair just before Shelley sits on them. "Listen to this." As we settle in beside her with our muffins and lattes, Megan launches into a riff about Angelina and Brad's latest scuffle and Suri's outlandish birthday party. Then she starts in on Jimmy. "Red Lobster. Seriously. I'm wearing an Hervé Léger bandage dress cut up to my ass, and he wants to take me to Red-fucking-Lobster!"

I believe everyone deserves that one outrageously bold friend who simultaneously mortifies and electrifies, the friend whose crude comments send us into fits of hysteria while we look over our shoulders to make sure nobody's listening. Megan is that friend.

We met Meg two years ago through Shelley's younger sister, Patti. Patti and Megan were roommates in Dallas, training to be flight attendants with American Airlines. But in the final week of training, Megan wasn't able to reach a bag wedged in the back of an overhead bin. Her arms were decidedly too short for the job, an imperceptible flaw Megan is now obsessed with. Mortified, she fled to Chicago to become a realtor, and met Jimmy during her first sale.

"I can't lie, I love those Red Lobster biscuits, but come on!"

Finally, Shelley interrupts. "Megan, I told you, Brett needs our help."

Megan taps her iPad into submission and folds her hands on the table. "Okay, I'm all yours. What's the problem, chica?"

When it's not all about her, Megan can be an excellent listener. And judging by her folded hands and fixed gaze, today she's giving me the floor. Taking full advantage, I spill every detail of my mother's ploy to destroy my life.

"So that's the deal. No income, no job. Just ten asinine goals I'm expected to complete in the next year."

"That's bullshit," Megan says. "Tell the attorney to go fuck himself." She plucks the list from my hand. "HAVE A KID. GET A DOG. GET A HORSE." She lifts her Chanel sunglasses and gazes at me. "What the hell was your mother thinking? You'd up and marry Old MacDonald?"

I can't help but smile. Megan can be self-centered, but at times like this when I need a laugh, I wouldn't trade her for a dozen Mother Teresas.

"And Andrew's about as far from Old MacDonald as you can get," Shelley says, pouring another packet of sugar into her coffee. "What does he think of all this? Is he prepared to step up? Give you babies?"

"Buy you a horse?" Megan adds, erupting in high-pitched giggles.

"He is," I say, pretending to examine my spoon. "I'm sure he is."

Megan's eyes dance. "I'm sorry. I just don't see how you're going to manage a horse in the middle of downtown Chicago. Does your building allow pets?"

"You're hilarious, Meg." I rub my temples. "I'm beginning to think my mom was out of her mind. What fourteen-year-old doesn't want a horse? What little girl doesn't want to be a schoolteacher and have babies and a dog and a beautiful house?"

Shelley wiggles her outstretched fingers. "Let's see that list again." I pass it to her, and she mumbles as she peruses it. "STAY FRIENDS WITH CARRIE NEWSOME, FALL IN LOVE, HAVE A RELATIONSHIP WITH MY DAD." She looks up. "These are a cinch."

I narrow my eyes. "My father's dead, Shelley."

"She obviously wants you to make peace with him. You know, visit his grave site, plant some flowers. And look, you've already accomplished number seventeen, fall in love. You're in love with Andrew, right?"

I nod, though for some reason my insides freeze up. I can't remember the last time we actually spoke the words *I love you*. But that's perfectly natural. After four years, it's implied.

"Then go to Mr. Midar's office and tell him. And tonight, look up this Carrie Newsome chick on Facebook. Send a few messages. Reconnect. Bingo! Another score."

My breath catches. I haven't spoken to Carrie since she left my house, hurt and humiliated, nearly nineteen years ago. "What about number twelve, help poor people? That's not so hard. I'll donate to Unicef or something." I look to my friends for reassurance. "Don't you think?"

"Absolutely," Megan says. "You'll finish quicker than a horny frat boy."

"But that damn baby," I say, pinching the bridge of my nose. "And the live performance and the teaching job. I swore I'd never again set foot on a stage or in a classroom."

Megan grips her wrist and pulls, an annoying habit she thinks will lengthen her arms. "Forget about a teaching job. Just sub for a few days, maybe a week or two. You get through it, and voilà! That one's in the bag."

I mull it over. "A substitute teacher? My mom never said I had to have my own classroom." A slow smile makes its way across my face. I lift my latte. "Here's to you, girls. On Monday afternoon, martinis are on me. By then I'll have an envelope or two from Mr. Midar."

CHAPTER FIVE

I stop at the florist Monday morning and pick up a bouquet of wildflowers before heading straight to Mr. Midar's office. I figure I'll treat myself each time I accomplish one of *that girl's* life goals. On impulse, I pick up a bouquet for Midar, too.

As the elevator rises to the thirty-second floor, a mixture of anticipation and excitement bubbles up inside me. I can't wait to see his face when I tell him what I've accomplished. But when I burst into the swanky office and stride up to Claire's desk, she looks at me as if I'm insane.

"You want to see him now? Absolutely not. He's working on a huge case."

As I turn to leave, Midar shoots from his office like a jackrabbit from its hole. He searches the waiting room and breaks into an adorable grin when he spots me. "Ms. Bohlinger! I thought I heard your voice! Come in."

Claire looks on with her mouth agape as Mr. Midar waves me into his office. I hand him the wildflowers as I pass in front of him.

"For me?"

"I'm feeling generous."

He chuckles. "Thank you. Decided not to splurge on a vase, though, huh?"

I fight back a smile. "You're on your own. I'm unemployed, as you probably know."

He searches the office until he lands on a ceramic urn of silk flowers. "Yeah, that's a bummer about the job. Your mother plays hardball." He yanks out the artificial flowers and tosses them into his wastebasket. "Gotta get some water. Be right back."

He takes the urn with him and I'm left alone in his office, giving me a chance to check out his digs. I pass by the floor-to-ceiling window, admiring a southern view that spans from Millennium Park all the way to the Adler Planetarium. I slow when I near his massive walnut desk, littered with three substantial sets of files, his computer, and a coffee-stained mug. I search for framed pictures of the beautiful wife, the adorable child, and requisite golden retriever. Instead, I see a snapshot of a middle-aged woman and someone who looks to be her teenage son, lounging on the deck of a sailboat. His sister and nephew, I'm guessing. The only other picture is of Brad, in his cap and gown, squeezed between two beaming adults I presume are his parents.

"All set," he says.

I turn to see him kick the door shut behind him. He places the urn of flowers on a marble-topped table. "Beautiful."

"I've got some good news, Mr. Midar."

"Please," he says, waving me over to a pair of leather club chairs, cracked and weathered to perfection. "We'll be working together for the next year. Call me Brad."

"Okay. And I'm Brett."

He takes a seat in the chair adjacent to mine. "Brett. I like that name. Where'd it come from, anyway?"

"Elizabeth, of course. She was a fan of American literature. I was named after Lady Brett Ashley, the little tart in Hemingway's *The Sun Also Rises*."

"Great choice. And Joad? Wasn't that the family in Steinbeck's *Grapes of Wrath*?"

"You got it. Jay was named after Jay Gatsby, Fitzgerald's character."

"Clever woman. I wish I'd known her longer."

"Me too."

He gives my knee a sympathetic pat. "You okay?"

I nod and try to swallow. "As long as I don't think about it."

"I understand."

There it is again, the bruised look on his face I saw last week. I want to ask him about it, but it feels too intrusive.

"I've got good news," I say, sitting up straight. "I've already accomplished a life goal."

He raises one eyebrow but says nothing.

"Number seventeen. I've fallen in love."

He inhales audibly. "That was quick."

"Not really. My boyfriend, Andrew ... well, he and I have been together nearly four years."

"And you love him?"

"I do," I say, bending down to remove a tiny leaf stuck to my shoe. Of course I love Andrew. He's smart and ambitious. He's a superb athlete and flat-out gorgeous. So why do I feel like I'm cheating on this goal?

"Congratulations. Let me get your envelope."

He stands and moves to the file cabinet beside his desk. "Number seventeen," he mumbles as he searches. "Ah, here we go."

I rise from the chair and reach for the envelope, but he holds it protectively against his chest. "Your mother instructed me —"

"Oh, God! What now?"

"I'm sorry, Brett. She made me promise to open each envelope for you and read it aloud."

I plop back down in the chair and cross my arms over my chest like a sulky teenager. "Go on then, open it."

It seems to take him forever to open the envelope and remove the letter. Out of curiosity, my eyes trail to his left hand in search of platinum, but I see nothing but tanned flesh and a spattering of masculine hair. He pulls his reading glasses from his shirt pocket and takes a deep breath.

"'Hello, Brett,'" he reads. "'I'm sorry you made the trip across town to tell me you're in love with Andrew. You see, I'm waiting for that heart-stopping, *I'd die for you* kind of love.'"

"What?" I throw up my hands. "She's insane! That kind of love only exists in romance novels and the Lifetime channel. Any fool knows that."

"'We often choose relationships that mirror our past. In Andrew, you've chosen a man much like your father, though I know you'll disagree.'"

I gasp. The two men couldn't be more different. Unlike Andrew, who admires a powerful woman, my dad was threatened by my mother's achievement. For years, she was forced to downplay her success, laughing it off and calling her business her "hobby." But eventually the orders came in faster than she could fill them. She had to rent a space and hire employees. Suddenly she was living *her* dream. That's when their marriage fell apart.

"'Like your father, Andrew is ambitious and driven, but rather stingy with his love, wouldn't you agree? And oh, how it pains me to see you toil for that acceptance, just as you toiled for your father's. In vying for his affection, I fear you've abandoned your authentic self. Why is it that you feel unworthy of your own dreams?'"

Tears sting my eyes and I blink them away. An image springs to mind. It's dawn, and I'm making my daily trek to swim practice, dreading the frigid black water, but desperate to make my father proud. Years later I even minored in science, my least favorite subject, hoping to find common ground with the man, I eventually came to realize, I would never please.

"'I only want you to be happy. If indeed you are convinced Andrew is your love, then share this life list with him. If he is willing to be your partner in accomplishing these goals, I underestimated your love, and his, and you can consider this goal achieved. But whatever the outcome, please know that love is the one thing on which you should never compromise. Come back when you've found your love, my darling. It'll be worth it.'"

I rub the knot in my throat and try to look cheery. "Great. I'll be back in no time."

Brad turns to me. "You think he'll go for it, then? The baby? The dog?"

"Absolutely," I say, gnawing my thumbnail.

"'I love you,'" Brad says.

I snap to attention, but realize he's only resumed his reading. "'PS: You might want to begin with number eighteen: PERFORM LIVE, ON A SUPER BIG STAGE.'"

"Oh, right. I'll just sign myself up for the Joffrey Ballet. Has she completely lost it?"

"'I wonder what you had in mind. Ballet, I'm guessing, but perhaps a dramatic role. You adored your children's theater troupe nearly as much as your dance classes. But you quit both for the sake of cheerleading. And though I supported this endeavor, I tried to convince you to audition for the school plays, to join the choir or band. You wouldn't hear of it. Apparently your new friends did not favor these pursuits, and sadly that mattered to you. Where did she go, that fearless, self-assured girl who loved to entertain?'"

A searing memory surfaces, one I'd kept submerged for twenty years. It was the morning of my modern dance recital — the first time I'd be on stage without Carrie. She'd moved two months earlier, just weeks after my parents separated. In a sudden fit of loneliness, I lifted the phone to call her. But before I had time to punch in her number, I heard my mother's voice through the receiver.

"Charles, please. She's counting on you."

"Look, I said I'd try. The grant is due next week."

"But you promised her," my mother pleaded.

"Well maybe it's high time she realized that the world doesn't revolve around her." He huffed then, with a mocking tone I'll never forget. "Let's get real, Liz. The girl's not exactly Broadway-bound."

I waited thirty minutes before calling him, relieved when his answering machine picked up. "It's me, Dad. There's some sort of electrical outage at the auditorium. My recital's been canceled."

That day marked the last time I ever set foot on stage.

I swallow hard. "Where did she go? She went where every little girl with big dreams goes. She grew up. She got real."

Brad gives me a quizzical look, as if he wants me to elaborate, but continues reading when I don't. "'Given the time constraints, I suggest your performance be short and sweet, but something that nonetheless steals you from your rather stunted comfort zone. Do you remember celebrating Jay's birthday last June at Third Coast Comedy? When the MC was plugging their upcoming amateur night, you leaned over and told me you'd rather tackle Mount Everest in a pair of Christian Louboutins. It struck me then, how timid you'd become. At that moment I chose to keep this goal on your list, and decided a stand-up comedy routine would be the perfect antidote for your meekness. You'll be on stage, fulfilling both your wish and mine.'"

"No! Never!" I turn to Brad, desperate to make him see things my way. "I can't! I won't. I'm not the least bit funny."

"Maybe you just haven't worked at it lately."

"Look, I don't care if I'm Ellen-friggin'-DeGeneres, there's no way in hell I'm going to do stand-up. It's time we moved on to Plan B."

"Brett, there is no Plan B. If you want to honor your mother's wishes — and receive your inheritance — you must complete the list."

"No! Don't you get it? I don't want these damn wishes!"

He rises and goes to the window. Silhouetted before the neighboring skyscrapers with his hands planted in his pockets, he looks like a Greek philosopher, contemplating the mysteries of life. "Elizabeth made me think she was doing you a favor with these goals. She told me you might be reluctant, but I had no idea." He rakes a hand through his hair and turns to me. "I'm really sorry."

Something about his tenderness, his undisguised angst makes me bend a little.

"How could you have known? She did think she was doing me a favor. This was her last-ditch effort to change the trajectory of my life."

"She didn't think you were happy?"

I lower my eyes. "Apparently not, which is crazy. My mother rarely saw me without a smile on my face. She used to boast that I came out of the womb smiling."

"But behind the smile?"

The softly spoken, straightforward question catches me off-guard. For some reason, I choke up. My mind goes to little Trevor, and the red splotches of joy that flood his chubby face when he's laughing. My mom once told me I was just like him when I was a kid. I wonder where it goes, that kind of bliss? Perhaps the same place youthful confidence goes.

"I'm perfectly happy. I mean, why wouldn't I be?"

Brad gives me a rueful smile. "Confucius say: The route to happiness is found in stand-up comedy."

I can't help but smile at his lame Chinese accent. "Uh-huh. Confucius also say: Woman without humor should stay away from comedy club."

He chuckles and makes his way back to where I sit. He perches on the edge of his chair, his folded hands so close to my leg they're almost touching me. "I'll be right there with you," he says, "if you want me to be."

"You would?" I look at him as if he's just agreed to a double suicide. "Why?"

He leans back and cradles his neck in his fingers. "It'll be a blast."

"So we'd be like a comedy act . . . a duo?"

He laughs. "Oh, hell no! I said I'd be with you, meaning, I'll watch you — from the audience. This body won't be anywhere near the stage."

I narrow my eyes. "Wimp!"

"You got that right."

I study him. "Why are you being so nice to me? Did my mother put you up to this? Is she paying you or something?"

I expect him to laugh, but he doesn't. "In a way, yes. You see, last spring your mom came to an Alzheimer's fund-raiser I was co-hosting. That's how we met. My dad was diagnosed three years ago."

So that's where the sadness comes from. "I'm so sorry."

"Yeah, me too. Anyway, with the economy in the tank, it looked like we'd fall short of our projections. But your mom stepped in. She made a huge contribution and pushed us over the goal line."

"And so now you feel obligated? That's crazy. My mom did things like that all the time."

"The following week a package was delivered to my office. Soaps, shampoos, lotions, a whole slew of stuff from Bohlinger Cosmetics. It was addressed to my mother."

"Your mother? Wait, I thought you said your dad —"

"That's right."

It takes a second before the puzzle pieces fall into place. "Your mom was also a victim of Alzheimer's."

"Exactly. She cried when I gave her the package. As his caretaker, her needs were pretty much ignored. Your mom knew she needed comfort, too."

"That's my mother. She was the most sensitive woman I ever met."

"She was a saint. So when she made me executor of her estate and explained her plan for you, I gave her my word I'd see it through." His face is fixed with ironclad determination. "And believe me, I will."

CHAPTER SIX

*U*nemployment has its benefits, especially for one who needs to prepare a comedy routine by the month's end. I'm tempted to steal lines I've heard on Comedy Central, but I know Mom wouldn't approve. Instead I spend the week scouring the city. Anything I hear or see that's remotely funny becomes possible fodder for my act. In the hope of overcoming — or at least minimizing — the odds that I'll make a complete ass of myself in public, I spend hours in front of the mirror working to perfect my material. All the while my stomach knots into a tight little rock, and dark circles form tree-rings beneath my eyes.

It occurs to me that this could have been my mom's intention all along. By putting the live performance at the top of my list, she thought I'd be too anxious and preoccupied to think about her. In truth, it's had the opposite effect. Elizabeth Bohlinger loved nothing more than a good laugh. Each time I see someone acting silly, or hear something that makes me grin, it's my mom I want to share it with. If she were alive, I'd call and say, "Have I got a story for you."

That was all she needed to hear. She'd either beg me to tell it on the spot or, more often than not, invite me to dinner later. Once our wine was poured, she'd lean in and tap my arm. "Your story, darling. Please, I've been waiting all day."

I'd embellish the tale, using accents and dialects for effect. Even now I can hear the lilt of her laughter, see her dab tears from the corners of her eyes . . .

I catch myself smiling, and realize that, for the first time since her death, her memory makes me happy, not sad.

And that's just the way she'd want it, the woman who loved to laugh.

The night before my performance I lie awake, restless and edgy. A slice of streetlight finds its way through the wooden blinds and lands on Andrew's rib cage. Propping myself on one elbow, I gaze at him. His chest heaves in perfect synchronicity with the little popping noise that escapes his lips each time he exhales. It takes every bit of strength in me not to run my hand over the buttery smoothness of his skin. His hands are crossed over his flat stomach and his face is serene, not unlike my mother's manufactured death pose.

"Andrew," I whisper. "I'm so scared."

His inert body invites me to continue, or so it seems. "I'm going to perform at a comedy club tomorrow night. I want so badly to tell you, so you can be there with me, or wish me luck. You used to be so good at making me feel safe. Remember how you stayed on the line with me the entire night before my presentation in Milan, just so you'd be there, next to my pillow, in case I woke up?" My voice catches. "But if I told you about this comedy act, I'd have to tell you about this ludicrous list Mother wants me to complete, and I can't do that." I lift my head up to the ceiling and squeeze shut the tears in my eyes. "My life list is so different than yours would be." I start to say, *I love you,* but the phrase gets stuck in my throat. I mouth the words instead.

He stirs and my heart misses a beat. Oh, God, what if he saw me? I sigh. What if he did? Would it really be so bad if the man I live with, the man I share a bed with, knows I love him? I shut my eyes and the answer comes to me full force. Yes it would be. Because I'm not sure he'd be able to say it back.

I plop against the pillow and stare at the ceiling vents. Andrew loves my success and my status, but that's vanished. Does he truly love *me*? Does he even know me — the real me?

I cross an arm over my forehead. It's not his fault. My mother was right. I've kept my true self hidden. I've abandoned my dreams and morphed into exactly the kind of woman Andrew wants me to be — unconventional, undemanding, and unencumbered.

I glance over at my sleeping boyfriend. Why have I given up on the life I once wanted? Is that little girl still rambling around inside me, feeling unworthy? Is my mother right? Have I forsaken my own dreams in a desperate attempt to win Andrew's approval — the approval I never received from my father? No, that's ridiculous. I decided years ago my father's approval meant nothing to me. So why haven't I fought for my dreams? Because Andrew had different aspirations, and I chose to follow his? No, that's just the bighearted, self-sacrificing version of me I like to imagine. As much as I hate to admit it, there's something else, something much less noble . . .

I'm afraid. As weak and gutless as it may sound, I don't want to be alone. Leaving Andrew would be a huge gamble at this stage of my life. Sure, I might meet someone else, but at thirty-four, starting over seems too speculative, like transferring my life savings from a steady money-market account to a risky hedge fund.

True, the gains could be enormous, but the loss could wipe me out entirely. All that I've worked for could vanish in a flash, and I could end up with nothing.

At half past two, I finally pull myself from bed and lumber downstairs to the sofa. From the coffee table my cell phone flashes. I pick it up and read a text message, sent at eleven fifty. *Relax. You're going to be great. Get some sleep now.*

It's from Brad.

A slow smile crosses my face. I crawl under the chenille blanket and snuggle up to the sofa pillow. As if I'd just been kissed on the forehead and given a glass of warm milk, my heart slows and I feel safe again.

The way Andrew used to make me feel.

The size of a ballroom, Third Coast Comedy hosts a raucous, standing-room-only crowd tonight. Round tables fill the main floor, positioned before a wooden stage rising two feet high. Against the back wall, people gather three-deep at the bar, craning their necks to see the act. What's up with all these people on a Monday night? Don't they have jobs, either? From across the table, I grip Brad's arm, shouting to be heard over the roar of the audience.

"I can't believe I let you talk me into this! Couldn't you have found some little hole in the wall?"

"Seven minutes and you'll have goal eighteen behind you," he hollers back to me. "Then you can move on to the other nine."

"Oh, like that's an incentive! Check this one off so I can get my horse and make some sort of peace with my dead asshole of a father?"

"Sorry." He points to his ear. "I can't hear you."

I gulp my martini and turn to my friends. "You look cute tonight," Shelley shouts over the din.

"Thanks." I look down at my T-shirt. Across the front it reads NEVER TRUST A PREACHER WITH A BONER.

I hear another bout of laughter and turn my attention to the stage. Just my luck, I have to follow the crowd favorite, a lanky redhead who's on a riff about bimbos and boobs. I watch a chubby guy at the front table with a beer and three shots lined up in front of him. He whistles and whoops and pumps his fist in the air.

The master of ceremonies jumps onto the stage and grabs the microphone. "Let's give it up for Steve Pinckney." The crowd goes wild.

My heart pounds and I suck in a giant breath.

"Good luck, sis," Shelley shouts.

"Make me laugh, chica," Megan adds.

Brad squeezes my arm. "Liz would be proud of you." This makes my chest ache. From the corner of my eye I spot Bill, the manager, waving me to the stage.

Time folds in on itself. I creep toward the stage like an inmate heading to the electric chair.

"Next we have Brett—" The MC pauses for the ruckus to die down. "Our next guest is first-timer Brett Bohlinger. Let's give him a hand."

I climb the steps to the stage. My legs shake so violently I fear they'll buckle beneath me. Somehow I make it to the microphone, and once there grab hold of the metal stand with both hands to steady me. A bright white spotlight blinds me and I squint into the crowd. Acres of faces stare up at me expectantly. I'm supposed to make a joke now, aren't I? What was it? Help me, God! No, help me, *Mom*! After all, you're the one who put me up to this crazy stunt. I close my eyes. As if we were sitting at her dining room table, I imagine her voice. *Your story, darling. Please, I've been waiting all day.* I take a deep breath and dive into the shark-infested waters of Third Coast Comedy.

"Hello everyone." My tremulous voice is squelched by an obnoxious screech from the microphone. The drunk at the front table groans and covers his ears. I snatch the mike from its cradle. "Sorry," I say. "It's been awhile since I've been on stage. I didn't realize I'd be heckled by the microphone." I chuckle nervously and sneak a peek at my friends. Megan has a counterfeit grin on her face. Shelley records me on her iPhone, and Brad's knee bobs like he's got palsy.

"Um, you-you probably expected a guy when you heard the name Brett. I get that all the time. It's not living — I mean, it's not easy living with a boy's name. You wouldn't believe how mean kids can be. I'd run home from school crying after being teased, and I'd beg my brother, Tiffany, to beat them up."

I shade my eyes and gaze out at the crowd, waiting for the laughter. But all I hear is a little spatter of high-pitched giggling from Megan. "That's right," I say. "My brother, *Tiffany.*"

"You're not funny," the drunk yells out in a singsong voice.

I gasp, as if I'd been kicked in the gut. "And, uh, would you believe all that teasing and tormenting about my name occurred at a Catholic school? H-how many of you are the product of a Catholic school?"

A small portion of the crowd claps, and I take that for encouragement. "The-the nuns at my school were so strict, recess at Saint Mary's was the bathroom break we got after lunch."

Brad, Megan, and Shelley laugh especially loudly at this one. But the rest of the crowd sits watching me, some smiling politely, others checking their watches or cell phones.

"You forgot the punch line," someone hollers.

I think I'm going to vomit — or worse yet, break into tears. I glance at the digital clock positioned at the foot of the stage. Only two minutes, four seconds have passed. Jesus, I've got five more minutes up here! What's next? Oh, God! I don't remember a single joke. Horrified, I wipe my sweaty palms on my jeans and reach into my back pocket for the last resort.

"Aw, Jesus, note cards!" a voice shouts from the back. "Are you fucking kidding me?"

My lip quivers. "Back at Saint Mary's . . ."

The crowd moans. "Enough with the Catholic jokes!" someone shouts.

I can barely hold on to my note cards, my hands shake so violently. "Not only was it a Catholic school, but it was an all-girls school too. Kind of a two-for-one torture chamber."

The crowd boos. My eyes tear up and I fumble through the cards. Oh, Jesus, help me! People begin talking aloud now, no longer disguising their boredom. Others head to the bar or to the restroom. I see Shelley lower her phone, no longer capturing this fiasco on film. The drunk at the front table leans back in his chair, a longneck bottle clenched in his chubby fist.

"Next!" he shouts, lifting his arm and pointing to the stage, beckoning the next act.

Screw this! I'm outta here! I spin around, ready to bolt. But standing at the bottom of the stage steps, I see Brad.

"Shake it off, B.B.," he hollers over the noise. "Keep going."

I love him so much at this moment that I want to leap off the stage and throw my arms around him. I also want to choke him. He — and my mother — are the ones who forced me to do this.

"You can do it. You're almost there."

Fighting every impulse to run for my life, I turn back to the audience — the abusive barbarians who think it's intermission time.

"The nuns . . . they did everything in their power to keep us girls pure of thought." Nobody listens, not even my support team. Megan is talking to some guy at next table, and Shelley is sending a text. Nobody except Brad. I glance over at him and he nods.

"We had this, this big crucifix in our classroom. Sister Rose —" I rub my aching throat. "Sister Rose actually put a pair of pants over Jesus's loincloth."

"Twenty more seconds, B.B.," he shouts.

"My friend Kasey . . . won't even change her baby boy's diapers without closing her eyes."

"Sit down, lady," someone shouts. "You're killing us."

Brad begins a countdown. "Seven, six, five . . ."

I hear "zero" and slam the mike in its cradle. Brad whoops. When I leap from the stage, he grabs me in a hug. But I'm sobbing now. I break free and I race for the exit.

The night air is crisp and burns when I suck it in. Through tears I stagger across the parking lot until I find my car. I drop my arms on the rooftop and bury my head.

A moment later I feel a hand on my shoulder.

"Don't cry, B.B. You did it. It's over now." Brad rubs circles on my racking back.

"I sucked!" I say, pounding my fist on the roof. I spin around and face him. "I told you I wasn't funny."

He pulls me into his arms. I don't resist.

"Damn my mother," I say against his wool coat.

Silently, he rocks me.

"Why did she make me do this? I was a laughingstock — no, not a laughingstock . . . that would imply someone actually laughed."

He steps back and removes a pale pink envelope from his pocket. "Shall we let her defend herself?"

I wipe my nose with the back of my hand. "You're giving me the letter?"

He smiles and dabs a tear from my cheek. "I'm thinking you earned it, big time."

We get in my car and I crank the heat. In the passenger seat beside me, Brad slides a finger beneath the seal of envelope number eighteen and begins to read.

"'My Dearest Girl,

"'You're upset because you failed? Nonsense.'"

"What?" I say. "She knew I'd —"

Brad doesn't let me finish. He just keeps reading. "'At what point did you decide you must be perfect? For the life of me, I can't pinpoint it. But somewhere along the road, you lost your chutzpah. That happy little girl who loved to tell stories and sing and dance became anxious and unsure.'"

Pressure builds behind my eyes. *It wasn't you who silenced me, Mother.*

"'But tonight you were alive, my little performer, just as you used to be, and for that I'm so very pleased. I believe such passion — even passion born of fear and anxiety — is far better than a life of banality.

"'Let tonight's tale serve as a reminder of your spunk, your fortitude, your bravery. When you're fearful, grab hold of this courage and shake it loose, because now you know it's yours, just as I've known all along.

"'Eleanor Roosevelt once said, "Do something every day that scares you." Continue to push yourself to do those things that scare you, darling. Take those risks and see where you land, for they are the very things that make this journey worthwhile.'" He pauses for a moment. "'With all my love and pride, Mom.'"

I take the letter and re-read it, running my fingers over my mom's words. Just what is it that she's urging me to do? I think of Andrew, and the teaching job, and Carrie. I shudder. But as scary as those things are, there's one thing that terrifies me more. I push it from my thoughts. It's true, I failed tonight and lived through it, but I'm not ready for a repeat performance.

CHAPTER SEVEN

Dressed in my favorite Marc Jacobs suit, I'm sipping a latte at The Bourgeois Pig when Megan arrives midmorning. "Not another crossword puzzle!" She plops her purple Dolce & Gabbana tote on the table and snatches the puzzle out from under me. "I finally realize why your mother gave you a fucking deadline. Have you done a goddamn thing since that comedy act last week? When she told you to go after your dreams, I don't think she meant napping in the park." She points to my suit. "You've haven't even told Andrew yet!"

She tosses my newspaper aside and pulls the laptop from my satchel. "Today we're going to find your old friend."

"I can't just contact Carrie out of the blue. I need to figure out a plan first." I push the computer away and rub my temples. "I'm telling you, this list will ruin my life."

Megan studies me with a furrowed brow. "You're a strange

bird, Brett. I've got a feeling those goals might actually make you happy. It's Andrew's life you're afraid of ruining, not yours."

I'm taken aback by her candor and insight. "Maybe. But either way, I'm screwed. I'll lose my boyfriend, and I still won't be able to knock off these goals by next September."

Ignoring my little rant, she slides back her chair. "I need caffeine. You get on Facebook while I get my fix."

While Megan stands in line at the counter, I log on to Facebook. But instead of searching for Carrie, my fingers type BRAD MIDAR into the search bar. It's a cinch to spot him, even in the one-square-inch profile picture. Staring at his photo, I catch myself smiling. It occurs to me to send him a friend request, but he might think that's crossing a professional line — as if text messages and hugs don't. And then I think of my own boundaries. What would Andrew think if he knew I was searching out a friendship with the attorney I've kept secret from him?

I grip two fistfuls of my hair. What's wrong with me?

"Did you find her?" Megan says, coming up behind me with a macchiato and a scone. I slap shut the laptop. "Not yet."

I wait until Megan is on the other side of the table before I open the computer again, this time typing CARRIE NEWSOME in the search bar.

With her chair scooted next to mine, we wade through several pages, and then I spot her. Sporting a Wisconsin sweatshirt, she's remarkably unchanged. Still athletic looking, still wearing glasses, still smiling. Guilt takes hold of me. How could I have been so cruel?

"That's her?" Megan asks. "No wonder you wanted to lose her. Don't they sell tweezers in Wisconsin?"

"Stop it, Megan." I stare at her photo through a teary haze. "I loved this girl."

Growing up, Carrie and her parents lived two blocks away from us on Arthur Street. We were opposites, she the spunky tomboy, me the skinny girlie-girl. One afternoon when I was five years old, she sauntered past my house toting a black-and-white ball. When she saw me, a girl about her age, she recruited me to play soccer with her. I suggested we play House instead, but she wouldn't hear of it. So we walked to the park and climbed the monkey bars and swung and giggled the rest of the afternoon. From that day on, we were inseparable — until years later, when I abandoned her.

"I have no right to expect a friendship from this woman. And what's worse, I'm only doing it now because I have to."

"Really?" She tugs her arm. "Because I'd say she has no right to expect a friendship from you."

I shake my head. Megan would never understand that a person who looks like Carrie just might be out of our league.

"Jesus, Brett, what's the big fucking deal?" In an instant, she's hijacked the cursor and clicked ADD FRIEND.

I gasp. "I can't believe you did that!"

"Way to go, chica!" She raises her coffee cup, but I don't lift mine. At any moment now, Carrie Newsome will receive a cruel reminder of the once loved friend who betrayed her. I feel sick, but Megan's already moving on. She rubs her hands together.

"Okay, we're on a roll now. Let's go to the pet store and find you a dog."

"Forget it. Dogs smell bad. They mess up the house." I sip my coffee. "At least that's Andrew's take."

"What's Andrew got to do with it?" She breaks off a corner of her scone. "Brett, I'm sorry, but do you really think Andrew's part of your life plan? I mean, your mother basically told you he's history. Are you willing to ignore her last wish?"

Megan has found my Achilles' heel. I park my elbows on the table and pinch the bridge of my nose. "I've got to tell Andrew about this damn list. But he'll go ballistic. He wants to buy a plane someday, not a horse! Kids aren't part of his plan. He made that perfectly clear early on."

"And that was okay with you?"

I look out the window, my mind stretching back to another time, a time when I was bold and fearless, and certain my dreams really would come true. But then it happened, as it must, and I learned that the world didn't revolve around me.

"I convinced myself it was okay. Things were different back then. We traveled a lot . . . he'd join me on business trips. Our lives were so full it was hard to imagine having a child."

"And now?"

She's asking for the updated version of my life. The version where I eat alone most nights in front of the television and the last trip we took was to his sister's wedding in Boston two years ago. "I've just lost my mother and my job. I can't deal with more loss. Not yet."

She dabs her mouth with the napkin, and I notice her eyelashes are spiked with tears. I grab her hand. "I'm sorry. I didn't mean to unload on you."

Her face crumples. "I can't go on like this."

Oh. She's not crying for me. She's crying for herself. But I'm a fine one to talk. I've been so self-absorbed lately I make Megan look like a guidance counselor. I take her hand.

"More text messages on Jimmy's phone?"

"Worse. They were having sex in our bed when I got home yesterday. Our goddamn bed! Thank God I was able to get the hell out before they saw me."

"That jackass! Why would he bring her home, of all places? He knows you don't keep a regular schedule."

"He wants me to catch him. He doesn't have the balls to break it off, so he's hoping I will." She tugs her left wrist and heaves a sigh. "It's these damn arms. I'm deformed."

"That's ridiculous. You're beautiful and you need to dump his ass."

"I can't. What would I do for money?"

"You'd start selling houses."

She waves me off. "Phssh. I'm telling you, Brett, I must have been royalty in my past life, because I just can't get used to this idea of working for a living."

"Well, you can't just sit there and take it. Maybe if you confront him —"

"No!" she says, nearly shouting. "I can't confront him until I have another option."

At first I don't understand, but then it dawns on me. Megan wants a replacement before she gives up the original. She's like a terrified child, hoping to find a new family to take her in before she becomes an orphan.

"You don't need someone to take care of you. You're a smart woman. You can make it on your own." I hear my own words, and wonder if I'm speaking to Megan now, or to myself. I soften my tone. "I know it's hard, Meggie, but you can do it."

"Not happening."

I sigh. "Then you need to put yourself out there. Maybe go online to one of those match sites."

She rolls her eyes and pulls a tube of lip gloss from her purple bag. "Seeking gorgeous millionaire. Must like short arms."

"I'm serious, Megan, you'll have somebody new in no time. Someone much better." A thought occurs to me and I snap my fingers. "Hey, what about Brad?"

"Your mom's attorney?"

"Yeah. He's really nice. And cute, too, don't you think?"

She dabs her lips with gloss. "Uh-huh. There's just one teensy problem."

My nostrils flare. "What? He's not rich enough?"

"Nope." She smacks her lips together. "He's already in love with you."

My head snaps back as if I've been hit. Oh, my God! Could he be? But I've got Andrew. Sort of.

"Why do you think that?" I ask when I finally find my voice.

She shrugs. "Why else would he be so hell-bent on helping you?"

I should be relieved. What I need from Brad is friendship, not romance. But strangely, I deflate. "Nope. He's on Team Elizabeth. He's only helping me because he promised my mother he would. Trust me. I'm just his charity case."

Instead of arguing with me, as I hoped she would, she nods. "Ah, got it."

I hang my head. Am I no different than Megan, searching for a replacement before I lose the original?

My hands tremble when I open the letter. I read her words one more time. *Push yourself to do those things that scare you, darling.* Why, Mother? Why are you making me do this? I tuck the letter into my pocket and enter the gate.

It's been seven years since I've been to Saint Boniface Cemetery. That last time was with my mom. We were going somewhere — Christmas shopping, I think — but she insisted we make a quick detour first. It was a frigid afternoon. I remember watching the wind whip across the street, changing what little snow we had into angry, whirling eddies of ice. My mother and I fought the gales, and together we fastened an evergreen wreath to my father's headstone. I returned to the car then and turned the key in the ignition. Clouds of heat billowed from the vents. I warmed my hands and watched my mom standing silent, her head bowed. Then she dabbed her eyes with her glove and made the sign of the cross.

When she turned back to the car, I pretended to fiddle with the car radio, hoping to spare her dignity. I was embarrassed for her, a woman who still harbored devotion to the husband who'd abandoned her.

Unlike that day seven years ago, it is a glorious autumn day, the sky so pure and blue that winter's threat seems laughable. Leaves play tag with the soft breeze, and other than the squirrels searching for nuts beneath walnut trees, I'm alone in the beautiful hillside cemetery.

"You probably wonder why I'm here, after all these years," I whisper to the headstone. "Do you think I'm just like Mother? Unable to hate you?"

I brush dried leaves from the base of his headstone and perch on the marble slab. Reaching into my purse, I search out his picture from my wallet, wriggling it from between my library card and gym membership. It's dog-eared and faded, but the only picture I've kept of the two of us. Mother snapped the photo Christmas morning when I was six years old. Dressed in red flannel pajamas, I'm propped at the edge of his knee, my hands folded, as though praying I could leave the precarious spot. He rests one pale hand on my shoulder; the other hangs limply at his side. An uncertain smile hovers at his lips, but his eyes are flat and empty.

"What was it about me, Dad? Why couldn't I make you smile? Why was it so hard to put your arms around me?"

My eyes sting and I lift my head to the sky, hoping for that rush of peace my mother must have envisioned when she left this item on my list. But all I feel is the warm sun on my face and an open wound in my chest. I stare down at the picture. A teardrop lands on my pixie face, magnifying my injured eyes. I blot it with my shirtsleeve, leaving a warped ripple in its wake.

"Do you know what hurts most, Dad? It's feeling that I was never good enough for you. I was just a little girl. Why couldn't you tell me, even once, that I was good, or smart, or pretty?" I bite my lip until I taste blood. "I tried so hard to make you love me. I really did."

Tears stream down my cheeks. Pulling myself from the slab, I stare at the headstone as if it were my father's face. "This was Mother's idea, you know. She's the one who wants me to establish a relationship with you. I'd given up on that dream years ago." I run my fingertips over the engraved CHARLES JACOB BOHLINGER. "I wish you peace, Dad."

I turn and walk away, then break into a run.

*I*t's five o'clock by time I reach Argyle Station, and I'm still shaken. But I'll be damned if I'll let that bastard get to me. The El is packed and I'm sandwiched between a teenage girl whose iPod blares so loudly I can hear the lyrical obscenities through her earbuds, and a man wearing a baseball cap that says GODHEARSU.COM. I want to ask him whether God uses a Mac or a PC, but something tells me he wouldn't find it amusing. I lock eyes with a tall, dark-haired man in a khaki Burberry trench coat. His eyes are laughing, too, and there's something familiar about him. He leans in, both of us towering over the two young girls between us. "Technology's amazing, huh?"

I laugh. "No kidding. Confessional booths may soon be a thing of the past."

He grins, and I can't decide whether to focus on the golden flecks in his brown eyes or his soft, sensuous mouth. I spy a black thread on his tan coat and it hits me. Could this be the Burberry man I used to watch from the window of the loft, coming into the building every evening at seven? I dubbed him the Burberry man because he always wore a Burberry trench coat — just like the one he's wearing now. Though I never actually met him, I harbored a secret crush on him for a month or two — before he disappeared as quickly as he came.

I'm about to introduce myself when my phone rings. I see Brad's office number and pick up.

"Hello, Brett. It's Claire Cole. I got your message. Mr. Midar could see you October twenty-seventh at —"

"The twenty-seventh? That's three weeks away. I need . . ." My voice trails off. *I need to see him* sounds too impassioned, too desperate. But after today's cemetery visit, I'm on an emotional ledge, and I know Brad would talk me down. "I'd like to see him sooner, like tomorrow."

"I'm sorry. He's completely booked for the next week, and then he's going on vacation. He could see you on the twenty-seventh," she repeats. "He's got an eight o'clock opening."

I sigh. "If that's the first he's got, I'll take it. But if anyone cancels before then, call me. Please."

My stop is announced. I tuck my phone into my coat pocket and make my way toward the door.

"Have a good one," Burberry says to me as I squeeze past him.

"You, too."

I dash from the train, but not before a wave of melancholy catches me. Brad Midar is going away, and I don't like it one bit. I wonder where he's going. Is he traveling alone, or with a girlfriend? So far, the time has never felt quite right to ask him about his relationship status, and he's never offered. And why should he? I'm his client, for God's sake! But he's also my only link to my mother. I fear I've developed an unnaturally strong bond with him, as her messenger. Like a motherless baby duckling, I've imprinted on the first kind face I've found.

CHAPTER EIGHT

When my mother was alive and healthy, Thursday night was traditionally family night for the Bohlingers. We'd gather around her dining room table, where the conversation flowed as easily as the Sauvignon Blanc. With Mom seated at the head, topics shifted seamlessly from current events to politics to personal interests. Tonight, for the first time since her death, Joad and Catherine are boldly attempting to re-create the magic.

Joad kisses me on the cheek when I arrive. "Thanks for coming," he says, his suede blazer sheltered beneath a black-and-white-striped apron.

I slip off my shoes and sink into the sumptuous white carpet. Though Joad's taste in décor leans traditional, Catherine adores contemporary. The result is an immaculate, sparsely decorated condo in shades of whites and beiges, punctuated with fabulous original paintings and modern sculptures. The rather sterile place is definitely cool, if not inviting.

"Something smells delicious," I say.

"Rack of lamb, and it's just about ready. C'mon, Jay and Shelley are already on their second glass of Pinot."

As we should have anticipated, Mom's absence is as pronounced as a southern drawl. The five of us sit in Joad and Catherine's formal dining room overlooking the Chicago River, pretending not to notice the missing energy that was our mother. Instead, we cloak the awkward silence with idle chatter. After Catherine's twenty-minute riff about BC's third-quarter earnings and her plans for future expansion, the topic turns to me. She wants to know why Andrew isn't with me. Jay wonders if I've found a teaching job. Each question rocks me, like the aftershock following an earthquake. In need of a breather, I excuse myself the minute Joad heads to the kitchen to caramelize his famous crème brûlée.

As I travel down the hall toward the bathroom, I glance in at Joad's den. The small, cherry-paneled room is my brother's home office as well as his sanctuary, and I'd never enter uninvited. Behind locked cabinets he hides his collection of single-malt scotches and, though Catherine abhors smoking in the house, a humidor filled with Cuban cigars. As I pass, something on his desk catches my eye. I backtrack.

It takes a second for my eyes to adjust to the shadowed hue. I blink several times. There, atop a file folder on Joad's mahogany desk, sits the red leather journal.

What the hell? I step into the room. When I asked about the missing book, everyone, including Joad, denied having seen it. I pick it up, the cover no longer hidden by my mom's note. Her handwriting greets me and my chest tightens. *Summer of 1978*— the summer before I was born. No wonder Joad wanted it. This book is priceless. But surely he knows I'd share it with him and Jay.

Before I have time to open it, I hear footsteps coming down the hall. It's Joad. I freeze. I want to tell him I found my book and I'm taking it back, but something tells me to keep quiet. He obviously doesn't want me to have it. He passes the office without so much as a glance and I breathe a sigh of relief. Stuffing the book beneath my sweater, I leave the room as soundlessly as I'd entered.

I'm buttoning my coat when I step into the dining room.

"I'm sorry, Catherine. I'm going to skip dessert. I'm not feeling well."

"Wait, we'll drive you," Shelley says.

I shake my head. "No, thanks. I'll catch a cab. Tell Joad goodbye for me."

I'm out the door before Joad knows I've left.

The elevator doors slam shut and I let out a breath. God help me, I'm a thief! But a righteous thief. I pull my treasure from beneath my sweater and hug the little book to my chest, as if it's my mother I'm clinging to. I miss her so much right now. How like her to know exactly when I'd need her.

The elevator jerks to life. Against my better judgment telling me to wait until I'm under covers with my bedside lamp aglow, I open the cover for a quick peek.

By the time the elevator doors slide open, I'm transfixed. I stagger to a chair in the corner of the lobby, stunned and bewildered, and unravel the mystery that has puzzled me all my life.

*I*t could have been minutes. It could have been hours. Just how long I'd been sitting here when I hear my brother's voice, I couldn't say.

"Brett," Joad says, keeping his voice low as he trots toward me. "Don't open that book!"

I can't respond. I can't move. I'm numb.

"Jesus." He squats down beside me and takes the open journal from my lap. "I was hoping to reach you before you read it."

"Why?" I ask through a blurry haze. "Why would you keep this from me?"

"For just this reason," he says, brushing back my tear-soaked hair. "Look at you. You just lost Mom. The last thing you needed was another shock."

"I had a right to know, damn it!"

The marble floor amplifies my voice. Joad looks around, nodding sheepishly to the concierge at the front desk. "Let's go upstairs."

"No." I sit up, speaking to him through clenched teeth. "You should have told me. Mom should have told me! I struggled with that relationship my entire life. And this, *this* is how she tells me?"

"You don't know for sure, Brett. This journal tells us nothing. In all likelihood, you were Charles's daughter."

I jab a finger at him. "I was never that bastard's daughter. Never. And he knew it. That's why he never loved me. And Mom didn't have the guts to tell me!"

"Okay, okay. But maybe this Johnny Manns was an asshole. Maybe she didn't want you to find him."

"No. It's perfectly clear. She left me the journal. She left goal nineteen on my list. She wants me to find my real father, to have a relationship with him. Mom may have been a coward while she was alive, but at least she had the decency to leave me her story — *my* story — when she died." My eyes bore into his. "And you, you were going to keep it from me! Just how long have you known?"

He looks away and rubs a hand over his shiny scalp. Finally, he drops into a chair beside mine and stares down at the journal. "I found this years ago, when I was helping Mom move into Astor Street. It made me sick. She never knew I saw it. I was shocked when it surfaced again the day of the funeral."

"It made you sick? Don't you see how happy she was in these pages?" I take the book and open to the first entry.

"'May third. After twenty-seven years of slumber, love has arrived and awakened me from my sleep. The old me would say it's wrong, it's immoral. But the woman I've become feels helpless to stop it. For the first time, my heart has found its rhythm.'"

Joad holds out a hand, as if he can't bear to hear any more. My heart softens. It can't be easy finding out your mother had a lover.

"Who else knows?" I ask.

"Only Catherine. And she's probably telling Jay and Shelley now."

I let out a deep breath. My brother was doing what he thought was best. He wanted to protect me. "I can handle this, Joad." I blot my eyes with my shirtsleeve. "I'm furious with Mom for not telling me years ago, but I'm glad she finally did. I'm going to find him."

He shakes his head. "I figured you would. I suppose I can't talk you out of it."

"No way." I smile up at him. "You really were going to give this back to me, weren't you?"

He smooths my hair. "Of course. Once we figured out how to deal with it."

"Deal with it?"

"Yeah, you know, we can't just spring this on the public. Mom was a brand. The last thing the company needs is to have her spotless reputation tarnished by an illegitimate daughter."

The breath is knocked out of me. My brother's intentions weren't so noble after all. To him, I'm the illegitimate daughter who might just tarnish the Bohlinger Brand.

That night while Andrew sleeps, I creep from our bed, grab my laptop and my robe, and head for the sofa. Before I have time to Google Johnny Manns, I find a Facebook message from my old friend Carrie Newsome. I stare at the picture of the earthy-looking woman in the sweatshirt who was once my best friend.

Brett Bohlinger? My long-lost friend from Rogers Park? I can't believe you remembered me—let alone found me on Facebook! I have so many fond memories of you. Believe it or not, I'm going to be in Chicago next month. The National Association of Social Workers conference is at McCormick Place on November 14. Would you have time to meet for lunch, or better yet, dinner? Oh, Bretel, I'm so glad you found me! I've missed you!

Bretel. The old nickname she'd given me when we were kids. She'd compiled a list of possibilities after I'd complained for a week straight about having a boy's name. "How about Bretchen? Bretta? Brettany?" she asked. We finally settled on Bretel, a name that conjured images of candy houses and quick-witted children. And it stuck. To everyone else I was Brett. But to my dearest friend, I was Bretel.

It was a gilded autumn morning when Carrie announced her mother was taking a job at the University of Wisconsin. Dressed in plaid kilts and white blouses, we strolled down the sidewalk toward Loyola Academy, our new high school. I can almost hear the leaves crunching beneath our feet and see the canopy of reds and golds overhead. But the pain I feel over losing Carrie isn't imagined. I really do feel an ache in my heart, as if, after all these years, it's still bruised.

"My dad's taking me to dinner tonight," I told Carrie.

"That's great," she said, always my biggest ally. "I bet he misses you."

I kicked a pile of leaves. "Yeah, maybe."

We walked on in silence for half a block before she turned to me. "We're moving, Brett."

She didn't use my nickname then. Alarmed, I looked into eyes flooded with tears. Still, I refused to understand. "We are?" I asked, in all sincerity.

"No!" Through her tears, she laughed, sending a missile of snot blasting from her nose.

"Gross!" I cried. We doubled over with laughter, pushing each other into the leaves, not wanting the merriment to end. Because when it finally did, we were left staring into each other's empty faces. "Please, tell me you're not."

"I'm sorry, Bretel. We are."

My world ended that day. Or so I thought. The girl who could read my thoughts, challenge my thinking, laugh at my dim-witted jokes was leaving me. Madison seemed as far from Rogers Park as Uzbekistan. Five weeks later I stood on her porch stoop and waved good-bye as the moving van pulled away. For that first year, we wrote to each other like faithful lovers. Until one weekend she came back to visit, and we never spoke again. For all the atoning I've done, I've never forgiven myself. And for all the new friends I've made, I've never loved another like I loved Carrie Newsome.

Her message stares at me like a hungry puppy beside the dinner table. Doesn't she remember how I treated her the last time I saw her? I bury my head in my hands. When I finally lift my head, I type as fast as I can.

I miss you, too, Care Bear, and I'm so sorry. I'd love to see you on the 14th. Your hotel?

I push ENTER.
Next, I type JOHNNY MANNS.

CHAPTER NINE

$\mathcal{B}$rad and I sit in the matching leather chairs. I sip a cup of tea while he drinks from a water bottle and tells me about his trip. I can smell his cologne, and up close I notice he once had a pierced ear.

"San Francisco's awesome," he says. "Ever been there?"

"Twice. It's one of my favorite cities." I hide my face in my teacup and ask, "Was it business or pleasure?"

"Pleasure. My girlfriend Jenna moved out there last summer. She got a job with the *San Francisco Chronicle*."

Perfect. We're both in relationships. We won't have that distracting sexual tension between us. So why did my heart just take a nosedive?

"Wonderful!" I say, trying my damnedest to sound excited.

"It is. For her. She's loving it, but it puts a strain on our relationship."

"I can imagine. Being two thousand miles apart can't be easy, not to mention the two-hour time difference."

He shakes his head. "Or the eleven-year age difference."

I quickly calculate and guess Jenna must be about thirty. "Eleven years isn't such a huge gap."

"Exactly what I tell her. But she gets freaked out now and then." He goes to his desk and retrieves the photo of the woman and her son — the one I mistook for his older sister and nephew. "This is Jenna," he says. "And that's her son, Nate. He's a freshman at NYU."

I study the woman with a bashful smile and bright blue eyes. "She's really pretty."

"She is." He smiles at the picture, and I feel a pang of envy. How must it feel to be so adored?

I straighten in my chair and try to look officious. "I've got some news to report."

He cocks his head. "You and Andrew are having a baby? Buying a horse?"

"No. But I have made my last visit to Charles Bohlinger's grave site."

He raises his eyebrows. "You've already made peace with him?"

I shake my head. "Charles Bohlinger wasn't my real father, and I need you to help me find the man who is." I tell him about my mother's journal and the man she fell in love with the summer before I was born. "The final entry is on August twenty-ninth, the day Charles discovered the affair and Johnny left town. My mother was devastated. She wanted to leave Charles, but Johnny made her stay. Even though he loved her, he had dreams of being a musician. He couldn't settle down. Whether or not she knew she was pregnant, I'll never know. But she was — about two months' along. With Johnny's baby." I notice Brad's furrowed brow. "Trust me, Brad. Charles and I looked nothing alike. We had absolutely no connection. There's not a doubt in my mind that Johnny Manns is my father."

Brad sucks in a breath. "That's a lot to take in. How do you feel about this?"

I sigh. "Hurt. Deceived. Furious. I can't believe my mother didn't tell me, especially once Charles died. She knew how much I wanted a father. But more than anything, I feel relief. It explains so much. I finally understand why my father disliked me. It wasn't because I was a horrible girl, like I always thought. It was because I wasn't his daughter." I swallow and lift a hand to my mouth. "I've held so much anger for him. Now that I know the truth, that anger is fading."

"That's huge. And just think, you have a father out there somewhere."

"Yeah, that's the scary part. I have no idea how to find him." I bite my lip. "I also have no idea how he'll respond when I show up on his doorstep."

Brad squeezes my hand and looks directly into my eyes. "He'll love you."

My foolish heart skips a beat. I reclaim my hand and fold it on my lap. "Think you could help me find him?"

"You bet." He leaps to his feet and moves to his computer. "Let's start by Googling him."

"Wow!" I say, in mock admiration. "Google him? You think of everything. Give yourself a raise!"

He turns to me and his smile vanishes. But his eyes crinkle at the edges, and I know he gets me. "Smart-ass."

I laugh. "You think I haven't already Googled him? Come on, Midar."

He returns to his seat and crosses a leg over his knee. "Okay, so what'd you find?"

"I thought I'd found him right off, a band leader named Johnny Mann. But he was born in 1918."

"Yeah, that'd make him a pretty old geezer, even in 1978. Besides, this guy was Manns, not Mann, right?"

"That's how she wrote it in her journal. But I'm not ruling out Mann. I've also tried John, Johnny, and Jonathan. The problem is, there are over ten million Google entries! There's no way I can find him without narrowing the search."

"What else did she say about him? Was he from Chicago?"

"He was from North Dakota. I'm guessing he was my mom's age from the way she describes him, though I don't know for sure. He sublet the apartment above theirs when they lived on Bosworth Avenue, in Rogers Park. He was a musician, and he worked at a bar called Justine's just down the street."

He snaps a finger and points at me. "Bingo! We're going there now — to Justine's! We'll ask around, see if anyone remembers him."

I look at him and roll my eyes. "Remind me from which online university you earned your law degree."

"What?"

"We're talking over thirty years ago, Brad. Justine's isn't even Justine's anymore. It's a gay bar called Neptune."

He narrows his eyes at me. "You've already checked it out, haven't you?"

I fight a smile. "Okay, I admit it. I'm as dim-witted as you." I throw up my hands. "Obviously, we can't do this alone. We need an expert, Brad. Don't you know someone who can help?"

He goes to his desk and returns with his cell phone. "I do have someone I use occasionally with divorce cases. Steve Pohlonski. He's pretty good at detective work. But I can't guarantee he can find Johnny Manns."

"He's got to!" I cry, suddenly desperate to find my father. "If he can't, there's got to be someone else who can. I won't stop until I find this man."

Brad studies me and nods. "Good for you. This is the first time I've seen you embrace a goal with enthusiasm. I'm proud of you."

He's right. It's no longer my mom pushing me to accomplish goal number nineteen. It's no longer that girl's goal. A relationship with my father is something I want with all my heart, something I've wanted my whole life.

I leave the office wondering why it is I have this strange need to please Brad. Like my mother, he seems certain I can obtain these goals. Together, maybe we really will make my mom proud. Before I have time to ponder further, my phone rings. I open the double doors to Randolph Street and fish my phone from my purse.

"Brett Bohlinger? This is Susan Christian from the Chicago Public Schools. We've received your application and immunization records, and we've conducted your background check. I'm happy to say everything looks satisfactory. You're now eligible to substitute-teach. Congratulations."

A blast of October wind smacks me in the face. "Uh, okay, thanks."

"We need a fifth-grade sub tomorrow at Douglas J. Keyes Elementary, in Woodlawn. Are you available?"

I'm lying in bed with my novel, reading the same paragraph for the third time, when I hear the door open. I used to be so happy to see Andrew at the end of the day. Now my chest constricts and I have trouble breathing. I need to tell him the truth, but at ten o'clock at night, when he's exhausted and needs to relax, it hardly seems the time. At least that's how I rationalize it.

I slap shut my book and listen to him rifle through the cabinets and the fridge. Next I hear the sound of his feet slogging up the stairs to our bedroom as if he's wearing forty-pound boots. I can always gauge Andrew's mood by the sound of his feet as they climb the steps. Tonight he's exhausted and discouraged.

"Hey," I say, tossing aside my book. "How was your day?"

He plops down on the edge of the bed holding a bottle of Heineken. His face is ashy, and dark circles hover like crescent moons beneath his eyes. "You're in bed early."

I glance at the bedside clock. "It's almost ten. You're just later than usual. Can I get you some dinner?"

"I'm okay." He slides his tie down his chest and unbuttons his miraculously crisp blue shirt. "How was your day?"

"Fine," I say, feeling my blood pressure soar at the thought of tomorrow's substitute-teaching assignment. "But tomorrow's going to be a bitch. Big meeting with some new clients."

"You'll adjust. Your mother handled it. You will, too." He takes a swig of beer. "Catherine being helpful?"

I wave dismissively. "She runs the place, just like she always did." Dear Jesus! I'm walking a wire, and I need to get off before I slip! I gather my knees to my chest and lock them in a hug. "Tell me about your day."

He rakes a hand through his hair. "It sucked. Got a client who's accused of murdering a nineteen-year-old for throwing a rock at his Hummer." He sets his beer on a coaster and goes to his closet. "Makes running a cosmetics company look like a day at Disney."

Though I'm not running the company, nor am I even a menial advertising exec, the insult hits its mark like a knuckle sandwich. As far as he knows, I'm the president of that cosmetics company. Therefore I'd appreciate a modicum of respect, and frankly, a bit of awe and admiration as well. I open my mouth to defend myself, but snap it shut before I utter the first word. I'm the liar in this scenario, and the only thing worse than a liar is a self-righteous liar.

He must see that I'm offended, because he comes up beside me and squeezes my arm. "Hey, I didn't mean anything by that. I'm just saying, you've got a good gig."

My heart speeds. Now is the time. I take a deep breath. "But I don't have a good gig, Andrew. I've been pretending —"

"Would you stop with the second-guessing already? I get it. You feel like an imposter. We all do, sometimes. But you've got to step up, babe, show that you're up to the task. Stop doubting yourself. You're coming into your own now, becoming the woman your mother — and I — always knew you could be."

Oh, Jesus! I can't tell him the truth now. "Um, well, I don't know about that."

"There's not a doubt in my mind." He pulls a cedar hanger from the closet and slides his suit coat over it. Then he removes his pants, finds their crease, and clips them to the hanger, bottomside up. I study his smooth, tan skin and rippled abs. Along with his clothing and his physique, Andrew expects perfection in everything — including his girlfriend. A pit forms in my stomach.

"I've been thinking more and more about Bohlinger Cosmetics. I'd like you to consider bringing me aboard."

I gasp. "I . . . I'm not sure that's such a good idea."

He shoots me a look. "Really? What's changed? At one time you were all for it."

Three years ago I went to my mother, asking her to create a position for Andrew. But she refused. "Brett, darling, I simply won't consider it unless the two of you are married. And even then, you'd have a hard time convincing me to hire Andrew."

"Why? He's brilliant. Andrew works harder than anyone I know."

"Andrew would be an asset to many corporations, no doubt. But I'm not sure he's a good fit for BC." She locked eyes with me then, the way she always did when she had something difficult to say. "My sense is that Andrew is a bit more aggressive than is necessary for a business such as ours."

I swallow hard and force myself to look at Andrew. "But Mother was against it, remember? Besides, you've said many times what a good decision that was. You admitted you'd never be happy at a cosmetics company."

He moves to the bed and leans over me, positioning one bare arm on either side of me. "But that was before my girlfriend was president of the company."

"Which confirms the fact that you shouldn't work there."

He lowers his body, planting kisses on my forehead, my nose, my lips. "Imagine the fringe benefits," he whispers, his voice husky. "We create an adjoining office next to your corner suite. I'm your company's attorney as well as your private sex slave."

I giggle. "You're already my sex slave."

Nuzzling my neck, he lifts my nightshirt. "There's nothing sexier than a powerful woman. Come here, Madame President."

But if you knew I was a powerless substitute teacher, would you still find me sexy? I grope for the lamp switch, grateful when the room goes black, and lie still as he makes his way down my body.

My good angel reminds me that I need to tell him the truth, and soon. My bad angel tells her to mind her own business, and wraps her legs around his naked back.

I arrive at Douglas Keyes Elementary clad in black slacks and a black sweater, wearing my bright orange shoes in honor of Halloween season. Children love teachers who dress in holiday themes, though I refuse to wear the requisite appliqué pumpkin sweatshirts until I'm at least fifty.

Principal Bailey, an attractive African American woman, leads me down a terrazzo hallway toward Mrs. Porter's classroom.

"Woodlawn is home to several housing projects and a variety of street gangs. Not the easiest group to teach, but we're up for the challenge. I like to think Douglas Keyes Elementary serves as a safe haven for our youngsters."

"Nice."

"Mrs. Porter went into labor early this morning, three weeks earlier than expected. Unless it's a false start, she'll be out the next six weeks. Are you available to substitute long-term should we need you?"

My breath catches. "Uh, let me think . . ."

Six weeks? That's thirty days! My temples throb. Atop a set of double doors at the end of the hall, I see a bright red EXIT sign. I'm tempted to make a dash for it, never to return. But I think of that girl's list. If I serve my time for the next six weeks, I can achieve goal number twenty. Even Brad would agree I gave it a fair shot. I think of my mother's — or rather, Eleanor Roosevelt's — words. "Do something every day that scares you."

"Yes," I say, peeling my eyes from the EXIT sign. "I am available."

"Terrific," she says. "It's not easy to find substitutes for this building."

A mixture of panic and regret runs through my every nerve fiber. What the hell have I committed to? Mrs. Bailey unlocks the door and finds the light switch.

"You'll find lesson plans on Mrs. Porter's desk. If there's anything else you need, just ask." She gives me a thumbs-up before she pivots, and I'm left alone in my classroom.

I breathe in the scent of dust and musty old books, and gaze at a pasture of wooden desks. An old but familiar fantasy washes over me. For the first twenty years of my life, I dreamed of teaching in a classroom just like this.

The shrill sound of a school bell rings out, knocking me from my reverie. My eyes shoot to the clock above the chalkboard. Oh, dear God! School's about to start.

I rush to Mrs. Porter's desk and search for lesson plans. I lift the attendance book and scramble through a stack of worksheets, but find no lesson plans. I yank open the desk drawer. Nothing. I plow through the wooden cabinet. Still nothing! Where the hell are my lesson plans?

From down the hall I hear the rumble of an army stampeding

toward the classroom. My heart races and I snatch a file folder from a metal basket. The loose papers spill onto the floor. Damn! I catch a glimpse of LESSON . . . before it cascades to the floor and lands upside down under my desk. My lesson plan. Thank you, Lord!

The army is closer now. My hands tremble as I gather the fallen papers. I've retrieved most of them, except the most important one, the lesson plan wedged under Mrs. Porter's desk. On my hands and knees, I crawl toward it, desperate to retrieve it. But it's too far back. That's when my students arrive, my hindquarters providing the first impression of their substitute teacher.

"Nice ass," I hear somebody say, followed by hearty laughter all around.

I pull myself from under the desk and smooth down my slacks. "Good morning, boys and girls." I raise my voice so I can be heard over the morning chatter. "I'm Ms. Bohlinger. Mrs. Porter isn't here today."

"Cool!" a freckled redhead says. "Hey everyone. We got a sub today! Sit anywhere you want." Like in a game of musical chairs, my students leap from their desks and fight to capture a new seat.

"Back to your own desks! Now!" But my words are swallowed by the chaos. It's only eight twenty and I've already lost control of my classroom. I turn my attention to the back of the room where a girl with Medusa braids screams at a brown-skinned boy who looks to be about twenty.

"Stop it, Tyson!"

Tyson twirls while pulling her bright pink scarf, winding it around his waist tighter and tighter.

"Give me my fucking scarf!" Medusa says.

I march over to them. "Give her the scarf, please." I reach for it, but he shimmies from me and continues to spin in circles, stretching the scarf like he's pulling taffy. "C'mon now. Pink's not even your color."

"Yeah," the freckled boy shouts from across the room. "Whatcha want with a pink scarf, Ty? You gay or something?"

Tyson springs to life. He's almost as tall as I am, and a good twenty pounds heavier. He leaps over row after row of desks in search of the redhead.

"Stop!" I rush down the aisle as quickly as I can, but I can't leap the rows like he does. He's already got the kid by the throat, shaking him like a martini. My God, he's going to kill this kid! And it'll be my fault! Could I be charged with manslaughter? I call to Medusa, "Get the principal!"

By the time I reach the scuffle, the boy's freckled face glows red and his eyes are frantic. He's struggling to wedge Tyson's fingers from his neck. I yank on Tyson's arm, but he jerks away. "Let go!" I scream. But my voice doesn't seem to penetrate.

Kids gather around the fight, whooping and hollering, escalating the frenzy.

"Sit down!" I shout. But they don't flinch. "Stop it! Now!" I work to peel Tyson's fingers from the boy's neck, but they're like steel pipes. Just as I open my mouth to scream, a stern voice calls out from the doorway.

"Tyson Diggs, come here. Now!"

Instantly Tyson lets go of the boy's neck. I nearly collapse with relief, and turn to see Mrs. Bailey in the doorway. At once, the students retreat to their seats, silent and orderly.

"I said come here," she repeats. "You, too, Mr. Flynn."

The boys skulk forward. She claps a hand on each of their shoulders and nods to me. "Proceed with your lesson, Ms. Bohlinger. These young men will be spending the morning with me."

I want to thank her. No, I want to bow down and kiss her feet. But I don't trust my voice. I simply nod, hoping she can identify the gratitude in my face. She closes the door behind them. I take a deep breath and turn to my class.

"Good morning, boys and girls," I say, leaning one hand on a student's desk to steady myself. I try out a shaky smile. "I'm your substitute teacher."

"Duh!" a girl who looks seventeen says. "We know that."

"When's Mrs. Porter coming back?" another girl asks, her sequined T-shirt identifying her as a PRINCESS.

"I don't know, exactly." I look around the room. "Any more questions before we get started?" Started on what? The damn lesson plan is still under my desk.

The princess raises her hand. I lean in to read her name.

"Yes, Marissa? You have a question?"

She cocks her head, pointing her pencil at my orange Prada flats. "Did you actually pay for those?"

All I can hear is high-pitched, juvenile laughter, and I'm back at Meadowdale. I clap my hands. "Enough!" But my words are swallowed by the chaos. I need to get these prepubescent monsters on track, now. I spot a girl in the front row, presumably named Tierra. "You," I say. "Help me."

The volume in the classroom is mounting, and I don't have a moment to spare. "I need my lesson plan, Tierra." I point to the white sheet of paper wedged under the desk. "Can you climb under there and get it, please?"

Possibly the only obedient child in the room, she gets down on all fours and burrows under Mrs. Porter's desk, just as I'd done earlier. She's smaller than I am, and she reaches the paper easily. I watch as she plucks it up, and immediately I see the heading, LESSON 9—SILENT "E." It's not my lesson plan! It's a friggin' spelling list!

"Damn!" I say without thinking.

Tierra's head jerks to attention, slamming against the underside of the desk and sending a boom like a thunderclap throughout the room.

"Get the nurse!" I scream to whoever might be listening.

_A_fter an interminable six hours and forty-three minutes, I shuffle the students from the classroom. I want nothing more than to race from the school grounds and throw back a strong martini, but Mrs. Bailey has summoned me to her office. With lavender reading glasses balanced on the end of her nose, she hands me a stack of papers and her pen.

"I need you to sign off on these incident reports." She nods to the chair in front of her desk. "You might want to sit down. This could take a while."

I slide into a vinyl chair and scan the first report. "You must be incredibly busy, dealing with these incidents all day long."

She peers at me over her glasses. "Ms. Bohlinger, you sent more students to my office today than most teachers send in an entire school year."

I cringe. "Sorry about that."

She shakes her head. "I sense you've got a good heart, I really do. But your classroom management skills . . ."

"Once I get the hang of things, it'll get easier." *Like hell it will.* "Have you heard from Mrs. Porter? Did she have her baby?"

"She did indeed. A healthy baby girl."

My heart sinks but I paste on a smile. "I'll be back Monday then, bright and early."

"Monday?" She pulls off her glasses. "You don't think I'd allow you back in that classroom, do you?"

My first instinct is to be elated. I'll never have to teach those little hoodlums again! But rejection growls in my face. This woman doesn't want me in her building. I need to prove to her, and to my mother, and to that little girl with the silly dreams, that I can teach.

"Yes. I just need another chance. I can do better. I know I can."

Mrs. Bailey shakes her head. "I'm sorry, sugar. No deal."

———

Whether Brad really was available, or whether Claire sensed I was having a breakdown and hastily cleared his schedule, I'm not sure. Regardless, he's waiting for me when I arrive at his office. My hair, wet from the afternoon downpour, clings to my skull, and I reek of damp wool. He wraps an arm around my shoulder and leads me to the familiar leather chair. He smells like evergreen trees. I close my eyes and begin to cry.

"I'm a loser," I blubber. "I can't teach. I can't finish those goals, Brad. I can't."

"Stop," he says softly. "You're okay."

"Have you heard anything from Pohlonski?"

"Not yet. I told you, it'll be awhile."

"I'm losing it, Brad. I swear I am."

He holds me at arm's length. "We'll get you through this, I promise."

His placating tone infuriates me. "No!" I say, pulling away from him. "You don't know that! I'm serious. What happens if I can't complete this list?"

He rubs his chin and looks me squarely in the face. "Honestly? I guess you'd be just like millions of other folks out there, beating the bushes for a job and trying to make ends meet. But unlike most people, you'd have no debt to deal with . . . no retirement account to worry about . . ."

His words shame me. I've been so laden in self-pity that I'd forgotten how lucky I am — even now. I lower my eyes.

"Thanks. I needed that." I sink into the chair. "You're absolutely right. I'll find another advertising job. It's time I got on with my life."

"Your old life, you mean? With Andrew?"

A wave of sadness comes over me, imagining the rest of my

days spent in a passionless job, and my evenings alone in a cheerless condo I can't even call my own.

"Sure," I say. "It's the only one I've got."

"That's not true. You've got options. That's what your mother is trying to show you."

I shake my head, feeling my frustration mount again. "You don't get it! It's too late to start over. Do you know what the odds are of meeting the love of my life, and finding out he wants kids and a dog and a friggin' pony? And my clock is ticking, Brad — that cruel, one-sided woman-hating biological clock."

Brad perches on the chair facing mine. "Look, your mother thought completing that life list would lead to a better life, right?"

I shrug. "I guess."

"Has she ever let you down?"

I sigh. "No."

"Then make it happen, B.B."

"But how?" I nearly scream.

"By channeling that bold little girl you used to be. You criticize your mom for being a coward, but you're no different. You want those wishes, I know you do. But you're too damn scared to take a chance. Go make your dreams happen, B.B. Do it! Now!"

CHAPTER TEN

A ndrew's asleep on the sofa when I step into the loft, the il-
luminating flicker from the television playing hopscotch on his
face. He must have knocked off early today. I want nothing more
than to tiptoe past him, change my clothes, and pretend I just got
home from a long day at the office, but I don't. My heart thrums
in my chest. It's time.

I switch on a lamp and he stirs.

"When did you get home?" he asks, his voice groggy.

"Just a few minutes ago."

He checks his watch. "I was hoping we could beat the crowd at
The Gage."

"Sounds great," I say, hearing the slight tremor in my voice,
"but first I have something to tell you." I take a deep breath. "I've
been lying to you, Andrew. It's time you learned the truth."

I sit down on the sofa beside him, and reveal the wishes of a
girl I once knew.

———

$\mathcal{M}$y throat aches by the time I've finished. "So, that's the deal. I'm sorry I didn't tell you sooner. I was afraid you'd . . . I was afraid of . . ." I shake my head. "I was simply afraid of losing you."

Andrew props his elbow on the arm of the sofa and kneads his temple.

"That's pretty shitty of your mom."

"She thought she was doing me a favor." I find myself defending my mother, which seems simultaneously crazy and absolutely right.

Finally, he turns to me. "I'm not buying it. Elizabeth wouldn't keep you from your inheritance. In the end, there'll be a fortune, with or without meeting those goals. Mark my words."

I shake my head. "I don't think so. Neither does Brad."

"I'll do some checking. So far you haven't gotten a dime?"

"No, and there's no time to investigate. I have to complete this list by September."

His jaw drops. "Next September?"

"Yes." I take a deep breath. "So, I need to know, how do you feel about all this?"

"How do I feel about this? It's fucking nuts!" He repositions himself so that he faces me. "You need to do what you want, babe, not what your mother wants you to do. Granted, I didn't know you when you were fourteen, aspiring to teach school and have babies." He raises an eyebrow and grins at me. "All I know is the accomplished woman you are today, or rather, the woman you'll be once you land your next big position — if that's what you choose."

He grazes my cheek with his thumb. "Look, I know it's not perfect, but what we've got is pretty damn good. Sure there's stress with our careers, but it's nothing compared with our friends who have kids. And add to that a dog, and a horse, and social obligations." He shakes his head as if horrified by the thought. "I cannot imagine. I happen to love our life together, the way it is now. I thought you did, too." He tucks a lock of hair behind my ear. "Am I right?"

My face burns but he won't let go of my gaze. If I answer truthfully, I'll lose Andrew. My mother's words call to me as if she were shouting them from above: *When you're fearful, grab hold of this courage and shake it loose, because now you know it's yours, just as I've known all along.*

"No," I whisper. "My mother is right."

"Jesus."

Tears spill over my lids and I brush them away. "I'll make plans to move out this week."

I start to rise, but he grabs my arm.

"You're telling me this is the only way you can get your inheritance? There's no other option?"

"Yes, that's exactly what I'm telling you."

"How much are we talking about? Five, six mil?"

Is he talking about my inheritance? At first I'm taken aback, but I'm asking him to be my partner in this endeavor. Doesn't he have a right to know? "Yeah, something like that. I won't know for sure until I get my envelope." For some reason, I don't tell him about the exorbitant trusts my brothers received.

He exhales loudly, making his nostrils flare. "This sucks, you know that?"

I nod and swipe my nose with the back of my hand.

"Fuck!" he says. Finally he looks at me. "All right, damn it, if that's what it takes to keep you, I guess we'll have to do it."

He wants to keep me? Does he understand the stakes? I stare at him, my mouth agape. "You — you'll help me reach my goals, all of them?"

He shrugs. "I don't have a choice, do I?"

It strikes me as an odd response, since he's the only character in this play who actually *does* have a choice. But the bottom line is, he's willing to help me accomplish my goals! We're going to have a family! For the first time, Andrew is putting my needs ahead of his own. Or is he? An uneasy feeling comes over me, but I tamp it down, hoping against hope that my instincts are wrong. What right do I have to second-guess his motive?

With a blessed sense of relief, I'm alone in the loft Sunday afternoon. Since our decision Friday night, Andrew's been colder than the gales of Lake Michigan. So today, when he grumbled about having to go into the office, I tossed him his coat and shooed him out the door before he had time to change his mind. But I can't blame him for being upset. He was blindsided by this crazy life list, just as I was. And just like me, it'll take time for him to get used to the idea of a different lifestyle.

I take my laptop to the dining room table and log on to Facebook. One message. A reply from Carrie Newsome.

Hooray! I can't wait to see you on the 14th! Thanks for suggesting the hotel for dinner. It'll be easier than trying to schlep across town. Six o'clock is perfect. I hadn't realized how much I've missed you, Bretel.

Not one mention of my disloyalty. Who could be that forgiving?

The last time I saw Carrie I was a sophomore at Loyola Academy. She'd been in Madison for a year, and for her birthday her parents bought her a bus ticket to come see me. She seemed surprised when she saw me, so much had happened in those twelve months. I'd made the cheerleading squad that year and was immediately catapulted to the cool crowd. I'd gotten my braces off and wore makeup. My hair was cut in the new Rachel style, which I painstakingly straightened each morning. But Carrie was exactly the same — plain, stocky, and unadorned.

We sat on my bedroom floor, listening to a Boyz II Men CD and thumbing through my yearbook. When I saw Joni Nicol's picture, I pointed to it. "Remember Joni's brother, Nick? I've got a humongous crush on him. Are there lots of cute guys in Madison?"

She looked at me as if she was surprised by the question.

"I don't know. I haven't paid much attention."

My heart broke. Carrie had never had a boyfriend. I kept my eyes on the yearbook, embarrassed for her. "Someday you'll meet someone great, Care Bear."

"I'm a lesbian, Bretel." She said it without shame or regret, as if she were telling me her height or her blood type.

I stared at her, praying she'd bust out laughing. "You're joking."

"Nope. I told my parents a few months back. I've known pretty much all my life."

My head spun. "So, all those times we were together, those times you spent the night . . ."

She laughed. "What? You think I was hitting on you? Don't worry, Bretel, it's not like that!" I must have looked upset, because she stopped laughing then, and reached out a hand to touch my sleeve. "Hey, I didn't mean to spook you. It's still me — Carrie. You get that, right?"

"Yeah," I mumbled. But my narrow, fifteen-year-old mind didn't get it. My best friend wasn't normal. I studied her short hair and clipped nails, her barren face and baggy sweater. She looked foreign to me all of a sudden, masculine and odd.

I didn't take her to Erin Brown's party that night, like we'd planned. I was afraid my new friends would discover the truth. And if they did, they might think I was gay, too. Instead I feigned a headache and we stayed home and watched videos. But rather than sitting side by side sharing Doritos and a blanket, like we usually did, I sat in my dad's old recliner. Later, when my mom came in and saw Carrie asleep on the sofa, I put my finger to my lips. "Don't wake her. She's comfortable." My mother laid a blanket over Carrie and quietly left the room. I tiptoed to my bedroom, and lay awake the rest of the night.

The next morning while I was showering, Carrie called the bus station. She left at noon, a day ahead of schedule. I'm ashamed to admit the relief that swept over me when that Greyhound bus rounded the corner of the station and headed north.

The following week a letter arrived from Carrie, apologizing for springing her "freaky nature" on me without warning. She hoped our friendship would never change. She ended the letter with, "Please write back soon, Bretel! I need to know what you're thinking."

I hid the letter beneath a stack of *Seventeen* magazines while I thought about how to respond. But weeks turned into months, and then years. By the time I finally had the heart to deal with her sexual orientation, I didn't have the backbone. I was too much of a coward to resurrect the memory of that awkward weekend or, more accurately, my disloyalty. My insensitivity burns me with shame.

*I*t's Monday and I've just hung up from a call with the Chicago Public Schools when Brad texts me. His meeting on the North Side was canceled, and he wonders if I can meet him for lunch at P. J. Clarke's. Just as he promised my mother, he's keeping close tabs on me, making sure I'm inching closer to my goals.

I dab some gloss on my lips, pour my freshly brewed coffee into a to-go cup, and head down the stairs. As I waltz out of the building, I nearly collide with a tall, dark-haired man. Coffee sloshes onto my coat.

"Shit!" I say without thinking.

"Oh, Jesus. I'm so sorry." His contrite voice suddenly turns chipper. "Hey! We meet again!"

I break from dabbing my coat and look up, into the gorgeous eyes of the Burberry man.

"Well hello," I say, grinning like a silly teenager who's just been noticed by the football star.

"Hello." He points back to the building. "You live here?"

"Uh-huh. Do you?" *Phony! You know damn well he does!*

"Not anymore. I rented here for a couple of months while my condo was being renovated. I'm just stopping by to get my security deposit." His eyes land on the coffee stain. "God, I ruined your coat. C'mon, let me buy you another cup. There's a Starbucks right around the corner. It's the least I can do."

He introduces himself, but I don't hear a word he says. My mind is still languishing on the invitation for coffee. Oh, hell yes! But wait . . . I'm supposed to meet Brad. Just my luck.

"Thanks, maybe another time. I have a lunch date."

His smile fades. "Okay then, have a nice lunch. Again, I apologize for the coffee stain."

I want to call after him, to explain that my date is just a friend, that I'm free for coffee later. But that's despicable. Brad *is* just a friend . . . but Andrew's not.

"*H*ow's everything in your world?" I ask Brad after we've ordered our BLTs. "Planning your next trip to San Francisco?"

"I'm hoping to go Thanksgiving weekend," he says. "Nate will be with his dad. But Jenna hasn't decided what she's doing."

I nod, but inside I worry that Brad's being jerked around.

"How about you?" he asks. "Made any headway on the list?"

I scoot to the edge of the booth and prop my head high. "As a matter of fact, I have. Remember Mrs. Bailey, that principal I told you about from Douglas Keyes? Well, she recommended me for this homebound job — that's where you teach sick kids at their houses or in the hospital."

"Cool. Like one-on-one teaching?"

"Exactly. I have an interview tomorrow morning."

He lifts his hand for a high-five. "Awesome!"

I wave him away. "Don't get too excited. I'll never get the job. But for some reason, Mrs. Bailey thinks it might be a good fit for me."

"Well, I'm rooting for you."

"Thanks. And that's not all." Our sandwiches arrive and I tell him about my dinner date on the fourteenth with Carrie. "She lives in Madison. She is a social worker now, and she's in a relationship. I can't believe she has three kids."

"It'll be good to catch up with her, huh?"

I feel my face heat. "Yes, but I was a rotten friend. I have a lot of making up to do."

"Hey," he says, and covers my hand with his. "You're making headway. I'm proud of you."

"Thanks. And guess what else? I finally told Andrew about the list. He's on board!"

Instead of cheering, Brad gives me a sidelong glance. "Really?"

I wipe my mouth on my napkin. "Yes, really. Why is that so surprising?"

He shakes his head as if he's trying to clear it. "I'm sorry. No, that's great."

"Have you heard anything more from that detective? Steve what's-his-name?"

"Pohlonski," he says, downing his sandwich with a shot of Diet Coke. "Not yet. But I'll let you know the minute he has something."

"It's been over a week. I'm thinking it's time to cut him loose, hire someone else."

He wipes his mouth. "I know you're anxious about this, Brett, but he's working on it. Like I said, he found ninety-six Manns born in North Dakota between 1940 and 1955. He's whittled it down to six who might be possibilities. In the next week he's going to call each one."

"That's what you told me three days ago! How long does it take to make a phone call? Give me the list. I'll call them this afternoon."

"No. Pohlonski says it's best to have a third party make the initial contact."

I sigh. "Well, he better have news for me by Friday or he's off the case."

Brad laughs. "Off the case? Someone's been watching too much *CSI*."

I try to maintain my pout, but inside I'm thinking how much I like this guy. "You're annoying as hell, Midar."

The sky is the color of a newborn's eyes, and the surf foamy white atop smoky gray breakers. Meg, Shelley, and I power-walk past Grant Park, taking turns pushing baby Emma in her stroller.

"My IQ has dipped twenty points since I quit my job," Shelley says, a bit breathlessly. "It's been weeks since I've read a newspaper. And the mom cliques in the neighborhood — it's worse than middle school!"

"Maybe staying home isn't for you," I say, striding beside her.

"I'm telling you, I've never seen such competitive women. The other day at the park, I happened to mention that Trevor can count to thirty. Not bad for a three-year-old, right? Wrong. Melinda immediately piped in, 'Sammy counts to fifty.' And Lauren, the blond bitch, pursed her lips and gestured to little Kaitlyn. 'One hundred,' she whispered. 'In *Mandarin*.'"

Megan and I burst out laughing. "Speaking of competition,"

Megan says, swinging her fists in front of her. "Any luck finding that teaching job, Brett? The one where you don't step foot in the classroom?" She erupts in giggles.

"Actually, I have."

Shelley and Megan turn to me.

"I was offered a job this morning."

"That's great!" Shelley says. "See, and you didn't think you'd be competitive."

I bite my lip. "I was the only applicant."

"In this job market?" Megan asks, tugging her arm as she strides.

"Uh-huh. It seems that two ninety-nine's a difficult zone in the Chicago Public School District — that's what the personnel director told me. He said you have to be a bit of a risk taker." I tell them about the homebound position, teaching sick kids in their homes or at the hospital, one-on-one.

"Wait." Megan pulls me to a stop. "You'll be going into houses? On the South Side?"

My stomach aches and I start walking again. "That's right."

Megan keeps pace beside me, her eyes huge. "No fucking way! Girl, we're talking housing projects . . . tenement buildings. Nothing but roach-infested shitshacks."

"Megan has a point," Shelley says. "You sure it's safe?"

"Of course," I say, wishing I felt as sure as I sounded.

"Listen," Megan says. "Take the fucking job if you must, but then quit the minute it looks legit for Brad."

"Can you believe it? I might actually accomplish goal number twenty." I turn a circle and walk backward, facing them. "And guess what else, Shelley? Andrew hired Megan. We're going to buy a house."

"Get this," Megan says, flipping Shelley's arm with the back of her hand. "They're buying a house on the lake. Cha-ching!"

"No," I say. "Discourage the McMansions, Meg. Those houses are obnoxious."

"If you say so. Of course, that kind of commission would be nice." She bites her bottom lip, as if mentally computing her 6 percent cut.

"Forget it. We can't afford it."

"Andrew told me you're going to get a fucking fortune. He also told me about your profit sharing. Trust me, you won't have any problem getting a loan."

I shake my head. "Any profit sharing goes straight into my retirement account. I'd get killed on taxes if I touched it. And he's forgetting, we'll have a child's future to think about. Try to find something cute, something with a little backyard, maybe near a park."

She looks at me as if I'm insane, but eventually she nods. "Absolutely. I'm on it."

"It's amazing how far Andrew's come," I continue. "Everything's falling into place. I bought a book the other day, *What to Expect When You're Expecting*. It's so fun to think that I could be pregnant soon, and —"

"When's the wedding?" Shelley interrupts.

I move faster, keeping my eyes on the sidewalk. Shelley's the one person who would know that in a perfect world, I'd like to be married when I have a baby. "Marriage wasn't on the life list."

"I wasn't asking about the list."

Finally, I come to a halt and wipe the perspiration from my brow. "Truth is, Shel, I don't know."

"You need to tell Andrew he —"

I shake my head. "Look, life isn't perfect. We're all just getting through this journey as best we can. Admit it, Meg, you're with Jimmy because you're afraid of being poor."

She scowls, but then shrugs. "You're right. I'm basically a prostitute. But I can't help it. I just hate working."

"And face it, Shel, you're miserable since you quit your job." I sling an arm around her. "Honestly, I don't know if Andrew's going to marry me. But he is willing to do other things for me, important things, like have a baby. For now, maybe that's enough."

Shelley sniffs. "It's that obvious I'm miserable?"

I smile. "Remember when I fell down the stairs at Mom's funeral? Yes, I was wasted, but I was also trying to stuff my feet into shoes that didn't fit. I worry that you're trying to squeeze yourself into being a stay-at-home mom, when that's clearly not the right fit for you."

She looks up at me. "Yeah? Well I worry that you're trying to squeeze yourself into a size Andrew, when he's clearly not the right fit for you."

Touché. If I had the guts, I'd admit that I worry, too. I'd confess that sometimes, when Andrew's distant and I'm lonely, I wonder if there's still enough time to meet someone else before next September, someone I could fall in love and have babies with. But of course, there's not. I wonder what my mother would think if she knew that her little plan has made me more dependent on Andrew than ever.

CHAPTER ELEVEN

My first days on the job pass in a blurry haze. Since Wednesday I've been tagging along with Eve Seibold, the sixty-something who'll be vacating the position as soon as she thinks I'm the least bit competent. So far, she hasn't mentioned a date. We sit in the homebound office on the third floor of the administration building Friday afternoon. Compared with the spacious suite I had at Bohlinger Cosmetics, this cement-block room feels like a custodian's closet. But a nice window overlooks East 35th Street, and after I fill the ledge with my mother's potted geraniums, the place looks almost cheery.

I sit at the computer table perusing student files while Eve cleans out her desk. "Ashley Dickson sounds pretty straightforward," I say. "Two more weeks of maternity leave and she'll go back to school."

Eve chuckles. "Trust me, they're never straightforward."

I set aside Ashley's file and open another, this one for a sixth-grader. "Mental illness at age eleven?"

"Ah, Peter Madison." Eve pulls two notebooks from her desk and crams them into a cardboard box. "Crazy as a bedbug. His shrink wants to talk to you. Dr. Garrett Taylor. He's got a signed release from Peter's mom." She points to a phone number scrawled on the top of the folder. "The doc's number's right there."

I flip through the file and land on Peter's psychiatric report. Acts of aggression in the classroom . . . expulsion for the remainder of the semester. And I was worried about shabby houses? "What's wrong with him?"

"LSS," she tells me. "Little Shit Syndrome." She pulls a smashed Twinkie from the back of her drawer, contemplates it for a moment, and then chucks it into the metal waste can. "Dr. Taylor calls it conduct disorder, but I'm no fool. The kid's just like hundreds of others from these parts of Chicago. No dad, family history of substance abuse, not enough attention, yada, yada, yada."

"But he's just a kid. He should be in school. They can't deny him his education."

"That's where you come in. Give him homebound services twice a week and he's considered educated. Illinois Public Act Ninety-something-or-other. Make sure you call Dr. Taylor before you leave tonight. He'll fill you in."

By the time I've finished reading all seven student files, it's almost six o'clock. Eve left an hour ago, taking with her two large boxes crammed with everything from candy dishes to framed photos of her grandchildren. I gather my notes and my purse, suddenly anxious to start my weekend, too. Just as I'm about to turn out the lights, I remember I'm supposed to call Peter's psychiatrist. Damn. I trudge back to my desk. At this hour on a Friday, he'll be gone, but I'll feel better if I leave a quick voice mail. I punch in his number and mentally rehearse the message I'll leave.

"Garrett Taylor," a melodious baritone answers.

"Oh . . . hello. I, um, I wasn't expecting you to answer. I was planning to leave you a message."

"Another ten minutes and you would have. How can I help you?"

"My name is Brett Bohlinger. I'm the new homebound teacher. I'll be working with Peter Madison."

"Ah, yes, Brett. Thank you for calling." He chuckles. "You were expecting my voice mail; I was expecting a male voice."

I smile. "Good one. Just one of the pitfalls of having a man's name."

"I like it. Isn't there a Hemingway character named Brett?"

I lean back in my chair, impressed that he's made the connection. "Yes, Lady Brett Ashley from *The Sun Also Rises*. My mother —" I realize I'm rambling. Do psychiatrists have this effect on everyone? "I'm sorry. You're about to leave. Let me get to the point."

"Take your time. I'm in no rush."

His voice has a friendly, familiar tone, and I feel like I'm talking to an old chum rather than a medical doctor. I grab a piece of paper and lift my pen. "I'm calling about this student, Peter Madison. What can you tell me about him?"

I hear what sounds like Dr. Taylor settling back in his chair. "Peter is a very unusual boy. He's extremely bright, but very manipulative. From what I understand, he was wreaking havoc in his classroom. The school district wanted a complete psychiatric workup, which is why they enlisted my help. I've only been working with him since September, so you and I will both be learning about Peter as we go."

He tells me of Peter's escapades in the classroom, everything from bullying a student with cerebral palsy, to tormenting the classroom hamster, to cutting a student's hair.

"He gets pleasure from the reaction he receives from others. He enjoys inflicting emotional pain. In fact, he's highly stimulated by it."

Outside the wind howls and I wrap my sweater across my chest. "What caused him to be this way? Was he abused or something?"

"His mother is somewhat limited, but seems to be concerned. Dad's not in the picture, so there could be some emotional trauma associated with that. Or it's possible Peter's psychological disturbances are simply the result of an unfortunate genetic endowment."

"You mean he was just born this way?"

"It's possible."

Nothing I've read in *What to Expect When You're Expecting* has touched on this. I imagine a chapter titled "Unfortunate Genetic Endowments."

"But you'll find that Peter can be quite charming when he wants to be."

"Really? Like when he's putting scissors to my hair?"

He chuckles. "I'm afraid I've frightened you. You'll do fine. You sound very capable."

Uh-huh. So capable my mother fired me.

"You'll be the eyes and ears of the house, which will be extremely helpful. I'd like you to call me after each visit. Is that possible?"

"Yes, I can do that. Eve and I are supposed to see him Monday." *Unless I can come up with an excuse.*

"My last session ends at five on Monday. Would you be able to call me sometime after that?"

"Sure," I say, but his words barely register. Every cell in my brain is consumed with the fact that in three days, I'm going to be teaching the future Hannibal Lecter.

———

I take special care dressing Monday morning, finally opting for a pair of navy wool slacks to match the heather-gray cashmere sweater my mother bought me last Christmas. Not only do I want to make a good impression on my new students today, I also want to look my best when I meet Carrie. I think about her all the way to my office, hoping work goes smoothly and Eve doesn't yammer endlessly at the end of the day. I want plenty of time to get to McCormick Place and find the restaurant in the Hyatt before Carrie arrives.

When I get to my office, I learn that Eve's chatter would have been the least of my problems. Mr. Jackson, my supervisor, finds me before I've even turned on my computer.

"Eve called this morning," he says, his large frame filling the doorway to my office. "She had a family emergency and won't be back. But she's confident you'll be fine on your own. She told me to wish you luck." He gives me a terse nod. "Good luck."

I shoot from my desk, snagging my sweater on the splintered edge of my desk. So much for good impressions. "But Eve was going to introduce me to the students today, help me get the hang of things."

"I'm sure you can manage. Did you drive or take the bus?"

"I-I drove."

"Well then, you're all set." He turns to leave. "Be sure to keep track of your mileage. We do reimburse you, you know."

Mileage reimbursement? I don't give a rip about mileage. My life's at stake! I trail him as he walks away.

"Mr. Jackson, wait. We have this student, Peter Madison. He sounds like he could be trouble. I don't think I should see him alone."

When he wheels around, the crease between his brows is angled like a tree branch. "Ms. Bohlinger, I'd love to provide a personal bodyguard for you, but unfortunately our budget won't allow it."

I open my mouth to object, but he's already marching back to his office, leaving me alone to gnaw on my thumbnail.

$\mathcal{M}$y first student today is Amina Adawe, a third-grader who lives on South Morgan. I'm shocked when I spy an abandoned tenement with Amina's house number dangling above the entry door. I slow to a stop. People actually live in this place? The splintered door pushes open and a toddler waddles out, followed by a woman gabbing on her cell phone, dressed like she's ready to go clubbing. Apparently, they do.

I make my way up the cracked sidewalk, thinking of my private office at Bohlinger Cosmetics, with its lush green plants and my little fridge stocked with fruit and bottled water. A familiar anger rises in me. Why has my mother placed me in this predicament?

I take a deep breath and, using my coat sleeve, twist the doorknob. Before stepping inside I look around one more time, as if it might be my final glimpse.

It's murky and dank in the narrow hallway, and stinks of dirty diapers and garbage. I worm my way down the hallway, littered with food wrappers and cigarette butts. Rap music blares so loudly from one of the units I swear the floor is palpitating. Please tell me it this isn't Amina's apartment.

The apartment numbers on this floor are double digits. Amina's unit, number four, must be in the basement. My heart pounds in my chest and I inch down a flight of stairs. Who'd ever find me if I disappeared inside this hellhole? How long must I keep this damn job before I can convince Brad to check it off my list? Another week, I decide — two at the most. By Thanksgiving I'm finished.

I reach the bottom of the stairwell. An exposed lightbulb overhead flickers, creating a frenetic light show. From behind the closed door of apartment number two, obscenities storm me, ugly and foul. I freeze. I'm just about to race back up the steps when a door swings open at the end of the hall. A thin woman with caramel skin and kind gold eyes appears, a silk hijab covering her hair.

"I-I'm looking for apartment four," I enunciate slowly, holding out my staff ID. "Amina Adawe. I'm her teacher."

She smiles and waves me inside. When she closes the door behind us, the shouting and stench vanish. The tidy apartment smells of baked chicken and exotic spices. She nods when I remove my shoes, and leads me into the living room where a tiny girl rests on a threadbare sofa, her plastered leg propped on pillows.

"Hello, Amina. I'm Miss Brett. I'll be your teacher while you're recuperating."

Her dark eyes take me in bit by bit. "You very pretty," she says with a lovely Arabic accent.

I smile. "You are, too."

She tells me in broken English that she moved here from Somalia last winter, that she had one leg that was too short, so the doctor fixed it. She's very sad to be missing school.

I pat her hand. "We'll work together. When you return to school, you'll be right on track with the rest of the class. Shall we begin with reading?"

I pull her reading text from my leather bag and a small boy rushes into the room. He clutches the cotton fabric of his mother's jilbāb.

"Hello," I say. "What's your name?"

He peeks at me from behind his mother's dress and whispers, "Abdulkadir."

I repeat the multisyllabic mouthful and he blossoms into dimples. Amina and her mother giggle, their faces ripe with pride. With Amina propped on the bed and her brother sitting on his mother's lap, the three sit rapt while I read a story about a princess who couldn't cry. They study the pictures, stop to ask questions, giggle and clap.

Here I am, in my very own one-room schoolhouse! And this time, every student is ravenous to learn. This is a teacher's dream. This is *my* dream!

*T*wenty minutes later I'm driving through Englewood. I try to focus on the fact that one of my favorite singers, Jennifer Hudson, grew up here, and ignore the fact that her family was murdered in this very place. A shiver goes through me. I'm relieved when I pull up to a large green house on Carroll Avenue that looks perfectly safe. But what's with the sign in the front yard?

It's hard to believe Sanquita Bell, three months' pregnant and suffering from kidney disease, is a senior. The girl who looks to be of mixed race is as tiny as a twelve-year-old. Her wan face is barren of makeup, and her skin is silky and shiny, like pulled toffee. But it's her hazelnut eyes that break my heart. They're the weary eyes of a much older woman — one who's seen far too much of a cruel world.

"I'm sorry I'm late," I say, shedding my coat and gloves. "I saw the sign for Joshua House, and I thought I had the wrong address. What is this place?"

"A shelter for homeless women," she says matter-of-factly.

I stare at her, thunderstruck. "Oh, Sanquita, I'm sorry to hear that. Has your family been here long?"

"My family ain't here." She rubs a hand over her still-flat belly as she speaks. "My mom, she moved to Detroit last year, but I refuse to live there. My baby ain't gonna have that kinda life."

She doesn't define *that kind of life,* and I don't ask her. I bite my lip and nod.

She crosses her arms over her chest defensively. "Don't go feeling all sorry for me. Me and my baby's gonna be just fine."

"Of course you are." I want to wrap her in my arms, this poor homeless girl, but I wouldn't dare. It's obvious this young lady doesn't take kindly to comfort. "I don't have parents, either. It's hard, isn't it?"

She lifts her shoulders dismissively. "I wanted my baby to know her daddy, but that ain't gonna happen."

Before I have time to reply, a short brunette rounds the corner, a baby on her hip.

"Hey, Sanquita. This your new teacher?" The woman takes my elbow. "I'm Mercedes. C'mon. Me and Sanquita will show you around."

Sanquita lags behind while Mercedes leads me from the utilitarian kitchen into a spotless dining room. Two women fold laundry at a dining room table. In the living room, two more sit in front of an old television, watching *The Price Is Right*.

"This is nice," I say, and look back at Sanquita. She looks away.

"Nine bedrooms in all," Mercedes tells me, her voice tinged with pride.

We stop outside an office door, where an imposing black woman sits behind a desk, punching numbers into an adding machine.

"This is Jean Anderson, our director." Mercedes knocks on the open door. "Miss Jean, come meet Sanquita's teacher."

Miss Jean raises her chin. After giving me a thorough once-over, she lowers her eyes to her adding machine and resumes punching numbers. "Hello," she mumbles.

"Hi," I say, leaning in with my hand outstretched. "I'm Brett Bohlinger. I'll be working with Sanquita while she's out of school."

"Sanquita," she says without looking up. "You need to get that prescription filled today. Don't forget."

My arm falls to my side and Sanquita glances at me awkwardly. "Uh, okay. See you later, Miss Jean."

We climb the stairs, Sanquita a step ahead of Mercedes and me. "Miss Jean's cool," Mercedes tells me. "She just don't trust white people much."

"Gee, you'd never guess."

Mercedes busts out laughing. "You're sassy. You and Sanquita are gonna get along just fine, aren't you, Quita?"

Sanquita doesn't respond.

Mercedes and I are still chatting when we reach the top of the stairs. I look up to see Sanquita standing at a bedroom door, drumming her fingers on one of her crossed arms.

"Thanks for the tour," I tell Mercedes, and hurry into the bedroom.

A weathered bedside table separates a set of twin beds, made up with faded blue bedcovers. Two mismatched dressers sit on either side of a window that overlooks the street. Sanquita takes a seat on the bed. "We can work here. Chardonay's at work."

There's no chair, so I perch beside her on the bed, careful not to stare at her swollen hands, her eyelids puffy with fluid, or the patches of pink skin on her arms and hands that look as if they've been scratched raw.

"How do you like it here?" I ask, fishing her folder from my satchel.

"It's straight. Not too much drama. That last place I stayed didn't have no rules. I got my purse stole there, and some crazy lady thought I was messing with her. She tried to fight me."

"Oh, my gosh. Were you hurt?"

"I didn't care about me. I was just worried about my baby. That's when I came here."

"I'm glad you're in a safe place now. How are you feeling?"

She shrugs. "Okay. Just tired, that's all."

"Take care of yourself. Let me know if there's anything I can do for you."

"Just help me get my diploma. My baby's gotta know her mama was smart."

She says it as if she won't be around to tell the baby herself, and I wonder just how sick this girl actually is. "It's a deal," I say, and pull a chemistry book from my bag.

After an hour, I have to force myself to leave Sanquita. I could spend all day teaching this child. Chemistry is especially difficult for her, but she listens carefully as I explain, and keeps trying until she finally succeeds.

"I usually suck at science, but today I actually get it."

She doesn't attribute her success to me, nor should she. Still, I nearly burst with pride. "You're a hard worker," I say, and slide her folder into my satchel. "And you're one smart girl."

She studies her fingernails. "When you coming back?"

I open my planner. "Well, when would you like to see me again?"

She shrugs. "Tomorrow?"

"You'll be finished with your homework by tomorrow?"

Her eyes go cold and she slaps shut her chemistry book. "Never mind. I know you only gotta see me two times in the week."

"Let's see," I say, studying my calendar. The only unscheduled slot tomorrow is an hour at noon reserved for lunch and paperwork. "I can come at noon. Does that work for you?"

"Yeah. Noon's okay."

She doesn't smile. She doesn't thank me. But still, I leave feeling warm.

I call Brad on my way to Wentworth Street and leave him a message. "This job was made for me, Brad! I'm on my way to Peter's house, so wish me luck."

When I arrive, an obese woman opens the door, a telephone at her ear and a cigarette between her fingers. This must be Autumn, Peter's mother. She's wearing a baggy T-shirt with a picture of Sponge Bob. I smile at the whimsical character, but she simply jerks her head, which I take as a gesture for me to enter.

The stench of cigarette smoke and cat urine nearly knock the breath from me. A black wool blanket tacked over the picture window blocks any natural light from infusing the stuffy room. On the wall I can make out a framed picture of Jesus, his eyes beseeching and his bloody palms outstretched.

Autumn snaps shut her phone and turns to me. "You Peter's teacher?"

"Yes. Hi, I'm Brett Bohlinger." I take out my ID photo, but she doesn't bother to look at it.

"Peter! Get out here!"

I smile nervously and reposition my satchel on my shoulder. Autumn plants her fists on her hips. "Goddamn it, Peter. I said get out here, now!" She barrels down a hallway and I hear her pound on a door. "Your teacher's here. Get your ass out here before I break down the damn door!"

Peter obviously doesn't want to see me. The rant continues until finally I step toward the hallway. "Look," I say. "Why don't I come back another time . . ."

Suddenly the door swings open. At the end of the gloomy hall, a figure takes shape. A large boy, with shaggy brown hair and a sprout of fuzz on his chin, lumbers toward me. Instinctively, I take a step backward.

"Hi, Peter," I say, my voice shaky. "I'm Miss Brett."

He breezes past me. "No shit."

The one-hour session with Peter seems more like three. We sit at the Madisons' sticky kitchen table, but he refuses to look at me.

Within earshot, Autumn yaks on the phone to someone named Brittany. Her gravelly voice competes with mine, and I deliver my instructions loudly, determined to win this contest. Peter simply grunts, as if I'm a huge annoyance he's forced to endure. I consider myself lucky when I get an occasional terse, one-word answer. By the end of the session I've learned far more about Brittany than I have about him.

Freshly fallen snow covers the windy city like a layer of white frosting, and the entire region slows to a crawl. It's nearly five o'clock when I trudge up the stairwell and unlock my office door. I turn on the light switch and spot a fabulous vase of orchids on my desk. How thoughtful of Andrew. I tear open the enclosure card.

> Congratulations on your new job, Brett.
> Couldn't be happier for you.
>
> Best Wishes,
> Catherine and Joad

What was I thinking? Andrew's never been a flower kind of guy. I tuck the card back into its envelope and make a mental note to invite Catherine and Joad for Thanksgiving dinner.

The red light on my office telephone blinks and I lift the receiver to check my messages.

"Hello, Brett. It's Garrett Taylor. Just feeling a little anxious, wondering how it went today with Peter. My four o'clock canceled, so I'm available whenever you are."

I dial his number and he picks up on the first ring.

"Hello, Dr. Taylor. It's Brett Bohlinger."

I hear him sigh. It sounds like a sigh of relief rather than annoyance. "Hi, Brett," he says. "And it's Garrett — no need to call me Doc."

I like his informal tone, like we're colleagues.

"Everything go all right today?"

"I still have my hair, so I'm considering it a success."

He laughs. "That's good news. So he wasn't so bad?"

"Oh, no, he was a complete asshole." I slap a hand over my mouth and my cheeks flame. "I'm so sorry. That was totally unprofessional. I didn't mean —"

Dr. Taylor laughs. "It's fine. He can be an asshole, I agree. But maybe, just maybe, we can help this little asshole develop some social skills."

I tell him about Peter's reluctance to come out of his room.

"But he finally came out when he heard you say you were leaving. That's positive. He wanted to meet you."

The dark cloud that's been trailing me since I left Peter's house lifts. We discuss Peter for another ten minutes before the conversation takes a personal turn.

"Were you a classroom teacher before you took this homebound job?"

"No. I'm a disaster in the classroom."

"I doubt that."

"Trust me." I lean back and prop my feet on my desk. Without meaning to, I plunge into the story of my day substituting at Douglas Keyes, embellishing it for entertainment purposes. It's freeing, hearing him laugh at my tale, like a lead balloon miraculously rising and floating off into the heavens. I'm guessing this hour would cost me a couple hundred bucks if I were sitting in his office.

"I'm sorry," I say, suddenly embarrassed. "I'm wasting your time."

"Not at all. I've seen my last patient, and I'm enjoying this. So, even though your day as a substitute was a challenge, you knew teaching was your passion."

"Honestly, it's my mother who insists it's my passion. She died in September and left me instructions to try it again."

"Ah. She knew it suited you."

I smile. "I guess so."

"I have great respect for your profession. Both my older sisters are retired schoolteachers. My mother taught, too, for a short time. Believe it or not, she actually taught in a one-room schoolhouse."

"Really? When was that?"

"Back in the forties. But as soon as she got pregnant, she was required to resign. That's how it was done back then."

Shamelessly, I do a quick calculation. His oldest sister was born in the forties . . . he's pushing sixty, minimum. "That's not fair," I say.

"Certainly not, although I never sensed she regretted it. Like most women during that era, she spent the rest of her life as a homemaker."

"What made you choose your profession?"

"My story is a bit different than yours. My father was a physician — a cardiac surgeon. Being the only son, I was expected to join him after med school, and eventually take over his practice. But somewhere between med school and my internship, I realized I craved relationships with my patients. During rotations it was always the same issue, 'Taylor,' my supervising physician would say, 'you can't make money talking to patients. Get the facts and shut the hell up.'"

I laugh. "Too bad. I wish more doctors cared."

"It's not that they don't care. It's just that medicine has become an assembly line of sorts. The doctor's got twenty minutes to get the patient diagnosed and out the door, with either a prescription in hand or a referral for further testing. Then it's on to the next patient and the next. It wasn't my style."

"Well, from what I can sense, you chose the right specialty."

It's six thirty when we finally hang up, and I'm as relaxed as a cat in the sun. Peter will challenge me, no doubt about it. But I have an ally now, in Garrett.

Mine is the only car left in the dimly lit parking lot. Without an ice scraper, I use my mitten to brush the snow from the windshield. But beneath the snow lurks a layer of ice, too thick to crack with my hands.

Sitting in my car with the defroster blasting, I spy the red flash from my cell phone. Four text messages: one from Meg, one from Shelley, and two from Brad. Each is a similar version of the same message. *How was ur day? How was crzy kid?* I type a quick reply to each, feeling a lump in my throat swell until I can barely swallow. I rub it down and work to breathe.

Nothing from Andrew. Not even a simple, *U ok?*

The drive home is akin to an obstacle course. Drivers aren't used to winter conditions yet, and every block or two it seems I have to swerve around a fender-bender, or double back to avoid a traffic standstill. Finally, at eight twenty, I pull into the parking structure. Just as I turn off the ignition, the date on my dashboard catches my eye. I rotate the key and the dashboard lights up again. November 14.

"Shit!" I pound my fist on the steering wheel. "Shit! Shit! Shit! Shit! Shit!"

November 14, my date with Carrie Newsome.

CHAPTER TWELVE

✦

Carrie is so gracious when I call her hotel room that I'm actually tempted to drive back to McCormick Place and see her. "Absolutely not," she says. "I've been listening to the news and it sounds horrific out there. I worried you'd had an accident."

I shake my head. "I almost wish I had. At least then I'd have a good excuse."

She laughs, the same friendly, easy laugh of her youth. "Don't worry about a thing. I had a nice glass of wine in the dining room. It was heaven."

"I'm usually more organized than this. I just started a new job and . . ." I trail off, not wanting to confess I was chatting it up with my student's shrink while she was sitting alone in the hotel restaurant. "I'm so sorry." I take a deep breath. "For everything, Carrie."

"Forget about it. Tell me about this new job."

My heart speeds, but I have to do this. "I've never forgiven myself for how awful I was, that time you came to visit. You trusted me, and I let you down. I never even replied to your letter."

She laughs. "What? Brett, that was years ago! We were kids."

"No. I'm so ashamed. That must have been such a confusing time. I should have been there for you."

"Honestly, Brett, I understand. Sure, I was hurt. But I got over it. I can't believe you've been torturing yourself all these years."

"I should have written back immediately, begging *your* forgiveness. I was such a coward."

"Stop. I forgave you years ago." She laughs. "Now will you please forgive yourself?"

"Okay," I say. "But there's one more thing you should know."

I reveal my initial motivation for contacting her after all these years. "So you see, it started as an order from my mom, but once I found you, I realized how much I'd missed you."

She's silent, and I think she's about to tell me off. "Your mother was so wise," she finally says. "I wish I could thank her."

My heart is lighter than it's been in years. Until now, I hadn't realized just how laden with shame it was. I dab the corner of my eye and smile. "So tell me what I've missed out on these past eighteen years."

She tells me about the loves of her life: Stella Myers, her partner of eight years, and their three adopted kids. It strikes me how Carrie's lifestyle — the one I once thought abnormal and odd — is so much more conventional than mine.

"I'm so happy for you," I say. "And your parents, how are they?"

"As kooky and lovable as ever. Hey, remember their annual Christmas brunch?"

"Absolutely. Best brunch ever."

"They still have them, and I was thinking, if you're free, you and your boyfriend should come. This year it's on Sunday the eleventh. Madison's only a two-hour drive."

Memories come flooding back, Mr. Newsome in his Birkenstock sandals, a scotch in one hand and his camcorder in the other, and Carrie's mother strumming her guitar, playing Christmas carols and old folk songs.

"I've told Stella all about you. You'll love her, Brett. She's a teacher, too. And my parents would be thrilled to see you. My dad has some great videos of us. He always liked you — your mom, too. Please, say you'll come."

Suddenly I'm so homesick for my old friend that I'd drive across the country to see her. I cradle the phone with my shoulder and grab my calendar. "Okay," I say, grinning. "It's on my calendar in bold letters. And this time, Care Bear, I'll be there for you. I promise."

I fall asleep at the kitchen table while writing out a menu for Thanksgiving dinner. That's where Andrew finds me when he gets home from work.

"Hey," he says, gently nudging my arm. "Time for bed, sleepyhead."

I wipe a string of drool from my mouth. "What time is it?"

"Only ten fifteen. You must be exhausted. Let's get you up to bed."

I push myself from the table and spy my partially completed menu. "I want to have Thanksgiving this year," I say. "At Mother's house. I'll make all her traditional dishes. What do you think?"

"Suit yourself. I told you Joad and Catherine won't be around, didn't I?"

I frown. "No. I didn't know that."

He opens the refrigerator. "Joad left a message the other day. They're going to London. A business trip, apparently."

"On Thanksgiving? That's crazy. I'll call Catherine and see if they can get out of it."

He lands on a block of cheese and a bottle of Heineken. "You really think they're going to ditch London for a turkey dinner?"

I'm caught off-guard by a surge of loneliness. I assumed we'd all be together for our first holiday without Mother, helping to shore one another up. But in reality, I'm probably the only one who'd need shoring up. I let loose a sigh.

"You're right. I guess it'll be just us then, and Jay and Shelley and the kids." I brighten and turn to Andrew. "Hey, let's invite your parents. Think they'd come?"

"No chance. Too much traveling for them."

"Boston's not that far."

"Still, it's a hassle." He slams shut the refrigerator door with his hip and pulls a knife from the drawer.

I stare at him. "Is that how it's going to be with us one day? When our children grow up and invite us to Thanksgiving, you'll think it's a hassle?"

He slices a wedge of Asiago and pops it into his mouth. "Children?" he asks, one eyebrow raised. "I thought you said you had to have a child. Singular."

"Whatever. You get my point."

He swallows his cheese with a swig of beer. "If we have *a* child, I assume you'll want to spend every holiday with him. That's fine."

A bitter taste fills my mouth. I don't want to hear the answer to the next question, but still, I have to ask. "What about you? Will you want to spend time with our family?"

"Jesus!" He slams his beer bottle on the granite counter. Like his temper, it bubbles over. "It's not enough that I'm willing to have a kid. No. You expect me to be Cliff Huxtable." He shakes his head, and when he speaks again the volume is lower and I know he's trying to contain his frustration. "I'm changing my entire life to make this damn fairy tale come true, Brett, and still I fall short."

"I'm sorry. I appreciate all you're doing, I really do." My chin starts to tremble and I lift a hand to cover it. "This isn't what you want. I know that."

The room fills with the stench of uncomfortable silence. He picks up the beer bottle and studies it. Finally, he rubs a hand over his face. "Can we talk about this another time? It's been a hell of a day."

I nod, but I know *another time* must happen soon. It's just as selfish of me to expect him to share my dreams as it was for him to expect me to share his.

It's Friday afternoon and I've purposely scheduled Peter's appointment last, knowing how easily he can hijack my mood. Autumn points me toward the kitchen, where Peter sits at the cluttered table. Though he comes out of his room without a battle now, he's still rude and sullen, not unlike his mother. Today she sits in the living room, infusing our session with the voice of Maury Povich and the smell of cigarette smoke.

I fumble through my bag and retrieve an algebra book. "We're going to focus on math today, Peter. Most sixth-graders don't do algebra. You should be proud to be in the honors section."

I open to the chapter on polynomials. "Let's see, Mrs. Kiefer wants us to review dividing polynomials today. Let's take a look at number one. Can you give it a try for me?"

He studies the page, then knots his brow and scratches his head. "Too hard." He slides the book to me. "Show me."

I'm being duped, I know. Mrs. Kiefer assured me Peter would breeze through this assignment. But I find my pencil and paper. "It's been a long time since I've worked with polynomials." I copy the problem and silently berate myself for not having studied the lesson beforehand.

It isn't long before I fish my calculator from my bag. I punch numbers, scribble digits on the paper, erase, punch in more numbers, and erase again. All the while, Peter watches me with a smug smile on his face.

After a good five minutes, I have my answer — and an exhilarating sense of accomplishment. I blow up the bangs from my forehead and turn to him, smiling.

"I've got it. The answer is 3y over 8x to the negative fourth power." I position the paper in front of him. "Now let me explain how I got my answer."

He looks down his nose at my work like an arrogant professor. "Did you invert the negatives?"

My face heats and I examine my work. "Invert . . . what exactly . . . You mean, did I . . . ?"

Peter sighs. "When finding the quotient of polynomials, negative numbers need to be inverted. A negative numerator becomes a positive denominator. You knew that, right? The correct answer is 3y over 8x to the eighth."

I lean my elbows on the table and massage my temples. "Yes, of course. You're absolutely right. Good for you, Peter."

I feel his eyes on me as he scratches his left arm, slowly and methodically, until finally I look over at him.

"Stupid itch," he says, his eyes locked on mine.

Stupid bitch is what he's saying.

The sky has darkened to a smoky gray when I drive away from the old white house. After a few blocks, I stop the car in front of a deserted playground and pull my cell phone from my purse.

"Hello, Doc — Garrett. It's Brett."

"Hey. I was just thinking of you. How'd it go today?"

I lean my head against the headrest. "I just lost at *Are You Smarter Than a Seventh-Grader?*"

He laughs. "You're dealing with a sixth-grader," he reminds me. "Don't get cocky."

Despite my horrible session, I crack up. Then I suck up my pride and tell him about the math lesson —*my* math lesson.

"When he asked if I'd inverted the negatives, I looked at him like, *Duh? Invert what?*"

He roars with laughter. "I've been there. It's humbling to be outsmarted by a kid."

"Yeah, Peter's probably thinking I'm the cafeteria lady, that the school couldn't afford a real teacher."

"You are the best thing the school could have sent, of that I'm certain."

My heart does a little jig. "And I'm thinking he's pretty lucky to have you for his doc. Want to hear part two of my tale of humiliation?"

"Absolutely."

I tell him about Peter's scratching and his rude comment. "Clearly, he was calling me a stupid bitch."

"Clearly, that couldn't be farther from the truth."

I smile. "Yeah, well, you've never met me."

He chuckles. "But I hope to someday. And when I do, I'm sure my hunch will be confirmed."

My shitty day just improved a hundredfold. "Thanks. You're really nice."

"Yeah, well, you've never met me."

We laugh. "All right," he says, "I better not keep you. It's officially the weekend."

A wave of sadness hits me. I want to tell him it's okay, that I'd rather sit here in my cold car talking to him than go home to the empty loft. Instead, I say good-bye.

Tiny flakes of snow skitter and flit through the chilly November air. Barren oak trees line both sides of Forest Avenue, their gangly branches stretching toward one another like beseeching lovers.

The manicured lawns of summer are hidden beneath a layer of snow, but each drive and sidewalk is perfectly clear. A few weeks ago I'd have gazed in admiration at the stately brick Tudors. But today the gaping contrast between this idyllic Evanston neighborhood and the South Side streets of my students unsettles me.

In the backyard, Jay and Trevor build a snowman while Shelley and I sit at her kitchen table, snacking on Cabernet and Brie. "This cheese is delicious," I say, slicing off another wedge.

"It's organic," Shelley says.

"Huh, I thought all cheese was organic."

"Nope. These cows were raised on a grass-fed diet. I learned this from the mom clique."

"See, and you thought stay-at-home mothering offered no mental stimulation."

She rolls her eyes and pours herself another glass of Cabernet. "I just don't fit in with these women. It's all about their kids, which is great, who can fault them for that? But come on! I asked one woman what she likes to read, and with a perfectly straight face she told me Dr. Seuss."

I burst out laughing. "Oh, yeah, *Green Eggs and Ham* is a real page-turner."

Shelley howls. "And that plot twist in *Horton Hears a Who* — brilliant!"

We're doubled over laughing — until Shelley's guffaws morph into sobs. "I love my kids," she says, swiping her cheeks. "But —"

The back door pushes open and Trevor rushes into the kitchen. "Snowman all done, Auntie Bwett."

Shelley spins around. "It's Brrrett," she snaps. "*Rrr*. Can't you hear that?"

Trevor's face collapses and he rushes back outside. I turn to her.

"Shelley! Trevor's three years old. He's not supposed to say his *R*'s yet, and you know it. You're the speech pathologist."

"*Was* the speech pathologist," she says, slouching in her chair. "I'm nothing anymore."

"That's not true. You're a mother, the most important —"

"I suck at motherhood. God, look at the way I just yelled at Trevor." She clutches her head. "I'm going nuts here. I know I should be thankful I get to stay home with my kids, but if I have to go on one more playdate, I swear I'll lose it."

"Go back to work," I say softly.

She rubs her temples. "And your brother's losing interest in me."

"What? No way."

She slices another chunk of cheese, stares at it a moment, then plops it back on the plate. "I have nothing to share anymore. I'm boring and exhausted, and a shitty mom to boot."

"Go back to work."

"It's only been a couple of months. I have to give it a fair shot."

"Then maybe you two need to get away — without the kids. Plant yourselves on some tropical island. Drink cocktails with little umbrellas in them, soak up the sun."

She raises her arms and stares down at herself. "Oh sure. Stuffing this body into a swimsuit's going to cheer me right up."

I look away. Poor Shelley. What could be worse than feeling like your IQ has shrunk while your rear end has expanded? "Okay, so skip the Caribbean. How about New York, or Toronto? See some shows, do some shopping, have some uninterrupted sex."

She finally grins. She goes to the counter and brings back her calendar. "Maybe we could go somewhere for my birthday in February. Someplace different and fun, like New Orleans."

"Perfect. Make a plan. Oh, and your calendar reminds me, I thought we'd have Thanksgiving at Mom's, you know, so she could kind of be there with us."

Shelley raises her eyebrows. "So you've forgiven her?"

"No. My blood still boils when I think of how she kept my

identity secret." I shake my head. "But she is our mother, and I want her to be included in our holidays."

She bites her lip. "I've been meaning to tell you, Patti invited us to Dallas."

My heart plummets, but I don't say anything.

"I haven't spent Thanksgiving with my family in three years, Brett. Don't make me feel guilty."

I shake my head. "I'm sorry. Of course you should go. I'll miss you, that's all."

She pats my hand. "You'll have Andrew, and Catherine and Joad. That'll be fun, right?"

"Actually, Joad and . . ." I stop myself. The last thing Shelley needs is more guilt. "You're right, it'll be fun."

CHAPTER THIRTEEN

The night before Thanksgiving, Andrew and I load the car with a fresh turkey, three DVDs, two bottles of wine, and Andrew's laptop. I've already stocked Mom's kitchen with everything else we'll need. But as soon as we pull out of our parking garage, the car skids across the ice, just missing the curb on the opposite side of the street.

"Jesus!" Andrew holds tight the wheel and reins in the car. "I don't get why you're so hell-bent on having this at your mother's house. It would be a whole lot easier to have it here."

Here? Andrew never calls the loft *our* house or *our* place. And technically, he shouldn't. It isn't our house, it's his. Which could explain why I insisted the dinner be at Mom's brownstone, the only place that feels like home lately.

It takes us nearly thirty minutes to make the three-mile trek, and Andrew's temper gains momentum with each passing minute. "The weather's only going to get worse, with this freezing rain. Let's just turn back."

"I need to do the prep work tonight. All the food is at Mom's."

He curses under his breath.

"We're almost there," I say. "And if we're stranded at Mom's it'll be a blast. We'll roast marshmallows in the fireplace, play cards, or Scrabble . . ."

He keeps his eyes on the road. "You're forgetting, one of us has work to do." Without looking at me, he clamps a hand on my leg. "Have you had a chance to talk to Catherine yet?"

My stomach twists, as it does each time he mentions working for Bohlinger Cosmetics. "She's in London, remember?"

"They just left yesterday. You didn't call her Monday?"

"She's been so busy preparing to get out of town."

He nods. "You'll talk to her next week then?"

Ahead, Mother's house comes into view like a lighthouse in a storm. Andrew pulls up to the curb. I let out a sigh and throw open my car door. "Ah, we're here."

I grab the grocery bag and clamber up the porch steps, praying the unanswered question won't follow us inside.

By the time I finish the cranberry sauce and slide my pecan pie into the oven, the house smells almost like it did when Mother lived here. Tossing my apron over a bar stool, I stroll into the living room. Miles Davis pours from the speakers and the room glows with the amber light of the fire and Mother's Venetian lamps. I sidle up to where Andrew sits on the sofa with his laptop.

"What are you working on?"

"Just seeing if anything new came on the market."

My chest tightens. The house again. I see the price range he's searching and nearly gasp. Resting my head on his shoulder, I gaze at the screen. "Too bad the mortgage on the loft is upside down."

"Megan doesn't know what she's talking about."

"But for now maybe we should look for something smaller. Something we can afford if we pool our savings."

"I never realized you were such a piker. Jesus, you're about to inherit a fortune."

My stomach clenches. As much as I'd like to avoid it, it's time to ask the question that has been burning in me for weeks.

"What if there was no inheritance, Andrew? Would you still agree to help me with this list?

He lifts his face and scowls. "Is this some sort of a test?"

"There's a chance I won't get it, you know. I have no idea where my father is, thanks to my mother's secrecy. I may not get pregnant."

He turns his attention back to the laptop. "Then we'd fight it in court. And we'd win."

Stop. That's good enough. You're only going to make him angry if you keep pestering him.

"So your willingness to help me," I say, my heart battering against my rib cage. "It has nothing to do with money?"

His eyes flash with anger. "You think I'm after your money? Christ, I'm practically begging for a job here. And you still haven't told me you'll help! I'm doing everything you've asked, Brett. I've agreed to your dog, your teaching job, every damn request. I'm just asking for one thing in return: a job in the family business and the salary to go with it."

That's two things, I think to myself. But he's right. Begrudgingly or not, Andrew's doing everything I've asked of him. So why am I not satisfied?

"It's tricky," I say, grabbing his hand. "Mom didn't like the idea, and she rarely made a poor business decision."

He yanks his hand from mine. "Is your mother going to dictate our lives forever?"

I finger my necklace. "No . . . no. In the end, it would be Catherine's call."

"Bullshit. You have the power to bring me on board and you know it." He glowers at me. "I'm helping you with your goals, and I need to know you'll help me with mine."

I look away. He's not being unreasonable. It would be so easy to tell him yes. I could call Catherine on Monday and within a week or two she'd find a place for him in the company. He's an attorney, after all, an easy fit with our legal team, the finance department, or even HR. I hold the power to change the ugly mood of this evening with one simple declarative sentence. *Yes, I will help.*

"No," I say softly. "I can't help you. I don't feel right going against Mother on this one."

He rises from the sofa. I reach out my hand to him, but he jerks away, as if my touch burns. "You used to be so easy, so agreeable. But you've changed. You're not the girl I fell in love with."

He's right. I'm not. I swipe a tear from my cheek. "I'm sorry. I didn't mean to ruin the evening."

He paces the length of the room, dragging a hand through his hair. I know this look. He's making a decision. He's deciding whether or not I'll be part of his life. As if rendered impotent, I stand watching him, unable to speak and barely able to breathe. Finally, he stops in front of the bay window, his back to me. His shoulders fall, as if a mighty tension just left his body. He turns to me.

"Ruin the evening? You just ruined your life, baby."

*I*t seems treasonous to sleep in Mother's bed tonight. She's the enemy, after all. Because of her, I've lost my job, my home, and all hope. Yes, Andrew was difficult — even a jerk sometimes — but he was my jerk, and without him I'll never get pregnant.

I drag a comforter down the stairs and heave it onto the sofa. It takes a moment to adjust to the ambient glow from the streetlights. From across the room my eyes meet my mother's. The photo was taken at an awards ceremony two years ago when she was named Chicago's Businesswoman of the Year. Her salt-and-pepper hair is cut in her signature style, a boyish crop of layers I used to say nobody but she and Halle Berry could pull off. She's stunning, yes, with her high cheekbones and flawless olive skin. But beyond her physical beauty, I always felt the shot captured Mother's very essence, her wisdom, her serenity. Rising, I cross the room and snatch the photo, plunking it on the coffee table in front of the sofa. I settle back under the comforter and stare at her.

"Did you plan to ruin my life, Mom? Is that what you wanted?"

Her green eyes penetrate mine.

I move the photo nearer to me and glare at her. "Who are you, anyway? Not only did you lie to me your entire life, but because of you, I've lost Andrew, the one person who could help make my dreams come true."

Tears slide past my temples, into my ears. "I'm all alone now. And I'm so old." I choke on the words. "And you were right. I want a baby so badly it hurts. And now . . . now my dream's been yanked away like some cruel prank."

I bolt upright and jab a finger at her smiling face. "Are you happy now? You never liked him, did you? Well, you got your way. He's gone. Now I have nobody." I slam the photo facedown on the coffee table with such force I'm sure I've cracked the glass. But I don't check. I roll over and cry myself to sleep.

Mercifully, the first hint of dawn creeps through the bay window, giving me permission to rise from my fitful sleep. The first thing I do is hunt down my cell phone from beneath the rumpled comforter and check for messages. I hate myself for it, but I'm hoping for a message from Andrew. I stare into the phone, but the only message I have is a text from Brad, sent at midnight, Pacific time. *Happy Turkey Day*.

I type back, *U, 2*. He's in San Francisco with Jenna, and suddenly I miss him ferociously. If he were in town, I'd invite him to dinner. I'd pour out my heart to him, and then I'd listen as he shared his frustrations with Jenna. Just like Andrew and me, he and Jenna are having a rough go. "A couple of magnets," he tells me. "One moment locked in attraction, the next repelling each other." We'd open the wine while preparing sage stuffing. We'd laugh out loud, eat too much, watch movies . . . everything Andrew and I were supposed to do. But when I imagine it with Brad, it's casual and breezy rather than forced and stilted.

I'm about to send the text when I notice my mother's photo, facedown on the coffee table. I lift it. Her eyes tell me she's forgiven me for yelling at her. Pressure builds behind my eyes. I kiss my finger and touch it to the glass, leaving a fingerprint on her cheek. Her face shows encouragement today, something akin to prodding, as if she's trying to nudge me forward.

I gaze down at my phone, my index finger positioned on the SEND button. As if of their own volition, my fingers return to the keyboard and type one more sentence.

Miss u.

Then I press SEND.

It's only six o'clock in the morning. The entire day looms ahead of me like the wastelands of Siberia. I check my phone again, then, in frustration, heave it across the room. It lands with a dull thud on Mom's Persian rug. I plop down on a chair and rub my temples. If I stay in this house checking my phone every thirty seconds I'll lose my mind. I grab my jacket and scarf, wedge my feet into a pair of Mother's rubber boots, and trudge out the door.

In the east, pinks and oranges mop up a gunmetal-gray sky. A bitter wind cuts from the east, knocking the breath from me. I cover my nose with my scarf and pull up my hood. Across Lake Shore Drive, I'm greeted by the haunting howl of Lake Michigan. Angry waves slap the shore, retreat, and crash again. I traipse along the Lakefront Trail, my hands buried deep in my coat pockets. The path that hosts fitness buffs and tourists all summer long has lost its clientele this morning, a depressing reminder that everyone in the entire city is celebrating with friends and family. Households are waking, chatting over coffee and bagels, dicing celery and onions for their stuffing.

I round the bend of the Drake Hotel and head south. An empty Ferris wheel comes into view, like a ring on the finger of the Navy Pier. The abandoned wheel looks as forlorn as I feel. Will I be alone forever? Guys my age are already married, or dating twenty-year-olds. In the dating meal of life, I'm a leftover.

A jogger runs toward me, his Labrador leashed before him. I move aside to let them pass and the dog sizes me up with friendly eyes. As the runner passes I spin around. He's clad from head to toe in black Under Armour, but still, there's something familiar about him. He's looking back at me, too, and for a moment our eyes lock. He hesitates, as if he'd like to run back and talk to me, but then thinks better of it. He smiles and raises his arm in greeting, then turns and continues on. I watch him move into the distance. Finally, it hits me. I think that was the Burberry man — the man I spoke to on the train . . . and on my way out of the building! Or was it?

"Hey!" I call, but the roar of the tide swallows my words. I break into a run. The last time I saw him I was leaving for a lunch date. I'll let him know I'm single now. I need to catch him! But my clunky boots make it impossible to gain on him. He's a good fifty yards away now. Faster! Suddenly, the toe of my boot catches on something and I fall flat on my ass. I sit on the cold concrete, watching the Burberry man disappear down the trail.

Oh, God, I've reached a new low. Andrew and I just broke up last night. And here I am this morning, chasing — yes, chasing — after a man whose name I don't even know. Could I be any more pathetic? As if my biological clock weren't enough pressure, my mother has strapped a ticking time bomb on my back, and it's due to explode next September.

The day has officially clocked in by the time I wander back to Mother's house, but typical of November in Chicago, thick gray clouds have moved in, holding the sun hostage. Tiny specks of snow flutter in the air, instantly vanishing when they land on my wool coat. A foreboding feeling comes over me as I climb the concrete steps to my mother's door. I don't want to be alone today. I can't bear the thought of being that pitiful character you see in the movies, cooking for one on Thanksgiving Day.

I clear the dining room table I'd set last night, carefully folding Mother's treasured napkins and tablecloth. She bought the hand-embroidered linens when we visited Ireland three years ago, and insisted we use them at every family celebration. Tears stream down my face. We never imagined our family celebrations would vanish so quickly.

To further torture myself, I second-guess my relationship with Andrew. Why aren't I lovable? Fresh tears sting my eyes. I picture him moving on without me, finding a woman who's absolutely flawless, someone who could make him happy. Someone he'd want to marry.

Through a teary haze, I manage to stuff the turkey and push it into the oven. Mechanically, I peel potatoes and mix the ingredients for my mother's sweet potato casserole. By the time I slice fruit into a bowl, I'm no longer crying.

Three hours later, I remove the most gorgeous turkey I've ever prepared. The skin shines crisp and golden, and juices bubble from the bottom of the roaster. Next, I take out the sweet potato casserole and breathe in the familiar aroma of nutmeg and cinnamon. From the refrigerator, I grab the fruit salad and cranberry sauce. I slice the remaining tomatoes into the salad and set it next to my pies. After I've double-wrapped everything, I load the food into picnic baskets and cardboard boxes retrieved from the basement.

On my way, I call Sanquita at Joshua House. She's waiting at the door when I arrive.

"Hi, sweetie. Take this, can you?" I hand her the basket and turn back to the car. "I'll be right back."

"You brung us Thanksgiving dinner?" she asks, eyeing the picnic basket.

"Uh-huh."

"Miss Brett's brung us dinner," she calls to her housemates. She peers inside the basket. "Not just turkey loaf, like we had earlier, but real turkey with all the fixin's."

It takes me three trips to get everything into Joshua House. Sanquita helps me pile it on the kitchen counter, where the other women gather like ants to a sugar cube. By now I recognize most of their faces and even know a few names. Tanya, Mercedes, and Julonia unload the food while the others lean in.

"The stuffing's right inside the bird, just the way I like it."

"Umm um! This casserole smells delicious."

"Check it out — pecan pie!"

"Enjoy, ladies," I say, gathering the empty baskets. "I'll see you Monday, Sanquita."

"You don't gotta go," Sanquita mumbles, staring down at her feet. "I mean, you could eat something if you wanted."

I'm stunned. The girl who doesn't trust people is opening the door to me — just a crack. As much as I'd like to enter, I can't today. "Thanks, but I've had a long day. I need to get home." Which is where, exactly? Maybe I should ask about vacancies here.

She straightens her shoulders and hardness returns to her face. " 'Course you do."

I run a finger beneath my eyes and find flakes of dried mascara. "I'm not feeling so great." I look into her puffy face, and notice a patch of skin on her forehead that's been scratched raw, a cruel side effect of waste buildup. "How about you, kiddo? How are you feeling?"

"Good," she says, not meeting my eyes. "I feel fine."

Just then Jean Anderson, the grouchy director, steps through the front door. The pocket on her wool coat is torn and she's clutching a vinyl overnight bag.

"Miss Jean," Sanquita says. "You ain't supposed to be here today."

"Lisa called in sick." She shimmies out of her coat. "Funny how sickness always strikes on holidays."

"But your daughter's here from Mississippi," Mercedes says, "and your grandbabies."

"They'll still be here tomorrow." She reaches into the closet for a hanger, and when she turns back around, she spots me. Her face turns to stone. "What are you doing here?"

Before I can answer, Sanquita claps her hands. "Miss Brett brung us turkey and fixin's. Come see."

She eyes me and doesn't budge. "Are you all set then, Ms. Bohlinger?"

"Uh, yes. I'll get going." I pat Sanquita's arm. "See you Monday, sweetie."

I'm three blocks away when I screech to a halt and whip a U-turn. I pull up to the curb and dash up the porch steps, straight into Joshua House. Miss Jean stands at the kitchen counter slicing the turkey.

"Umm um. This bird is a beauty. Mercedes honey, will you set the table, please?" Her smile vanishes when she sees me.

"Forget something?"

"Go home," I tell her, breathless. "I'll stay tonight."

She gives me a once-over, then turns her attention back to the turkey.

I run a hand through my ratty hair. "I just got hired with the school district. They did a thorough background check. I'm safe, I promise."

She sets her knife on the cutting board and scowls at me. "Why would someone like you choose to spend your holiday at a homeless shelter? Don't you have kin at home?"

"I like it here," I say, honestly. "And I adore Sanquita. Besides, my family is out of town and I'm alone. You, on the other hand, have a houseful of guests. You need to be with them."

"Go home, Miss Jean," Mercedes tells her. "We'll be fine."

She rakes her teeth over her bottom lip. Finally she throws her head toward the office. "Follow me."

As I trail Miss Jean down the hall, I glance over my shoulder. Sanquita stands watching, her arms crossed over her chest. Have I crossed a boundary? Am I invading her personal space by staying tonight? Our eyes meet. One hand emerges from within her crossed arms. I see a clenched fist, then a thumb. She raises it, giving me a thumbs-up. I could cry.

Although Joshua House is at full capacity tonight, it's free of drama, as far as Miss Jean can tell — no threatening ex-boyfriends, no addicts. "The guests — that's what we call them — have the run of the house until seven P.M. After that, the kitchen's off-limits. Children need to be in bed no later than nine o'clock. The television goes off at eleven thirty and everyone must retreat to their own quarters." She points to a twin bed against the wall. "You'll sleep here. We change the sheets on this bed daily, so in the morning you'll strip it. Amy Olle will relieve you in the morning, eight A.M." She lets out a sigh. "I think that about covers it. Any questions?"

I want to put her at ease, so I don't pummel her with the choir of questions in my head. Is anyone dangerous? Is there a security alarm on this house?

"I can handle it," I say, with more conviction than I feel. "Get going."

Instead of leaving, she stands facing me with her hands on her hips.

"I don't know what your motive is, but if I find out you're exploiting these women, I'll have you tossed out of here before you can say *designer handbag*. Do you understand me?"

"Exploit? No. No, I don't understand."

She crosses her arms across her bosom. "Last spring a pretty white woman much like yourself showed up wanting to volunteer. Of course I let her. We need all the help we can get. It wasn't a week later that the video crew came a-calling. Little Miss Pretty was running for circuit court judge. She wanted the city to see what a swell lady she was, volunteering with the poor black folks on the South Side."

"I would never do that. I promise you."

We stare at each other until finally she lowers her eyes to her desk.

"My home phone number is right here," she says, pointing to a Post-it note. "Call if you have any questions."

She grabs her purse and strides from the room without a good-bye or a good luck. I sink into a chair, trying to drum up a reason to be thankful today.

❖

CHAPTER FOURTEEN

*B*rad calls me Monday morning, asking if I can stop by his office on my way home from work. All afternoon my hunch gains momentum, and now, as the elevator climbs to the thirty-second floor, it's no longer a hunch. I'm certain he's got news about my father.

He looks up when he sees me and smiles. "Hey, B.B." He crosses the room and gives me a hug. "Thanks for coming in." He pulls back from me and scowls. "Everything okay? You look kind of tired."

"Exhausted. I can't seem to get enough sleep these days." I rub my cheeks, hoping to stir some color to their pale surface. "So tell me, what's going on?"

He walks me to the set of chairs and heaves a sigh. "Have a seat." His voice sounds flat and defeated, and I push back the dread that's threatening to invade me.

"Did Pohlonski find my dad?"

He plops down in the chair next to mine and runs a hand over his face. "He struck out, Brett."

"What do you mean, struck out? I thought he had six possibilities."

"He called each one. There was one guy he thought might be the one. He was in Chicago during the summer of '78. But he didn't know your mom."

"Maybe he just forgot. Does this guy play the guitar? Tell him to ask him about Justine's."

"He was a grad student at DePaul at the time. Never heard of Justine's. No musical ability whatsoever."

"Damn!" I pound the edge of the chair. "Why didn't my mother tell me about Johnny while she was alive? She must have had more information about him. But no, she was too damn selfish. She was more concerned with protecting herself than helping me." I turn to Brad, trying to tamp down my anger. "So, what's Pohlonski's plan now?"

"He's done everything he can, I'm afraid. He tried tracking down the owners of Justine's but they've both passed away. It's likely Johnny was paid under the table, because Steve can't find any tax records. He even located the property owner of the place on Bosworth."

"The landlord? That's good. He must have an old lease from Johnny Manns, right?"

"No. Nothing. The old man's living in a nursing home in Naperville now and has no recollection of Johnny Manns or your parents."

"He's got to keep trying. I'll keep paying him."

Brad's silence makes me nervous, so I fill it. "Maybe he wasn't born in North Dakota, after all. We'll widen this search. We'll check different spellings, too."

"Brett, he's reached a dead end. There's just not enough information to go on."

I cross my arms over my chest. "I don't like this guy, Pohlonski. He doesn't know what he's doing."

"You're free to find someone else, but take a look at these records." He hands me a spreadsheet showing the search for Jon, John, Jonathan, Jonothon, or Johnny Manns. Some names are circled; some are crossed out. Notes are scribbled in the margins, indicating dates and times of phone calls. One thing is obvious: This Pohlonski guy has been trying his damnedest to find my father.

"Okay then, tell him to keep trying. Johnny's out there somewhere."

"I've decided to exempt you from this goal."

I turn to him. "Exempt me? You're telling me I should give up?"

He lifts the spreadsheet from my lap. "You don't have to give up. I'll leave that up to you. But I'm not going to hold you to this one, Brett. You've tried, but this search is going nowhere."

I lean in. "Well, I'll tell you right now, I'm not giving up. Pohlonski needs to try harder. We need a bigger age span. Maybe my father was older . . . or younger."

"B.B., this could take years. It'll cost you a fortune. I think you should focus on your other goals for now."

"Forget it. I'm not giving up."

He frowns at me. "Brett, listen to me. I know you're running low on cash and —"

"Not anymore," I say, interrupting him.

His eyes land on my naked wrist. "Oh, hell. Where's your Rolex?"

I rub the place where my watch used to rest. "I didn't need it. My cell phone keeps better time than that old watch ever did."

His jaw drops. "Jesus, you pawned it?"

"Sold it. On eBay. Some jewelry, too. Next will be my suits and some purses."

He takes a deep breath and runs a hand over his face. "Oh, B.B., I'm so sorry."

He thinks I'm wasting my money. He thinks I'll never find my father. I clutch his arm.

"Don't be sorry, because I'm not. I have money now. I can keep searching for my father. And finding him, my friend, is priceless."

He offers me a sad little smile. "Fair enough. I'll tell Pohlonski to keep looking."

I nod and swallow hard. "How was San Francisco?"

He takes a deep breath and sighs. "Not the easiest trip. Jenna was a little preoccupied with a story she's working on."

He tells me about the day trip they took to Half Moon Bay, but I have a hard time focusing. My mind is on my father. Does he look like me? What kind of a man is he? Will he like me, or will he be ashamed of his illegitimate daughter? What if he's dead? My heart sinks.

"Can Pohlonski check death records?"

"What?"

"I need to find Johnny, even if he's dead. Tell Pohlonski to check death records as well as birth records."

He looks at me, his eyes heavy. When he makes a note on his legal pad, I know he's doing it to appease me.

"How was Thanksgiving?" he asks.

I tell him about my breakup with Andrew. He tries to appear neutral, but I can see approval in his face.

"You deserve someone who shares your dreams. And remember, your mother was never convinced he was the one."

"Yeah, but now that I'm alone, my goals seem even more impossible."

He looks directly in my eyes. "You won't be alone forever. Trust me."

My heart does a two-step and I curse myself. Brad has a girlfriend. He's off-limits. "Whatever," I say, and look out the window. "After he left, I spent Thanksgiving at Joshua House."

"Joshua House?"

"A women's shelter. I have a student living there. You wouldn't believe how great these women are — all except for the director, who despises me. Anyway, a couple of them suffer from mental illness, but most are just normal women who've fallen on hard times."

He studies me. "Is that right?"

"Yeah, like Mercedes. She was a single mother who got suckered into an adjustable mortgage. When her interest rate went through the roof and she couldn't sell her house, she had to walk away. Luckily, someone told her about Joshua House. Now she and her kids have a place to stay."

Brad watches me with a smile on his face.

"What?"

"I really admire you."

I wave him off. "Don't be ridiculous. Hey, I've signed up to volunteer on Monday nights. You should stop by next week and meet these women — especially Sanquita. She's still hard as nails, but she actually invited me to stay for Thanksgiving dinner."

He holds up an index finger and gets to his feet. Standing at his file cabinet, he removes my mother's envelopes and returns to where I sit.

"Congratulations." He holds out envelope number twelve: HELP POOR PEOPLE.

I don't reach for it. "But I didn't . . . I wasn't . . ."

"You did it effortlessly, without ulterior motives. That's exactly what your mom would have wanted."

I think of the five minutes I spent making a donation to Heifer International last week, thinking that might qualify me for my envelope. Even then I knew Mother wanted more from me, but I had no idea what, or where. Serendipitously, Joshua House found me.

"Shall I open it?" he asks.

I nod, not trusting my voice.

"'Darling Brett,

"'Perhaps you remember the story I used to tell you of the old man in search of happiness. He wanders the world, asking everyone he meets to share with him the secret to a happy life. But nobody is able to articulate what the secret is. Finally, the old man meets a Buddha who agrees to reveal the secret. The Buddha leans down and takes hold of the old man's hands. He looks into his weary eyes and says, "Don't do bad things. Always do good things."

"'The old man stares at him, confused. "But that's too simple. I've known that since I was three years old!"

"'"Yes," the Buddha says. "We all know this at age three. But at eighty we have forgotten."

"'Congratulations, my daughter, for doing good things. It is indeed, the secret to a happy life.'"

I burst into tears and Brad crouches at my side, pulling me into his arms. "I miss her," I say though my sobs. "I miss her so much."

"I know," he says, rubbing my back. "I know just how you feel."

I hear the catch in his voice. I pull back and dab my eyes. "You miss your dad, don't you?"

He rubs his throat and nods. "Yeah, the man he was."

This time, it's me rubbing his back and whispering comfort.

I'm exhausted. I'm weepy. I think my boobs are a bit tender. Even though Andrew and I had sex only twice since my last period, I can't help but wonder if . . . no! I can't even go there. I'll jinx it if I do. Still, every now and then a bubble of joy rises in me so pure and strong that it nearly lifts me off my feet.

But Wednesday afternoon, that joy is nowhere to be found. It's four o'clock when I arrive at Andrew's loft. Lugging empty boxes, I let myself in and grope for the light switch. It's chilly in the lifeless space, and a shiver wriggles through me. I toss my coat and gloves onto the sofa and dash up the stairs to the bedroom. I want to be out of here before Andrew gets home from work.

Without taking care to fold or sort, I stuff my clothes into the empty boxes, clearing the armoire first, and then my closet. When did I accumulate all this stuff? I think of the women at Joshua House, with their three drawers and a shared closet, and feel repulsed by my gluttony. I drag four boxes to my car, drive to my mother's with the trunk tied down, dump the boxes in her foyer, and return for the next load.

By eight o'clock I'm out of steam. I've emptied the loft of every last article of clothing, makeup, lotion, and hair product belonging to me. With car keys in hand, I meander through the loft one last time. Mentally, I begin to note all the things I brought to the house, everything I purchased since we've lived here. Was I trying to fill this loft with pieces of me, hoping it would make it feel like home? Along with paying half the mortgage and utilities, I bought the dining room table, the sofa and love seat, and two high-def TVs. Climbing the stairs, I remember purchasing the bedroom set the first week we moved in. A maple sleigh bed, a chest of drawers, two bedside tables, and the antique armoire I said I couldn't live without. In the bathroom I spot my sumptuous Ralph Lauren towels, and the Missoni bath mat I found at Neiman Marcus. Shaking my head, I turn out the light and walk downstairs. I step into the kitchen and open the cupboard, spying my Italian dishes, All-Clad pots and pans, Pasquini espresso maker. I put a hand to my mouth.

Everything in this place, it seems, is mine. There must be tens of thousands of dollars' worth of inventory! But I cannot empty Andrew's house. He'd be livid. And really, what would I do with a houseful of furniture now? I'd have to put it in storage until I have my own place. And what if I really am you-know-what? Is it possible I'd move back in?

I close the kitchen cupboard. He can have it. He can have everything. It'll be my peace offering.

I'm buttoning my coat when I hear his key in the door. Shit! I turn out the kitchen light and step into the hallway when the door swings open and I hear a woman's voice.

I slip back into the kitchen and plaster myself against the wall, next to the fridge. My heart's pounding so frantically I'm afraid they'll hear it.

"I'll take your coat," Andrew says.

She says something, but I can't make out the words. But it's a woman's voice. No mistaking that. I stand frozen, debating what to do. Why didn't I just let Andrew know I was here? If I step out now, it'll look like I've been spying. But if they find me in here hiding, I'll look like his stalker ex-girlfriend.

"I like having you here," he says. "You brighten the place."

She lets loose a high-pitched giggle and I gasp. I clap my hand over my mouth to keep from crying out.

I hear him rifle through the liquor cabinet. "C'mon," he says. "I'll show you the upstairs."

She breaks into a fresh giggle.

From the darkness of the kitchen I watch Andrew chase Megan up the stairs, a bottle of Glenlivet in one hand, and two glasses in the other.

The following afternoon I meet the moving van at Andrew's. Three burly men wearing Carhartt coveralls and leather gloves greet me.

"Whatcha got for us today, Miss?" the oldest one asks.

"I want you to move everything out of unit four."

"Everything?"

"Yes. Except the brown chair in the living room." I open the door to the building. "On second thought, leave the mattress, too."

I fill boxes with towels and sheets, dishes and cookware and silver. The movers tackle the big items. It takes the four of us three hours, but we finish before Andrew is home. I look around. The house that never felt like home is completely emptied of me.

"Where we taking this stuff?" the man with the goatee asks.

"Carroll Avenue. The Joshua House."

On the morning of December 11, armed with a trunk full of gifts and a full tank of gas, I set out for the Newsomes' annual Christmas brunch. Two hours later, exhausted and queasy, I pull up to the curb alongside a dozen other cars and stare up at a pretty yellow ranch. A yard sign, barely visible in the snowy grounds, reads ANOTHER FAMILY FOR PEACE. I smile, glad to know some things remain constant.

Footprints of various sizes on the snowy sidewalk tell of people coming and going. I lift my trunk and hear the sound of the front door opening. A woman dressed in jeans and a fleece vest darts from the house and races down the walk. As she nears me, she slips and nearly falls. I catch her and we burst out laughing.

"Bretel!" she cries. "I can't believe you're here!"

She folds me into her arms and squeezes. My eyes flood with tears.

"It was worth it," I whisper. "If only for this."

She holds me at arm's length. "Wow. You're even prettier than your pictures on Facebook."

I shake my head, taking in the woman before me. Her brown hair is cut short and she carries an extra fifteen pounds on her large frame. Her translucent skin glows pink, and from behind her glasses blue eyes shine big and bright and utterly gleeful. I brush the snow from her sleeve. "You're beautiful," I say.

"C'mon," she says. "Let's get you inside."

"Wait. Before we go in, I need to do this." I take her by the arms and look into her eyes. "I am so sorry for the way I treated you, Carrie. Please forgive me."

Her face turns pink and she waves me off. "You're ridiculous. There's nothing to forgive." She grabs my elbow. "Now c'mon. Everyone's so excited to meet you."

The scent of freshly brewed coffee, the background hum of laughter and chatter, take me back to the Newsomes' old bunga-low on Arthur Street. Carrie's three biracial children sit around an oak table with needles and thread, stringing popcorn and cranberries. I crouch beside nine-year-old Tayloe.

"I remember stringing popcorn with your mother and your grandparents one year. We'd gone up north to Egg Harbor." I turn to Carrie. "Your grandparents' old log cabin. Do you remember?"

She nods. "My parents own it now. My dad's been pulling out old videos all week, in honor of your visit. I'm sure he's got some footage of us at Egg Harbor."

"He really should have been a filmmaker. He always had that camera with him. Remember when he filmed us sunbathing while there was still snow on the ground?"

We're laughing when Stella steps into the kitchen. She's short and slim, with close-cropped blond hair and dark-framed glasses. She looks smart and serious, like a fitness trainer. But the mo-ment she smiles, her face softens.

"Hey, Brett! You made it!"

She plunks her coffee cup on the counter, then rushes in to shake my hand. Looking me straight in the eyes, she smiles brightly. "Oh, and by the way, I'm Stella."

I laugh with joy, sensing that Carrie has chosen well. Instead of taking her hand, I open my arms to her.

"I'm so glad to know you, Stella."

"Same here. Carrie's been watching out that window for you

all morning. I haven't seen her this excited since we got the kids."
She winks at Tayloe and chuckles. "How about a cup of coffee?"

Carrie raises her eyebrows. "Or a Bloody Mary? We also have
Mimosas, or my mom's famous brandied eggnog."

I glance at the kids with their mugs of hot chocolate. "Do you
have any more cocoa?"

"Cocoa?"

I place a hand on my stomach. "I'm probably being overly
cautious."

Carrie's eyes travel to what I'm convinced is a baby bump.
"Are you — ? Could you be?"

I laugh. "Maybe. I don't know for sure, but I'm ten days' late.
And I'm constantly tired . . . my stomach's always upset . . ."

She throws her arms around me. "That's wonderful!" She
pulls back and looks at me. "It is wonderful, isn't it?"

"You have no idea."

Carrying a mug of hot cocoa, I follow Carrie into the family
room where an eclectic mix of young and old mingle and chat. A
misshapen Christmas tree takes up an entire corner of the room,
and a real wood fire crackles in a mammoth fieldstone fireplace.

"Holy Toledo!" Mr. Newsome calls when he sees me. "Pull out
the red carpet. I do believe a Hollywood starlet just arrived!"

He hugs me and we spin until I nearly collapse. I gaze up at
him through a haze of tears. His beard is streaked with gray, and
his once thick ponytail is now a short thatch of silver hair, but his
smile remains radiant.

"It's so good to see you," I say.

A lovely woman stands behind him, her sandy hair still thick
and curly. "My turn," she says, stepping forward and pulling me
into her arms. Her embrace is snug and safe, the first mother's
hug I've had in months.

"Oh, Mrs. Newsome," I say, catching a whiff of her patchouli
oil. "I've missed you."

"I've missed you, my dear," she whispers. "And for goodness' sake, we've known you almost thirty years. Call us Mary and David. Now let me get you a plate. David made a terrific mushroom quiche. And you've got to try my pumpkin bread pudding. The caramel sauce is sinful."

It feels like a homecoming. I bask in the love and attention of this eccentric couple, dressed in their ragg wool sweaters and Birkenstock sandals. My heart, empty after my mother's death and Andrew's betrayal, begins to fill.

By early afternoon, my throat aches from talking and laughing. The crowd has cleared, and Carrie, Stella, and I stand in the kitchen with Mary, chatting and putting away leftover food. From the next room, Carrie's dad calls us into his den.

"Come see what I've got here."

We make our way to the cozy, knotty-pine den, and Carrie's kids gather around the television as if they're expecting a Disney DVD. Instead, a freckle-faced girl and her dark-eyed friend spring to life. Carrie and I sit through two tapes, mesmerized, laughing and poking fun at ourselves.

David goes to his cabinet, studying shelves lined with DVDs. "Took me about six months to convert my old VHS film onto DVD." He lands on a disc and pulls it from the shelf. "Here's one you won't remember." He slides the disc into the slot and presses PLAY.

A pretty young brunette with a Farrah Fawcett haircut waves into the screen. She's wearing a navy maxi coat that won't button over her belly, pulling two towheaded boys on a sled. I leap from the sofa and kneel in front of the television set, my hand over my mouth.

"Mom," I say, my voice thick. I turn around. "That's my mother! And she's pregnant . . . with me."

Carrie hands me a box of Kleenex and I dab my eyes.

"She's beautiful," I whisper. But close up, her gorgeous face is etched with sadness. "Where did you get this tape?"

"Shot it back when we all lived on Bosworth Avenue."

"Bosworth? You mean Arthur Street."

"Nah. We were friends from way back. We were your mother's first customers."

The hair on the back of my neck rises. I turn to him. "When, exactly, did you meet my mother?"

"We moved in Easter weekend . . . that would have been spring of . . ." He looks at his wife.

" 'Seventy-eight," Mary says.

I clutch my throat, paralyzed with a mix of urgency and fear. "Johnny Manns," I say. "Do you remember him?"

"Johnny? Oh, hell yes! Played guitar at Justine's."

"He was a huge talent," Mary said. "And gorgeous, to boot. Every woman on the block was a little in love with him."

Here, in this very room, are two people who know my father.

CHAPTER FIFTEEN

"Tell me about him," I say, barely breathing. "Please. Tell me everything."

"I can do you one better," David says, rifling through his DVD library. He pulls a plastic case from the cabinet and studies it while he walks to the television. "I filmed him back when I tended bar at Justine's. We were all sure this guy was going places."

He presses PLAY, and my heart hammers. A crowd of young faces is pressed into a small, dimly lit bar. I scoot closer to the screen, watching as the camera focuses on a man, sitting on a stool. He has a head of shaggy black hair and a full beard and mustache. The camera zooms in, and the man's brown eyes meet mine. I know those eyes. They're the same eyes I see every time I look into the mirror. A moan rises from my chest and I clap a hand over my mouth.

"This next song is from the Beatles' double album known as *The White Album*," Johnny says. "Though credits cite Lennon and

McCartney, it was actually written by Paul while he was in Scotland during the spring of 1968. The escalating tension back in the States between the black folks and the whites inspired him to react." He strums a chord. "In England, the word *bird* is slang for 'woman.'"

He picks the notes to the introduction riff. When he opens his mouth, the voice of an angel rings out. I let out a mangled sob. He sings of a blackbird with broken wings, longing to fly, longing to be free. The bird's been waiting all her life for one single moment to arrive.

I think of my mother, saddled with two young children and a husband she didn't love. She, too, must have longed for wings.

I think of myself, having waited all my life for this moment to arrive. The moment I could look into the kind eyes of a man, and know he is my father.

Tears slide down my cheeks. The song ends. The disc cuts to another scene at Justine's, this time with a female singer. I don't ask, I simply press REWIND and watch again, and again. I listen to my father's voice, his words. I reach out and touch his beautiful face, his exquisite hands.

After watching four times, I sit silent. Sometime during the viewing, Mary has positioned herself beside me on the floor. David sits at my other side. He places the DVD in my lap.

"This belongs to you, doesn't it?"

I trace my finger over the disc and nod. "He was my father."

"C'mon, kids. Let's play Uno," Stella says. "First one to the kitchen table gets to deal."

Once Carrie and her crew are out of earshot, Mary takes my hands in hers. "How long have you known?"

"I just found out. She left me her journal." My eyes travel from her face to David's. "Did you know?"

"No. Of course not," David says. "Your mother was too classy to kiss and tell. But everyone knew he was smitten with her."

A cry escapes me, a cry of relief and heartbreak. Mary pats my back until I can breathe again. "Was he a good man?"

"The very best," she says.

David nods. "Johnny was the real deal."

I hold my breath. "Where is he is now?"

"Last we knew he was living out west," Mary says. "But that's been fifteen years."

"Where?" I ask, suddenly light-headed. "LA?"

"San Francisco for a while. But we lost track of him. He may have moved on."

"This will help. I've hired a detective who's been trying to find him for months. You wouldn't believe the number of Johnny Manns in this country."

David snaps to attention. "Darling, his name was never Johnny Manns. It was Manson. He used Manns as his stage name on account of the mass murderer. The Manson name carried a horrible stigma in the seventies."

The words settle on me in bits and spurts. "Johnny Manson? Oh, my God. Oh, my God! Thank you!" I hug David, then Mary. "No wonder I couldn't find him."

"Your mother probably never knew his real name. I only knew because I was the bartender that summer and I did the payroll."

"I would have been searching forever if I hadn't seen you again."

A shiver makes its way up my spine. Goal number nine led me to Carrie, and Carrie led me to my father. Did Mother know this would happen? A lifelong friendship *and* a clue to my father. A twofer.

While Carrie and I trek to my car with Mary's leftovers, I punch Brad's number into my phone. "Do you mind?" I ask Carrie. "I'll only be a sec."

"Of course not," she says, carrying a paper bag filled with homemade blackberry jam.

"I'll put him on speaker so you can meet him. He's a doll."

Carrie raises her eyebrows. "Really?"

I bat my hand at her, and then I hear Brad's voice.

"My dad is John Manson, not Manns," I say. "And he's living somewhere out west. You've got to tell Pohlonski. I just watched a video of him. He's beautiful."

"Where are you, B.B.? I thought you were in Wisconsin."

"I am. I'm with Carrie now. You're on speaker. Say hi."

"Hey, Carrie."

Carrie laughs. "Hi, Brad."

"Okay, listen. Carrie's parents lived on Bosworth Avenue. They knew Johnny Manns!" I give him a condensed version of the morning's events. "Can you believe this? I'd never have known if I hadn't reconnected with Carrie." I look over at her. "She's a gift, in so many ways."

"This is a huge break. I'll leave Pohlonski a message as soon as we hang up."

"How long do you think it'll take to find him?"

"I couldn't say, but let's assume it won't happen overnight. Even now with this new information, it could take months."

I bite my lip. "Tell him to hurry, okay?"

"I will. Hey, want to catch a movie when you get home? Or dinner? Or better yet, just come here. I'll have dinner waiting."

My heart goes out to him. I know how endless Sundays can seem when you're alone.

"Option three sounds great. Oh, and I got a message from the animal shelter. My application was accepted. Want to help me pick out my pup next week?"

"Love to. Drive safely, B.B."

When I hang up, Carrie gives me a sidelong glance. "Are you two dating?"

"No," I say, placing a container of cookies on the passenger seat. "Just great friends. It's really nice."

"Careful, Bretel. I'm thinking this guy wants you."

I shake my head and take the sack from her. "Brad's got a girl-friend."

She smiles at me. "Keep his friendship. You look happy when you're talking to him."

"I will," I say. "And I am."

Brad's cozy duplex on North Oakley is a welcome respite after the long drive. Eva Cassidy plays on the stereo and I sit on a bar stool watching Brad shave cheese onto a Caesar salad. He keeps his eyes downcast, and when he laughs at my stories of Carrie and her brood, I can tell it's forced. Finally, I hop from my stool and take the cheese grater from his clutches.

"Okay, Midar, what's going on? Something's bothering you, I can tell."

He rubs the back of his neck and blows out a huff of air. "Jenna decided we should take a break."

I'm ashamed to admit, a part of me shouts *Hooray!* We're both single now, and who knows what might happen down the road. But looking at him, I see the pain in his face. He's obviously in love, and it's not with me.

"I'm so sorry." I pull him into my arms and he clings to me. "You know," I say quietly, "you could do something big, some-thing that will prove you're serious and committed."

He pulls back. "Like proposing?"

"Yes! If you want her, Midar, make it happen, just like you told me to do. To hell with the miles and years between you — ask her to marry you!"

His turns his back to me and braces his hands on the counter. "I did. She said no."

"Oh, God. I'm so sor —"

He lifts a hand to stop me. "Enough whining." He wipes his hands on a dish towel and tosses it on the counter. "We have reason here to celebrate."

He strides through the kitchen, into the adjoining living room, and lifts a pink envelope from the coffee table. "I stopped by the office this afternoon," he says, shaking the envelope at me. "Thought you might want this."

GOAL #9, STAY FRIENDS WITH CARRIE NEWSOME FOREVER. I rush to him and stare at the handwritten envelope, desperate to hear my mother's words. But I can't celebrate when Brad is feeling so low.

"Not today," I say. "Let's save it for a time when you're feeling better."

"No way. We're opening it now."

He tears the seal, and I collapse onto the sofa, clinging to his arm as he reads.

"'Dear Brett,

"'Thank you, dear, for granting my wish (and yours, as well) by rekindling your friendship with Carrie. I'll never forget how devastated you were when the Newsomes moved to Madison. I watched helplessly while dust gathered on your heart. Perhaps you understood then that true friendships were hard to come by. After she came to visit you, you two drifted apart, though you never told me why.

"'Sadly, I don't believe you've ever had another friend as true as Carrie. It wasn't until I became ill that I realized what a shallow pool of true confidantes you have. Aside from Shelley and me, I don't detect any other genuine friends.'"

"She didn't mention Megan," I say. "Or Andrew. Do you think she knew, even then, that they weren't real friends?"

Brad nods. "I suspect she did."

He returns to the letter. "'I'm hopeful Carrie will fill this void.

Enjoy and nurture this friendship, my dear daughter. And please, make a point to say hello to Carrie's parents. David and Mary were my first customers when we all lived on Bosworth Avenue. They were fans of your father's, too.'"

I clap a hand over my mouth. "She's talking about Johnny, not Charles. She's giving me a clue here, just in case I'd missed it." I turn to Brad. "Why the hell didn't she just tell me flat out? Why is she putting me through this scavenger hunt?"

"I admit, it does seem strange."

"She was always so straightforward — or at least I thought she was. Why all this nuance and innuendo? She's making me crazy." I take a breath and unclench my fist. "On the bright side, I'll finally find him now."

"Let's not get too excited. It's still a long slog. It could take months . . . or longer."

"We're going to find him, Brad." I grab my mother's letter and shake it at him. "She might be playing games with me, but she would never set me up for a disappointment this big."

"Let's hope you're right." He slaps my knee. "C'mon, dinner's ready."

CHAPTER SIXTEEN

I'm just turning out the lights to my office Friday afternoon when Megan calls. Since spying her at Andrew's loft, I've ignored her calls and messages. I'm about to pitch the phone back into my satchel but at the last minute decide, *What the hell.*

"Hey, chica," she says with her aging-cheerleader voice. It's hard to imagine I actually found that voice cute at one time. "Shel tells me you're getting a dog today."

I slide my key into the lock and twist it until it clicks. "That's the plan."

"Perfect. I've got this client who's buying a condo on Lake Shore Drive, but the building doesn't allow pets. He's sick about it, but he has to get rid of Champ. And Champ is, like, a fucking show dog. He's a purebred greyhound. Very classy. Anyway, he said you could have him. Can you believe it? He's giving you his fucking show dog!"

I throw open a set of double doors. "Thanks, but I'm not interested."

"What? Why? This dog is valuable."

I dance down the stairs and breeze out the door. Brilliant sunlight brushes my face, along with a snap of December wind. "I don't want a show dog, Megan. Sure, they look great, but they're too high-maintenance. All that grooming, and training, and competing. It's exhausting, keeping up with their needs." My rant is gaining speed, but I can't seem to slow it down. "After a while you start to resent them — their finicky diets and their special soaps and their fancy shampoos. It's too much! And to top it off, they have a complete lack of respect for your needs! It's all about them! They're selfish and —"

"Jesus, Brett, calm down. We're talking about a damn dog here."

"We're talking dog all right," I lean against my car door and expel a deep breath. "How could you, Meg?"

She sucks in a breath, and I picture her inhaling a lipstick-stained cigarette. "What? You mean Andrew? Newsflash: You guys aren't together anymore. And when you were, I swear to God I never so much as peeked at his package."

"Oh, wow, what a pal!"

"I cannot believe you took all of his furniture. He was so fucking furious. And then you wouldn't return his calls. He threatened to have you arrested for home invasion."

"I heard the messages. I only took what was mine, Megan. He knows it."

"Lucky for you, I calmed his ass down. I told him he could afford new furniture. He's a goddamn attorney, for shit's sake." She pauses. "He does have money, doesn't he, Brett? I mean, last night when the waiter left our check, Andrew just sat there, like he expected me to pay." She giggles. "Of course, he thinks I'm loaded, being a successful Chicago realtor and all."

Ha! Megan will finally get what's coming to her. And Andrew, too. They're shallow and self-centered and materialistic and —

I stop myself. What right do I have to judge? Most of my adult life I've been a material girl, too, with my designer clothes and BMW, my expensive purses and jewelry. And wasn't I just as shallow and selfish when I abandoned Carrie at the time she needed me most? Yet she forgave me. Perhaps it's time I paid it forward.

"Meggie girl, set your goals higher. You're a beautiful woman with tons of potential. Find someone who adores you, someone who'll treat —"

She laughs. "Oh, Brett, stop being so fucking phony. I understand you're jealous, but get over it. He. Doesn't. Love. You!"

The wind is knocked from me. Pay it forward? Uh-uh. Not today.

"You're right. You two really are perfect for each other." I climb into my car. "And Megan, stop worrying about your short arms. They're the least of your problems."

With that, I'm off to find my lovable, loyal mutt.

Brad is waiting at the curb when I pull up to the Aon Center in my new/used car.

"What's up? The Beemer in the shop?" He gives me a quick peck on the cheek and buckles his seat belt.

"Nope. I traded it in."

"You're kidding. For this?"

"And some much-needed cash. It just seemed wrong, driving a car like that when most of the families I work with don't even own one."

He whistles. "You are committed to this job."

"Yup, though I have to confess I'm pretty excited to have the next two weeks off. I'm officially on Christmas break."

He groans. "I want your job."

I laugh. "I really did get lucky. The kids are incredible. But I'm worried about Sanquita. She's not looking very healthy these days. She's four months along and it's hard to tell she's pregnant. She sees whoever's on duty at Cook County Health Department, but these are just regular doctors, with no expertise in kidney disease. I've made an appointment with Dr. Chan at University of Chicago Medical Center. She's supposed to be one of the best nephrologists in the country."

"And what's new with psycho dude?"

"Peter?" I let out a sigh. "I saw him this morning. He's smart as a whip, but I just can't seem to reach him."

"Still talking to his shrink?"

I smile. "Yeah. That's been a huge perk. Garrett's such a dear man. He's so wise and so skilled, yet at the same time he's completely approachable. We talk about Peter, but then we end up discussing our families or our dreams. I even told him about my mother's wishes."

"You like this guy."

If I didn't know better, I'd say Brad was jealous. But that's crazy. "I adore Dr. Taylor. He's a widower. His wife died of pancreatic cancer three years ago."

I cover my mouth and yawn.

"Tired?" Brad asks.

"Exhausted. I don't know what's wrong with me lately." *Except, perhaps, that I'm pregnant!* I turn to him. "Heard anything from Jenna?"

He stares out the window. "Nada."

I squeeze his arm. What a foolish woman.

Smells of wood shavings and animal dander assail us when we step through the doors of the Chicago Animal Rescue Shelter. A silver-haired woman wearing Wrangler jeans and a flannel shirt saunters over to us, swinging her arms with each stride. "Welcome to CARS," she says. "I'm Gillian, one of the volunteers. What brings you here today?"

"I've been approved for pet adoption," I tell her over background barking. "I'm here today to find my dog."

Gillian points a stubby finger at a gated section of the building. "Our registered dogs are in this area. These are the dogs with pedigrees and papers. They usually go very quickly. A gorgeous Portuguese water dog came in just last night. 'Course, he won't last but a minute. Ever since the Obamas chose Bo, the breed's been in huge demand."

"I'm looking for more of a mutt," I say.

She raises an eyebrow. "You don't say?" She pivots and makes a swooping gesture with her arm. "Mutts are terrific. The only problem with a mutt is that you don't know their family history. You've no idea of the temperament of the animal or chances for diseases, based on genetic stock."

Kind of like me. "I'll risk it."

It takes less than ten minutes to find him. Through a metal cage, a fluffy canine stares at me with coffee bean eyes that are at once friendly and pleading.

"Hello, boy!" I tug Brad's coat sleeve. "Meet my new dog."

Gillian opens the cage. "Hey, Rudy."

Rudy scampers to the cement floor, his tail flickering like a rattlesnake's as he sniffs us. He stares up at Brad, then me, as if checking out his prospective parents.

I scoop him up and he squirms in my arms. He licks my cheeks and I laugh with joy.

"He likes you," Brad says, scratching the dog's ears. "He's adorable."

"Isn't he?" Gillian agrees. "Rudy's a year and a half old, full grown. My best guess is that he's part bichon frise, part cocker, with a smidgen of poodle to complete the recipe."

Regardless, the final product is delicious. I nuzzle his soft fur. "Why would someone give away a dog like this?"

"You'd be surprised. Usually it's a move, or a new baby, or a clash in temperaments. If I remember right, Rudy's owner is about to marry someone who doesn't want a pet."

It feels like Rudy and I are a matched set: two homeless mongrels who've just lost the ones they loved — or thought they loved.

While I write the check for my new pup and all his accoutrements, Brad studies a flyer about the shelter. "Listen," he says. "CARS is committed to ending animal suffering and believes in no-kill communities to help the stray, abused, and neglected companion animals in urban areas, like Chicago."

"Cool," I say, scribbling the date on the check.

Brad taps a photo in the flyer. "Gillian, you actually adopt out horses?"

I lift my pen, midword, and narrow my eyes at him.

"We sure do," Gillian says. "Whatcha looking for?"

He lifts his shoulders. "I'm completely clueless. Give me an idea of what's out there."

"Are we talking for you, or your children?" Gillian asks, flipping pages in a three-ring binder.

"Never mind, Gillian," I say. "We're not getting a horse."

"Just us," Brad tells her. "For now, anyway."

For a sweet, fleeting instant, I imagine a child — my child — horseback riding. But that's years down the road. "We need to talk about this one," I say to him. "There's absolutely no way I can care for a horse."

"Here she is." Gillian positions the binder in front of us and taps a chipped nail on a picture. "Meet Lady Lulu. A thoroughbred gelding, fifteen years old. She was a racehorse early on, but now she's got some issues with arthritis and whatnot, so the owner won't keep her." She keeps her eyes on Brad, obviously sensing he's the only one with any interest. "Lulu would be perfect for pleasure or light trail riding. And she's a total sweetheart, just a baby. Come see her."

I tear the check from my checkbook and hand it to her. "Thanks, Gillian. We'll think about it."

"She's stabled in Marengo, at Paddock Farms. You really should take a look at her. She's a special one."

We head north on State Street, Rudy in the backseat secured in his crate. He peers out the window like a nosy tot, mesmerized by the honking traffic, the crowds darting in and out of stores, the Christmas lights twinkling from tree branches. I glance back at him and reach a hand to his cage.

"You doing okay, sweetie?" I ask. "Mommy's right here."

Brad swings around. "Hang in there, Rudy boy. We'll be home soon."

We sound like proud parents, bringing our newborn home from the hospital. Within the dark confines of the car, I smile.

"About the horse," Brad says, planting me firmly back in real time.

"Yes, about the horse. I think that's the goal I should be exempt from."

"What?" he asks. "You don't want a horse?"

"I'm a city girl, Midar. I love Chicago. And what kills me is that my mom knew this. Why would she keep such an absurd goal on my list?"

"Real nice. You're going to let Lady Lulu retire to the glue factory?"

"Stop. I'm serious. I actually called around about boarding a horse. It would cost a fortune, all the feedings, and supplements, and grooming. Really, it adds up to a monthly fee more than most people's mortgage. Do you realize what Joshua House could do with that money?"

"You've got a point. It is a tad wasteful. But it's not going to break the bank, B.B. You just sold your car. You've got the money now."

"No I don't! That money is for Pohlonski. My savings account is disappearing before my eyes."

"But that's temporary. Once you get your inheritance —"

"*If* I get my inheritance! Who knows when that will be? I can't possibly meet all these goals within the year."

"Okay. Let's just focus on one. It *is* possible that you could get the horse, right?"

"But I don't have the time. The closest place I found to board is an hour away."

Brad stares out the front window. "I think we've got to trust your mom on this one. So far she hasn't let us down."

"This goal isn't just about me. It's about an animal — an animal I don't have time to care for. I won't do that. A dog is one thing, but a horse is, well, a completely different animal."

He nods. "Okay then. Let's just put this goal out to pasture for the moment. Give you time to *rein* in your fears. I don't want to be a *neigh*-sayer."

I roll my eyes at him but it's good to hear him laughing again.

"Stop horsing around," I tell him, unable to resist his silly game.

"Good one!" He holds up his hand for a high five. "You've got good horse sense."

"You're a horse's ass," I say, trying to keep a straight face.

"Oh, get off your high horse," he says, busting himself up.

I shake my head. "You are such a loser."

Brad carries Rudy across my mother's threshold like his new bride. With his free hand, he drags a sack of dog supplies into the foyer while I click on lamps and plug in my Christmas tree. Smelling of pine, the room glows with the ethereal brilliance of the colored lights.

"This place is gorgeous," he says, lowering Rudy. Wasting no time, Rudy romps to the tree, sniffing at the red foil packages beneath it.

"Come here, Rudy. Let's get you some food."

Brad fills the water dish and I empty kibbles into the dog bowl. We move about in the kitchen like Fred and Ginger, each with our choreographed duties. He dries his hands on a terry-cloth towel, and I rinse mine in the sink. I turn off the water and he hands me the towel.

"How about a glass of wine?" I ask.

"I'd love one."

I reach for a bottle of Pinot Noir, and notice Brad's eyes roving the kitchen like a prospective buyer's. "Ever think about buying this place?"

"This house? I love it here, but this house is Mother's."

"All the more reason to keep it." He leans against the center island. "To me, this house looks like you, if that makes sense."

I twist the corkscrew. "Really?"

"Really. It's elegant and sophisticated, but it also has a warm, mellow side."

Honey runs through my veins. "Thank you."

"You should think about it."

I pull a wineglass from the cupboard. "Could I even afford it? I'd have to buy it from my brothers, you know."

"Sure, you'll be able to afford it. Once you get your final inheritance."

"But you're forgetting, I need to fall in love and have babies. The love of my life might not want to live in my mother's home."

"He'll love this place. And there's a park just down the street, perfect for your kids."

He says it with such certainty I almost believe him. I hand him his wine. "Did my mom ever tell you why she wanted my brothers and me to keep the house for the first year?"

"Nope. But I'm guessing she knew you'd need a place to stay."

"Yeah, that's my guess, too."

"And she probably figured the place is so nice you'd never want to leave." He swirls his wineglass. "Which is why she included that thirty-day clause. She didn't want you to get too comfy."

"Wait . . . what?"

"That clause in the will. Nobody can stay more than thirty consecutive days. Remember?"

"No," I say honestly. "You mean I can't stay here? I have to find another place to live?"

"Yup. It's all in the will. You have your copy, don't you?"

I clutch my head. "I just bought a dog. Do you realize how hard it'll be to find a place that takes animals? And my furniture! I gave it all to Joshua House. I don't have money —"

"Hey, hey." He sets down his glass and seizes both my wrists. "It's going to be okay. Look, you spent the night at Joshua House last week, so technically the clock's just starting. You've got plenty of time to find something."

I pull free my wrists. "Back up a sec. You're saying because they weren't consecutive, technically I've only been here six days?"

"That's right."

"So, as long as I take a night or two away each month, like when I'm at Joshua House, I'll never go over the maximum?"

"Uh, I don't think —"

I break into a victorious smile. "That means I can stay here indefinitely. Problem solved!"

Before he has time to argue, I lift my water goblet. "Cheers!"

"Cheers," he says, clinking my goblet. "No vino tonight?"

"I'm not drinking these days."

His glass is almost to his lips when he lowers it. "Earlier, you said you've been exhausted lately, right?"

"Uh-huh."

"And you're not drinking alcohol?"

"That's what I said, Einstein."

"Holy shit. You're prego."

I laugh. "I think I am! I bought a pregnancy test but I'm too afraid to take it. I'll wait until after the holidays."

"You're afraid it'll be positive."

"No! I'm afraid it'll be negative. I'd be devastated." I look up at him. "It's not exactly the way I pictured it would be, being single and all. I'll let Andrew decide whether he wants to be part of his child's life. I won't ask for child support. This is my dream, after all. I'll raise my baby—"

"Whoa, whoa, whoa. Slow down, B.B. You're talking like this is a sure thing. Be careful you don't, well, put the cart before the horse."

"Stop with those silly horse puns."

He holds me at arm's length. "Seriously, Brett. I know you. You're getting excited. Until you know for sure, put the brakes on."

"Too late," I say. "I'm beyond excited. For the first time since my mother's diagnosis, I feel joy."

We take our drinks into the living room where Rudy lies stretched in front of the fire. Brad plucks an envelope from his back pocket before taking a seat on the sofa. Goal number six.

"Shall we hear what your mom has to say about Rudy?"

"Please." I sit down on an adjacent club chair, tucking my feet beneath me.

He pats his shirt pocket. "Damn. I don't have my reading glasses."

I leap from the chair and retrieve a pair of my mom's reading glasses from her secretary desk. "Here you go," I say, handing him a pair of fuchsia-and-periwinkle specs.

He scowls at the flashy frames, but puts them on anyway.

The sight of him in the gaudy women's glasses sends me into hysterics. "Oh, my God!" I say, pointing at him. "You look hilarious!"

He grabs me and pulls me down onto the sofa, securing me in a headlock. "You think this is funny, huh?" He rubs his knuckles on the top of my head.

"Stop!" I say between fits of laughter.

Eventually, we sober, but in the skirmish I've ended up next to him on the sofa, and his left arm is still wrapped around the back of my neck. A better woman would scoot away. After all, he's only on a break from his girlfriend. But me? I stay right where I am.

"Okay," he says. "Behave." With his right hand, he shakes the letter and manages to unfold it.

Snuggled next to him, I nod. "Okay, Granny. Read."

He snarls his lip at me but begins the letter.

"'Congratulations on your new dog, darling! I'm thrilled for you. You loved animals so much as a child, but at some point in your adulthood you must have tucked away that passion. I'm not sure why, though I have my suspicions.'"

"Andrew was a neat-freak. She knew that."

"'Do you remember the stray collie that befriended us when we lived in Rogers Park? You named him Leroy and begged us to let you keep him. You probably don't know this, but I went to bat for you. I pleaded with Charles to let you keep Leroy, but he was quite persnickety. He couldn't tolerate an animal in the house. Too smelly, he said.'"

I snatch the letter from Brad's clutches and re-read the last two sentences. "Maybe I really did choose someone just like Charles, hoping to make him love me."

He gives my shoulder a squeeze. "But you realize it now. You'll never have to please Charles Bohlinger — or any other man — to prove that you're lovable."

I let his words sink in. "Yeah. My mother's secret freed me. If only she'd told me sooner."

"'Take good care of your mutt — it is a mutt, isn't it? Will you allow your pet to sleep upstairs? If so, may I suggest you remove the duvet? It's very costly to have it dry-cleaned.

"'Go make memories with your pup, my love.

"'Mom.'"

I take the letter from Brad and quickly re-read it. "She knows I'm living in her house. How'd she know that?"

"I don't know. Maybe she connected the dots."

"Connected the dots?"

"Andrew didn't want a dog, so since you have a dog, you're not living with Andrew. If you're not living with Andrew, the logical place you'd be is right here."

I turn to Brad. "See, she wants me here. That thirty-day clause must have been a mistake."

My voice sounds certain, but inside I wonder if I'm fooling myself.

Brad and I lie slouched on the sofa, our stocking feet propped on the coffee table in front of us as the credits of *White Christmas* roll down the screen. Brad throws back the last of his wine and checks his watch. "Jesus, I better scoot." He gets to his feet and stretches. "I told my mom I'd get an early start tomorrow. Only two days until Christmas and she's waiting for me to help decorate the tree."

In a brick Colonial in Champaign, he and his parents will stumble through Christmas pretending not to notice that one family member is missing, just like I will.

"Before you leave, you have to open your Christmas gift."

"Aw, you didn't need to get me anything." He shoos his hand at me. "But since you did, let's have at it. Go now. Chop! Chop!"

I search out the rectangular box beneath the tree. When he opens the package, he simply stares at it. Finally, he pulls the wooden ship from the box.

"She's beautiful."

"I thought it was appropriate, you being at the helm of my lifeboat and all."

"Very thoughtful." He kisses my forehead. "But you're the captain of your ship," he says softly. "I'm just a member of the crew." He rises from the sofa. "Hold on."

He disappears to the coat closet, then moseys back to the sofa holding a tiny silver box.

"For you."

Inside the box, atop a blanket of red velvet, sits a gold charm — a miniature parachute.

"So you'll always have a safe landing."

I finger the charm. "It's perfect. Thank you, Brad. And thank you for being here these past three months. I'm serious. I couldn't have done any of this without you."

He tousles my hair, but his eyes are somber. "Sure you could have. But I'm glad you let me come along for the ride."

Without warning, he leans in and kisses me. It's slower, more deliberate than our usual pecks, and my breath catches. I scramble to my feet. He's had too much to drink, and the two of us, heartbroken and vulnerable, could be dangerous tonight. We walk to the foyer and I pull his coat from the closet.

"Happy Christmas," I say, trying to sound casual. "Promise you'll call the minute you get news about my father."

"I promise." But instead of taking his coat, he gazes down at me. Ever so gently, he reaches out and strokes my cheek with his knuckles. His eyes are so tender that, on impulse, I kiss his cheek.

"I want you to be happy."

"Ditto," he whispers, and takes another step closer to me. A little flutter invades my belly but I try to ignore it. He's in love with Jenna. He smooths my hair and his eyes rove my face, as if he's seeing me for the first time. "Come here," he says, his voice husky.

My heart batters in my chest. *Don't ruin your friendship. He's lonely. He's hurt. He's missing Jenna.*

Silencing all reason, I step into his arms.

He closes in around me and I hear him inhale, as if he's breathing in every bit of me. He presses his body against mine, and I feel his heat, his hardness, his strength. I close my eyes and nuzzle against his chest. He smells of pine, and I can feel his heart beating against his chest. I burrow closer, unable to ignore the passion igniting in me. His fingers weave through my hair and I feel his lips on my ear, my neck. Oh, God, it's been so long since I've been kissed like this. Slowly, I lift my face to his. His eyes, heavy with passion, fall closed and he lowers his lips to mine. His mouth is warm and wet and delicious.

With every bit of strength I have, I gently push away.

"No, Brad," I whisper, half hoping he doesn't hear me. I want this man, but it's wrong now. He and Jenna are taking a break. He needs to see that relationship through before he gets involved in another.

Finally, he disentangles his hands from my hair. Taking a step back, he rubs a hand over his face. When he looks up, his cheeks are marred with red splotches, whether from passion's heat or embarrassment, I'm not sure.

"We can't," I say. "It's too soon."

His eyes look bruised and he gives me a rueful smile. With one hand, he pulls my head to his lips and kisses my forehead. "Why do you have to be so damn practical?" he asks, his voice touchingly raw.

I smile, but my heart aches. "Night, Brad."

Standing on the concrete stoop in my stocking feet, I watch until his silhouette rounds the corner. As difficult as it was, I know I've made the right decision. Brad isn't ready for a new relationship.

I step inside the house and close the door. Instead of the gloom that shadowed me when I was alone at Andrew's, tonight I feel a glimmer of hope. Though Brad might not be ready to love again, the passion that stirred in me tonight tells me that perhaps I am. I turn to see Rudy, asleep on the rug. I've got a dog now. And by this time next year, I'll have a baby. I gaze down at my flat belly, imagining myself in a couple of months sporting maternity clothes and stretch marks. The thought fills me with such bliss my heart nearly bursts.

Christmas morning arrives and I wake to Rudy's snout ramming my rib cage. I scratch his head. "Merry Christmas, Rudy boy." Immediately a mental list unfurls, revealing everything I need to do to prepare for my family dinner. My stomach cramps into a tight little ball.

"Let's get moving, Rudy. We've got a party to give." I wince from another wave of cramps and pull myself to my feet. The pain eases, and I slip into my robe. But when I glance down at the crumpled sheet, I see it.

A bright red stain.

CHAPTER SEVENTEEN

For a moment my mind refuses to accept the truth. I simply stare at the stain. Then my ribs fuse and I can't breathe. I drop to my knees and bury my head in my hands. Beside me, Rudy barks and wedges his nose into my crossed arms. But I have nothing to give him right now. I'm empty.

After ten minutes of grief-stricken paralysis, I leap to my feet, yanking the sheets from the bed. Tears stream down my face and I unleash loud, ugly wails. Beads of perspiration gather at my hairline. I wad the sheets and stuff them into a laundry basket. With the basket on my hip, I yank open the bedroom curtain. A Christmas morning as perfect as a Norman Rockwell painting greets me. But I cannot appreciate the day's beauty. My soul is as hollow and barren as my womb.

I move through Christmas Day as if I'm anesthetized. Emma and Trevor are fascinated with my new puppy, and the three provide loads of entertainment for my siblings. But I watch vacantly, impervious to joy or laughter or even good food. Catherine takes a bite-sized portion from each dish on the table, while the others eat ravenously. I pick at my food indifferently.

The loss of my phantom child resurrects the memory of my mother's death, and I grieve anew for her. For the third time today, I've locked myself into the upstairs bathroom. I'm hunched over the sink splashing cold water on my face, telling myself I'll be okay.

I wanted that baby. I was sure I was pregnant. And my mother . . . she should be here, damn it. She, who always loved the holidays, deserved one more Christmas.

Last year we celebrated as usual, ignorant of the fate awaiting us in the New Year. Had I known it would be her last Christmas, I'd have given her something special, something that would have touched her heart. Instead, I bought her a panini grill from Williams-Sonoma. Even so, her face lit up with joy, as if it were the very gift she'd been hoping for. She pulled me into her arms that morning and whispered, "You make me merry, dear daughter."

Every unshed tear in my chest suddenly breaks anchor. I slide to the bathroom floor, sobbing. I need my mother's love so badly today. I'd tell her about the grandbaby I'd hoped to give her. She'd soothe me, and assure me there would be another sky.

"Brett," Joad calls. He raps on the door. "Hey, Brett. You in there?"

I lift my head and take in a breath. "Umm-hmm."

"There's a phone call for you."

I rise from the cold tile and blow my nose, wondering who's calling. Carrie and I chatted for twenty minutes last night. It's probably Brad, calling yet again to check on me, and to apologize once more for his "lecherous" behavior. I open the bathroom door and trudge down the hallway. Trevor meets me halfway up the stairs and hands me the phone.

"Hello," I say, patting the top of my nephew's head before he skips back down the stairs.

"Brett?" an unfamiliar voice asks.

"Yes."

Silence fills the air, and I wonder if I've lost the call.

"Hello?" I ask again.

Finally he speaks, his voice raw with emotion. "This is John Manson."

CHAPTER EIGHTEEN

I race back up the stairs, into my mother's bedroom. I close the door behind me and sink to the floor, my back against the door.

"Hello, John," I say when I finally find my voice. "Merry Christmas."

He chuckles, a low sweet sound. "Merry Christmas to you."

"You must think this is all very strange," I say. "I'm just getting used to it myself, and I found the journal two months ago."

"Yes. But it's also very cool. I wish Elizabeth had contacted me, but I understand why she didn't."

You do? I want to ask. Because I'd love to know. But this conversation can wait for another time — a time when we're sitting across from each other holding hands, or snuggled together on a sofa, his arm slung around my shoulder.

"Where do you live?"

"Seattle. I have a little music store here, Manson Music. I even manage to get a guitar gig a couple times a month."

I can't stop smiling, picturing this wonderful, musical man who is my father. "Tell me more. I want to know everything about you."

He chuckles. "I will, I promise. But I'm a bit rushed at the moment —"

"I'm sorry," I say. "It's Christmas. I won't keep you. But I'd love to see you. Any chance you could come to Chicago? I'm off work until after the New Year."

He sighs. "I'd love to see you, but the timing couldn't be worse. I've got a twelve-year-old daughter. Her mother moved to Aspen awhile back and I have custody."

"I have a sister?" Strangely, in all my father–daughter fantasies, this never occurred to me. "That's awesome. What's her name?"

"Zoë. And she is awesome. But she's been coughing today. I'm afraid she's coming down with a cold. Traveling right now is out of the question."

"That's too bad." A thought occurs to me, and I instantly blurt it out. "Why don't I come to Seattle? That way Zoë won't have to travel and —"

"I appreciate the offer, but it's not the time." His voice is stern now. "I need to keep Zoë away from people, just to be cautious."

At once I realize what's happening. My father is making excuses. He doesn't want to see me. He doesn't want his impressionable young daughter to know his shameful secret. Why didn't I see this coming? "Okay, some other time then. You better get back to Zoë now."

"Yes, I'd better. But Brett, I'm happy to know you. I look forward to meeting you, just not now. You do understand?"

"Of course," I say. "Give Zoë my love. Tell her I hope she feels better."

I lay the phone at my side. I've finally found my father. And I've got a half sister, to boot. So why do I feel more rejected than ever?

———

*A*ll eyes are on me when I stride into the living room. "That was my dad," I say, trying to sound chipper. "John Manson."

Shelley rouses from her snooze. "How was he?"

"Wonderful. He seems really great. He's kind, I can tell."

"Where does he live?" Joad asks.

I plop down in front of the fire and hug my knees. "Seattle. And he's still making music. Isn't that cool?"

"Did you make plans to see him?" Shelley asks.

I search out Rudy's sweet face and scratch his chin. "Not yet, but we will soon."

"Invite him to Chicago," Jay says. "We'd all like to meet him."

"I will, as soon as his daughter gets well. Right now she's a little under the weather. Can you believe it? I have a sister!"

Joad holds his Bloody Mary aloft and raises an eyebrow. "He's got a real family then?"

My breath catches. "What do you mean, *real* family?"

"Nothing. I just meant . . ."

"What Joad means," Catherine says, "is that he has a family he lives with, a family he knows."

Jay sidles up next to me on the floor, resting a hand on my shoulder. "You're his real family, too. But you need to brace yourself, sis. It'll be different with you and Johnny, trying to bond now, after thirty-four years. He's never rocked you to sleep, or climbed in bed with you when you had a nightmare . . ."

Or worried about me when I had the sniffles.

Joad nods. "A woman in my office had a son she'd given up for adoption. When he looked her up nineteen years later, it was terribly disruptive. She had two young children then, and suddenly this stranger wanted access to their lives. She felt a complete disconnect from him." He shakes his head, as if trying to clear the nightmarish image. Then he sees me. "It won't be that way for you, though."

A thick fog rolls into my chest. The father I've been searching for doesn't want to meet me. He has another daughter, a *real* daughter he adores. And I'm the contagion he fears might harm their twosome. Did my mother anticipate this? Is this why she never told me about him?

At nine o'clock I stand at the front door with my shoes in my hand, exhausted and heartsick, shuffling my siblings from the house. Joad and Catherine are the last to leave, but standing in the foyer, Joad seems hesitant. He fumbles with his car keys before handing them to Catherine. "Go start the car, hon. I'll be right there."

Once she leaves, he turns to me. "I've been meaning to ask, how much longer do you plan to live here, in Mother's house?"

His tone makes my pulse quicken. "I . . . I'm not sure. I don't have anywhere else to go at the moment."

He rubs his chin. "Mother stipulated a thirty-day max. You've been here since Thanksgiving, right?"

I stare at him, incredulous. At this moment, every good gene from my mother's DNA is hidden, and all I can see is Charles Bohlinger. "Yes, but she said thirty *consecutive* days. I spend every Monday at Joshua House."

His mouth doesn't smile, but his eyes do, in a mocking way that makes me feel silly. "And what? You think the clock starts over each week?"

That's exactly what I think. But the smirk on his face lets me know he disagrees. "What do you want me to do, Joad? I'm living on a teacher's salary. I have no inheritance. I've given away all my furniture."

He throws up his hands. "Okay, okay. Forget it. I just thought you, of all people, would want to follow Mother's rules. Stay as long as you like. Makes no difference to me." He pecks me on the cheek. "Thanks for a great day. Love you."

I slam the door behind him, but the massive rosewood door is so heavy it doesn't even catch. I march toward the living room, then turn around and heave my shoes at the door. "Damn you, Joad!"

Rudy bolts from his rug and peels toward me. I plop down in front of him. "And you," I say, nuzzling his fluff. "Thanks to you, we have to find an apartment that takes scruffy ol' mutts. What are we going to do?"

I'm emotionally drained, and want nothing more than to sink beneath my mother's sumptuous sheets and drift off to dreamland. Instead I lie awake at three in the morning, my mind leaping from thoughts of my father, to my childless womb, to the reality check from my sibs. The instant love I felt for my half sister has vanished, leaving in its wake a disturbing wave of jealousy and self-loathing.

I roll onto my side and my mind shifts to Joad. I play his words — his accusation — over and over in my mind until finally I throw back the covers and shuffle down the stairs. I find my laptop on the kitchen counter.

Within ten minutes, it's painfully apparent that my meager income and furry friend will be significant obstacles to finding my new digs. After scouring pages of spiffy rentals that would eat up my entire month's salary, I take a deep breath and revise my search. I can live without that second bedroom. But the prices for one-bedroom units are still too high. There's only one solution: I have to move south. The desirable northeast neighborhoods where I've spent my entire life are just too pricey. What does it matter that everyone in my entire world lives north of the Loop?

I press ENTER and realize I was right. Rentals south of the Loop are much, much cheaper . . . but *still* not cheap enough for someone with a first-year teacher's salary. Without dipping into my retirement fund or subletting with a slew of strangers, my only option is to live south of the Eisenhower Expressway — an area I never, ever imagined I'd live.

I can't do this! I can't live in an area that's foreign to me — an area riddled with crime and corruption. Again, I'm baffled. What the hell was my mother thinking?

CHAPTER NINETEEN

The sun crowns over the horizon when, red-eyed and rumpled, I pick up Sanquita at Joshua House for her appointment
with Dr. Chan. It's a frigid morning — the kind of morning you
remember by sound rather than sight . . . crunching snow beneath boots, cracking plates of ice on Lake Michigan, humming
of furnaces running nonstop. Sanquita sits in the passenger seat
wearing a velour running suit and a cropped jacket with a faux-
fur hood, rubbing her bare hands in front of the heat vent.

"According to *U.S. News & World Report*," I tell her, "University of Chicago Medical Center has one of the best nephrology
programs in the nation."

She pulls down the visor to shield the sunlight and leans back,
tucking her hands under her legs. "I still don't get why you're
doing this. Don't you got better things to do?"

"I care about you." She rolls her eyes, but I keep talking. "I know you don't want to hear it, and I know you don't trust me yet, but it's the simple truth. And when you care about someone, you want to help them."

"Thing is, I really don't need your help. Soon as the baby comes I'll be better."

"I know," I say, wishing I believed my words. But I don't. She looks waxen in the harsh morning light, and judging from her belly she's not gaining enough weight.

"Do you have any names picked out?" I ask, hoping to lighten the mood.

"Uh-huh," she says, scratching her legs with both hands. "I'm gonna name my baby after my little brother."

"Your brother must be a special guy."

"He was. Smart too."

"Was?" I ask softly.

"He died."

"Oh, honey. I'm sorry." I know enough now not to pry. As soon as things get personal, Sanquita shuts down. We ride in silence for another minute when, to my surprise, she continues.

"I was in sixth grade. Deonte and Austin, they was the only kids at home. The rest of us was in school. They got hungry. Deonte climbed up on the counter. He was trying to reach a cereal box."

The hairs on my arms rise and I want to tell her to stop. This time I don't want to hear what happens next.

She gazes out the passenger window. "He didn't know the stove was on. His pajamas caught fire. Austin tried, but he couldn't do nothing."

She shakes her head, her eyes focused on the horizon.

"I probably been mad at my mom ever since. Them people from the county said it wasn't her fault, but I know why she didn't wake up when my brothers screamed. When I got home from school I flushed everything down the toilet. No way was we going to foster care. Sometimes I wonder why I did that."

My gut wrenches. Marijuana? Cocaine? Meth? I don't ask. I reach over and gently place a hand on her arm. "I'm so sorry, sweetie. Deonte will live on through your baby. That's so thoughtful."

She looks at me. "Uh-uh. Not Deonte. I'm gonna name him Austin. Austin wasn't never the same after that day. My mom, she made him think it was his fault. He turned real quiet. He had all kind of problems. He stopped going to school when he was fourteen. About two years back he shot hisself with my uncle's pistol. After he seen Deonte die, living was just too hard for him."

Aside from the nurses and the chipper receptionist sitting behind a glass panel, we're the first to arrive at Dr. Chan's office. Sitting beside me in the sterile reception area, Sanquita completes her paperwork.

"Sanquita Bell," a nurse calls from an open door.

Sanquita gets to her feet. "You coming?"

I look up from my magazine. "It's okay, I can stay here."

She bites the side of her lip but doesn't move.

"Or I can come in, if you want me to. It's up to you."

"That'd be straight."

I can hardly believe it. She wants me with her. I toss aside my magazine. Placing a protective hand on her shoulder, we follow the nurse into the exam room.

Wearing a flimsy green hospital gown, Sanquita sits atop the examination table with a sheet covering her skinny bare legs. With her hair tied back in a rubber band and her face absent any makeup, Sanquita looks like a child waiting to see her pediatrician. We hear a gentle knock on the door, and Dr. Chan steps into the room. She introduces herself to Sanquita, and turns to me. "You are?"

"I'm Brett Bohlinger, Sanquita's teacher — and friend. Her mother lives in Detroit."

She nods, as if the vague answer suffices. After a thorough examination, multiple blood draws, and an exhausting array of questions, Dr. Chan peels off her latex gloves and tells Sanquita to get dressed. "I'll meet you across the hall, in my office."

We sit facing the doctor's desk, and she wastes no time before getting to the point. "You have a very serious condition, Sanquita. And the pregnancy adds a significant complication. The tenuous condition of your kidneys is further compromised by the stress of your pregnancy. When your kidneys don't function properly, your potassium levels rise, as I suspect they have. When this happens, you risk going into cardiac arrest." She shuffles some papers on her desk, and I can't decide if she's uncomfortable or impatient. "I want to see you again once I receive the lab results, but time is of the essence. I suggest you abort the fetus as soon as possible."

"What? No!" Sanquita turns to me as if I'd betrayed her. "No!"

I press a hand to her arm and turn to the doctor. "She's well into her second trimester, Dr. Chan."

"Late-term abortions are performed when the mother's life is at risk. In this case, it is."

Sanquita pulls herself to her feet, obviously ready to have this conversation behind her. But I remain seated. "What's her prognosis if she doesn't?"

She looks directly at me. "She has a fifty–fifty chance. The baby's chances are more like thirty percent."

She doesn't say *of survival.* She doesn't have to.

Sanquita sits with her eyes fixed out the front window of my car, her face set like granite. "I'm not going back there. I won't. That lady wants me to kill my baby. That ain't gonna happen."

"Sweetie, it's not what she wants, it's what she thinks is best for you. Your life is at stake. Do you understand?"

"Do *you* understand?" She glares at me. "You ain't got no kids. You got no right telling me what to do!"

My heart shatters. The red bloodstain comes back to me full force. I work to keep my breathing steady. "You're right. I'm sorry."

She stares out the passenger window and we drive in silence for several miles. We're almost to Carroll Avenue when she finally speaks, her voice so soft I can barely hear her. "You wanted kids, didn't you?"

She says it as if it's too late, as if I've lost my window of opportunity. And in her world, thirty-four sounds ancient. "Yes, I did — I do — want kids."

She finally turns to me. "You would've made a good mom."

It's both the sweetest and the cruelest thing she could have said. I reach over and squeeze her hand. She doesn't pull away. "You will too, someday when you get your kidney problem resolved. But right now . . . I just don't want to lose you."

"Ms. Brett, don't you see? My life don't mean nothing if I don't have my baby. I'd rather die than kill this baby."

The *I'd die for you kind of love.* Sanquita has found it. And true to an obsessive love, it might just kill her.

It's only ten in the morning when I drop Sanquita off at Joshua House. I'd planned to spend the morning with her, stopping for breakfast, doing a bit of baby shopping, but the mood is so far from celebratory I don't even suggest it.

As I back out of the driveway, I catch sight of the pages I'd printed during my late-night apartment search, strewn on the backseat. I pull over to the curb and thumb through them, look-ing for that nice brick house I saw in Pilsen. Maybe I'll drive by it, just to see. Then I can tell Joad and Brad I've been looking.

I rifle through the pages. I see the six places in Little Italy, the four apartments in University Village, but I can't find that pretty place in Pilsen. I know I printed it. Where did it go? On my lap, the other pages seem to beg for my attention like neglected chil-dren. What the hell . . . here goes nothing.

I try to cheer myself with the idea that I'll be closer to work and Joshua House. But I'm not cheered. These South Side neigh-borhoods look dismal and depressing . . . even borderline danger-ous. I perk up when I enter the Italian American village of Little Italy, with its vibrant shopping area and some of the best restau-rants in the city. This could work. I search out the first address with my fingers crossed. But rather than one of the cute houses I'd seen in the village, I see a cement-block building with its front window boarded up like a patched eye. My God, this dump looks nothing like the picture on Craigslist. My anger mounts when I move on to Loomis Street, where the FOR RENT sign is lost in a yard littered with everything from old car tires to a rusted ironing board. Is this what my mother had in mind? I can't decide if I'm hurt or offended or enraged. I decide I'm all three.

It's five o'clock on New Year's Eve, and I'm propped in the window seat of Mom's brownstone clutching a bag of M&M's. Outside, the sun is losing its battle to the moon as the city pre-pares for its annual hullabaloo. With Rudy curled at my feet, I give Carrie the latest update on the phone. I tell her about San-quita's doctor's visit and Joad's interrogation about my living situation.

"And Johnny called again last night. As usual, he only wanted to talk about Zoë. Her cold is worse. He's worried. I want to say, *I get it. You don't have to worry. I'm not going to show up on your doorstep."*

"Don't go jumping to conclusions. Once Zoë is healthy, he'll be able to focus on you. Trust me. I know what it's like to have a sick child. They become your world."

I start to grouse that it's just a cold, for God's sake, but I stop myself. Sanquita was right. I don't understand. I don't have kids.

"So, how are your kids?" I ask.

"Great. Tayloe had a dance recital Thursday night. I'll send you the video. She's the tall one in the back who's constantly out of step, just like I always was."

We giggle. "What are you doing tonight?" she asks.

"Nothing. Jay and Shelley are at some swanky party. I offered to watch the kids, but Shelley hired a sitter. So, I've rented every old Meg Ryan film I could find." I traipse over to the stack of DVDs on the coffee table. "There's *Sleepless in Seattle, You've Got Mail* . . . Want to come over?" I tease.

"If you've got *When Harry Met Sally,* I'm there."

"First one I picked."

We laugh. "God, Bretel, I miss you. We're going to a party with some of Stella's work friends. Truth be told, I'd trade my night for yours. Sometimes I really envy you."

"Don't," I say, returning to my window seat. "There's nothing enviable about my life." My throat seizes up. "It's depressing being alone, Car. I walk down the street and see these young couples — more often than not pushing a baby carriage — and I feel so old. What if I never meet anyone? What if I never have kids? Will the neighbor children race past my house, afraid of the crazy old lady who lives all alone?" I grab a tissue and dab my nose. "Jesus, am I going to die here alone, in my mother's brownstone."

"No. You're not allowed to live there, remember? More likely you'll die alone in some shabby rental."

"Oh, real nice."

She's laughing. "You're going to be fine, Bretel. You're thirty-four, not ninety-four. And you will meet someone." She pauses. "In fact, I'm guessing you already have."

"Really?" I stuff my tissue into my pocket. "And who might that be?"

"Your mother's attorney."

My heart pitches. "Brad? No way."

"Have you ever thought about it? And don't lie to me."

I sigh and grab another handful of M&M's. "Okay, maybe." I tell her about the last time I saw him, and his halfhearted attempt to seduce me. "He and Jenna are on a hiatus. He was lonely and a little drunk. It would've ruined everything if we'd hooked up."

"Their relationship's been on and off for months. You told me so yourself. Look, I've been thinking. You know how you wondered why your mom hired Brad, instead of using that old fart she'd used for years?"

"Yeah?"

"I think she was setting you up with Brad."

I sit up. "You think she wanted Brad and me to get together?"

"Yup."

Like a burst of sunshine splitting a stormy sky, I'm suddenly illuminated. I can't believe I didn't figure this out sooner. Mother chose Brad Midar to handle her estate, rather than Mr. Goldblatt, knowing we would fall in love. She orchestrated an entirely new relationship for me with a man she knew and respected. The red journal wasn't her last gift to me, after all!

I stare at the phone and mentally rehearse what I'm going to say for the forty-seventh time. My hands are shaking, but I also feel strangely calm. I'm not alone. My mom is with me on this, I can feel it. I finger the little gold charm, my parachute, to ensure soft landings. I take a deep breath and punch in the number. He picks up on the third ring.

"It's me," I say.

"Hey, what's up?" He sounds groggy, and I picture him stretching and grappling for the clock to check the time. I'm tempted to tease him about what a couple of losers we are, alone on New Year's Eve, but now's not the time for joking. I swallow hard.

"Would you like some company tonight?"

There could be no mistaking my message. He doesn't say anything at first, and my heart sinks. I'm about to laugh and tell him I was only joking when I hear his voice, soft and warm like a glass of sherry on a frigid night. "I'd love some."

Dainty flakes fall from the sky like sifted flour. I turn right on Oakley and cruise down the quiet street, softly lit by streetlamps. Miraculously, I find a parking spot just a block from his duplex. A good omen, I decide. I step from my car and as I near his house, I break into a trot. All is the way it should be. Together, we'll accomplish every last goal, including the dreaded horse. Even my false pregnancy seems less devastating now. Brad will make a terrific father, much better than Andrew ever would. I'm giddy now, thrilled to start my new year, my new life.

I stop when I reach his porch. What if my hunch was wrong, and Carrie's, too? My heart pounds in my temples. Am I making a mistake? Before I have time to rethink things, the door swings open and our eyes meet. He's sporting a pair of jeans and a cotton shirt, untucked. He looks so gorgeous I want to throw my arms around him. But I don't have time. He beats me to the punch.

He kicks the door shut behind us and flattens me against the wall. My breath comes fast and my head spins. I wriggle out of my coat and lock my arms around the back of his neck. Cupping my face with his hands, he kisses my neck, my lips, his tongue mingling with mine.

He tastes faintly of bourbon and I want to drink him up. I run my fingers through his hair. It's thick and soft — exactly how I imagined it would feel. His hands travel down my body. He lifts my sweater and his fingers find my bare skin. My body erupts in gooseflesh.

He pulls my sweater over my head and slips his hands beneath my bra, cupping my breasts. "Oh, God," he whispers against my neck. "You're so beautiful."

I'm on fire now. I reach down and blindly fumble with his belt buckle. I find the leather strap and pull it free. Then I yank open the buttons of his jeans.

And from the other room, I hear his phone ring.

His body stiffens and his fingers come to a halt on my nipples. It rings again.

With every instinct I possess, I know it's Jenna. And I know Brad knows it, too.

"Ignore it," he whispers, kneading my breasts. But his fingers are clumsy now, as if they've lost their rhythm — or their interest.

I bury my head against his chest and listen to the phone ring again. Finally, his hands fall to his side.

A sick feeling comes over me. I am such a fool. What was I thinking? I disentangle myself and cross my arms over my bare chest. "Go," I say. "Answer the phone."

But the ringing has stopped now. The only sound is the despondent moan of the furnace and Brad's heavy breathing. He stands before me, his pants unbuttoned and his shirt rumpled, and rubs the back of his neck. He reaches out for me, and there's no mistaking the heavy look in his eyes. It's a tender gaze that says he doesn't want to hurt me. A look that tells me his heart belongs to someone else.

I try to work my lips into a smile, but the corners tug downward with a will of their own. "Call her," I whisper, and bend down to get my sweater.

I hear him calling to me as I dash down the porch steps. I reach the sidewalk and break into a run, terrified my world will fall out from under me if I stop for even the briefest moment.

CHAPTER TWENTY

Mercifully, the Christmas holiday ends and my teaching job resumes. Who would have thought my life could be so pathetic I'd rather be at work than on break? I hoist my leather satchel on one shoulder and my overnight bag on the other. "Have fun at Aunt Shelley's, Rudy boy. I'll see you tomorrow."

I'm on the road before the clock strikes six, but already the predawn traffic is cranky. I mentally review the long day ahead of me. What in hell possessed me to keep my Monday-night shift at Joshua House on my first day back at work? Though truth be told, it's probably better that I'm at the shelter, rather than at home lamenting the baby who wasn't, the new love who wasn't, and the father who might not be.

I turn on the overhead lights and my office wakes from its slumber. On the windowsill, I spy my geraniums. The blooms have gone to seed and the leaves are brittle and yellowed, but they've managed to survive the two-week hiatus — just as I have. I switch on my computer. It's not quite seven, which means I have two glorious hours to get organized before my busy day begins. First-semester final exams start tomorrow, and Sanquita will be taking five before the week's end.

The blinking red light of my telephone tells me I've got messages. I grab my notepad and listen. The first two are new referrals. The third message is from Dr. Taylor, sent on December 23. I sit down when I hear his voice and nibble on my pencil eraser.

"Hey, it's Garrett. Just in case you happen to retrieve your messages during your break, I wanted to give you my cell phone number. It's 312-555-4928. Call me anytime. I'll be around. Holidays can be difficult, especially your first Christmas without your mom." He pauses. "Anyway, I just wanted you to know how to reach me. And if it's the New Year when you're listening to this message, I'm glad you survived the holidays. Congratulations and happy New Year. Let's talk soon."

I drop my pencil and stare at the phone. Dr. Taylor genuinely cares about me. I'm not just the teacher of his patient. I listen a second time, just to hear his voice, and I catch myself smiling for the first time in days. I dial his number, hoping he's an early bird, too.

He is.

"Happy New Year, Garrett. It's Brett. I just got your message."

"Hey! Well, I just . . . I wasn't sure if . . ."

He sounds embarrassed, and I smile. "Thank you. I really appreciate it. How were your holidays?"

He tells me he spent Christmas with his sisters and their families. "We had dinner at my niece's house in Pennsylvania."

"Your niece's house?" I'm thrown off for a moment. But of course, unlike baby Emma, his niece is an adult, maybe even my age. "How nice."

"Melissa's my oldest sister's daughter. Hard to imagine she has two kids in high school now." He pauses for a moment. "How were your holidays?"

"Lucky for you I didn't get your message until today. If I'd had your number, it would have been programmed to speed dial."

"That bad, huh?"

"Yeah. That bad."

"My first patient doesn't arrive until nine. Do you want to talk about it?"

I spare him the details about starting my period on Christmas Day and the humiliating episode with Brad, but I give him a snapshot of my holidays — the mourning of my mother, my futile search for an apartment, and Sanquita's doctor's appointment. It goes without saying he's an excellent listener. He is, after all, a shrink. But this doctor who specializes in mental illness makes me feel like I'm normal, not like some psycho-freak bordering on dysfunction, the way I sometimes feel. He even has me laughing . . . until he asks if I've heard anything from my father.

"As a matter of fact, he called Christmas Day. He has another daughter," I blurt out. "Someone he knows and adores. He's not nearly as anxious to meet me as I am to meet him." The minute I've uttered the words, I regret it. I shouldn't be jealous of my sister. She's not feeling well. I should be more understanding.

"You haven't made plans to meet?"

"No." I pinch the bridge of my nose. "Zoë's got a cold. He doesn't want her to travel, and he doesn't want to expose her to any germs I might carry."

"And that feels like rejection to you." His voice is soft and kind.

"Yes," I whisper. "I thought he'd catch the first flight to Chicago. Maybe he doesn't want to upset Zoë by bringing me into the fold. Who knows? I feel so selfish, but I've waited so long. I just want to know him — and Zoë, too. She's my sister."

"Of course you do."

"I feel like . . . like I'm some gift I gave my father, but it's a gift he didn't need after all. I gave him a duplicate, and he's crazy about the original." I squeeze shut my eyes. "The simple fact is, I'm jealous of Zoë. I know I shouldn't feel this way, but I do."

"There are no *shoulds* when it comes to our feelings. They are what they are." His voice is a cool washcloth on my fevered forehead. "It must feel as if your father is protecting your sister, but not you."

I start to choke up and fan my face. "Um-hmm." I glance at the clock. "Oh, my gosh. It's eight thirty. I need to let you go."

"Brett, your feelings are normal. Like every healthy person, you crave a relationship where you feel nurtured, protected, cared for. And you had great expectations that your father would fill those needs. And maybe he will. But those needs can be met in other ways, too."

"Is this where you prescribe Xanax or Valium or something?"

He chuckles. "No. You don't need meds. You just need more love in your life — be it from your father, or from a lover, or from another source, perhaps yourself even. What's lacking is a basic human need. Believe it or not, you're one of the lucky ones — you admit you need it. There are a whole lot of unhappy folks out there who've stuffed away their needs. Seeking love creates vulnerability. Only healthy people can allow themselves to be vulnerable."

"I don't feel so healthy at the moment, but since you're the expert, I'll take your word for it." I glance at my calendar and see that I have a nine fifteen appointment with Amina. "I really have to go, and so do you. But thank you for the session. Am I going to get some big fat bill at the end of my treatments?"

He laughs. "Maybe. Or maybe I'll just make you treat me to lunch one day."

I'm caught off-guard. Is Dr. Taylor hitting on me? Hmm. I've never dated an older man. But I must admit, I'm not exactly a dating tour de force with men in my age bracket. Could Garrett be the Michael Douglas to my Catherine Zeta-Jones? The Spencer Tracy to my Katharine Hepburn? My mind races for something clever to say, something light but substantial that will imply the door is open — even if only a crack.

But I've waited too long.

"Get to work," he says, more business-like than usual. "Please, call me after your next session with Peter, will you?"

"Yes. Yes, of course."

I want to get back to the topic of lunch, but he's already saying good-bye, and next thing I know we're disconnected.

Literally and figuratively.

All day long, a fine mist sprinkles the city like holy water, and now the temperatures are falling, creating havoc with traffic. As usual, I've scheduled Peter's session last, knowing he has the power to ruin even my best day.

Today's session is no different from the others. As usual, he refuses eye contact and grunts his answers through clenched teeth. Still, I can't help but feel sorry for him, a bright child cooped up all day long in this smoke-filled house. As we finish our session, I pull a stack of books from my satchel.

"I was at the bookstore the other day, Peter. I thought you might like something to read, you know, to keep your mind busy." I look up at him, hoping to see a flash of anticipation or excitement on his face. But he simply stares down at the table in front of him.

I pull my favorite from the stack. "I know you like history. This book is about children of the Dust Bowl." I reach for another. "And this one tells all about Lewis and Clark's expedition."

I'm about to choose another when he yanks the books from my grasp.

I smile. "That's right. Take them. They're yours."

He lifts the entire stack and holds them protectively to his chest.

My heart sings. It's the first time our session has ended positively.

It's still drizzling when I creep down the porch steps. I grip the iron rail, noting the coat of slush on the cement steps. My feet have reached the driveway when I hear the door open behind me.

I turn around. Peter stands on the porch in the rain, cradling his new books in his arms. He stares at me, and I wonder if he wants to thank me. I wait a moment, but he doesn't say anything. He probably feels embarrassed. I wave and turn back toward my car. "Enjoy your books, Peter."

A loud smacking sound startles me, and I spin around. Peter stands watching me with an evil grin on his face. The brand new books are splayed on the porch, soaking up the sloppy wet puddles.

I unlock the door to my office, toss my wet bag on the floor, and rush to the telephone. It rings four times before he picks up.

"Garrett, it's Brett. Do you have a minute?"

My voice is still shaking when I describe Peter's cruel reaction to the books.

I hear him sigh. "I'm so sorry about this. I'll make some phone calls tomorrow. His behavior at home is escalating. It's time we found another placement for Peter."

"Another placement?"

"Homebound isn't the answer for this kid. Cook County has a first-rate program for mentally ill teens. New Pathways. The student-to-staff ratio is two-to-one, and students receive intensive therapy twice daily. Peter's a tad young, but I'm hoping they'll make an exception."

I'm at once relieved and disappointed. Peter may soon be off my caseload. But it feels like I'm abandoning a mission, like I'm walking out on a play just before the ending. And who knows? Perhaps the ending would have been redeeming.

"Maybe he just thought those books were silly, or insulting," I say. "Maybe he was offended that I'd bought him presents, like he was a charity case."

"This has nothing to do with you, Brett. He's not your typical kid. I'm afraid you're not going to win him over, no matter how hard you try. He wants to hurt you. So far it's just emotional pain, but it concerns me that it could get worse."

I remember Peter's grin, cold and heartless. A shiver goes through me.

"I've frightened you, haven't I?"

"I'm fine." I gaze out at the dreary street below. I'd planned to stay here all evening, until my nine o'clock shift at Joshua House. But my cozy office suddenly feels isolated and ominous.

"Remember that lunch you mentioned earlier?"

Garrett hesitates. "Yes."

I take a deep breath and squeeze shut my eyes. "Would you want to meet for coffee, now? Or maybe a drink?"

I hold my breath while I wait for his answer. When he speaks, I think I hear a smile in his voice. "I'd love to meet for a drink."

Traffic is horrendous, as I knew it would be. Rather than the trendy places Andrew and I used to frequent, I choose Petterino's, a forties-style bar and restaurant near the Loop, where I think Garrett will feel comfortable. But it's five forty and I'm still on the South Side, miles from the theater district. I'll never make it by six. Why did I delete his message this morning before jotting down his cell phone number?

When my phone rings, I assume it's him, telling me he's stuck in traffic, too. But it can't be. He doesn't have my cell phone number, either.

"This is Jean Anderson from Joshua House. You're expected to be here at nine, but I need you to come early."

My hackles rise. What is it with this woman, thinking she can order me around? "Sorry, I've got plans. I could probably be there around eight, but I can't promise."

"It's Sanquita. She's bleeding."

I toss my phone onto the passenger seat and whip a U-turn. Two cars blast their horns at me, but I ignore them. All I can think of is that girl with the hazelnut eyes and the baby she's willing to die for.

"Don't let the baby die," I pray aloud, over and over until I reach the center.

Jean jumps from her white Chevrolet when I pull up to the curb. She trots over to meet me as I race up the driveway.

"I'm taking her to Cook County Memorial," she says. "I've left a note with all the instructions for tonight."

I reach the car and open the back door. Sanquita lies in the backseat, massaging her belly. Her bloated face glistens with sweat, but she smiles when she sees me. I squeeze her hand.

"Hang in there, sweetie."

"You coming back tomorrow? I gotta take those exams."

Despite all she's going through, she's still determined to finish school. I swallow the lump in my throat. "Whenever you're ready. Don't you worry. Your teachers will understand."

Her eyes implore mine. "Pray for my baby, Miss Brett."

I nod and close the car door. As the car pulls away, I say another prayer.

I find Jean's note in the office, along with details of a feud that's brewing between two of the guests. She's hoping I can mediate, if time allows. But before I do anything, I need to call Petterino's and page Garrett. I'm searching the desk for a phone directory when I hear shouting from the TV room. I leap from my chair, throw open the office door, and step into a battlefield.

"You got no business gettin' in my shit!" Julonia screams, her face crimson. She's inches from Tanya's face, but Tanya's not backing down.

"I told you, I ain't been in your drawer. Get a life."

"Calm down, ladies," I say, but my voice is shaking. "Just stop right now."

Like my students at Douglas Keyes, they pay no heed. Guests scurry in from other rooms to watch the spectacle.

"I got me a life!" Julonia says, her hands on her hips. "I don't gotta steal other people's money! I got me a job, unlike you, who do nothing 'cept sit on yo fat ass all day."

A collective "Oooh" goes out from the spectators. In the background Judge Judy gives someone a severe reprimand on television. I try to channel her authority.

"Ladies, stop!"

Tanya starts to walk away, then backs up a step. With the agility of an acrobat, she pivots and drives her fist into Julonia's jaw. Momentarily stunned, Julonia dabs at her mouth. When she lowers her hand, she sees blood on her fingers.

"Bitch!" She grabs a fistful of Tanya's hair and yanks. A chunk of Tanya's weave falls to the carpet.

Tanya screams obscenities and lunges for her. Lucky for me, Mercedes grabs Tanya from behind. I seize Julonia's arm and, with a strength that stuns me, pull her into the office. I kick shut the door and lock it behind us with trembling hands. Julonia curses and the veins in her forehead bulge, but at least she's contained. From beyond the door I hear Tanya, still hollering, but her voice is losing its fire. I drop onto the desktop and point to the bed.

"Sit down," I say, and draw in a ragged breath.

Julonia perches on the edge of the bed, raking her teeth over her bottom lip and clenching her fists. "She stole my money, Ms. Brett. I know she did."

"How much are we talking?"

"Seven dollars."

"Seven dollars?" I'd assumed it was hundreds, judging by the fury. Once again, I'm humbled. To someone who has nothing, seven dollars is their fortune. "What makes you think Tanya took it?"

"She the only one who know where I keep my cheddar."

I look at her blankly.

"My bills. My money."

"Oh. Well, maybe you spent it and forgot. That happens to me all the time. I open my wallet and think money's missing, but when I really stop and backtrack, I realize I just spent it."

She cocks her head at me and scowls. "Uh-uh. That don't happen with me." She lifts her face to the ceiling and blinks quickly. "I was gon' buy Myanna a new book bag. Hers be all tore up. They got one at the Walmart cost fourteen dollar. I be halfway there 'fore that lazy ho stole it from me."

My heart breaks for her. I want to open my wallet and give her all I have, but that's against the rules. "I tell you what. I'm going to find you a little safe. I'll drop it off tomorrow. That way nobody can take your cheddar."

She smiles at me. "That'd be straight. But that still don't bring me back my money. You got any idea how long it took me to save up seven bills?"

No, I don't. For reasons I cannot explain or possibly justify, I was dealt a lucky hand, a hand that included love and money and education. I'm flooded with guilt and gratitude, humility and heartbreak.

"This book bag you're looking at, what color is it?"

"She want the purple one."

"And it's from Walmart, in the kids' department?"

"That right."

"Julonia, I think I've got that very book bag. I bought it for my niece, but she already had one. It's never been used. Would you like it?"

She studies me, as if deciding whether I'm telling the truth. "The purple one?"

"Uh-huh."

Her face blooms. "That'd be real nice. Right now Myanna be carrying her books in a plastic bag. She need her a book bag."

"Okay then, I'll bring it tomorrow."

"The safe-bank, too?"

"Yes, the safe-bank, too."

I sit at the desk and massage my temples. Finally, I find the strength to retrieve an incident report and begin to fill it out. Date: January 5. Time: I look at the clock and start to write seven fifteen. Then I drop my pencil. "No!" I fling open the desk drawer and yank out the telephone book, scanning it as quickly as I can. Finally, I find the number to Petterino's.

"Hello," I say to the maître d'. "I was supposed to meet a friend tonight. I'm hoping he's still there. Dr. Garrett Taylor. He's a gentleman . . ." It occurs to me, I have no way to identify Garrett. "He's alone."

"Might you be Ms. Bohlinger?"

I laugh, relief pouring over me. "Yes. Yes, I am. Could I please speak with him?"

"I'm sorry, Ms. Bohlinger. Dr. Taylor left five minutes ago."

CHAPTER TWENTY-ONE

I call the hospital nearly every hour. By three A.M., Miss Jean assures me that Sanquita will be fine. The next morning, I'm loading breakfast bowls into the dishwasher when I hear her car pull into the drive. I dash from the kitchen. Before the ignition's off, I throw open the car door. Sanquita lies slumped in the back-seat, her head propped against the window.

"Hello, sweet pea. How are you feeling this morning?"

Dark circles shadow her glassy eyes. "They give me some medicine to stop the contractions."

With her arms draped around our necks, Jean and I hoist San-quita up the porch steps and into the house. When we reach the stairs, I lift Sanquita into my arms. She feels lighter than Rudy. I take her to her room and lay her on her bed.

"I gotta take my exams," she mumbles.

"We'll worry about those later. Get some sleep now." I kiss her forehead and turn out the lamp. "I'll be back later to check on you."

When we reach the bottom of the stairs, Jean pulls off her head scarf, setting free a bonnet of black curls.

"I've tried to reach her mother all night, but her phone's out of service," she says. "That poor girl's all alone."

"I can stay with her."

She removes her boots and slips into a pair of practical black pumps. "Don't you have other students?"

"Yes, but I can reschedule them."

She waves me off. "Nonsense. I'll be here today. Just stop by later if you can."

She turns in the direction of her office, but stops, keeping her back to me. "Sanquita talked about you last night. Said you took her to a specialist."

I shake my head. "I apologize for that. I didn't realize Dr. Chan would recom —"

"And she said you've been providing homebound services every day, not just the two appointments required."

My defenses rise. What is she implying? "I have no problem giving up my lunch hour. Look, if there's a problem —"

"She told me nobody's ever cared about her like that." She shuffles away. "That child thinks you're mighty special. I figured you should know."

My throat constricts. "I think she's mighty special, too," I whisper, but Miss Jean is already halfway down the hall.

On my way to Amina's, I phone Dr. Taylor's office. Like before, his machine picks up. I hang up without leaving another message. Damn.

I go through my daily motions in a mechanical way, my mind

filled with thoughts of Sanquita and the baby. At the end of the day, I hustle back to Joshua House gripped with anxiety. I race up the stairs expecting to see a failing patient, but instead Sanquita sits propped against her pillow in the brightly lit room, sipping a glass of juice. Tanya and Mercedes loiter at her bedside, telling stories of their own labor. Sanquita's eyes go wide when she sees me at the door.

"Hey, Ms. Brett. Come in."

"Hi, ladies." I bend down to hug Sanquita. Instead of the stiff, awkward response I usually get, she hugs me back. "You're looking much better, sweet pea."

"I feel better, too. I just have to stay off my feet, that's what them doctors told me. If this baby can just wait till the end of April, around my thirty-sixth week, everything'll be all right."

"Wonderful," I say, trying to believe it.

"You got my exams?"

I laugh. "Don't worry about your exams. I spoke to your teachers. We agreed you should focus on your health for now."

"Ain't no way I'm giving up now. I'm about to graduate. You told me you'd help me."

"Okay, okay," I say, smiling. "If you're sure you can manage, we'll start your exams tomorrow."

She grins. "I can manage, you'll see."

I wrap her in my arms. "You're something special, you know that?"

She doesn't say anything in return. And I don't expect her to. It's enough that she lets me hug her.

Before leaving the house, I knock on Julonia's bedroom door.

"Julonia?" I say, pushing past the partially open door. I step inside the spotless room and walk to a set of twin beds. On the green quilt I position a sturdy little safe-bank. On the Snow White bedspread, I leave Myanna's new purple book bag.

I'm meeting Brad for dinner at Bistrot Zinc, a cozy French restaurant on State Street. Since our New Year's Eve fiasco we've talked on the phone, but aside from letting me know he and Jenna are "working things out," we've kept the conversation focused on my life list. Tonight we'll actually meet face-to-face, which has me jittery. Oh, God! Even now I cringe, thinking of that lonely, reckless girl driving across town with such high hopes.

On my way to the restaurant I call Garrett's office again. *Come on. Answer the phone, Garrett.*

"Garrett Taylor," he says.

"Garrett, it's Brett. Don't hang up."

He chuckles. "Don't worry. I wouldn't hang up on you. I got your message this morning, and I see you called about seven more times today."

Great. He's just added obsessive-compulsive to my list of diagnoses. "Yeah, sorry about that. I just wanted to explain what happened."

"You did. And I completely understand. How's the young lady doing — Sanquita?"

I let out a sigh of relief. "Much better, thank you. I just left her. Have you heard anything about placement for Peter?"

"Yes. I spoke with the director of special education this afternoon. The age requirement at New Pathways is still an issue. I'm afraid it could be a while."

"That's okay. I need a little more time with him."

I pull my car over to a curb and we chat for another five minutes. Finally he asks, "Hey, you're in your car, right?"

"Right."

"And you're finished with work for the day?"

"Uh-huh."

"What do you say we go have that drink now?"

I smile, and it hits me: I've got a crush on Garrett Taylor. And I think he's got a crush on me, too.

"I'm sorry," I say, hearing the silly smile in my voice. "I'm meeting a friend for dinner tonight."

"Oh, right. Okay then. I'll talk to you after your next session."

I'm taken aback by how abruptly he ends our conversation. I guess he didn't have a crush on me after all. My chest tightens. Will I ever find someone?

I replay our conversation . . . *I'm meeting a friend.* Oh, no! Garrett thinks I've got a date. And that smile in my voice probably sounded mocking. I need to set him straight!

I grab the phone, too anxious and impatient to wait for our next phone conversation. Maybe we can meet tomorrow night. What should I wear? Punching in his number, I catch sight of myself in my rearview mirror. My eyes look wild, and my face has a frantic look of desperation.

I drop my phone and knead my forehead. Jesus, have I sunk so low I'm hustling a sixty-something? This damn list is making me crazy. I'm sizing up every guy I meet, like a director searching for the perfect character to play the role of husband and father in her play. This isn't what my mom wants.

I click off my phone and toss it into my bag.

Brad sits at the bar drinking a martini, looking especially handsome in his powder-blue shirt and black cashmere jacket. But as always, his hair is a little mussed, and today a mustard-colored stain dots his tie. My heartstrings tug. God, I've missed him. He rises when he sees me and holds out his arms. Without hesitating, I fill them.

Our hug is especially fierce, as if we're both trying to squeeze the love and friendship back into our twosome. "I'm so sorry," he whispers in my ear.

"Me too."

I slip off my coat and find the hook under the bar for my purse. Once settled, there's an awkward silence between us, a disturbing lull that's never been there before.

"Want a drink?" he asks.

"Just water for now. I'll have a glass of wine with dinner."

Brad nods and sips his martini. The television over the bar is tuned to CNN, but the volume is muted. I stare at it anyway. Have I ruined everything? Will our friendship forever be tainted by that mortifying make-out session?

"How's Jenna?" I ask, breaking the silence.

He drags the toothpick of olives from his martini and stares at it. "Good. We seem to be back on track."

A branding fork sears my heart. "Good."

His eyes are as tender as a koala bear's. "If our timing had been different, I think you and I could have been pretty amazing."

I force myself to smile. "But as they say, timing is everything."

The silence returns. Brad senses the change between us, too, I can tell. He plays with his toothpick, dunking the olives into the martini and dredging them back to the surface. Dunking. Dredging. Dunking. Dredging. I can't let this happen. I won't let this happen! I love our friendship too much to let it slip away because of a twenty-minute mistake.

"Look, Midar. You've got to know, I was feeling a little desperate that night."

He looks over at me. "Desperate, huh?"

I punch his arm. "It was New Year's Eve, after all. Give a girl a break."

Laugh lines crease the corners of his eyes. "Ah. So I was just your booty call?"

"You got that right."

He grins. "Real nice, B.B. I should've known."

My smile fades and I run a finger over the rim of my water

glass. "Honestly, Brad? I thought maybe it was part of my mom's plan. You know, sort of a postmortem fix-me-up, just like she's doing with the rest of my life."

He swivels on his stool to face me. "Your mom knew I was unavailable, Brett. She met Jenna that same night she met me. She wouldn't have done that to you, or to me."

I feel like I've been sucker-punched in the gut. "Then why, Brad? Why did my mom hire you? Why did she insist you open every letter? Why did she make sure we were in constant contact if she knew you weren't available?"

He shrugs his shoulders. "Beats the hell out of me. Unless, maybe, she actually liked me, and thought you might, too." He rubs his chin in thought. "Nah, that's too far-fetched."

"Way!" I tease. "Seriously. I thought for sure my mom was orchestrating our romance. Otherwise, I'd never have had the nerve to . . ." I feel heat rise to my cheeks and I roll my eyes. "The nerve to do what I did."

"Seduce me?"

I sneer at him. "Ah, as I recall, you tried to seduce me, just a week earlier."

He chuckles. "Let's not go tit-for-tat here. Besides, it was the holiday season. Give a guy a break."

And just like that, we're back to the old Brad and B.B.

"Jenna's coming here in two weeks. I'd love for you to meet her, if you're okay with it."

I smile, and it actually feels genuine. "I'd like that."

He looks over my shoulder and tips his head. "Looks like our table's ready."

We move to our table by the window, and I break into a riff about Peter, Sanquita, and my other students. "They've got her on terbutaline to stop contractions, but I'm still worried."

Brad watches me, grinning.

"What?"

"Nothing. Everything." He shakes his head. "You're so different from that woman sitting in my office last September. You really like this job, don't you?"

"I do. I love it. Can you believe it?"

"After all your whining and bellyaching, Elizabeth was right."

I narrow my eyes at him and he laughs.

"Hey, the truth hurts."

"Maybe. But what if I hadn't gotten this homebound job? What if I was forced to teach in the classroom? I would have had a breakdown. Seriously. My mom just lucked out."

He pulls a pink envelope from his pocket. Goal number twenty.

"You've been teaching almost three months. You've earned your envelope." He opens the seal.

"'Congratulations, dear daughter! Oh, how I'd love to hear all about your new job. I wonder where you're teaching. I suspect it's not a conventional assignment, since you were never much of a disciplinarian.'"

I gasp.

"'Don't be insulted, darling. Maria let those von Trapp children run wild and we loved her for it.'"

I smile, picturing my mother and me snuggled on the sofa, sharing a bowl of popcorn, watching our favorite movie, *The Sound of Music*.

"'Like Maria, you're an idealist, which is wonderful. You think if you're kind, others will be kind in return. Instead, children often challenge those who seem sensitive, especially in front of an audience of their peers.'"

I think of the kids at Meadowdale, and Douglas Keyes Elementary, and Peter. "Yeah, they do."

"'I envision you teaching small groups of children, or perhaps tutoring. Is that what you're doing? How I wish I knew! No matter, I know you're terrific. I know your students are benefiting from your patience and encouragement. And darling, I'm so very proud of you. You were a fine advertising executive, but you're a superb teacher.

"'I bet your life on it.'"

I stare at the last line, my eyes swimming in tears. Yes, she did. My mom took a huge gamble, trying to fix a life she thought was broken. She wanted to ensure my happiness, plain and simple. I just hope she doesn't lose the bet.

The following week I'm driving to work when my phone rings. From the caller ID, I see it's Johnny. What now? His princess still has the sniffles? As I pull over to the curb, I realize it's not even dawn on the West Coast. I shiver with the first prickle of fear.

"Hey, Brett." His voice sounds gravelly, like he's exhausted. "Just wanted to let you know, Zoë's in the hospital."

My breath catches. *No! Zoë has a cold. You don't go to the hospital for a cold!* I grip the phone. "Why? What's wrong?"

"She's got pneumonia — exactly what I feared. The poor kid's been plagued with respiratory problems since birth."

I hang my head in shame. My sister is sick — extremely sick. And all I could think about was myself. I cover my mouth. "Oh, John. I'm so sorry. Is she going to be okay?"

"She's a fighter. She'll get through it. She always does."

"What can I do? How can I help?"

"There's nothing to do now but wait. But keep her in your thoughts, will you?"

"Always," I say. "Please, give her a hug for me. Tell her to stay strong, and that I'm praying for her."

"And, Brett, if you would, keep sending those cards. She in-

sisted on taking them with her. She's got every card you've sent on
her hospital nightstand."

I close my eyes. I'd begun doubting whether he was even giving those cards to Zoë. Tears of shame and sorrow trail down my
face. My sister is seriously ill and, until now, I hadn't trusted her
or my father.

CHAPTER TWENTY-TWO

*T*hough technically the shortest month, February with its gray, blustery days seems endless. Along with cards, balloons, and flowers, I call every day to check on Zoë. She was discharged last Friday, only to be readmitted the following Monday. The poor girl can't seem to gain strength and I feel helpless, being two thousand miles away.

It's my thirteenth consecutive day at my mother's house, since by my rules the clock starts over every time I'm at Joshua House. But still, my stomach roils every time I think of Joad's words: *I thought you, of all people, would want to follow Mother's rules.* Could he be right? Would Mother want me out of her house? It seems so cruel, given all I've lost. And my mother was never, ever cruel.

With his words ringing in my ears, I drive to Pilsen on Saturday morning. I'll do a quick cruise through the little burb, and when I get home I'll email Joad and Brad. I'll tell them about my fruitless search. We'll all feel better.

The village is bustling this morning. I've been told Pilsen has the most authentic Mexican restaurants in the city, and as I travel down the commercial streets, it's easy to see the Hispanic influence. A Mexican bakery sits on one corner, a Mexican grocery store on the other. And everywhere, I see beautiful Mexican artwork. The place has a nice, ethnic feel to it, as if it's filled with people searching for a better life . . . people like me.

I turn right on West 17th Place and creep down the potholed street. Like most of Pilsen, the houses on this street are mostly wood-framed, prewar homes in various stages of disrepair. I pass an empty lot littered with soda cans and liquor bottles and decide I've seen enough.

I let out a sigh. Good. Now, I can honestly say I've tried again. But before I have time to celebrate and hightail it out of here, a FOR RENT sign comes into view. I edge toward it and spy a pretty red-brick house . . . the very house I saw on the Internet six weeks ago! I can't believe it's still for rent. That can only mean one thing. It's a disaster inside. But from the outside it looks lovely.

I slow to a stop. Decorative cornices painted a buttery yellow top each of the five windows, and a wrought-iron fence surrounds the perimeter. A dozen concrete steps lead to dual front doors, where urns filled with plastic poinsettia blossoms frame each door. I smile. Really? Plastic flowers? But it's clear. Whoever owns this place takes great pride in it.

I drum my fingers on the steering wheel. Sure, it looks sweet, but do I really want to trade my mother's gorgeous brownstone for this place? I'm so comfortable on Astor Street, so safe and settled. Surely that's what my mother would want.

Just as I pull away from the curb, a young woman steps from the left-side front door and locks it behind her. I stop the car and watch her. Her red heels must be four inches high. I wince as she skips down the steps, praying she won't twist an ankle and tumble down. Her thick body is packed into a pair of skinny black jeans, and she's sporting a shiny gold jacket that seems insufficient for such a chilly day.

She makes it down the stairs without incident, and gets only a few paces when she spots me sitting in my car staring at her. Before I have time to look away, she smiles and waves, a gesture so open and trusting that on impulse, I take her cue and roll down the passenger-side window.

Up close I see BJHS MARCHING BAND printed on the left side of her jacket. Benito Juarez High School.

"Hi," I say. "Sorry to bother you, but is this place still for rent?"

She takes a wad of gum from her mouth and tosses it into a snowbank, then leans her arms on the open window. Thick gold hoops dangle from her earlobes, along with at least six other earrings of various sizes and shapes. "Yes, it's for rent, but why do you say *still*?"

"I saw it on Craigslist a few weeks ago."

She shakes her head. "Not this place. We just put the sign up two hours ago. And trust me, my mom has no clue how to use Craigslist."

I'm sure she's mistaken, but still, the hairs on my arms rise. "Your mom's the landlord?"

"Yeah, the absolute best!" She breaks into a grin. "At least, that's what I tell her she'll be. We just finished redoing the upstairs last week, so we've never actually rented it before."

I smile, catching the contagion of her energy. "It's a beautiful house. You'll have no problem renting it."

"You looking for a place?"

"Uh, sort of. But I've got a dog," I add quickly.

She clasps her hands so tightly I fear one of her orange nails will pop off. "We love dogs — as long as it's not aggressive. We've got a Yorkie. He's just adorable. Fits in my purse, like Paris Hilton's Chihuahua. Come in. My mom's home now so you can meet her. The apartment is awesome! Wait till you see it."

Her speech is so rapid-fire it takes a moment for me to process. I peek at my watch. It's not even noon. What else have I got to do?

"Well, okay. Sure. If you're sure your mom won't mind."

"Mind? She'll be totally stoked. But one thing . . . she doesn't speak much English."

*B*lanca and Selina Ruiz look more like sisters than mother and daughter. I shake Blanca's soft brown hand and she leads me up a walnut staircase. Atop the landing, she unlocks a door, and then she steps aside and makes a sweeping gesture with her hand.

The tiny apartment reminds me of a miniature doll's house, but on this chilly gray day it feels more cozy than cramped. Empty, it has a decent-sized main room with an old marble fireplace on one wall and an immaculate kitchenette in the back. Adjacent to the kitchenette is a bedroom the size of my mom's walk-in closet. Off the bedroom, a pink-and-black-tiled bathroom boasts a pedestal sink and claw-foot tub. The entire apartment would fit into my mother's living room, and as in Mother's room, the floors are hardwood while the walls are topped with cove moldings. Blanca looks on, nodding and smiling, while Selina points out every detail.

"I picked out this bathroom cabinet. It's from Ikea. They make really good stuff."

I open the cabinet and peer inside, as if its quality could sway my decision. But it wouldn't matter what the cabinet looked like. I've already made up my mind.

"You like this light fixture? I told my mom no brass."

"I love it," I say, embellishing my enthusiasm.

Blanca claps her hands together, as if she understands, and says something in Spanish to her daughter. Selina turns to me.

"She likes you. She wants to know if you'd like to live here."

I laugh. "Yes. I would. *Sí! Sí!*"

———

While I sign the lease, Selina tells me that she is the first of her family to be born in America. Her mother grew up in a rural village outside Mexico City, and came to the United States with her parents and three younger siblings when she was seventeen.

"Before she could enroll in high school, she found out she was pregnant with me. We lived with my aunts and uncle and grandparents in a tiny house just around the corner. *Mis abuelos*— my grandparents — they still live there."

"When did you move here?" I ask.

"About a year ago. My mom, she's a cook just down the block at El Tapatio. She always told me we'd have our own house someday. When this one went into foreclosure a year ago, she couldn't believe she'd saved enough money for the down payment. It took us seven months to fix up the apartment, but we did it, didn't we, Mama?"

She throws an arm around her mother's shoulder and Blanca glows with pride, as if she secretly understood the entire exchange.

Their story seems so similar to my mother's that I start to tell them. But then think better of it. In truth, it's a vastly different story, and once again I'm humbled at how very fortunate I am.

I spend the rest of the weekend packing my clothes and ferrying boxes to Pilsen. On Monday afternoon, the same movers who emptied Andrew's loft last November load up a few meager furnishings from Astor Street and deliver them to my new apartment. I was tempted to take Mother's iron bed, but it's much too big for my tiny apartment. Besides, it belongs at Astor. That way, when I visit it'll be waiting for me, just like Mom always was.

Instead, they carry my old double bed up the stairs, along with my cherry dresser. I direct them to position our old love seat from Arthur Street in front of the fireplace, framed by a couple of mismatched end tables. A scratched coffee table from my mom's attic is perfect in front of the sofa, and the seventies terra-cotta lamp I found at a thrift shop looks almost hip now.

From a cardboard box, I lift four bowls and plates I borrowed from my mom's cabinet. I put them in my new cupboard, along with some spare utensils and a couple of pots and pans. Moving to the bathroom, I arrange my cosmetics and three sets of towels in the lovely Ikea cabinet.

When the movers leave and every last box is unpacked, I light half a dozen candles and open a bottle of wine. The room glows amber from the candles and terra-cotta lamp. With Rudy at my feet, I curl up on the sofa with my book. Music from my laptop floats through the room. Within minutes I'm fast asleep in my snug little apartment in Pilsen.

March is just around the corner, and panic is setting in. I'm nearly halfway to my September deadline, with only five of my ten goals completed. I'm hopeful that I can establish a relationship with my dad, but those other four goals seem impossible. In the next six and a half months I must fall in love, have a baby, buy a horse, and get a beautiful house. Aside from the ludicrous horse goal, these goals are out of my control.

In need of a distraction, I drive to Evanston. Though the Saturday temperature is still below freezing, the brilliant sunshine teases of springtime. With my car window cracked, I breathe in the crisp air and suddenly long for my mother. She'll miss her favorite season this year. The season of hope and love, she always said.

Shelley greets me at the door wearing a crisp white blouse and leggings. I notice a sheen of gloss on her lips; her curls fall softly at her chin.

"You look cute," I tell her, taking my sleeping niece from her arms.

"You want to see cute?" she asks, leading me into her sun-drenched kitchen. "When Trevor wakes from his nap I'll have him sing you this song we learned, '*Five Little Rabbits.*' It's adorable." She chuckles. "Of course, he says *wabbits.*"

I'm surprised to hear Shelley make light of the once sensitive issue. Encouraged, I take it a step farther. "But can he sing it in Mandarin?"

She grins. "There will be no more talk of Mandarin or mom cliques." She fills a teapot. "I called my old supervisor yesterday. I'm going back to work in May."

"Oh, Shelley, that's terrific! What was the final straw?"

She drags two cups from the cupboard. "I guess it was that weekend in New Orleans you suggested. Jay and I were an actual couple again, not just a mommy and a daddy. As we were packing up to head home, I started to cry." She looks up at me. "I wouldn't admit this to anyone but you and Jay. I love my kids dearly, but the thought of going back to those endless days of reading *Dora the Explorer* and *Cat in the Hat* were too much. I confessed that I wasn't happy in this new role. Your brother simply said, 'Go back to work.' No judgment, no guilt trip. Last week he met with the chair of his department. He was granted a leave of absence. He'll finish the semester, and then he's off for a year. We'll see how it goes from there."

"So, Jay's going to be a stay-at-home dad?"

She shrugs. "He's going to give it a try. And you know what? I think he'll be great. God knows he has more patience than I do."

We're sitting at the kitchen table, sipping tea and laughing like old times, when Jay breezes in, wearing a pair of running pants and a Loyola sweatshirt. His face is flushed from his run, and he grins when he sees me.

"Hey! How's my favorite sister?" He plops his iPod on the counter and moves to the sink. "Hon, did you ask Brett about next Saturday?"

"I was just about to." She turns to me. "We've got a proposition for you. There's this new guy in Jay's department, Dr. Herbert Moyer. He's some hotshot prof they recruited from Penn."

Jay chugs a glass of water and swipes his mouth. "The world's expert on the Byzantian conquest of Bulgaria."

I shoot Shelley a look that says *WTF*? She grins and shrugs. "He hasn't made many friends in Chicago yet."

"Shocking," I say.

Jay doesn't seem to notice my sarcasm. "We thought it'd be nice to introduce you. You know, maybe have the two of you for dinner."

A blind date with a Byzantine geek is about as appealing to me as the mom clique is to Shelley. "Thanks, but I don't think so."

Shelley gives me a sidelong glance. "What, you're dating someone?"

I smooth down Emma's hair and consider my love life since breaking up with Andrew. One measly false alarm with Brad . . . and that's it. Not a single date. I couldn't be more pitiful! I straighten in my chair, trying to muster up a shred of pride. Dr. Taylor springs to mind, just in time.

"There's this man I've been talking to on the phone. He's my student's doctor. We tried to get together a couple of times, but so far it hasn't worked out."

Shelley scowls. "That widower you were telling me about? You're not serious."

I raise my chin. "He happens to be really nice."

Jay tousles my hair. "So is Regis Philbin." He grins and slides into the chair beside me. "Just meet Herbert. It won't kill you. Besides, time is of the essence, isn't it?"

"Don't remind me." I blow out a huff of air. "These last five goals are killing me. Falling in love and having a baby are two of the biggest events in a person's life. You don't just decide you're going to do it and *wham!* it happens. These are matters of the heart. They can't be checked off, like eggs and cheese on a grocery list."

"Exactly," Shelley says. "That's why it's important to get back out there. It's a game of odds. The more men you meet, the better your chances of finding one you actually love."

"Oh, now that's romantic." I kiss Emma's head. "So who is this guy, Herbert? And who names their kid Herbert, anyway?"

"Apparently rich people," Jay says. "His father has over thirty patents. They have houses on each coast, along with a private island in the Caribbean. Herbert's an only child."

"He's not going to be interested in someone like me. I'm a schoolteacher. I live in Pilsen, for God's sake."

Shelley waves me off. "That's just temporary. Jay told him all about the delayed inheritance."

My mouth drops. "What?" I turn to Jay. "Why would you do that?"

"You want him to know you're in his league, don't you?"

An uneasy feeling comes over me. Is this how I used to be? Did I judge people on where they lived, or how much money they made? As much as I hate to admit it, I think I did. Wasn't *What do you do for a living?* one of the first questions I'd ask when meeting someone new? Was it just coincidence that all of the friends Andrew and I hung out with were wealthy and fit and attractive? I shudder. No wonder my mother forced me to shift lanes, away from that superficial, fast-paced freeway I was barreling down. The lane I'm in now may be slower, and the scenery not nearly as glamorous, but for the first time in years I'm enjoying the ride.

"If he wouldn't be comfortable dating the woman I am now, I don't want to meet him."

Shelley shakes her head. "Now *you're* being judgmental. Lighten up. It's just one night. I'm thinking next Saturday —"

Lucky for me, my cell phone interrupts further plotting. I peek at the caller ID.

"I'm going to take this. It's Johnny."

Jay takes Emma from me and Shelley moves to the sink to refill the teapot.

"Hello, John," I say into the phone. "How's Zoë?"

"Hi, Brett. I've got great news. I think this revolving door is finally going to stop. Zoë is coming home, this time for good."

"Fantastic!" I say. I turn to Shelley and give her a thumbs-up. "You must be so relieved."

"I am. And we'd love it if you could come visit us."

I pause. "Really?"

"It would be easier if you'd come our way this time, if that's okay. I'll send you the airfare."

"No, no, that's no problem."

"Listen, I insist. What do you say? Any chance you could get away?"

I bite my lip to keep my smile from hijacking my entire face. "I've got a couple of personal days I could use. Maybe sometime in March, once Zoë's had time to settle in?"

"Sounds like a plan. We're dying to meet you. Listen, I better get back to Zoë. Her doctor should be in any minute with the discharge papers. Check out the flights and let me know what you decide."

I hang up the phone. My head feels light, as if I might faint.

"You okay?" Jay asks.

I nod. "I'm finally going to meet my dad! And my sister, too!"

Shelley rushes to me. "Oh, Brett! That's wonderful."

"Good going," Jay says. "Now meet Herbert and make it a trifecta."

CHAPTER TWENTY-THREE

The following Saturday, I take the forty-minute combined bus–train trip uptown to find a good bottle of wine for tonight's dinner with Jay and Shelley . . . and Herbert. My stomach pitches every time I think of this damn date. I'm too old for first dates. And even when I was dating, blind dates were excruciating. They're the lowest rung on the dating ladder. Blind dates are nothing more than a lesson in humility, a time when you actually get to see what other people think you deserve.

The arduous trip uptown is successful, and by one o'clock I leave Fox & Obel toting a 2007 bottle of Argentinean Malbec. Clutching my conspicuous brown-paper bag, I trudge back to the train station.

The station is abuzz at midday. I'm carried along with the crowd until we reach a bottleneck at the turnstile. That's when I spot him. The Burberry man! The guy who spilled coffee on me. I haven't seen him since Thanksgiving morning, running along

Lake Michigan with his black Lab. He's through the turnstile and already making his way down the stairs to the station.

Time crawls as I maneuver past the crowd and through the metal turnstile. I work my way toward the stairs, zigzagging though a gaggle of tourists, craning my neck to catch a glimpse of Burberry. My heart pounds in my temples. Where did he go? I join the herd moving en masse down an escalator. Stepping to the left, I hustle past idle riders, all the while keeping an eye out for Burberry. I'm halfway down the escalator when I hear the rattle of a train. I watch the mob on the left side of the platform come alive. People pick up their bags, end their phone calls, and gravitate toward the approaching train.

There he is! He's standing on the platform waiting to board the northbound train. He's holding his cell phone at his ear, smiling. My heart does a little cartwheel. Maybe I can catch this train. Who cares that it's going in the opposite direction? I can finally meet this man!

"Excuse me," I say to the girl in front of me. She's listening to her iPod and can't hear me. I tap her shoulder and she curses as I press past her. Squeezing against and around lollygaggers, I'm almost down the escalator when the doors to the train open. Passengers exit, and for a moment I've lost Burberry. A ripple of panic spreads over me. But then I find him. He's taller than most of the others, and his wavy hair is a very dark brown. He stands aside while an older woman boards. I dash down the final steps. The last passengers board the train. My feet hit the concrete and skitter down the narrow platform toward Burberry's compartment.

I hear the double bells and the recorded voice announce, "Doors closing." I run faster, nearly full out.

Just as I reach the door, it slams shut. I slap the Plexiglas window.

"Wait!" I say aloud.

The train shoots off, and from the window I swear I see Burberry. I think he's watching me. Yes, he is! He lifts his hand and waves.

I wave back, wondering whether we're waving hello or goodbye.

Thoughts of this mystery man trail me as I drive to Shelley and Jay's. What if I arrive and discover the gorgeous man in the Burberry coat is none other than Herbert Moyer? In a couple of weeks I'm meeting my father and sister — so anything is possible! I laugh at my foolishness, but my stomach knots the moment I pull into Jay and Shelley's driveway. It's been so long since I've been on a date. What will we talk about? What if he's disappointed?

I make my way up the walk, my heart pounding beneath my black trench coat. Why did I agree to this? But of course I know the answer. I agreed to meet Herbert because in the next six months I'm required to fall in love and have babies. I blow out a huff of frustration and ring the bell.

"Anyone home?" I call, opening the door.

"Come in." Jay steps into the foyer and gives me a once-over. "Wow! If you weren't my sister, I'd say you looked hot."

I'm wearing a black skirt and tights, with a clingy sweater and my cruel black pumps. I kiss his cheek and whisper, "All this effort for a guy named Herbert. Dinner better be good."

I hear footsteps approach. When I spin around, an absolute god appears in the foyer.

"Dr. Moyer," Jay says. "Meet my sister, Brett."

He moves toward me with his hand outstretched. It's large and soft and manly, all at once. His clear blue eyes meet mine as we shake hands. All thoughts of the Burberry man vanish.

"Hello, Brett." He smiles and his chiseled features become warm and friendly.

"Hi, Herbert." I stare up at him stupidly. So this is the kind of guy my brother thinks I deserve? I'm most definitely flattered.

Dr. Moyer's manners are as impeccable as his Armani sports coat. I watch as he swirls his after-dinner brandy, the stem of the crystal snifter casually planted between his index and middle fingers. Refined, white bread. Not a grain of chaff.

Miles from their conversation about ancient Greece, I sip my brandy, thinking how completely incongruent his name is with that gorgeous exterior.

"Herbert," I mumble.

Three pairs of eyes turn to me.

With the permission of two glasses of wine and a brandy, I bluntly ask, "Where did you get that name? Herbert?"

Across the table, my brother's eyes go wide in disbelief. Shelley pretends to read the label on the brandy bottle. But Herbert just laughs.

"It's familial," he says. "I was named after my grandfather Moyer. I tried using nicknames from time to time, but Herb seemed too botanical, and Bert, well, that wasn't an option. You see, my best friend all through school was a guy named Ernest Walker, and we weren't exactly the coolest sodas in the fridge. You can only imagine the Bert and Ernie jokes we would have endured had I insisted on Bert."

I laugh. What do you know? Gorgeous *and* funny.

"And when you used your full names, the idiots never made the *Sesame Street* connection?" Jay asks.

"Nope." He leans into the table and holds up his index finger, as if he's standing at a lectern. "Though technically they were morons, not idiots. You see, an idiot is a dumb person whose mental age is less than three years, while a moron is a dumb person whose mental age is between seven and twelve."

The three of us stare at him, speechless. Finally, Jay laughs and slaps his back. "Get a life, you repugnant pedant!" He shakes his head and reaches for the brandy bottle. "Another drink?"

*I*t's after midnight when we say good-bye to Jay and Shelley. Herbert walks me to my car. We stand under a star-strewn sky, and I plant my hands in my coat pockets.

"That was fun," I say.

"It was. I'd love to see you again. Are you free at all next week?"

I wait for my heart to leap from my chest, but it just keeps beating its regular steady rhythm. "I'm free Wednesday night."

"Could I take you to dinner, say, sevenish?"

"Sounds great."

He leans over and pecks me on the cheek, then opens my car door. "I'll call you Monday to confirm. Drive safely."

I drive away, wondering what my mom would think of Herbert. Would he be the kind of man she would choose for my future husband and the father of my children? I think so. Did she play a part in setting me up with him? I'm guessing she might have.

I look both ways at an intersection and see it on my passenger seat. The bottle of Malbec I journeyed uptown for. I forgot to take it in. What a pointless trip — except for that glimpse of my Burberry man.

*T*he next three weeks dissolve as quickly as the last patches of snow. As planned, Herbert and I have dinner Wednesday night, which leads to dozens of phone calls and six additional dates, each one a bit more interesting than the one before. He has so many qualities I genuinely love, like when I'm telling a funny story and the corners of his lips curl into a smile before I even reach the punch line. Or the way he makes sure I'm his final telephone call, because he wants me to be the last person he talks to before he drifts off to sleep.

But other things — small, insignificant, quirky things — nearly derail me. Like the way he refers to himself as *Doctor* Moyer to everyone he meets, as if the waitress or the maître d' actually needs to know his title. And when they assume he's a medical doctor rather than a man with a doctoral degree in history, he doesn't correct them.

But wasn't I the one who told Megan and Shelley that life isn't perfect? That we're all just getting through this journey as best we can, and we need to compromise? And it's hardly fair to call Herbert a compromise. In every objective way, he's a catch-and-a-half.

Yesterday we celebrated Chicago's favorite and most raucous holiday, Saint Patrick's Day. But rather than swilling green beer with a mob of friends alongside the emerald-dyed river, like Andrew and I used to do, Herbert served me Irish fondue by candlelight. It felt very grown-up and dignified. He chose the movie *Once* to watch afterward, a romantic musical set in Dublin. I lay cuddled in his arms on the sofa, marveling at his thoughtfulness. Later, we stood on his deck and gazed out at a moonlit Lake Michigan. A breeze blew in and he wrapped me in his coat. Holding me snug against his chest, he pointed out the constellations.

"Most people refer to the Big Dipper as a constellation, but it is actually an asterism. The stars of the dipper are part of the larger constellation Ursa Major."

"Huh," I said, studying the star-strewn heavens. "Just think, next Thursday I'll be up in that very sky, on my way to Seattle."

"I'll miss you," he said, brushing his cheek against my hair. "I'm growing quite fond of you, you know."

A snicker burst from my chest before I had time to tamp it down. "C'mon Herbert, growing quite fond? Who uses terms like, *growing quite fond*?"

He stared at me, and I thought I'd gone too far. But then his face flooded with humor and he offered up his dazzling white grin. "All right, smarty-pants, so I'm not exactly hip. Welcome to the world of nerd dating."

I smiled. "Nerd dating?"

"That's right. In case you haven't heard, we nerds happen to be the best-kept secret in the dating world. We're smart, successful, we never cheat. Hell, we're just happy someone actually likes us." He turned his gaze to the lake. "And we make excellent marriage material."

For four years I couldn't get Andrew to utter the *M* word. And there was Herbert, hinting at it after only six dates.

I pressed closer to him. "I think I'm going to like nerd dating," I said. And I meant it.

The bright morning rays stream through my office window, and I hum while I pack my satchel for the day ahead. I'm searching for a watercolor paint set for my new kindergartner when the telephone rings. It's Garrett.

"I'm glad I caught you before you left the office. Peter had another violent outburst last night. Autumn couldn't contain him. Luckily, the neighbors heard the ruckus and came to help. I'd hate to think what Peter might have done."

"Oh, no! Poor Autumn." I rub my arms, imagining the horrible scene.

"I just got off the phone with the folks at New Pathways. They've agreed to open a spot for him. He'll start later this week, but as of today there will be no more homebound visits."

A surprising melancholy comes over me. Against all odds, I

was still hoping for a happy ending — an ending where Peter made progress and was able to return to his old school, the one with ordinary kids who don't need therapy two times a day.

"But I never even got to say good-bye."

"I'll be sure to tell him for you."

"And remind him how smart he is, tell him I wish him luck."

"Absolutely." He pauses, and when he speaks again, his tone is gentle. "You learn with these cases that you can't save them all. It's a tough lesson, especially for someone like you, who's young and idealistic. I was the same way when I first started my practice."

"It feels like I'm deserting him," I say. "Maybe if I'd had more time . . ."

"No," he says firmly. "I'm sorry, Brett, I'm not going to let you second-guess yourself. You did everything you could to help Peter, and then some. And you've been a tremendous help to me. I've really enjoyed working with you."

"I liked working with you, too." My voice breaks. I'm shocked at how choked up I am, knowing I'm losing my connection to this man I've come to love and trust. I clear my throat. "I want to thank you. You were really there for me, not just with Peter, but with everything I was going through."

"It was a pleasure. Truly." He hesitates a moment, and when he speaks his tone is lighter. "You do realize, don't you, that you still owe me a drink?"

The question catches me off-guard. It's been weeks since we last mentioned that drink. I've come a long way since those bleak days last January when I was frantic to find a man and fall in love. Now I'm dating, arguably, the most eligible man in Chicago. Still, a part of me is curious about Dr. Taylor. I rub my temples.

"Um, yeah, sure."

"Everything okay?" Garret asks. "You seem hesitant."

I blow out a stream of air. Hell, I've told the man everything else, I may as well be upfront now. "I'd love to meet you for a drink. It's just that I started seeing someone recently . . ."

"Not a problem," Garrett says. He's so gracious that I feel silly now. He probably had no romantic intentions whatsoever, and thinks I'm full of myself for assuming he did. "I hope things work out for you, Brett."

"Yeah, well, thanks."

"Listen, I'll let you go. Let's keep in touch."

"Yes, let's," I say, knowing that we won't.

I hang up from the last conversation I'll have with Dr. Taylor. Like the final chapter of a book, it's bittersweet. There will be no more help from Garrett, and certainly no romance. And deep inside I realize it's probably for the best. I've got Herbert now, and a new family I'm about to meet. Maybe Dr. Taylor really was a character in my mother's play. He entered at a critical point, just when I needed him, and exited stage right, exactly as the script intended.

I find the paint set I was searching for and grab my coat. I turn out the lights and close the door, making sure to lock it behind me.

CHAPTER TWENTY-FOUR

I watch the city of Seattle take shape from the window of the 757. It's a cloudy afternoon, but once we begin our descent, the ribbons of Lake Washington appear. It's beautiful, this jigsaw piece of land surrounded by threads of blue water. I search the cityscape and nearly cry out when I spy the Space Needle. The plane descends and miniature blocks of houses emerge. I stare, mesmerized, knowing somewhere down there, in one of those little blocks of concrete and wood, lives a man and his daughter, my father and my half sister.

Along with the other passengers, I traipse to baggage claim, where hordes of people await their travelers. I search out the faces. Some seem impatient, holding up hand-printed signs with names on them. Others seem excited, bouncing on the balls of their feet while seeking out the passengers. One by one, everyone around me seems to claim their friends and relatives. But I stand alone, sweaty and nauseous.

I scan the crowd for a dark-haired man with a twelve-year-old girl. *Where are you, Johnny and Zoë?* Did they forget I was coming today? Could Zoë have fallen ill again? I pull my cell phone from my purse. I'm checking for messages when I hear my name.

"Brett?"

I spin around. In front of me stands a tall, silver-haired man. He's clean-shaven and borderline preppy. His eyes find mine, and when he smiles I see the man from the video, the man he was thirty-four years ago. I hide my trembling chin and nod.

As if he, too, doesn't trust his voice, he opens his arms to me. I step to him, closing my eyes and breathing in the scent of his leather coat. I let my head fall against the cool leather and he rocks me back and forth. For the first time, I know what it feels like to be held by my father.

"You're beautiful," he says, finally pulling away and holding me at arm's length. "You look just like your mother."

"But I got my height from you, I see."

"Your eyes, too." He takes my face in his hands and stares into it. "My God, I'm glad you found me."

Joy floods my soul. "Me too."

He tosses my carry-on bag over his shoulder and drapes his other arm around my shoulder. "Let's get your suitcase, then we'll pick Zoë up from school. She's nearly beside herself with excitement."

We talk nonstop on our way to Franklin L. Nelson Center, Zoë's private school. Every question he'd failed to ask during our phone conversations he asks now. I can't stop grinning. My father is actually interested in me, and what's more, there's an ease and familiarity between us that I hadn't even dared hope for. But when he veers down the tree-lined entrance to the school, the ugly jealous monster inside me springs to life again. As excited as I am to meet Zoë, I want more time with Johnny. Alone. When she climbs into the car, I'll be the outsider once again, a role I've grown weary of.

Nelson Center is a sprawling, one-story building, beautifully landscaped and tended. Tuition here must cost a fortune.

"School isn't over for another ten minutes, but Zoë wanted her classmates to meet her new sister. You don't mind, do you?"

"No, of course not."

He holds open one of the steel double doors and I pass through to a large vestibule. On a wooden bench, a little girl wearing a navy uniform sits swinging her legs in front of her. She jumps to her feet when she sees me, but then hesitates. When John moves through the door, she lets out a whoop.

"Daddy!" Her round face is utterly gleeful. She lumbers full force toward us and locks her pudgy arms around my hips. I hug her, but she only comes to my rib cage. John looks on, grinning.

"Okay, Zoë," he says, tapping the top of her head. "Better let your sister breathe."

She finally loosens her grip on me. "You my sister," she declares.

I squat down next to her and gaze into her smooth, alabaster face. How could I have ever resented this angel? Her shiny hair is dark, like her dad's and mine. But unlike our brown eyes, hers are green and shrouded with extra folds of skin.

"Yes, I am. We're sisters, you and I."

She smiles at me and the shiny, sea-green marbles become half-moon slits. Her thick pink tongue peeks out from between a vast overbite. I instantly love this girl who is my sister . . . this girl who has Down syndrome.

With one hand in John's and the other in mine, she pulls us down the hall toward her classroom. Along the way, John points out some of the special facilities at the school. One hallway is designed as a city street. Storefronts line both sides of the brick street, with traffic lights and crossing signals at each intersection.

"This area teaches the kids how to cross streets safely, how to interact with store clerks, how to figure money when purchasing items, and so forth."

When we finally reach Zoë's classroom, we step into a frenzy of activity as Miss Cindy, Zoë's bright-eyed teacher, and her assistant, Mr. Kopec, work to get their eight mentally challenged students ready for dismissal. Mr. Kopec zips the coat of a boy behind a walker. "Harvey, you need to keep your coat zipped, ya hear? It's cold out there today."

"Who's missing a scarf?" Miss Cindy calls from the coatroom, holding up a red snake of wool.

"Look," Zoë announces in her raspy voice. "This my sister." With that, her face erupts in joy, and she rubs her palms together like she's making fire. Gripping my hand, she leads me around the room, pointing to pictures on the wall, showing me the fish tank, telling me the names of her friends. In all my life, I've never felt more worshiped.

Before we leave, John drives us around the thirty-acre Nelson complex. Zoë points to the playground.

"Her favorite place," John says, reaching behind him to squeeze Zoë's leg. "And there's the greenhouse, where the kids learn to tend plants."

We cruise past clay tennis courts and a newly paved asphalt track. Passing a red barn, I spot a wooden sign: THERAPEUTIC HORSEBACK RIDING PROGRAM.

"What's that?"

"That was the equine center. The kids learned to ride horses. The original intent was to help with their balance and coordination, but you'd be amazed what it did for their self-confidence."

"Pluto!" Zoë cries from the backseat.

John smiles into his rearview mirror. "Yeah, you loved that

ol' horse, Pluto." He glances at me. "It was an expensive program. With budget cuts, they had to shut it down last fall."

In my mind, a lightbulb flickers to life.

As promised on SeattleTravel.com, the drizzle hasn't let up since I arrived. But that's fine with me. I'm perfectly content to stay inside John and Zoë's cozy brick ranch on Friday. Brightly colored rugs cover the oak floors, and wooden bookshelves span the walls. In every available space and cranny I find interesting paintings and artwork, all from places John visited when he was a traveling musician. Zoë was allowed to play hooky today, and the three of us sit on a Navajo rug playing Crazy Eights while obscure indie musicians seduce me on the stereo.

It's six o'clock in the evening, and John decides it's time to fix his famous eggplant Parmesan. Zoë and I follow him into the kitchen and make a salad.

"Okay, Zoë, now we shake it, just like this." I shake the salad dressing carafe and hand it to her. "Your turn."

"I make dressing," she says, shaking the glass container with both hands. But suddenly, the plastic lid loosens. Ranch dressing explodes, raining down the cabinets and pooling onto the countertop.

"I'm so sorry!" I cry. "I didn't check the lid." I grab a dishcloth, anxious to clean up the mess that I've created. But behind me, I hear laughter.

"Zoë, come take a look at yourself!"

I spin around and see John leading Zoë to the oven door, where she can see her reflection. Blobs of white dressing cling to her hair and dot her face. Zoë thinks it's hilarious. She scoops a dab from her cheek and licks her fingers.

"Yummy yummy."

John laughs and pretends to snack on a lock of her hair. She squeals with delight. I watch this father–daughter scene, so unlike any in my memory, and work to etch it forever into my mind.

When we finally sit down to eat, John lifts his wineglass. "To my beautiful daughters," he says. "I am a lucky man."

Zoë lifts her tumbler of milk, and we all clink glasses.

After lighthearted dinner conversation, we loiter at the oak table, listening to tales of John's early days after leaving Chicago. When he sees Zoë rubbing her eyes, he pushes back from the table.

"Let's get you into your PJs, sleepy girl. It's bedtime."

"No. I stay with my sister."

"Zoë?" I ask. "Can I help you get ready for bed tonight?"

Her eyes go wide and she slips from her chair, grabbing me by the hand. We're nearly out of the kitchen when she glances back at her dad. "You stay. My sister help me."

John chuckles. "Okay, Miss Bossy Pants."

She leads me into her cotton-candy palace of lavenders and pinks. Tieback lace curtains frame the windows, and her small bed is a jungle of stuffed animals.

"I love your room," I say, clicking on her bedside lamp.

She changes into purple Tinker Bell pajamas and I help her brush her teeth. Then she climbs into her twin bed and pats a place beside her. "You go sleep now."

"Can I read you a story?"

"Libya!" she says. "Libya!"

I crouch down in front of her book nook and search the titles for a story about Libya, to no avail. Finally, I spot a story about a pig named Olivia.

"This one?" I ask, holding up the book.

She grins. "Libya!" I snuggle up beside her and lay my head on the pillow next to hers. She turns to me, smelling of peppermint toothpaste and vanilla shampoo, and kisses my cheek. "Read," she commands, pointing to the book.

Midway through the story, her breathing slows and her eyes fall shut. Taking great care, I unbraid my arm from beneath her neck and douse the bedside lamp. The room glows pink from her Little Mermaid night-light.

"I love you, Zoë," I whisper, bending down to kiss her cheek. "What a lesson you are to me."

When I return to the kitchen, the table is cleared and the dishwasher hums. I refill my wineglass and move to the living room, where John sits with his guitar perched like a toddler on his knee. He smiles when he sees me.

"Have a seat. Can I get you anything? More wine? A cup of coffee?"

I lift my glass. "All set." I sit down on the chair next to his, admiring the dark glossy wood-and-ivory inlay of his guitar. "That's beautiful."

"Thanks. I love this old Gibson." He plucks a few notes before ducking out from under the leather strap. "It's what kept me sane during those times in life when the waters were rising faster than I could bail." With the care of a lover, he places the instrument in its metal cradle. "Do you play?"

"I'm afraid that gene sailed right past me."

He chuckles. "What were you like as a child, Brett?"

We settle back in our chairs and for the next two hours exchange questions and stories, tales and anecdotes, trying to fill in the missing pieces to a thirty-four-year puzzle.

"You remind me so much of your mother," he says.

"That's such a compliment. I miss her so much."

His eyes are heavy, and he looks down at his hands. "Yeah, me too."

"Did you ever try to keep in touch with her?"

His jaw twitches ever so slightly. As if it's his talisman, he pulls the guitar from its cradle and sets it on his knee. Keeping his eyes downcast, he picks at the strings, sending random, melancholy notes adrift. Finally he looks up at me.

"Charles Bohlinger was a piece of work." He blows out a stream of air as if he'd been holding it for three decades. "I wanted to marry your mother. Leaving her was the hardest thing I've ever done. I loved her the way I've never loved another woman. Ever."

I shake my head. "But you broke her heart, John. It was clear from her journal that she would have left Charles and followed you, but you didn't want to settle down."

He flinches. "That's not exactly true. You see, when your dad found out —"

"Charles," I say, interrupting him. "He was never a dad to me."

John looks at me and nods. "When *Charles* found out your mother and I had fallen in love, he was livid. He forced her to make a decision, either him or me. She looked him square in the eyes and said she loved me." He smiles, as if the memory is still sweet. "She marched out of the kitchen then. Before I could follow her, Charles grabbed me by the arm. He promised me that if Elizabeth left, she'd never see her boys again."

"What? He couldn't do that."

"Remember, that was back in the seventies. Things were different then. He swore he'd testify that she was a slut, an unfit mother. I smoked my share of weed back then, and he threatened to paint me as the pothead boyfriend. It wasn't hard to figure out whom the courts would side with. I was nothing but a liability to her."

"God, that's horrible."

"Losing Joad and Jay would have killed her. In the end I lied, so she wouldn't have to choose. I told her I didn't want a permanent relationship." He shakes his head, as if trying to clear a bad dream. "That nearly did me in. But I knew your mother. If she lost her boys she'd never recover.

"We stood on the front porch. It was hotter than hell that afternoon. All the windows in the house were open. I was sure Charles was listening. But I didn't care. I told your mother I loved her, that I'd always love her. But I just wasn't the staying kind. I swear to God she saw through me. When she kissed me good-bye for the last time, she whispered, 'You know where to find me.'"

I ache for the sad woman in the navy maxi coat, pulling her sons in the wagon. "She thought you'd come back for her."

John nods, composing himself before continuing. "God, I can still see those eyes, green as the Irish hills and unwavering in their belief in me."

I swallow the lump in my throat. "But they divorced later. Couldn't you have gone to her then?"

"I lost track of her. Once I left, I convinced myself I'd done the right thing. I tried my damnedest not to torture myself with what-ifs. For years this old guitar was about the only thing that brought me any pleasure.

"Fifteen years later I met Zoë's mother. We were together eight years, though we never married."

"Where is she now?"

"Melinda moved back to Aspen — that's where her family lives. Motherhood wasn't her thing."

I want to know more, but don't ask. I'm guessing a child with Down syndrome wasn't her thing.

"I'm sorry," I say, "for all your losses."

He shakes his head. "I'm the last person who deserves sympathy. Life is good, as they say." He reaches over and squeezes my hand. "And only getting better."

I smile at him. "I wonder why my mom didn't contact you when she divorced, or after Charles died."

"My guess is that in those early days she waited for me, expecting a letter or a phone call, some form of contact. But as time passed, and that letter never arrived, she decided I didn't love her after all."

A shiver goes through me. Did my mother die thinking the love of her life was a fraud? Suddenly I blurt out a question that has been plaguing me for weeks.

"John, why haven't you asked for a paternity test? Or maybe you do want one, which is fine with me."

"No. No, I don't. Not for a moment did I doubt you were my daughter."

"Why not? Everyone else questioned it. I could be Charles's daughter just as easily as I am yours."

He pauses and strums a random chord. "Charles had a vasectomy after Jay was born. Your mother told me about it soon after we became friends."

I blink, stunned. "He knew I wasn't his child? God, no wonder he didn't like me."

"And he'd only have to take a look at you if he needed further proof."

"I was an unwanted pregnancy. I never knew that."

"Now, that's where you're wrong. Your mother was devastated when she found out he'd had the procedure. She told me so. She'd wanted another child. In fact, she told me she'd always wanted a daughter."

"She did?"

"Very much. You can't imagine how thrilled I was when Mr. Pohlonski informed me I'd given her such a priceless gift."

I lift my hand to my mouth. "And she gave the gift back to us when she left me that journal."

His eyes smile and he reaches out his hand to me. "You're the gift that keeps on giving."

———

By Saturday, it feels like I'm leaving my family rather than the two strangers I met on arrival. I squat next to Zoë in the airport lobby and hug her to my chest. She clings to me, clutching my sweater. When she pulls away, she holds out her thumb.

"My sister."

I press my thumb against hers, our new ritual. "I love you, my sister. I'll call you tonight, okay?"

John pulls me into a giant bear hug. His arms are strong and protective, the way I always imagined a father's hug would be. I breathe deeply and close my eyes. The scent of his leather jacket mingles with his spicy cologne, smells that will forever be my dad's. Finally, he loosens his grip and holds me at arm's length.

"When can we see you again?"

"Come to Chicago," I say. "I want everyone to meet you and Zoë."

"We will." He kisses me and pats my back. "Now scoot, before you miss your flight."

"Wait. I have something for you." I reach into my bag and retrieve my mother's leather journal. "I want you to have this."

He nestles it in both his hands as if it were the Holy Grail. I see the little muscle in his jaw twitch, and I kiss his cheek.

"If you ever doubted her love for you, you won't once you've read this. All of Elizabeth's feelings are here, in black and white."

"Are there other journals? Did she continue to write after I left?"

"No. I searched the house wondering the same thing, but I never found another. I think her story ended with you."

Five hours later, the plane touches down at O'Hare. I glance at my watch. Ten thirty-five, twelve minutes early. I turn on my cell phone and discover a text message from Herbert. *Meet you at baggage claim.*

I've never dated a nicer guy. Now I won't have to hail a cab. I won't have to schlep these bags by myself. I'll get to see Herbert. But for the life of me, I can't muster any enthusiasm. I must be tired. All I can think about is getting home to my little apartment in Pilsen, climbing into bed, and calling Zoë.

As promised, I find him in baggage claim, sitting in a metal-and-Naugahyde sling chair, reading what appears to be a text-book. His face comes alive when he sees me. He jumps up and I step into the arms of the most gorgeous man in the airport.

"Welcome home," he whispers in my ear. "I've missed you."

I pull away and stare up at him. He's beautiful. Absolutely beautiful. "Thanks. I missed you, too."

We stand holding hands, watching the conveyer belt spit suit-cases. In front of us, a baby peers over her mother's shoulder, wearing a pink headband with a bright green daisy attached to it. With wide blue eyes, she stares at Herbert, quite possibly appreci-ating the view. Herbert leans in and smiles at her.

"Hey cutie," he says. "Aren't you a pretty girl."

Already a flirt, the baby breaks into a wet, dimpled grin. Herbert laughs aloud and turns to me. "Is there anything more transcendent than a baby's smile?"

It takes me a second to translate *transcendent*. I think he means extraordinary. And at this moment, I think he's transcendent, too. On impulse I lean in and kiss his cheek. "Thank you."

He cocks his head. "What for?"

"For picking me up at the airport. And for appreciating a baby's smile."

His face turns pink and he turns his attention to the carou-sel. "I heard something about a life list you're supposed to com-plete."

I groan. "My brother has a big mouth."

He chuckles. "One of your goals was to have kids, wasn't it?"

"Uh-huh," I say, trying to sound casual. But inside my chest there's a drummer on steroids. "What about you? Do you want kids someday?"

"Absolutely. I love kids."

My suitcase falls from the chute. I step forward to fetch it but Herbert grabs hold of my arm. "I've got it."

As he steps to the carousal, the baby's eyes find mine. She studies me, as if sizing me up, deciding whether I'd make a decent mommy. I'm reminded of my time line — the one imposed by both Mother Elizabeth and Mother Nature — and wait for the familiar wave of panic to strike. But this time it doesn't.

In one fell swoop, Herbert scoops up my bag and returns to my side.

"Are we all set?" he asks. "Do you have everything you need?"

I glance at the baby, as if for confirmation. A smile lights her face. I fit my hand into the crook of Herbert's elbow. "Yes, I believe I do."

After letting Rudy out for his four A.M. potty break, I fall back into bed, taking full advantage of Sunday by sleeping until nine o'clock. My excuse is that I'm still on Pacific Time. When I finally rise, I take my coffee into my sunny living room and work the *Tribune* crossword puzzle, feeling positively decadent and happy. Rudy lies curled on the rug beside me, watching me knock off the puzzle, square by square. Finally, I pull myself from the sofa and go to my closet, where I swap my pajamas for my sweats. I clip Rudy's leash to his collar, and he turns in circles, anticipating our outing. Clutching my iPod and sunglasses, I push open the front door and scamper down the stairs.

Rudy and I start off with a leisurely stroll. I lift my face to the sun, marveling at the cloudless blue sky and the promise of spring in the air. Gusts of Chicago wind lap my cheeks, but unlike the hateful, ill-tempered gales of February, the late-March winds are kinder, more charitable, almost tender. Rudy pulls ahead of me and I have to tug at his leash to keep him from dragging me away. I check my watch when I reach 18th Street, secure my earbuds, and break into a run.

Eighteenth Street is a bustling commercial corridor with Mexican bakeries, restaurants, and grocery stores on either side. As I jog along the sidewalk, I realize my mother was right to make me venture out of my comfort zone. I never dreamed I could call a place so modest and humble my home. I picture my mother in the heavens, perched in her director's chair with a bullhorn in her hand, calling the shots for each scene of my life. Now that Herbert's a character in my play, I can actually imagine falling in love and having babies — two goals I doubted I'd ever accomplish, let alone in a matter of months.

We're all the way to Harrison Park when Rudy finally poops out. We rest a minute, then stroll back toward home. Along the way, my thoughts linger on Herbert Moyer.

He's remarkable. Last night when we left the airport, it was clear he wanted me to spend the night. And I was tempted. But when I told him I needed to retrieve Rudy, that I was exhausted and wanted to sleep in my own bed, he completely understood. I'm convinced the term *gentleman* was coined for Herbert Moyer. What's more, he's the most doting man I've ever dated. He opens doors, pulls out chairs . . . I swear if I asked him, he'd carry my purse. I've never felt more adored.

So why, I ask myself now, didn't I spend the night with him? Dog or no dog, you couldn't have kept me away from Andrew. And it has nothing to do with Herbert's ability as a lover. He's wonderful — more attentive than Andrew ever was. Herbert is exactly the kind of man I'd hoped to find and everything my mother would have wanted for me.

But still, a part of me is resisting his love. I worry sometimes whether I'm capable of a "normal" relationship, because if I'm totally honest with myself, sometimes I find Herbert's attention and kindness suffocating. I'm worried that what feels normal to me, what I've grown most comfortable with, are cold, detached guys like Charles Bohlinger and Andrew Benson. But I cannot — I will not — screw this up. I'm wiser now, more aware, and I refuse to let my past destroy my future. Guys like Herbert Moyer are as rare as genuine Louis Vuitton handbags, and I need to thank my lucky stars that I've found the real deal.

In the distance my house comes into view. I unclip Rudy's leash and we race to the front door. From its place on the end table, the light of my cell phone blinks. Herbert wants me to help him pick out bar stools today. He's probably eager to get going. I click on the voice message.

"Brett, it's Jean Anderson. Sanquita's in labor. I'm taking her to Cook County Memorial. She's asking for you."

CHAPTER TWENTY-FIVE

*B*lood rushes to my head. I bound down the stairs and pound on Selina and Blanca's door, breathless, asking if they could keep Rudy. On the way to the hospital I call Herbert.

"Hey," he says. "I was just going to call you. Can you be ready in an hour?"

"Go ahead with your shopping plans without me. I'm on my way to the hospital. Sanquita's in labor."

"I'm so sorry. Is there anything I can do?"

"Say a prayer. She's still seven weeks from her due date. I'm so worried, for her and this baby."

"Of course. Let me know if I can be of any help."

The hospital entrance looms ahead and I slow down. "Thanks. I'll call you as soon as I can."

I punch off my phone, marveling at Herbert's compassion. Andrew would never understand my need to be here with Sanquita. He'd make me feel guilty for ruining his plans. Herbert is a prince, no question about it.

Miss Jean pushes herself up from a black vinyl chair and rushes to me when I enter the small waiting room. She grips my arm and we move as one into the hall.

"It's not good," she tells me, her lids hanging heavy over her eyes. "They're doing an emergency C-section. Her potassium level is too high. They're afraid she'll go into cardiac arrest."

Just as Dr. Chan warned us. "How's the baby?"

"Distressed as all get-out." She shakes her head and puts a tissue to her nose. "This shouldn't be happening. That girl has too much life in her. And that baby made it this far, it can't die now."

"They're not going to die," I say, with more conviction than I feel. "Don't lose faith now. Everyone's going to be fine."

She glares at me with knitted brow. "You people think every storm ends with a rainbow. It's not that way with black folk. This story isn't going to have a happy ending. You might just as well know that now."

I take a step back, stabbed by another blade of fear.

Twenty minutes later, a physician steps into the waiting room, plucking her paper mask from her face. She's a young brunette who looks like she should be cheering at a high school football game instead of delivering babies. "Sanquita Bell?" she asks, her eyes scanning the waiting room.

Jean and I bolt from our chairs and meet her halfway into the room.

"How is she?" I ask. My heart's drumming so fast I fear I might pass out before I hear the news.

"I'm Dr. O'Connor," she says. "Miss Bell delivered a two-pound, four-ounce baby girl."

"Healthy?" I manage to croak.

Dr. O'Connor takes in a breath. "She's extremely malnourished and her lungs aren't fully developed. I've ordered a CPAP until she can breathe on her own. They've taken her to NICU — the neonatal intensive care unit." She shakes her head. "All things considered, she's a miracle, that little peanut."

I cover my mouth and start to cry. Miracles do happen, I want to tell Jean. But now isn't the time to gloat. "Can we see Sanquita?"

"She's being transferred to the ICU. By the time you get up there she should be settled."

"Intensive care?" My eyes search the doctor's. "She's going to be okay, isn't she?"

Dr. O'Connor gives a tight-lipped smile. "We've witnessed one miracle today. We can hope for another."

Jean and I take what seems an interminable elevator ride to the fifth floor.

"C'mon," I say, punching the button again and again.

"There's something you should know."

The gravity in Jean's voice alarms me and I turn to her. Under the fluorescent light of the elevator car, every line on her face is visible and pronounced. Her black eyes stare at me, unflinching.

"Sanquita is dying. Her baby is likely to die, too."

I turn away and study the numbers above the elevator door. "Maybe not," I whisper.

"This morning she told me if she dies, she wants you to keep her baby."

I slump against the wall, and put my hands to my head. "I can't . . . I don't . . ." My face crumbles and I choke on my tears.

She shakes her head and stares at the elevator tiles in the ceiling. "I warned her you might not want a child of mixed race."

A jolt of electricity zaps me. Suddenly, every fiber and nerve ending is firing simultaneously. "That child's race has nothing to do with it. Do you understand? Nothing! I'm honored beyond belief that she'd even consider having me raise her child." I take a deep breath and rub the knot in my throat. "But Sanquita's going to live. They're both going to live."

The curtain around Sanquita's bed is pulled shut, along with her blinds, creating a murky den filled with wires and tubes and blinking lights. She's asleep, her chapped mouth slack and her breath catching in short jerky spasms. Filled with fluid, her face is stretched tight, like a blister dangerously close to popping. Her eyes are closed, but her puffy eyelids look like they've been blackened with charcoal. I take hold of her limp hand and brush back the hair from her lifeless face.

"We're here, sweet pea. You rest now."

The faint smell of ammonia fills my nostrils. Uremia, a buildup of waste in the blood, just like I'd read about. Dread fills me.

Jean trots around her bed, tucking in blankets and smoothing down her pillow. But once she's exhausted her to-do list, she simply stares at Sanquita.

"Go home," I tell her. "There's nothing we can do. I'll call you when she wakes up."

She checks her wristwatch. "I need to get back to the shelter, but first, you run down and check on that baby girl. I'll wait with Sanquita until you get back."

———

$\mathcal{A}$ pair of locked double doors prevents my entrance to the NICU. Beside the doors, an attractive nurse with strawberry blond hair sits behind a walled reception area. She smiles when I approach.

"Can I help you?"

"Yes. I'm here to see . . ." It strikes me, this baby doesn't even have a name. "I'm here to see Sanquita Bell's baby."

She scowls, as if she's never heard of Sanquita Bell, then slowly nods. "Her baby just came in, right? The homeless baby?"

My gut clenches. Born less than an hour ago, the child has already been labeled.

"Sanquita's baby, yes."

She lifts a telephone, and almost instantly a short, dark-haired woman appears, a medical chart in her hand. Her purple scrubs are decorated with Disney characters. "Hello. I'm Maureen Marble. And you are?" she asks, flipping open the chart.

"I'm Brett Bohlinger. Sanquita's teacher."

She studies her chart. "Ah, yes. Sanquita designated you as her support person. I'll meet you inside."

A buzz rings out and the doors click open. I step into a brightly lit hallway. Nurse Maureen reappears and leads me down the corridor. "We have nine nursery rooms in the NICU, each one houses eight isolettes. Sanquita's newborn is in room seven."

I follow her into room seven, where an older man and woman stand gazing at what I'm guessing is their new grandchild. Eight incubators, or "isolettes," line the perimeter of the large room. Above almost every isolette, I notice brightly colored banners taped to the walls, or whimsical letters spelling the baby's name. Isaiah. Kaitlyn. Taylor. I spy family photos displayed inside several isolettes, and soft, hand-knitted blankets that clearly didn't come from the hospital.

Maureen points to a lone incubator in the back corner, unattended and empty of any display of love.

"Here she is."

The crib card on the front of the isolette reads, BABY GIRL. I close my eyes. It may as well say BABY DOE.

I peer inside the plastic crib. A miniature baby about the length of a ruler lies sleeping, wearing only a doll-sized diaper and a pale pink cap. Three patches adhere to her chest and stomach, delivering wires to various monitors. An IV needle affixed with clear plastic tape protrudes from a vein in her foot, and a thin tube delivering white liquid snakes into her nostrils. Surrounding her apple-sized head are two elastic straps, holding in place a clear plastic apparatus that covers her mouth and nose.

I lift a hand to my chest and turn to Maureen. "Is she going to be okay?"

"She should be just fine. The mask you see is called a CPAP," Maureen tells me. "It provides continuous positive airway pressure. Her lungs aren't fully developed. The CPAP will assist her until she's able to breathe on her own." She turns to me. "Would you like to hold her?"

"Hold her? Oh, no. No, thank you. I'd probably unplug something." I try to hide my nervous laughter by clearing my throat. "I'll let Sanquita be the first to hold her."

She gives me a sidelong glance. "You take your time getting acquainted with Baby Girl. I'll be back."

I'm left alone, staring at this wrinkled newborn, a virtual pincushion with the plethora of needles and tubes. Her round face is pinched, as if she's a bit peeved about being away from her mommy. Caramel skin, still covered with downy hair, looks as if it's several sizes too big for her. She stretches and splays her fingers, and I see five little matchsticks. My throat swells.

"Baby Girl," I whisper, but the words sound cold and impersonal. I'm reminded of the heartbreaking story of Sanquita's brother, a boy too sensitive for the world he was born into. I kiss my finger and place it on the glass where I see Baby Girl's sleeping face. "Austin," I whisper. "Welcome, beautiful Austin."

For a little boy's past and a new baby's future, for reasons known and for reasons yet to be revealed, I close my eyes and weep.

Jean bounds from the reclining chair when I return to Sanquita's room. "How's that baby?"

"Perfect," I say, trying to sound more optimistic than I feel. "Go see her."

Jean shakes her head. "Sanquita had to choose one support person. She chose you."

I look for signs of disappointment or, worse, disapproval. But to my surprise, Jean's face shows neither. I step to Sanquita's bed. She lies sleeping on her back, exactly as she was when I left her, her bloated face a cruel caricature of the once lovely girl. "Your baby is beautiful, Sanquita."

Jean grabs her purse. "You'll be okay here by yourself?"

"I'll be fine."

She swabs her eyes with a handkerchief. "Call the minute she wakes."

"I will. I promise."

She leans in and rubs her cheek against Sanquita's. "I'll be back, baby cake." Her voice breaks. "You hold on, you hear?"

I turn to the window and clap a hand over my mouth, gulping back my own tears. Then I feel Jean beside me. She reaches out a hand to touch me, but draws back before she makes contact.

"You take care of yourself," she whispers. "I'm afraid that baby's going to need you."

———

*E*very thirty minutes a nurse comes in to check Sanquita's vitals, but nothing seems to change. The hours pass like sand through molasses. I scoot a wooden chair next to the bed, so close to Sanquita I can see each shallow intake of breath. Weaving my hand through the bed's metal bar, I find her hand. While she lies sleeping, I tell her all about her precious child and the wonderful mother she's going to be.

It's late afternoon when a young woman enters the murky room. She's wearing a white smock, with strands of stringy blond hair dangling from her blue bonnet. She rummages around Sanquita's bedside table and startles when she sees me on the opposite side of the bed.

"Oh, I didn't see you there. I'm looking for her menu. Did she fill one out?"

"She won't be eating tonight, thanks."

Her eyes search out the lifeless form of Sanquita. "Think she's gonna need any more menus? I mean, I can leave one each day, or I could just wait . . ."

Blood races past my temples. I rise and snatch the menu from the woman's hand. "Yes, she'll need tomorrow's menu. Leave one every day. Do you understand? Every day."

*A*t five o'clock I dash back down to the nursery to check on Austin. After being buzzed into the NICU, I make a beeline to room seven and scrub in. Striding straight to the back corner, I gasp when I discover Austin's isolette, lit up like a tanning booth. The CPAP still covers her nose and mouth, and now her eyes are hidden beneath a pair of blindfolds. What now? My heart thunders in my chest.

I wheel around. "Maureen?" But Nurse Maureen is across the room, busy talking to the elderly couple I saw earlier.

I spy a woman in a lab coat crossing the room. "Excuse me," I say, trailing her out the door. "Could you tell me what's going on with Austin — Baby Girl? Her isolette —"

She lifts her hand and strides away. "I've got an emergency. You'll have to speak to one of the nurses."

I dart back into the room. Finally, Nurse Maureen pulls herself away from the doting grandparents. "What is it, Brett?"

"What's wrong with Sanquita's baby? Her crib is all lit up. And she's wearing blindfolds."

A machine from across the room beeps like an ornery alarm clock, and Maureen jumps to attention. "She's undergoing bili light therapy," she tells me as she scurries across the room.

I return to Austin's crib, no closer to knowing what's wrong with her. The older man I presume is Grandpa sidles up beside me and peers in at Austin. "Is this little one yours?"

"No. Her mother is one of my students."

He scowls. "Your student? How old is she?"

"Eighteen."

He shakes his head. "What a shame." He shuffles back to his wife and whispers something I can't hear.

Is this how it's going to be for this baby? People treating her like she's a mistake, the unfortunate result of a reckless teen? People overlooking her because she's poor and homeless? I rub my temples, horrified at the thought.

A pretty, dark-skinned redhead with NURSE LADONNA on her name tag appears at a neighboring isolette. "Excuse me," I say, this time with the authority of someone's caretaker.

She looks up. "How can I help you?"

"Sanquita Bell's baby," I say, pointing at the isolette. "Why is she in the tanning booth?"

Nurse LaDonna grins, revealing a friendly, gap-toothed smile. "She's under bili light therapy for hyperbilirubinemia."

"Hyperbili . . . ?" I stop, unable to reiterate the unfamiliar word. I clear my throat. "Look, I don't care if it's hyper . . . billythekid. I just need to know what's wrong with Austin. In plain English, please."

I see humor in Nurse LaDonna's eyes, but she just nods. "Fair enough. Hyperbillythekid"— she winks —"is typically referred to as jaundice. It's very common in preemies. We treat it with special blue lights that help their little bodies eliminate the excess bilirubin. The lights aren't harmful, and Baby Girl isn't in any discomfort. Her bili levels should stabilize within a day or two."

I let out a sigh of relief. "Thank God." I look at her. "And thank you."

"My pleasure. Anything else?"

"No. Not right now." I start to turn back to the baby, but stop short. "There is one more thing," I say, returning my gaze to LaDonna.

"What is it?"

"Can we please call her Austin, not Baby Girl?"

She smiles. "Fair enough."

The evening sky is dark now. I walk to the window and call Herbert. While I wait for him to answer, I gaze out over the busy city. Outside, people go about their lives, buying groceries, walking dogs, preparing dinner. Suddenly everyday life seems miraculous. Do these people know how lucky they are? A day of shopping with Herbert seems so frivolous, so greedy now.

"Hello there," he says. "Where are you?"

"At the hospital. Sanquita's in ICU. She's developed heart failure."

"Oh, sweetheart, that's distressing news."

"There's nothing I can do," I say pinching a Kleenex to my nose. "Her baby's critical, too."

"Let me come get you. I'll make you dinner. We'll watch a

movie later, or take a stroll along the lake. I'll drive you back first thing in the morning."

I shake my head. "I can't leave her. She needs me. You understand, don't you?"

"Certainly. I'd like to see you, that's all."

"I'll call you later." I start to hang up when I hear him speak again.

"Brett?"

"Yes," I say.

"I love you."

I'm stunned. He chooses this moment to declare his love? My mind races and I can't think of an appropriate response . . . besides the obvious.

"Love you, too," I finally say, before deciding whether or not I actually do.

When I walk back to my chair, Sanquita's eyes are lucid and wide open, staring straight at me through the metal bars of her bed rail. I freeze. My mother died with her eyes open, too. But then I see the slight rise and fall of the blanket when she breathes. Thank God. I lean in over the bedrail.

"Congratulations, sweet pea. You've got a beautiful baby daughter."

Her eyes lock on mine, as if begging to hear more.

"She's doing great," I lie. "She's absolutely perfect."

Her puffy lip quivers, and her body trembles. She's crying. I brush back the hair from her forehead. Her skin feels like ice.

"You're freezing, sweetie."

Her teeth chatter, and she gives me the slightest nod. I look around, but find no spare blankets. What further torture must this child endure? And where's her mom, damn it? In all the years she's been ill, has anyone ever comforted this child? Has she ever felt a mother's loving embrace? I want nothing more than to take her in my arms, to make her feel warm and safe and loved. So I do.

I lower the bedrail and reposition the cords and tubes connected to her hands and chest. She feels almost weightless as I carefully slide her to one side of the bed. Then, inching my way ever so cautiously, I climb in beside her.

As tenderly as if she were made of crystal, I fold her into my arms. I smell ammonia again, heavier this time. Uremia. Is her body shutting down? Please, God, no! Not now.

I wrap the blankets tighter around her delicate frame. Her entire body trembles, as if she were electrified. I hold her close against my chest, hoping she'll capture the heat of my body. With my cheek resting on her head, I rock her, and softly sing my favorite lullaby against her ear.

"Somewhere . . . over the rainbow . . ."

I hope she doesn't notice the quiver in my voice, or how I have to stop every few words to dislodge the knot in my throat. Midway through the song, her quaking body settles into stillness. I stop rocking, suddenly seized with panic. But then I hear a voice, so hoarse and faint it's barely audible.

"Baby."

I gaze down at her, past a bald patch she'd scratched raw, and force my lips into a smile.

"Just wait until you see her, Sanquita. She's tiny, not much bigger than my hand, but she has a strong will, just like her mommy. You can see it even now. And she's got your pretty long fingers."

A single tear trails down her bloated face. My heart shatters.

I dab her cheek with the cotton sheet. "The nurses are taking great care of her until you get stronger."

"Won't . . . get . . . stronger," she whispers.

"Stop!" I bite the inside of my cheek so hard I taste blood. I can't let her know how scared I am. "You've got to fight, Sanquita! Your baby is depending on you."

With what seems to be Herculean strength, she lifts her face to mine. "You. Take . . . my baby. Please."

I swallow hard. "I won't need to. You're going to get better."

She glares at me, her eyes wild with desperation. "Please!"

A sob racks my body. I no longer try to hide it from her. She knows her fate. And she needs to know her baby's.

"I will take your baby," I tell her, choking on my sobs. "I'll make sure she has a wonderful life. We'll talk about you every day." I cover my mouth and a moan escapes me. "I'll tell her how smart you were . . . how hard you worked."

"Loved . . . her."

I close my eyes and nod until I can finally speak again. "I'll tell her you loved her more than life itself."

CHAPTER TWENTY-SIX

*S*anquita's funeral is a poor reflection of her courageous young life. She's buried in her gold cap and gown at Oak Woods Cemetery three days after her daughter's birth, surrounded by her friends from Joshua House, Jean Anderson, two teachers, and Herbert and me. Standing graveside, Jean's pastor prays over the coffin and gives an impersonal eulogy to the girl he never met. Afterward, the group splinters, Jean rushing back to Joshua House, the teachers back to their jobs. I watch Tanya, Julonia, and the rest of the women walk up the grassy hill toward East 67th Street to catch the bus. Tanya lights a cigarette, takes a long drag, and passes it to Julonia.

That's it. It's over. Sanquita Bell's eighteen years of life are now a memory, a memory that will fade a bit each day. The thought makes me shudder.

Herbert looks over at me. "Are you okay, love?"

"I need to get to the hospital." I reach for my seat belt, but he grabs my hand.

"You're running yourself ragged, between work and the hospital. I've barely seen you this week."

"Austin needs me."

He lifts my hand to his lips and kisses it. "Sweetheart, Austin is getting all the care she needs. Take a break today. Let me take you out for a nice dinner."

He's right. Austin probably wouldn't miss me. But the fact is, I'd miss her. I look into his eyes hoping he'll understand. "I can't."

Of course, he does. Without so much as a sigh of frustration, he slides the car into gear and heads to the hospital.

I rush to Austin's isolette, expecting to see the blue lights I've grown accustomed to. Instead, her blindfolds are off and the blue lights have vanished. She lies curled up on her stomach, her head on its side. Her eyes are open. I squat down and peer in at her.

"Hello, little one," I say. "You look so pretty."

Nurse LaDonna comes up beside me. "Her blood levels have normalized. No more bili lights! Would you like to hold her?"

For the past two days, while she's been under the lights, I've put my hands inside the isolette to rub her skin, but I've not yet held her.

"Uh, sure," I say. "If it's okay. I don't want to hurt her."

LaDonna chuckles. "You'll do fine. She's more resilient than you think, and she needs human touch right now."

The nurses have been especially kind to me since Sanquita's death. They know of my plans to adopt Austin, and I'm treated like a new mom now, rather than a visitor. But unlike the bright-eyed, confident new mothers I see around me, I feel clumsy and unprepared. Sanquita trusted me with her only child. The welfare of this rumpled little alien rests squarely on my shoulders. But what if I fail her, the same way I failed Peter Madison?

LaDonna raises the lid of the isolette and cradles Austin in her hands while adjusting the wires, the nasal feeding tube, and the CPAP mask. She repositions the photo I've placed in Austin's isolette — Sanquita's high school ID — and grabs a blanket. She wraps Austin into a tight little bundle. "Babies like to be swaddled," she tells me, and hands me the tiny papoose.

Austin feels almost weightless. She's lost two ounces since her birth, which LaDonna tells me is normal, but I can't help but worry. Unlike healthy babies, Austin has no weight to spare. I position her in the crook of my arm and she's practically lost. Her forehead scrunches, but because of the CPAP covering her mouth and nose, her cry is muted.

"She's crying." I hold the bundle out to LaDonna, wishing she'd take Austin back. But she doesn't. I jostle Austin and hold her closer, but the heartbreaking, silent whimper continues. "What am I doing wrong?"

"She's been fussy all day." LaDonna taps her chin with an index finger. "You know what I think?"

"Uh, that I suck at mothering?"

She bats a hand at me and shakes her head. "No! You'll be a fine mother. I think Austin needs some Kangarooing."

"Exactly what I thought!" I shake my head at her. "C'mon, LaDonna, you're talking to a newbie here . . . and I don't mean Austin. What the heck is Kangarooing?"

She laughs. "Kangaroo Care is skin-to-skin contact between the mother and the preemie, like a baby kangaroo in its mother's pouch. These babies need physical contact to bond, but studies also show that holding a preemie against her mother's chest stabilizes her respiratory and heart rates. It conserves calories so the baby gains more weight, and it even regulates her body temperature. The mother's body acts as the incubator."

"Really?"

"Yes. The mother's breasts actually change temperature in response to the baby's body temperature. Babies are more content, less apt to have apnea, all sorts of good things. Would you like to try it?"

"But I'm not the mother . . . the biological mother."

"All the more reason to strengthen the bond. I'll pull up some screens so you two can have your privacy. While I get them, you unswaddle Austin. Take everything off her except her diaper. Would you like me to get you a hospital gown, or would you prefer to unbutton your blouse?"

"Um . . . I'll just unbutton my blouse, I guess. Are you sure this works if it's not the real mother? I'd hate to have her catch cold because I wasn't able to properly Kangaroo."

LaDonna laughs. "It'll work." She cocks her head, serious now. "And Brett, remember how you asked me not to call Austin *Baby Girl*?"

"Yes."

"Will you please stop saying you're not the mother?"

I suck in a breath and nod. "Fair enough."

I lie in a reclining chair, surrounded by privacy screens. I've unbuttoned my blouse and taken off my bra. LaDonna positions Austin on my chest, the mound of my left breast serving as a cushion. Her downy hair tickles my skin, and I flinch. LaDonna settles a blanket over the baby.

"Enjoy," she says, and disappears behind the screen.

Wait, I want to call to her. *How long am I supposed to do this? Could you get me a book maybe, or even a magazine?*

I let out a sigh. Carefully, I slip my hand under the blanket and land on Austin's naked back. It's as soft as butter. I feel the rapid rise and fall of her breathing. Looking down I see her fine black hair. Her face, in profile, is no longer contorted in her silent wail. Her eyes blink, telling me she's awake.

"Hello, Austin," I say. "Are you feeling sad today, sweet pea? I'm so sorry your mommy died. We loved her so much, didn't we?"

She blinks, as if she's listening to me.

"I'm going to be your mommy now," I whisper. "I'm new at this, so you're going to have to cut me some slack, okay?"

Austin stares straight ahead.

"I'm going to make some mistakes, you might as well know that now. But I promise you, I'll do everything in my power to make your life safe, and sweet, and happy, and good."

Austin snuggles into my neck. I laugh softly and rub my cheek against her fuzzy head. "I'm so proud that you're my daughter."

Her breathing slows and her eyes fall shut. I stare at this amazing gift, and I'm overcome with a love so raw, so instinctual, that it takes my breath away.

In no time, LaDonna peers around the screen. "Visiting hours are almost over," she whispers.

I glance at the clock on the wall. "Already?"

"You've been in here almost three hours."

"You're kidding."

"Nope. Austin looks content now . . . and so do you. How did it go?"

"It was . . ." I kiss the top of Austin's head and search for the adjective. "Magical."

As I lay Austin in her isolette and kiss her good night, I spy Sanquita's plastic school ID — the only picture Jean could find of her. I prop the photo against Austin's isolette, directly in her line of vision. I make a mental note to bring another picture tomorrow.

This one of me.

Though my rational brain knows any warm body would have produced the same results, it's almost spiritual, watching Austin's transformation. After only seven days of the skin-to-skin Kangaroo Care, she's graduated from the CPAP to a nasal tube. I can finally see her pretty bowed lips and nuzzle her without the clunky plastic mask interfering. Since her birth nine days ago, she's gained back the weight she lost, along with another two ounces, and she's looking less and less like a little alien.

It's three o'clock in the afternoon, and I dash through the hospital parking lot, my cell phone at my ear. Every day since Austin's birth, I wake before dawn, arriving at my office before seven. I work through my lunch hour, and finish my last appointment by two thirty. This allows me four glorious hours to spend with Austin.

"This Kangarooing is a miracle," I tell Shelley on the telephone. "Austin's close to breathing on her own. And she's trying so hard to coordinate her sucking, swallowing, and breathing. She's almost got it, and then they'll wean her off the IV and feeding tube. She's so adorable, Shel. I can't wait for you to meet her. You've gotten the pictures I've sent, right?"

Shelley laughs. "Yes. She's darling. My God, Brett, you really sound like a mom."

I throw open the hospital door. "Yeah, well, let's hope I don't screw up the poor kid with all my fears and insecurities and neuroses."

"Good point. Here's hoping."

We share a laugh. "Listen, I'm here now. Give the kids my love. Tell Jay hello."

I thrust my phone into my pocket and make my way to the elevators. I smile, wondering what little surprise awaits us today. So far Herbert hasn't missed a day. Because he's not allowed to visit, he sends packages to the nurses' station, addressed to Austin and me. It's become quite the event, with the nurses, and even some of the other new mothers, huddled around to watch me unwrap Herbert's latest offering. I think they look forward to the surprises more than I do. LaDonna adores the silver key fob, hand-engraved with Austin's birth date. I love it, too, but my favorite was yesterday's picture of Austin and me. He printed two copies of a photo I'd sent him, and framed each one. My silver frame reads MOTHER AND CHILD, and Austin's pink-and-white frame says MOMMY AND ME.

But when I arrive today, it seems that the fifth floor has received a surprise of its own. Up ahead I see a woman, surrounded by LaDonna, Maureen, and a security guard. They're huddled just outside the locked entrance to the NICU. The woman's long yellow hair has the texture of late-August hay, and even with the bulk of a faux-fur coat she looks almost skeletal.

"I ain't going nowhere." Her words are slurred, and she wobbles on red heels. "I got a right to see my grandbaby."

Oh, dear, the poor woman must be drunk. How sad for her daughter and her grandbaby. LaDonna catches sight of me and gives me a sharp look of warning. I slow my pace and turn around, but the sounds of the scuffle trail me.

"Ma'am, you need to leave now," the guard tells her, "or I'll have to call the police."

"You ain't gonna call no police on me. I ain't done nothin' wrong. I come all the way from Detroit. I ain't leaving till I see her, you hear me?"

Oh, God! I turn the corner, out of sight, and slump against the wall. Could this be Sanquita's mother? Footsteps near and the shouts get louder. "Get your fucking hands off me! You wanna get sued, motherfucker?"

They round the corner and she's so close I catch a whiff of lingering cigarette smoke. Her face is nearly colorless, like oatmeal, and wadded into an angry snarl. I spy black, rotting teeth, and my first thought is *meth addict*. Was she? Is she? Sanquita's words come back to me. *I know why she didn't wake up when my brothers screamed. When I got home from school I flushed everything down the toilet.*

Gripping her arm, the guard nearly drags her toward the elevator, ignoring the obscenities being hurled at him. As she passes in front of me, she squints, as if to see me better. My breath catches and I step back. Does she know who I am? Does she know I'm going to be Austin's mom? An instinctive ripple of fear passes through me.

The guard yanks her onward, but she cranes her neck and glares back at me with cold gray eyes.

"What you looking at, bitch?"

My sympathy vanishes. In its place, something primal kicks in, some protective maternal instinct, and I know I would die — or kill — for Austin's life and safety. The thought leaves me horrified and astonished and strangely proud.

CHAPTER TWENTY-SEVEN

*T*he neonatal unit is abuzz with chatter. LaDonna grabs my elbow when she sees me, and leads me into a private corner. "We've got a problem," she whispers.

"Sanquita's mother?" I ask, already knowing the answer.

She nods and looks around to make sure nobody's within earshot. "Tia Robinson. She was so high or drunk or . . . who knows what . . . she could barely walk."

Another wave of panic floods me.

"She's come for her grandbaby." She shakes her head, as if the idea is crazy.

I clutch my throat, trying to keep the bitter bile from rising. "Could she? Is it possible she could get the baby?"

She shrugs. "I've seen stranger things happen. If a relative steps up and is willing to take the child, more often than not they get him. Just one less case the state has to worry about."

"No! Not her. I won't let that happen. I'm taking Austin. I told you, it was Sanquita's last wish."

She scowls. "Look, I think that's wonderful, but it's not your decision to make. Have you talked to Kirsten Schertzing, the hospital's social worker?"

"No," I say, feeling suddenly foolish. Why did I assume adopting this homeless, motherless child would be a cinch? "I've been playing phone tag with a woman from Social Services. And I've been meaning to contact the social worker here, but I've been so busy with Austin."

"I'll call Kirsten now. If she's available, maybe you can talk to her today."

She disappears behind the nurses' station, and returns a moment later with a Post-it note. "She's about to step into a meeting. But she can see you tomorrow at four. She's on the second floor, room two fourteen." She hands me the note. "I've written it down for you."

My head spins and I stare at the sticky note.

"You may have a fight on your hands. Ms. Robinson is determined this child is hers."

"Why?" I ask. "She didn't even want to raise her own daughter."

LaDonna gives a little huff. "That's a no-brainer. She wants the death benefits. Austin will receive about a thousand dollars a month in SSI for the next eighteen years."

A dark, atavistic fear mounts within me. This woman is hell-bent on getting my baby, with a motive as old and sinister as time. And she's Austin's maternal grandmother. I'm just Sanquita's teacher, someone she knew a scant five months.

I spend the next two hours behind the privacy screen with Austin at my chest, singing along with today's gift from Herbert — an iPod he's loaded with perfectly fitting songs for a new mother, like "I Hope You Dance," and "You Make Me Feel Like a Natural Woman." I'm touched. It must have taken him hours to compile. But will I ever be a new mother? My chest clenches. I peer down at Austin and try to sing along with Alison Krauss.

"It's amazing how you can speak right to my heart."

Her tiny fist pokes through the blanket, and she yawns and closes her eyes again. I laugh through tears and pat her back. Suddenly a hand on my own back startles me. "You have a visitor, Brett. He's waiting in the reception area."

I'm surprised when I see my brother just outside the NICU. He's wearing a suit and tie, clearly having come straight from work.

"Joad," I say. "What are you doing here?"

"You've been pretty hard to get ahold of the last couple of weeks." He leans in and pecks my cheek. "I hear you've got a new little friend. Catherine's gaga over those pictures you sent."

"Something horrible just happened. Sanquita's mom showed up today. She thinks she's going to take my baby." Hysteria mounts anew as I recall the horrible scene. "It's not happening, Joad! I won't let her."

He cocks his head, his forehead creased with worry lines. "Just how do you plan to stop her?"

"I'm adopting her."

"C'mon. Let's get a cup of coffee." He gives me a once-over. "Or better yet, dinner. When's the last time you ate?"

"I'm not hungry."

He shakes his head. "Let's go. You're going to eat, and then you're going to tell me what's going on." He tugs my arm, but I slip from his grasp.

"No! I can't leave her. That woman might come back and take her."

He stares at me, his eyes wide with alarm. "Get ahold of yourself. You look like hell. Have you slept in the last two weeks? This baby's not going anywhere." He gestures to Nurse Kathy at the reception desk. "We'll be back in a few."

"Tell LaDonna not to let Austin out of her sight," I call as Joad pulls me toward the elevator.

Sitting in a molded plastic booth in the back of the hospital cafeteria, Joad lifts a plate of spaghetti from an orange tray and places it in front of me. "Eat," he tells me. "And between bites, tell me what you mean to do with Sanquita's baby."

I don't like the way he says *Sanquita's baby,* as if Austin's fate were still arbitrary. I pull the paper ring from the napkin and find the fork and knife within. The spaghetti makes my stomach roil, but I fill my fork and lift it to my mouth. It takes all my strength to chew and swallow. I dab my mouth with the paper napkin and set down my fork.

"She's my baby. I'm adopting her."

He listens as I tell him about Sanquita and her last wish, Ms. Robinson and the scene earlier. "Tomorrow I'm meeting with the social worker. I'm going to save this child. She needs me. And I promised Sanquita."

He eyes me while he sips his coffee. When he sets down the cup, he shakes his head. "Mom really did a number on you with these goals, didn't she?"

"What do you mean?"

"You don't need this baby. You'll have your own kid eventually. It might take you a little longer, but it'll happen. You've just got to be patient."

I shake my head. "I want *this* child, Joad. It has nothing to do with Mother's goals. I need this baby, and she needs me."

He doesn't seem to hear me. "Look, you've got to be running low on cash about now. I'd be happy to loan —"

I stare at him, horrified. "You think I'm doing this to get my inheritance?" I lift my head to the ceiling. "Jesus, Joad! You must think I'm just as greedy as Sanquita's mother!" I push away my plate and lean in. "I don't give a damn about that inheritance. I'd give up every cent for this baby. Do you understand me? Every. Red. Fucking. Cent!"

He leans back, as if he's frightened of me. "Okay, so money's not the issue. I still think you're being shortsighted. Mother planted this seed, and now you're obsessed with it. That child doesn't look like us, Brett. What is she? Hispanic? Middle Eastern?"

At this moment I don't see my brother. I see his father, Charles Bohlinger, shaking his head, wondering why in hell I'd choose to go to the prom with Terrell Jones. My blood pressure soars. "Her mother was biracial. She was a poor, homeless girl from the Detroit projects. I don't know what race the baby's father is, because it was a one-night stand. There! Does that satisfy your curiosity?"

He pinches the bridge of his nose. "Jesus, some gene pool. What does Herbert think about this?"

I lean in. "Screw you, Joad. I love this baby. I *adore* this baby. And she's bonded with me now. You should see how she snuggles up to me when I hold her. And for your information, Herbert's completely supportive, though I don't know what difference that makes."

He blinks several times. "Are you serious? The man's in love with you. He's definitely thinking long-term."

I give him a dismissive wave. "That's a bit premature, don't you think? He's known me all of two months."

"When we were at Jay's last week, he pulled me aside. I don't know, maybe he figured since I was your oldest brother, I was like a surrogate father or something. Anyway, he told me he hopes to have a future with you. It was just short of asking for your hand."

I scowl. "Well, that'll be my decision, not yours, or Herbert's, or anyone else's."

"He's a great guy, Brett. Don't fuck this up. If you do, you'll regret it, mark my words."

I look him square in the eyes. "Mark my words, I won't." I throw my napkin onto the table and rise, leaving him to guess whether I won't fuck it up with Herbert, or whether I won't regret it.

That evening when I arrive home, I find a package gracing my porch, this one with a Wisconsin return address. Carrie. How sweet. I lug it up to my apartment and split the seam with a butter knife. Inside I find a menagerie of stuffed animals, hardback books, cotton sleepers, bibs, blankets, and booties. I hold each piece in front of me, imagining Austin when she's big enough to wear these clothes that would swallow her today. But then I remember the vulgar woman with the rotting teeth, and her wish to destroy my child's life. I pick up the phone and call Carrie.

"I just opened the fabulous package you sent," I say, trying to sound cheerful. "That was so thoughtful of you."

"It's our pleasure. When we first got the kids, Sammy was only a month old. We had no clue what we'd need. You'll love that Moby Wrap, just wait and see. And the —"

"Sanquita's mother wants Austin."

There's a moment of silence at the other end of the line. "Oh, Brett. I'm so sorry."

"I'd have sympathy for the woman if she weren't so horrible." I tell the story of Deonte and Austin. "She was stoned when Deonte died, but she laid the blame on Austin." My eyes flood with tears. "I'm terrified, Carrie. What if I don't get her? Austin's life will be hell."

"Pray," she tells me. "Just pray."

And I do. Just the same way I prayed my mother would live. And Sanquita would get healthy.

———

*T*he walls of Kirsten Schertzing's modest office are garnished with snapshots of smiling kids and families, old people grinning up from their wheelchairs, amputees happily waving into the camera lens. The officious social worker with the all-knowing eyes clearly has a warm side, though so far I haven't witnessed it.

"Thank you for coming," she says, closing the door behind us. "Have a seat."

Brad and I sit side by side on a love seat, and Kirsten sits in a wooden chair facing us, a plastic clipboard on her lap. She takes notes as I tell her about my relationship with Sanquita, and her dying wish that I keep the baby.

She lifts the page she's writing on and scans her own personal notes beneath. "According to her medical chart, Sanquita lapsed into a coma following her C-section. For the next thirteen hours leading up to her death, nobody reported her conscious . . . except for you."

Suddenly, this feels like an interrogation. "All I know is that evening, the same day she delivered the baby, she woke up."

She notes this. "Just long enough to tell you she wanted you to keep the baby?"

My pulse races. "Yes, that's right."

She writes with raised eyebrows. "Did anyone else witness this?"

"At the hospital, no. But that morning, on her way to the hospital, she told Miss Jean, the director of her shelter." I look away. "But I doubt she'd stand up for me in court." I clasp my clammy hands together. "Sanquita spoke to me. I know it sounds crazy. But it's true. She begged me to take her baby."

She sets down her pen and finally looks up. "It wouldn't be the first time someone's gained consciousness just long enough to say good-bye, or express a last wish."

"So you believe me?"

"What I believe is irrelevant. What matters is what the court believes." She stands and moves to her desk. "This morning a very coherent, extremely well-behaved Ms. Robinson came to see me."

I gasp. "What did she say?"

"I'm not at liberty to tell you. But it's important to note, in almost every case of child custody, the court rules in favor of the family. I'm not sure this is a fight you want to take on."

Brad clears his throat. "I've done a background check on Tia Robinson. She receives disability due to a history of mental illness. She's been in and out of rehab for alcohol and drug addiction. She lives in one of Detroit's most crime-ridden housing projects. Sanquita has three half brothers, each from a different fath —"

Kirsten doesn't let him finish. "Mr. Midar, with all due respect, the state is only interested in whether or not this woman — who happens to be the baby's maternal grandmother — has ever been convicted of a felony. And though she's had several misdemeanors, she's not a felon."

"What about the boy, Deonte, who died in the fire?" I ask. "What kind of mother sleeps while her kids are screaming for help?"

"I checked into that for you. There was no formal charge. The records from the county indicate that she'd briefly stepped into the shower. Sadly, accidents happen in the blink of an eye."

"No. She was high. Sanquita told me."

"Hearsay," Kirsten and Brad say simultaneously.

I stare at Brad like he's a traitor. But of course, he's right. My statement would never hold up in court. "But these other things," I say. "The addictions, the mental illness. Don't they matter?"

"Right now she's testing clean. Look, if we took children away from parents who were depressed or had prior addictions, half the city would be in foster care. Whenever possible, the state's goal is to keep children with their family. Period."

Brad shakes his head. "That's wrong."

Kirsten shrugs. "And what kind of society would we be if placement were based on who had the nicest house, or who was happiest?"

My mind races. I cannot allow this child to go to Ms. Robinson. I can't! I promised Sanquita. And I love that baby too much.

"Sanquita didn't want her baby anywhere near this woman," I say. "If it has to be a family member, let's find someone else, some relative without issues."

"Fine idea, but nobody else has come forward. Sanquita had no sisters, so the maternal grandmother is the closest of all relatives. And in this case, Grandma's only thirty-six years old, so it's not exactly a stretch to imagine this woman raising a baby."

Thirty-six? The woman I saw in the hallway looked fifty! I look up and Ms. Schertzing gives me a sympathetic smile. I'm losing this case. I'm letting Sanquita down.

"What can I do?"

Her lips tighten into a thin line. "Honestly? I suggest you start reining in your emotions as best you can. I have every reason to believe this is an open-and-shut case. Ms. Robinson will be granted custody of her granddaughter."

I cover my face and burst into tears. I feel Brad's hand on my back, patting me the same way I pat Austin.

"You'll be okay, B.B.," he whispers. "There will be another baby."

I'm crying so hard I can't tell him my tears aren't for me. It's true. I may have another baby. But Austin only gets one mother.

CHAPTER TWENTY-EIGHT

I spend the next week racing to the hospital every afternoon following my last homebound session. I don't care what the social worker said, I'm going to spend every last minute with this baby. Each time I touch her silky black curls or rub her downy skin, I pray these tender moments will somehow take root in her memory and trail her for a lifetime.

Nurse LaDonna sidles up to the reclining chair and bends down to take the baby from me. "Kirsten Schertzing just called. She'd like you to call her before five o'clock."

My heart soars. Maybe Ms. Robinson changed her mind! Or maybe the court denied her custody!

I race down the hall to a bench in front of a window that overlooks the city, the only place in the hospital that has decent cell phone reception. Austin is mine, I feel it. But didn't I also feel pregnant? And that Brad was the man of my dreams?

"Kirsten," I say, gripping the phone. "It's Brett Bohlinger.

What's going on? I'm here at the hospital now. I can come down to your office —"

"No. That's not necessary. I've just received information about the custody hearing. It's scheduled for tomorrow morning at eight o'clock. Judge Garcia at Cook County Courthouse will be presiding."

I let out a breath. "Nothing's changed?"

"Nada. Tia Robinson is back in town now. Short of a miracle, she'll leave the courtroom tomorrow with custody of her grand-daughter."

I clap a hand over my mouth to keep from screaming, and tears flood my eyes.

"I'm sorry, Brett. I just wanted you to know in case you're still determined to contest it."

I manage a thank you and punch off the phone. An elderly patient teeters down the hall, wheeling his IV pole alongside him.

"Bad prognosis?" he asks when he passes in front of me and sees the tears streaming down my cheeks.

I nod, unable to utter the word *terminal*.

When I return to the neonatal unit, Jean Anderson sits on a sofa in the reception area, holding a bright pink package on her lap. She startles when she sees me.

"Well, well," she says, pulling herself to her feet. "Look what the cat drug in." She thrusts the pink present at me. "From the women at Joshua House."

I take the gift, but I don't trust my voice to speak.

She narrows her gaze. "You all right?"

"Sanquita's mother is taking the baby."

She scowls. "But Sanquita wanted you to keep the baby. She told me."

"There's a hearing tomorrow morning with Judge Garcia. The woman is crazy, Jean. I'm so scared for Austin. Can you come tomorrow? Can you tell the judge what Sanquita told you?"

She huffs. "And waste my time?" She lets loose a cruel cackle. "It doesn't matter what Sanquita told me. It's all hearsay. We don't have a lick of proof. And because of that, grandmother trumps the schoolteacher, crazy or not."

I stare at her. "Then we've got to convince Judge Garcia it's in Austin's best interests for me to adopt her. We'll tell him how Sanquita didn't want her child to live in Detroit, and how . . ." My voice trails off when I see Jean shaking her head.

"You think everybody plays by the rules, don't you? You think if you smile real pretty and tell that judge the truth, he'll see things your way." Her eyes narrow, and she breathes heavily. "No. I'm afraid the truth won't set you free this time."

I break into tears.

"Look at me." She grips my arms so tightly they hurt. "Those crocodile tears probably worked wonders all your life, but they're not going to help you get that baby, you hear? If you want that child, you fight for her. Play hardball, don't you know?"

I sniff and wipe my eyes. "I will. Of course I will."

I'd love to play hardball. But the only equipment I've got is a plastic bat and a Nerf ball.

Painted the shade of a cardboard box, Cook County's musty old courtroom looks as lonesome and forsaken as I feel. Six empty rows of pine pews, separated by a center aisle, face the judge's bench and witness stand. To the right of the witness stand, the chairs reserved for jurors sit vacant today. This is a bench trial. Judge Garcia will decide this case.

Brad reviews his notes and I glance at the table to our right. Huddled together, Tia Robinson and her court-appointed attorney, Mr. Croft, speak in hushed tones. I look behind me at the empty pews. Nobody cares about this trial. Not even Miss Jean.

At precisely eight o'clock, Judge Garcia takes his place on the bench and calls the court to order. We learn that Ms. Robinson will not be testifying today. I'm no attorney, but even I know it's too risky to put that woman on the witness stand. Besides, it's an open-and-shut case. She has nothing to gain by testifying.

Suddenly I'm being called to the witness stand. I'm sworn in and Brad asks me to state my name and my relation to Sanquita Bell. I take a deep breath and make myself believe everything hinges on this testimony, that the case hasn't already been decided.

"I'm Brett Bohlinger," I say, working to steady my breathing. "I worked with Sanquita Bell the five months preceding her death. I was her homebound teacher and her friend."

"Would you say you had a close relationship with Sanquita?" Brad asks.

"Yes. I loved her."

"Did Sanquita ever mention her mother to you?"

I take care not to look at Tia Robinson, seated less than twelve feet from me.

"Yes. She told me her mother moved to Detroit, but she refused to go. She said she didn't want her baby to have that kind of life."

With one hand resting on the edge of the witness stand, Brad looks as comfortable as if we were chatting it up at P. J. Clarke's. "Can you tell me what happened at the hospital?"

"Yes," I say, feeling sweat trickle down the back of my neck. "It was after her surgery, about six o'clock in the evening. I was alone with Sanquita. She woke up suddenly. I went to her bedside and that's when she told me she wanted me to take the baby." I bite my lip to keep it from quivering. "I told her she wasn't going to die, but she was insistent." My throat tightens and my voice is strained. "She knew she was dying. She made me promise to take her baby."

Brad hands me a handkerchief and I blot my eyes. When I lower the hankie, my eyes lock on Tia's. She sits with her hands folded, showing not a trace of emotion for her daughter's dying words.

"I plan to keep that promise."

"Thank you, Ms. Bohlinger. No further questions."

Mr. Croft's sickly sweet cologne arrives at the witness stand ten seconds before he does. He hikes up his brown slacks before turning to me, his belly looking more impregnated than Sanquita's ever did.

"Ms. Bohlinger, did anyone hear Sanquita tell you she wanted you to take her baby?"

"No. We were alone in the room. But she did tell someone earlier, Jean Anderson from the Joshua House."

He wags his finger at me. "Please answer yes or no. Did anyone else witness this miracle you say happened, when Sanquita came out of her coma just long enough to tell you to keep her baby?"

He thinks I'm lying! I search out Brad's face, but he simply nods for me to continue.

I force myself to meet the runny gray eyes behind Mr. Croft's wire-framed glasses. "No."

"Did Sanquita know she was dying?"

"Yes."

He nods. "So she wanted to have all her ducks in a row."

"Exactly."

"Did Sanquita strike you as a smart girl?"

"Yes. She was very bright."

"Then naturally, she put her wishes in writing, yes?"

The air is sucked from the room. "No. Not that I know of."

He scratches his head. "That's extremely odd, don't you think?"

"I-I don't know."

"You don't know?" He paces in front of me. "A smart girl who knew she was going to die wouldn't plan ahead for her baby's future? Perplexing, wouldn't you agree? Especially when her home environment was as deplorable as you claim."

"I . . . I'm not sure why she didn't."

"This life that Sanquita referred to . . . the life in Detroit with her mother? Did she happen to mention that she was in Detroit when she became impregnated?"

"Yes."

"So you are aware that she slipped out of the apartment against her mother's wishes and had unprotected sex?"

I blink. "No. She never told me that. I don't think she slipped away, as you suggest."

His face is a portrait of self-righteousness, nose aloft and head angled so he's looking down at me. "Did she tell you she wandered down to the Detroit Jazz Festival that very night and had sex with a stranger? Someone whose name she didn't even remember?"

"It . . . it wasn't like that. She was lonely . . . and very upset . . ."

He raises one eyebrow. "Did she tell you she stayed six weeks? That she left Detroit only when she found out she was pregnant?"

"I . . . I didn't know she stayed six weeks. The point is, she left. Like I said, she wanted her baby out of that environment."

"And she wanted to get herself out of that environment as well, yes?"

"Yes, she did."

"Did she tell you that her mother wanted her to terminate the pregnancy?"

My head snaps to attention. "No."

"Sanquita's kidney disease was so severe, the doctor recommended an abortion in order to save Sanquita's life."

My mind reels. "That's what Dr. Chan told her, too."

"And did she listen to Dr. Chan?"

"No. She said she wanted the baby more than life itself."

He smirks in a way that makes me want to pinch it off his face. "The truth is, Sanquita was a stubborn girl. She refused to believe her mother had her best intentions in mind."

"Objection!" Brad cries.

"Sustained."

Mr. Croft continues. "Sanquita left Detroit the very day she and her mother argued about terminating the pregnancy."

I'm stunned. Could this be possible?

Mr. Croft turns to the judge's bench. "This has nothing to do with Ms. Robinson's home environment, Your Honor. Ms. Robinson was simply trying to save her daughter's life." He hangs his head. "I have no further questions."

My hands tremble so violently, it takes effort to fold them. They're making Ms. Robinson out to be Sanquita's savior . . . and Sanquita to be the wild child who refused to listen.

"Thank you, Mr. Croft," Judge Garcia says. He nods to me, indicating I can step down. "Thank you, Ms. Bohlinger."

"Would you like to call your next witness?" he asks Brad.

"Your Honor, I'd like to request that we take a break." Brad says. "My client needs a short recess."

Judge Garcia checks his watch, then slams down the gavel. "The court will resume after a fifteen-minute recess."

Brad practically drags me through the double doors and into the corridor. My body has turned to lead and I can't think straight. My baby is being given a life sentence. I need to save her, but I'm powerless. I'm the one person Sanquita trusted. And I'm forsaking her. Brad props me up against a wall and grips my arms.

"Don't you dare break, B.B. We've done everything we can. It's out of our hands now."

My breath comes out in jagged spurts and my head feels light. "He made Sanquita look like a juvenile delinquent."

"Could it be true?" he asks. "Is it possible she left Detroit over an argument about her health?"

I throw up my hands. "I don't know. It doesn't matter, anyway. What matters now is Austin. That woman didn't shed a tear when I described Sanquita's final moments. And you know what she did to her son. She's heartless, Brad!" I grab his jacket sleeve and stare into his face. "You should have seen her last week, when she was being hauled away by security. It was disgusting. We can't do this to Austin. We've got to do something."

"We've done everything we can."

I start to cry, but Brad shakes me. "Buck up, now. You'll have time to cry later. We need to finish this trial."

Fifteen minutes later, we shuffle back into the courtroom. I drop into my chair beside Brad. I've never felt so useless. My baby's life is about to take a horrific detour, and I can't do a thing about it. Garrett's words come back to me: *You can't save them all.* Just this one, I pray. Please, God, just this one.

As I pray, I work to breathe, but my lungs won't fill. Panic sets in. I'm going to pass out. I can't do this. I cannot survive another loss.

Just as the bailiff pulls shut the double door in the back, I hear her voice. My head snaps to attention and I spin around. Jean Anderson lumbers down the aisle, dressed in a smart wool suit. But the back of her hair is matted, and she's wearing sneakers instead of her usual pumps.

"Jean?" I say aloud. I turn to Brad.

"Just sit tight," he whispers.

Instead of scooting into one of the pews, Jean marches directly up to the judge's bench. She whispers something to Judge Garcia, and he mumbles something in return. Then she takes a paper from her purse and hands it to him. He puts on his reading glasses and examines it. Finally, he looks up.

"Will the counsel please approach the bench?"

The four of them mumble for what seems an interminable length of time. I hear Mr. Croft above the others, and the judge telling him to lower his voice. When they finally return to their seats, Brad and Jean are smiling. I warn myself not to get excited.

Judge Garcia holds the paper aloft for all to see. "It appears Ms. Bell put her request in writing, after all. We have a notarized statement dated March fifth, several weeks prior to her death." He clears his throat and reads aloud in a monotonous voice. "I, Sanquita Jahzmen Bell, being of sound mind, do hereby declare my intentions for my unborn child, should he or she outlive me. It is my heartfelt desire that Ms. Brett Bohlinger, my best friend and my homebound teacher, get sole custody of my child." He takes off his glasses. "It's signed, Sanquita Jahzmen Bell." He clears his throat.

"In light of this notarized request, I'm granting temporary custody to Ms. Bohlinger until adoption procedures are finalized." He slaps the gavel on his desk. "This court is adjourned."

I drop my head into my hands and sob.

I never ask Jean about the notarized paper. I don't want to know how she got it, or when. It doesn't matter. We've done right by Sanquita and her baby. That's all that matters. Brad suggests we three celebrate after the hearing, but I can't. I head straight to the hospital to see my baby. *My baby!* I round the corner and scurry down the hall. The doors to the neonatal unit open and I practically sprint to room seven. I enter and my heart skips a beat.

Dressed in khakis and a navy sports coat, Herbert sits in a rocking chair, with Austin in his arms. He's smiling down at her, watching her sleep. I come up behind him and kiss his neck.

"What are you doing here?"

"Congratulations, love," he says. "I came here as soon as I got your message. I knew you'd be right behind me."

"But who let you in?"

"Nurse LaDonna."

Of course she did. Every nurse in the unit is half in love with the incredible, gift-giving Herbert — and now that they've laid eyes on him, there will be no going back.

"Since you're now Austin's custodial parent," Herbert continues, "you're allowed one support person. You don't mind, do you?"

I push away thoughts of Shelley, or Carrie, or Brad, and stare down at my beautiful daughter. I wrap myself in a hug. "I can't believe it, Herbert. I'm a mother!"

"And a fine one you'll be." He rises and holds out the sleeping bundle to me. "Have a seat. Perhaps you want to properly introduce yourself to this little one."

Austin punches a fist into the air before settling back to sleep against my chest. Her eyes are at half-mast and I plant a kiss on her nose — a nose free of oxygen and feeding tubes. "Hey there, pretty girl. Guess what? I'm going to be your mommy. And this time I promise." Her eyebrows furrow, and I smile through tears. "What did I do to deserve you?"

With his camera poised before him, Herbert moves in to get a close-up. The camera seems intrusive at this moment of intimacy. But he's excited, and what more could I hope for than this kind of enthusiasm and support?

He retrieves sandwiches and coffee from the cafeteria, and we stay with Austin until visiting hours end. Strangely, it's easier to leave tonight, knowing she's mine. I'm not going to lose her, now or ever. As we walk to the elevator, Herbert stops suddenly and snaps his finger. "Forgot my coat. Be right back."

He returns — with a khaki Burberry trench coat draped over his arm.

I gasp. "That coat!" I say, staring at it as if it were a magician's cape.

He looks embarrassed. "Yes, well, it was a bit nippy this morning."

I laugh and shake my head. He's not the man from Andrew's building, the man I saw on the train, or on the jogging path. But maybe, just maybe, he's my Burberry man.

The April evening is warm, and the sweet smell of lilacs tints the air. To the east, a moon as slender as a fingernail clipping hangs low in the slate-colored sky. Herbert walks with me to my car, his Burberry coat slung over his shoulder.

"If she continues to thrive, she could come home within the next two weeks. I've got so much to do to get ready. I've asked for a leave of absence from work. School's going to be out in a few weeks and Eve said she'd substitute for me. I need to get the bedroom ready, a rug and some baby furniture. I'm thinking just a bassinet and changing table for now, since that's about all that'll fit in our tiny bedroom." I laugh. "And I thought —"

He turns to me and places his index finger on my lips. "Stop. I'm hearing too much about what *you* have to do. You and I are partners. Let me help you."

"Okay. Thank you."

"No need to thank me. It's what I want." He takes me by the arms and gazes into my eyes. "I love you. Do you realize that?"

I stare up at him. "I do."

"And if I am to believe what you've been professing, you love me, too."

I take a step back. "Uh-huh."

"Let's revisit this life list you're expected to complete."

I shake my head and turn away, but he moves closer. "Look, it doesn't scare me, if that's what you're afraid of. I want to help. You should consider each and every one of those goals accomplished, do you understand?"

Before I can answer, he takes my hands in his. "I realize we've only known each other a short time, but given the fact that you now have a child, as well as the fact that I am completely, head-over-heels in love with you, I think we should consider marriage."

I gasp. "You mean . . . you want . . . ?"

He chuckles, and gestures at the parking lot. "Don't worry, darling. I would never choose such an unworthy backdrop for an official proposal. I just want to plant the seed. I'd like you to mull it over, start thinking of us as a couple — a permanent couple — sometime down the road." He grins. "And I'd prefer it be an expressway rather than a meandering country lane."

I open my mouth to speak, but the words don't come.

He reaches out and touches my cheek. "I know it sounds crazy, but from the moment I met you, that very first night at Jay's, I knew you'd be my wife someday."

"You did?" My thoughts immediately turn to my mother. Is she responsible, in some way, for this man falling in love with me?

"I did." He smiles and kisses the tip of my nose. "But the last thing I want is to pressure you. Just promise me you'll think about it, won't you?"

His thick hair is mussed, and his eyes are like two sparkling sapphires. When he smiles, it's as if a lily has bloomed. This man is the closest to perfection I'll ever find. He's smart and kind, ambitious and loving. My God, he even plays the violin! And for some crazy reason, he loves me. And best of all, he loves my daughter.

"Yes," I say. "Of course I'll think about it."

$\mathcal{G}$ray clouds spritz a fine mist into the warm May air. Carrying my red umbrella, I sprint down my porch steps clutching Rudy's leash. Like a child of divorced parents, my poor dog has been shuttled back and forth between my apartment and Selina and Blanca's for the past six weeks. Lucky for me, my wonderful neighbors love the silly mutt as much as I do. But this weekend they're at a marching band competition in Springfield, so Rudy and I pile into the car and head to Brad's house.

"This will be the last time I abandon you, Rudy boy," I tell him as we travel north to Bucktown. "Tomorrow our baby's coming home."

Brad has coffee and warm poppy-seed muffins waiting when I arrive at his duplex. I sit at his kitchen table and, beneath a bowl of strawberries, spy two pink envelopes. Since Judge Garcia's decision, I've been expecting goal number one, but when I see the second envelope for goal number seventeen, FALL IN LOVE, my pulse quickens.

Brad sits down across from me. "Want these now, or after breakfast?"

"Now, please," I say, hiding behind my coffee cup. "But just envelope number one today."

He chuckles. "You said you're talking marriage now. That means you're in love, right?"

I pluck a strawberry from the bowl and study it. "I just want to spread them out a bit. There aren't many left."

He gives me a sidelong glance.

I thrust the first envelope at him. "Go on, open it."

He waits a beat, then slices the seam of envelope one with his finger. Before he has time to realize he's missing them, I go to the end table and fetch his glasses. He smiles at me.

"We're a pretty good team, huh?"

"The best," I say, and feel a small tug on my heartstrings. Could we have been a team, if our timing had been different? God, how awful of me to even consider what-ifs. I'm practically engaged to Herbert!

"'Dear Brett,

"'Someone once asked Michelangelo how he was able to create the amazing statue of David. He replied, "I didn't create David. He was there all along, in that massive block of marble. I just had to chip away to find him."

"'Like Michelangelo, I hope I've helped find you these last months — that I've chipped away at that hard exterior until the real you emerged. You're a mother, darling! I believe that nurturing, caring woman was in you all along, and I'm thrilled to have had a role in finding her.

"'I believe motherhood will be the seminal event in your life. You will find it in turns gratifying, frustrating, amazing, and overwhelming. It will be the most marvelous, challenging, vital role you'll ever play.

"'Someone once told me, "As mothers, our job is not to raise children, but to raise adults." I am confident your child will become a fine adult under your careful sculpting. And at some time or another, take a moment to imagine a world where, instead of teaching our children to be strong, we teach them to be gentle.

"'Now dry your eyes and smile. What a lucky child you have. If there's a heaven where I'm going, and if I'm entrusted with a pair of wings, I promise to watch over her and keep her safe.

"'I love you both more than I can ever express.

"'Mom.'"

Brad takes my soggy napkin and replaces it with a fresh tissue. Then he rests his hand on my back while I sob.

"I wish Austin could have known her."

"She will," Brad says. And he's right. She'll know my mother and hers, I'll make sure of it.

I blow my nose and look up at him. "She knew I'd have a daughter. Did you catch that?" I pull the letter from his hand and find the line. "Right here," I say, pointing. "'I'll watch over her and keep her safe.' How did she know that?"

He studies the letter. "I'm guessing that was inadvertent. She didn't mean to specify a gender."

I shake my head. "No. She knew it. She knew I would have a baby girl. And I believe she helped me get Austin Elizabeth. She softened Jean's heart."

"Whatever you say." He sets the letter aside and reaches for his coffee cup. "Do you think she'd be happy about your relationship with Herbert?"

For some reason, my heart stammers. "Absolutely." Rudy comes up beside me and I scratch his chin. "Herbert's exactly the kind of guy my mother would want for me. Why would you ask?"

He shrugs. "Oh, I just . . . I . . ." He shakes his head. "Look, I've only met *Doctor* Moyer once. You know him better than I do."

"That's right, I do. And he's awesome."

"Oh, I don't doubt that. I just . . ." His voice trails off.

"Look, Midar, if you have something to say, spit it out."

He looks me in the eye. "I just wonder if awesome is enough."

My God, he sees it. The tiny ripple in my gorgeous glass pond. The one I've been ignoring, hoping time will smooth out. I haven't told anyone — not even Shelley or Carrie. Because someday soon that ripple will fade, and once it does, I don't want anyone to doubt my love for him. I can — and I will — love Herbert.

"What are you implying?" I ask, keeping my voice casual.

He pushes aside the bowl of berries and leans in. "Are you happy, B.B.? I mean wigged-out, over-the-moon happy?"

I walk to the sink and rinse my cup. Along with Herbert, I think of every good thing in my life. Austin, and my job, my new friends and family . . .

I turn to him and smile. "You have no idea."

He studies me for a moment before finally throwing up his hands. "Okay then. It's settled. I'm sorry I ever doubted it. Herbert's the guy."

The following morning, Sunday the sixth of May, weighing in at four pounds, twelve ounces and wearing a pink layette from her aunt Catherine, Austin comes home. Herbert put up a ferocious battle, insisting the baby and I move back to Astor Street, but I wouldn't hear of it. Pilsen is our home for now, and besides, Selina and Blanca would be heartbroken. They've been gushing over Austin's pictures for the past month, buying her little sneakers and stuffed animals. Deserting them now is out of the question.

Herbert snaps pictures all the way down the hospital hallway and into the car. We giggle, struggling to get her miniature body strapped into her car seat. She looks lost in the plastic contraption, so I prop blankets around her to keep her from tipping.

"Are you certain this car seat is the right size?" Herbert asks.

"Yes. The hospital inspected it, and believe it or not, it's the size for her."

He looks skeptical but closes the door anyway before rushing over to my side to help me settle in beside her. He extends the seat belt and reaches over me to latch it, as if I'm the second child.

"Herbert, please. You're allowed to spoil the baby, not me."

"I beg to differ. I intend to spoil both my girls."

I loosen my seat belt strap, feeling suddenly cramped and caged. It touches me, his concern for Austin, but his devotion to me still feels overwhelming at times. I reach out to close the door. But Herbert has already closed it for me. I feel my blood pressure rise, and silently chastise myself. I'm the one with issues, not him.

When I enter my little apartment with my baby in my arms, I feel my mother's presence so deeply I want to call out to her. She'd love this moment, this baby, this woman I've become. She'd greet me with a kiss, then lean in to better see the baby, taking her from me as quickly as I'd allow it.

"Where would you like me to put this?"

I turn to see Herbert, holding the hospital bag aloft. He shouldn't be here. This scene belongs to my mom and Austin and me. He has invaded our special moment.

But he doesn't know that, and he looks so adorable, holding the pink-and-brown-polka-dot bag. I smile at him.

"Please, just set it on the counter. I'll get it later."

He's back in a flash, rubbing his hands together. "How about some lunch? I can whip up a delicious omelet . . . unless you'd rather have —"

"No!" I snap, followed by rush of guilt. What kind of cold, ungrateful person am I? I touch his arm. "I mean . . . yes. An omelet is fine, thank you."

I remember a line from the movie *Terms of Endearment*. "Don't worship me until I've earned it." That proud, independent sentiment always resonated with me. But why? Once again I wonder if the man who raised me left a scar so deep that, as an adult, I can't accept genuine affection. I was so desperate to "earn" Charles's approval — and Andrew's, too — that I sacrificed my true identity. And even then I fell short. It's different with Herbert. I can finally be myself, and he adores me — the real me. For the first time in my life, I'm in a healthy relationship, just as my mother had hoped.

Herbert peeks around the kitchen wall, an egg carton in one hand and a stick of butter in the other. He grins at me, a smile as sweet and unassuming as a schoolboy's. I step forward and take his face in my hands, and stare into his eyes so intensely that his face flushes. Then I lean in and kiss his mouth, long and deep and desperately. My spirit and soul and every drop of blood coursing through my veins cries out, *Love him!*

And with all of my being, I beg my heart to obey.

The spring daffodils fade, leaving a path of daisies in their wake. Summer's pace slows and I drink in every moment with Austin. I trade my heels and skirts for flip-flops and sundresses, and my three-mile runs become lazy strolls behind a baby buggy. Lucky for me, my daughter's a happy girl, and with the exception of a few bouts of sneezing, she's remarkably healthy. When I read and sing and talk to her, she listens, wide-eyed and focused, and I swear I see Sanquita in her curious little face. I've started a journal for Austin, pointing out their similarities and recording every detail I remember about the brave, beautiful woman who gave her — and me — life.

In honor of Austin's three-month birthday, I breeze down the familiar hallway toward the neonatal unit, my daughter snug against my chest in her Moby Wrap. LaDonna spots us from a distance and leaps from her perch behind the desk.

"Brett!" She throws her arms around me then peers into the sling. "Oh, my goodness, Austin Elizabeth! We've missed you so much!"

I kiss my baby's forehead. "We've missed you all, too." I lift Austin from the wrap and LaDonna takes her.

"Hello, cutie pie," she says, holding the baby out in front of her. Austin kicks her feet and coos. "Look how big you are!"

"Eight pounds, one ounce," I say, grinning. "We just came from Dr. McGlew's office. She's a picture of health."

LaDonna kisses her forehead. "That's wonderful."

I hold out a plate of cookies and a card, stamped in purple with Austin's footprint. "We made you some goodies for taking such good care of us all those weeks."

"Aw, Brett, thank you. You can put them on the counter. They'll be gone by the end of the day." I feel her eyes on me as I place the cookies on the nurses' station. "Motherhood suits you."

"Really? You like these dark circles under my eyes?" I laugh. "Honest to God, LaDonna, I have never been more exhausted in my life. Or more grateful." I glance down at the wonder I call my child. When she sees me, her face bursts with utter joy, like a blaze of sunshine, and I melt. "I say a prayer of thanks to Sanquita every day. Austin is the best thing that's ever happened to me," I say, my voice thick with emotion. "Ever."

LaDonna winks at me. "Good for you. Now, come sit down. Maureen and Kathy just left for break. They'll want to see the baby."

"We can't stay." I glance at the clock behind her desk. "We're on dinner duty tonight at Joshua House. But we'll be back another time."

"Well, before you leave, you have to tell me what's happening. Have you and Dr. Moyer gotten engaged yet?" She raises her eyebrows mischievously. "You know, every nurse up here had a bit of a crush on Hubert."

"Herbert," I correct her. "He was pushing for a small ceremony on August seventh, my mother's birthday, but it's too soon. For now, I just want to focus on this little pumpkin."

"Good move," LaDonna says.

I gaze down at my daughter. "It'll happen someday, of course. Herbert's wonderful with Austin. You should see them together."

She smiles and pats my hand. "Oh, Brett, I'm thrilled things worked out for you. The baby . . . your gorgeous beau. Your fairy godmother sure takes good care of you."

I think of my mother and Sanquita, and their roles in making my dreams come true. But that's only part of it . . .

"It's true, I'm incredibly lucky. But fairy godmothers can only do so much. I think we each hold the power to grant our own wishes. We just need to find the courage."

She smiles. "Well you've done it, girl. Good for you!"

A sinking feeling comes over me. Would my mother agree with LaDonna? Or am I giving up on the one thing she said I should never compromise on? Do I have the courage, this late in the game, to toss aside the prototypical Mr. Right in hopes of finding Mr. Absolutely Right? Or is that courage at all? Maybe it's stupidity, or immaturity. Just where is that line between courage and arrogance, between wanting what's right, and expecting more than we deserve?

After thirty minutes of gathering supplies, performing a last-minute diaper change, and packing my baby girl into her stroller, we're finally out the door. What did I possibly do with all the extra time before I became a mother?

Unlike most July scorchers, today's sky is overcast, and a gentle breeze tickles my bare arms. As we near Efebina's Café, I spy

Brad sitting under an umbrella table. He stands and greets me with a café con leche and a hug.

"How's my big girl?" he asks, lifting Austin from her stroller.

"Tell Uncle Brad how terrific you are, Austin. Tell him how you smile at your mommy."

"Are you a happy girl?" He coos and nuzzles Austin. With his free hand, he pulls an envelope from his pocket. Goal number seventeen.

"Fall in love," I mumble.

"Congratulations, B.B. Two months until September's deadline and you're right on track. It's time to move on and buy that horse and the house. You said Herbert's game, right?"

"Uh-huh."

Brad shifts closer to me. "Something wrong?"

"No. Nothing." I take my drowsy daughter from his arms and tuck her into her stroller. "Go ahead. Open it."

His gaze is laser-focused on me. "What is it about this one? You've always been raring to go when I offer an envelope. Last time I tried to open this, you wouldn't let me. What's going on?"

"Nothing. Open it."

He cocks his head in a way that tells me he's not buying it, but he opens the envelope nonetheless. He releases the folded pink page, sets it facedown on the table, and stares directly into my eyes.

"This is your last chance, B.B.," he says, gripping my arms. "If you aren't in love with Herbert, you need to tell me now."

My heart stammers. I stare back at him until I can no longer stand it. Four months of doubt and frustration rise to the surface. I plant my elbows on the table and drop my head in my hands. "I'm so screwed up, Brad. I thought I loved Andrew, the most self-absorbed man I've ever met. But for some reason I can't muster any depth of emotion for this great guy who'd do anything for me." I clutch two fistfuls of hair. "What's wrong with me, Midar? Am I still looking for someone I have to win over, like Charles?"

He tousles my hair. "Love is fickle. If we could choose who we fall in love with, do you think I'd choose a woman who lives two thousand miles away?"

"But Herbert is so good. He loves me. And he loves my baby. And he wants to marry me. What if I lose him? What if I never find anyone else who loves us the way he does? I could be alone forever, and Austin would be fatherless."

"That won't happen."

"You don't know that."

"I do. Your mother wouldn't have left the goal on your life list if you weren't able to accomplish it. She knows you'll meet someone."

I groan. "Now you sound as crazy as I do."

"I'm serious. It's occurred to me more than once that she's engineered some of these events."

"Well, if that's the case, maybe she engineered my relationship with Herbert. Maybe she guided him here to Chicago, into my brother's department, just so we'd meet and fall in love."

"I'm not feeling it."

"Why not?"

He gives me a wan smile. "Because you're not in love with him."

I look away. "But I should be. Maybe if I just try a little harder, give it a little more time . . ."

"Love is not an endurance test."

"But Herbert thinks we're meant to be together — and maybe we are." I sigh and rub my temples. "If only my mom would give me a sign. If only she'd send one huge, unmistakable signal telling me whether or not he's the one."

He stares at the folded letter on the table. "Shall we?"

The sight of the letter makes my heart leap. "I don't know. Would that be fair?"

"I think we can take a quick peek. Who knows? Maybe it'll shed some light on your feelings."

I let out a breath I didn't realize I'd been holding. "Okay. Go ahead."

Brad unfolds the letter and clears his throat.

"'Dear Brett,

"'I'm sorry, darling. This is not the man for you. You are not in love. Keep trying, my dear.'"

My mouth falls open and I let out a gasp of relief. "Oh, thank God!" I throw back my head and laugh. "She gave me my sign, Brad! My mother has spoken. I'm free!"

I feel Brad's eyes on me. He's no longer reading. He's folding the letter and sliding it back into its envelope. And where are his reading glasses? How was he able to read Mother's message without his glasses? My face falls.

"Oh, God. You made that up." I go to snatch the letter from him, but he holds it aloft.

"It doesn't matter now. You've got your answer."

"But he adores Austin. And he thinks we're going to be a family. He'll be crushed."

"You'd rather wait until he's on one knee, offering you a diamond ring?"

My stomach rumbles and I pinch the bridge of my nose. "No. Of course not." It takes me a minute before I'm able to lift my eyes to his. "I've got to break Herbert's heart, don't I?"

"Nobody said love was easy, kid." He stuffs the pink envelope into his shirt pocket. "We'll save this for another time," he says, patting his pocket. "I've got a feeling it'll be worth the wait."

My stomach is in knots as I wait for seven o'clock—and Herbert—to arrive. Just as I finish feeding Austin, the phone rings. I jump, hoping it's Herbert calling to cancel. But instead I hear Catherine's cool voice. She and Joad must be back from their week in Saint Bart. I put the phone on speaker and prop Austin on my shoulder.

"Welcome home," I say, patting Austin's back. "How was your trip?"

"Absolute perfection," she says. "The resort was an all-inclusive, I told you that, didn't I?"

"Yes, I think —"

"I'm telling you, Brett, we've never been so spoiled. We were able to choose from three five-star restaurants, all of which were divine. If it weren't for their state-of-the-art workout facility, I'd have gained ten pounds!" She laughs. "Our every need was met half an hour before we even knew we had it."

"Sounds wonderful," I say cheerfully, but inside I'm smacked with an image of my own all-inclusive — Hotel Herbert, asking if I need anything, wondering if there's anything he can do for me.

"It was. In fact, it was one of the best resorts we've visited, and we've stayed in some pretty spectacular places. You and Herbert really should go sometime. You'd have to be insane not to fall in love with this place."

A cramp seizes my stomach. I'm insane to break up with Herbert! Any normal person could love him.

Suddenly my mind shifts back to a time nearly thirteen years ago, when my mother and I were in Puerto Vallarta. She took me to the Mexican port town to celebrate my graduation from Northwestern. It was the first time either of us had stayed at an all-inclusive resort. And just like Catherine's experience, Grand Palladium Vallarta was a glimpse of heaven. A full-service day spa, three infinity pools, and more gourmet meals and umbrella drinks than we could possibly consume. But by the third day, I was desperate to escape. I felt horrible for not loving the manufactured paradise. It must have cost my mother a fortune.

She'd be devastated if she knew what an ungrateful daughter she'd raised.

But that afternoon, when the pool attendant asked us for the tenth time if we wanted another drink, or a dry towel, or a spritz of cool water, my mother shook her head. Ever the clairvoyant, I could swear she read my mind.

"Gracias, Fernando, but we don't need a thing. No need to check on us again."

She smiled graciously until he was out of earshot, then she turned to me. "I'm sorry, darling, but I'm going *loco* in this paradise."

To this day, I'm not sure whether she was being truthful, or if she claimed to be going crazy for my sake. Regardless, I nearly fell off my chaise laughing.

We ran up to our room then, giggling as we threw on sundresses and sandals. We took a rickety old bus to Viejo Vallarta — old town — and haggled with area vendors at the *mercado*. Later we stumbled upon a local joint. A mariachi band, dressed in silver-studded suits and sombreros, played on a dusty wooden platform. My mother and I sat at the bar drinking *cerveza*, yelling out with the band and the local patrons at each interlude. It was the best night of our trip.

The doorbell rings and my heart skips a beat. "Sorry, Catherine, Herbert's here. Glad you're back. Give Joad my love."

I walk to the door with Austin in my arms, grateful for the beautiful memory stirred by Catherine's call. Is it possible there are two types of people, those who adore all-inclusive resorts and those who find them stifling? And maybe, just maybe, those of us who consider 24/7 pampering oppressive aren't ungrateful fools, after all.

I wait until Austin is asleep. When I tiptoe back into the living room, I see Herbert on the sofa, sipping a glass of Chardonnay and perusing one of my novels. My chest clamps. He looks up and smiles when he sees me.

"Mission accomplished?"

I cross my fingers. "So far, so good."

I sit down beside him and check out what he's reading. Of all my wonderful books, he's selected James Joyce's *Ulysses*, arguably the most difficult read in English literature. "That was mandatory reading for me back at Loyola Academy," I say. "God, I hated—"

"It's been years since I've read this," he interrupts. "I'd love to read it again. May I borrow it?"

"Keep it," I say.

I lift the book from his hands and place it on the coffee table. As if this were his cue, he leans in to kiss me. With the desperate longing that this time my breath will catch and I'll feel a flutter of butterflies in my stomach, I let him.

It doesn't. And I don't.

I draw back. Like ripping off a bandage, I let loose the words in one quick swoop. "Herbert I can't keep seeing you."

He lowers his face to mine. "What?"

Tears well in my eyes and I cover my trembling mouth. "I'm so sorry. I don't know what's wrong with me. You're a wonderful man. The best guy I've ever dated. But . . ."

"You don't love me." It's a statement, not a question.

"I'm not sure," I say softly. "And I can't risk your happiness, or mine, waiting to find out."

"You are not risking . . ." He stops midsentence and lifts his head to the ceiling, biting his lip.

I turn away and squeeze shut my eyes. What the hell am I doing? This man loves me. I should jump up now, laugh and tell him this was all a joke. But I'm cemented to the sofa and my mouth is sealed shut.

Finally, he pulls himself to his feet. He stares down at me, and

I can actually see his face shift from sadness to anger. He's suddenly strong . . . stronger than I've ever seen him.

"What the hell are you looking for, Brett? Another asshole, like your last boyfriend? Really? What is it you want?"

My heart quickens. My God, Herbert has balls, after all. I've never even heard him swear before . . . and I kind of like it. Maybe I was too hasty . . . Perhaps this would work if . . .

No. I've made my decision. I can't unbake this cake.

"I . . . I don't know." How can I tell him that I'm looking for something so special, when it happens I won't have to wonder whether I've found it?

"You need to think about this, Brett, because you're making a huge mistake. Deep inside, you know it. I won't be available forever. You need to figure this out before it's too late."

His words suck the air from my lungs. What if he really is the one, and I find out too late? I watch, stupefied, as he crosses the room and drags his Burberry coat from the closet. With one hand on the doorknob, he turns around and searches out my tear-soaked face.

"I truly loved you, Brett. And Austin, too. Give her a good-bye hug for me, will you?" With that, he steps out the door and pulls it shut behind him.

I burst into tears. What the hell have I done? Did I just let the man of my dreams — my beautiful Burberry man — walk away? I curl up in the chair next to the front window and gaze out at the dusty sky, as if searching for an answer, hidden somewhere out there in the dark abyss. Is my mother watching over me right now? What is she trying to tell me? I sit there until two A.M., second-guessing my decision and waiting to hear my mother's words, "There will be another sky, my love."

The words never come.

✦

CHAPTER THIRTY

*I*nstead of preparing the August 7 wedding that Herbert once suggested, I plan a party for what would have been my mother's sixty-third birthday. On Friday morning, Zoë and John arrive at O'Hare airport, an arrival scene much different from the one in Seattle. After months of talking nearly every day, we greet one another like the family we've become, sharing kisses and tears and bone-crushing hugs. John and I talk nonstop on the drive to Brad's office, while Zoë sits in the backseat gabbing to Austin Elizabeth.

"You my knees," she says, taking Austin's hand in hers.

"Niece," John corrects her, and the two of us chuckle. Then he turns to me, serious. "How would you feel if Austin were to call me Grandpa? Or Papa?"

I smile. "I'd love it."

"And Brett, you can call me Dad, you know."

My cup runneth over.

___

$\mathcal{M}$y dad grips Brad's hand, and the two men in my life finally meet. But Zoë is much more interested in the view of the city than she is in meeting Brad. She stands before the floor-to-ceiling window, utterly fascinated, and I settle in at the mahogany table, the same table where I sat, bitter and heartsick, almost a year ago. I thought my life had fractured that day, and in truth it had. But just like a fractured limb, it's stronger now, in those broken places that have healed.

While my dad settles in beside me, Brad moves to the window and squats down next to Zoë.

"Hey, Zoë, want to take a ride on the elevator with me? I'll show you an even cooler window."

Her eyes go wide and she looks to her dad for permission.

"Sure, sweetie, but could you wait just a minute? Mr. Midar's about to read a letter from Brett's mom."

Brad rises and shakes his head. "Not this one. You two read it together, alone. I think that's the way Elizabeth would want it." With Zoë's hand in his, he steps from the office and closes the door behind them.

I pull the letter from its envelope and place it on the table before us. My father covers my hand with his, and together, we read the letter in silence.

> *Dear Brett,*
>
> *Thirty-four years ago I made a promise — a promise I have forever regretted. I told Charles Bohlinger I would never reveal the secret of your conception. In return, he promised he'd raise you as his own. Whether or not he upheld his end of the bargain is debatable. But I believe I've kept my promise, even now.*
>
> *So many times I have longed to reveal the truth. You*

struggled so with your relationship with Charles. I begged him to let me tell you, but he was adamant. Whether guided by shame or by foolishness, I felt I owed him his dignity. And without knowledge of your father's whereabouts, I feared it would only confirm your feelings of paternal rejection.

I hope you'll find it in your heart to forgive me, and Charles as well. Please understand, it wasn't easy for him. Instead of seeing the goodness and beauty in you, you were a constant reminder of my infidelity. But to me, you were a gift, a joy, a rainbow after a wretched storm. God knows I didn't deserve it, but a piece of the man I loved had returned to me, and once again, music infused my soul.

You see, my world went silent during those weeks after your father left me. It wasn't until years later that I understood the chivalrous, selfless deed he'd executed on my behalf. I loved him so desperately I would have done anything to stay with him — even something that would have eventually bankrupted my soul. But he spared me, and I'm forever grateful.

Though I tried, I've never been able to locate your father. I hired someone once, after Charles and I divorced, but it was a fruitless search. Somehow, as I write this, I know with certainty that you will find him. And when you do, celebrate. Your father is an extraordinary man. And though I know an illicit affair is a selfish and cowardly act, to this day I still believe that what I felt for your father was love — pure and true and strong as a prairie wind.

You often asked me why I never had another relationship after Charles and I divorced. I'd smile and tell you there was no need. I'd already had the love of my life. And it was true.

Thank you for bridging two lives, my beautiful daughter. Your spirit, your kindness, all the good in you comes from

*your father. I thank him — and you — every day for showing
me what love is.*

Forever yours,
Mom

Astor Street is a flurry of activity Saturday afternoon. Mother
would have adored this day, a day of love past and present, of
friendship old and new, and of family — lost and found. Carrie
and her brood arrive at noon, followed soon after by her parents,
Mary and David. While Carrie, Stella, and I prepare lasagna for
fourteen, Mary and David sip drinks in the sunroom with Johnny,
laughing and telling stories of old times in Rogers Park. In her
swing by the window, Austin gnaws on a rubber fish, watching
Carrie's kids play hopscotch with Zoë in the courtyard out back.

It's four thirty when Carrie decides to make her flourless
chocolate cake. "If my timing's right, it'll still be warm when I
serve it."

"I'm already salivating," I say. "The mixing bowls are on the
baker's rack."

"I'll set the table," Stella says. She disappears into the dining
room then calls to me, "Where do you keep your table linens, Brett?"

"Oh, no!" I bat my forehead. "I forgot to pick up the linens from
the dry cleaners."

She hauls a stack of damask place mats and napkins into the
kitchen. "It's okay, I found some."

"No, we have to use the hand-embroidered Irish linens today.
Mom always used them for special occasions, and what's more
special than her birthday?" I check the time. "I'll be back in thirty
minutes."

Like August days should be, today is bright, with jumbo-sized cotton clouds dangling from an azure sky. Though the forecast calls for falling temperatures and thunderstorms, you wouldn't know it now. Humming "What a Wonderful World," I stroll down the sidewalk with my dog promenading before me, and my daughter snuggled against my chest in her BabyBjörn.

Outside Mauer's Dry Cleaners, a glamorous blonde sits on a bench, clutching a leash attached to a black Labrador. Rudy sniffs the docile dog, then gives it a head butt, hoping to drum up playtime.

"Behave, Rudy," I say, looping his leash around a wooden rung on the bench. I smile at the woman but she's yakking on her cell phone and seems not to notice.

Bells jingle when I enter Mauer's. It's almost five — nearly closing time. I step in line behind the only other customer in the place, a tall guy with dark, wavy hair. He's listening as the white-haired woman behind the counter chats away. My eyes bore into the back of his head. *Come on, already!* He laughs at something she says, and finally hands her his ticket. She shuffles over to a mechanized rack in search of his dry cleaning, and returns a moment later with his garment, covered in clear plastic.

"Here we go," she tells him. She hangs the garment on a metal rod.

I stare at it . . . then at the man . . . then back to the garment.

It's a Burberry trench coat.

"Looks good," he says.

I'm suddenly light-headed. Could this be the Burberry man? Nah, what are the odds?

He hands her some cash and lifts his coat.

"Thanks, Marilyn. Enjoy your weekend."

He spins around. Brown eyes flecked with gold land first on Austin. "Hey cutie," he says to her. She stares up at him for a moment before breaking into a grin. Laugh lines shoot like fireworks from the corners of his eyes and he turns his gaze to me. I watch his face go from confused, to quiet recognition.

"Hey," he says, pointing a finger at me. "You're the woman I used to run into all the time. I spilled coffee on your coat outside your apartment building. I saw you that morning when I was jogging." The soft undercurrent in his deep voice makes me feel like I'm reuniting with an old friend when, of course, I barely know him. "The last time I saw you we were at Chicago station. You were so mad you'd missed your train . . ." He shakes his head as if he's embarrassed. "You probably don't remember."

My heart beats in my temples. I'm tempted to confess it was *his* train I wanted to catch, but I simply say, "I remember."

He steps closer to me. "You do?"

"Uh-huh."

His face softens into a smile and he offers his hand. "I'm Garrett. Garrett Taylor."

I stare at him, mouth agape. "You . . . you're Dr. Taylor? The psychiatrist?"

He cocks his head. "Yeah?"

Time folds in on itself. That voice. Of course! Garrett Taylor is the Burberry man! He's not some old geezer. He's a gorgeous forty-something, with a nose that's a bit crooked and a visible scar along his jawbone — the most perfect face I've ever seen. A dozen hummingbirds let loose in my chest. I throw back my head and laugh, then take his outstretched hand.

"Garrett, it's me. Brett Bohlinger."

His eyes go wide. "Oh, my God! I can't believe it, Brett. I've thought about you so often. I wanted to call you but it just seemed . . ." He draws back, leaving his sentence dangling in the air.

"But you're supposed to be old," I say. "Your mother taught in a one-room schoolhouse. Your sisters are retired schoolteachers . . ."

He grins. "There's a nineteen-year gap between my sisters and me. I was what you might call a surprise."

A surprise, indeed.

"Do you live around here?" I ask.

"Just over on Goethe."

"I'm on Astor."

He laughs. "We live only blocks from each other."

"It's actually my mother's house. I moved to Pilsen last winter."

He offers his pinkie to Austin and she latches onto it. "And you've got a new baby." A trace of sadness colors his voice. "Congratulations."

"Meet Austin Elizabeth."

He runs a hand over her silky curls. But when he smiles, his eyes have lost their cheer.

"She's adorable." He looks at me. "You're happy now. I can see that."

"I am. Deliriously."

"You've made some progress on that life list. Good for you, Brett." He nods curtly and grips my arm. "I'm so glad we finally had a chance to meet. I wish you every happiness with your new family."

He's moving toward the door now. He thinks I'm married. I can't let him leave! What if I never see him again? His hand lands on the doorknob.

"Remember Sanquita?" I nearly shout. "My student with kidney disease?"

He turns around. "The girl in the shelter?"

I nod. "She died last spring. This was her child."

"I'm so sorry to hear that." He wades toward me. "So, Austin's adopted?"

"Yes, after weeks of paperwork, it became final just last week."

He smiles down at me. "She's a lucky baby."

We stare at each other until finally Marilyn calls to us from behind the counter. "I hate to break up your little reunion, but we're about to close."

"Oh, sorry." I scramble to the counter and dig into my pocket for my ticket. I hand it to her and turn to Garrett.

"Listen," I say, hoping he can't see my heart's frenetic dance through my flimsy T-shirt. "If you're not doing anything tonight, I'm having a little party, mostly family and a few friends. We're celebrating my mother's birthday. I'd love it if you could stop over — One Thirteen North Astor."

He looks genuinely disappointed. "I've already got a commitment tonight." His eyes dart to the window for a blunt millisecond, and my eyes follow. The blonde with the black Lab no longer yaks on her cell phone. She stands at the window peering in at us, probably wondering what's keeping her boyfriend . . . or husband.

"Oh, no problem," I say, feeling heat rise to my cheeks.

"I should scoot," Garrett says. "Looks like my dog's getting restless out there."

A dozen comebacks spring to mind, and they'd be hilarious if I weren't standing here utterly mortified, looking at a woman who's as far from dog-like as anyone could possibly be.

Marilyn returns to the counter with my linens. "Seventeen fifty," she tells me.

I fumble for my money, then glance back at Garrett. "It was great to meet you," I say, trying my damnedest to sound lighthearted. "Take good care."

"You too." He hesitates for the briefest moment before opening the door and stepping out.

The clouds have thickened, brushing the sky with swirls of amethyst and gray. I can almost see the rain huddled in the menacing clouds, planning its assault. I breathe in the fusty scent of the approaching storm and pick up my pace, hoping to make it home before the clouds burst.

I curse myself all the way home. Why, oh why, did I open my big mouth? He must think I'm a nut, asking him to an intimate family birthday party when I barely know him. How could I be so stupid? A guy like Garrett wouldn't be single. He's a gorgeous doctor — and a nice one, too. No wonder we were never able to connect all those times we tried. Mother probably threw those roadblocks in front of us, desperate to keep his unavailable body away from mine. Am I ever going to meet a nice guy? A nice guy who's single? One who'll love both Austin and me?

An image of Herbert Moyer barges in and takes lodge in my brain.

The house smells of sautéed garlic, and laughter and chatter drift from the kitchen. I unclip Rudy's leash and work to banish all thoughts of my mortifying encounter with Garrett Taylor. It's Mother's birthday celebration, and I refuse to let anything ruin it.

Brad rushes in from the living room and takes the linens from my hand. "Jenna just called. Her flight arrived on time and she's on her way."

"Hooray! We're all here." I pull Austin from her front pack, then turn so Brad can unhook the BabyBjörn.

"And Zoë was just telling me about her horse, Pluto." He peers in at me over my shoulder. "According to your dad, some anonymous donor gave the Nelson Center a significant endowment to reinstate their therapeutic horseback riding program." He leans in and whispers in my ear, "What did you sell this time, B.B.? Another Rolex?"

"Actually, I took some money out of my retirement. Zoë's horseback program is worth the tax penalty."

"Well, congratulations. Goal number fourteen is in the bag — the feed bag!" He busts out laughing and I can't resist a smile.

"You are such a loser."

"No, the only loser in this story is Lady Lulu. Remember Lulu, the horse at the animal shelter Gillian wanted us to rescue?" He shakes his head and wipes an imaginary tear from his eye. "Poor ol' Lu's probably on her way to the glue factory as we speak."

"She is not. Lulu found herself a good home months ago."

"Wait. You actually followed up on Lady Lulu?"

I shrug. "Don't give me too much credit. You have no idea how relieved I was to find out she'd been adopted."

He laughs and lifts his hand for a high five. "I'm impressed, kid. That's another goal knocked off. You're almost there."

"Yeah, except for the very hardest one." My wounded ego flares and I shake my head. "Time's running out, Brad. I have one month to fall in love."

"Look, I've been thinking about this. You're in love with Austin, right? I mean, couldn't that be the *heart-stopping, I'd die for you* kind of love your mother was talking about?"

I gaze at the face of a baby I'd gladly die for. If I say yes, I'll get envelope number seventeen. I'll buy my mother's house and every last goal will be accomplished, right on schedule. Austin and I will get our inheritance and our futures will be secure.

I open my mouth to tell Brad yes, but I stop when a flash of the fourteen-year-old appears in my mind's eye, her wistful eyes begging me not to abandon her lifelong dream. I hear my mother's words, *Love is the one thing on which you should never compromise.*

I punch Brad's arm. "Gee, thanks for the vote of confidence, Midar."

"No, I'm just —"

I smile. "I know. You're just trying to help. And I appreciate it. But I'm going to finish this list, no matter how long it takes. It isn't about the inheritance anymore. I can't disappoint Mother — or that girl I once knew." I kiss the top of Austin's downy head. "We'll be fine, with or without our millions."

The lasagna is golden brown and bubbling. Mary places a silver bowl brimming with hydrangeas in the center of the dining room table, elegantly set with Mother's embroidered linens. Catherine lights the candles, and I dim the lights. The room takes on the lavender hue of the approaching storm. If Mother were here she'd clasp her hands and say, "Oh, darling, it's lovely!" I'm filled with pride, and a sudden, desperate longing for the woman I lost.

A crack of thunder startles me from my reverie, immediately followed by the sound of rain pummeling the windowpanes. Outside the window, Mother's oak tree sways with fury. I rub the gooseflesh from my arms.

"Dinner's ready," I announce.

I watch the people I love, the people who love me and love my mother, gather around her beautiful mahogany table. Jay pulls out a chair for Shelley, and as she goes to sit, he kisses the back of her neck. Shelley blushes when she realizes I saw the little act of affection, and I give her a wink of approval. Carrie and her family take up one side of the table, her children arguing over who gets to sit beside Zoë. Brad and Jenna claim the chairs next to Shelley, chatting about Jenna's flight. I take my dad's hand and lead him to the head of the table, right where he belongs. Mary and David slide in next to Joad. Beside him, my beautiful daughter dreams, nestled against her aunt Catherine's chest. I hear Joad suggest she lay Austin down while we eat, but Catherine won't hear of it. I catch Catherine's eye and we smile, the smile of two very different women with a common love.

At last, when everyone is settled, I take my place at the head of the table, opposite my father.

"I'd like to propose a toast," I say, lifting my wineglass. "To Elizabeth Bohlinger, the extraordinary woman some of us called Mother . . ." My throat seizes and I can't speak.

"Others called friend," David fills in, nodding at me and raising his glass.

"One called lover," John says, his voice thick with emotion.

"Some called boss," Catherine adds. We laugh then.

"And three will forever call Grandmother," Jay finishes.

My eyes land on Trevor and Emma, then move to Austin.

"To Elizabeth," I say, "the remarkable woman who touched each of our lives so profoundly."

We're clinking glasses when the doorbell rings. Trevor leaps from his booster seat and races Rudy to the foyer.

"Tell whoever it is we're eating," Joad calls.

"That's right," Catherine says, gazing down at the sleeping bundle in her arms. "Little Austin doesn't want to be disturbed during the dinner hour."

We're passing dishes when Trevor returns to the table. I add salad to Zoë's plate and glance at my nephew. "Who was it, honey?"

"Dr. Someone," Trevor says. "I told him go away."

"Dr. Moyer?" Jay asks.

"Uh-huh," Trevor says, tearing into a breadstick.

Jay cranes his neck and peers out the rain-soaked window. "Well, what do you know, Herbert's here!" He bolts from the table, nearly upending his chair, then pauses and turns to me. "Did you invite him?"

"No," I say, pushing back my chair and tossing aside my napkin. "But we've got plenty of food. You sit down, Jay. I'll invite him in."

During the twenty seconds it takes me to reach the front door, my mind skips and trips and stumbles over itself. My God, Herbert's back, on what could have been our wedding day. Is this a sign from Mother? Perhaps she didn't like the idea of Austin and me moving through life as a twosome. She wants me to give him another chance. And maybe this time she'll make sure the magic catches.

A gust of wind knocks the breath from me when I open the door. From the back courtyard, I hear the clashing of Mother's wind chimes. Craning my neck, I peer out at an empty porch. My hair flies in every direction and I harness it in my fist. Where did he go? Slashing rain stings my face like little zaps of electricity and I squint into the downpour. Finally, I edge back into the house. Just as I go to close the door, I see him. He's crossing the street under a big, black umbrella.

"Herbert!"

He wheels around. He's wearing his Burberry coat, clutching a bouquet of wildflowers. My hand flies to my mouth and I step outside, into the fury of the tempest. Through the pelting downpour, I see his beautiful smile.

Without wasting a second, I race down the porch steps. The rain drowns my silk blouse, but I don't care.

He runs toward me, laughing. When we meet, he lifts his umbrella to shelter me, pulling me in so close I can see a fresh knick from shaving on his chin.

"What are you doing here?" I ask.

Garrett Taylor smiles and holds out the weatherworn flowers to me. "I canceled my plans. I didn't postpone them. I didn't take a rain check. I canceled them. Permanently."

My heart dances and I bury my nose in a bright orange poppy. "You didn't have to do that."

"Yes. I did." He gazes down at me and gently tucks a lock of wet hair behind my ear. "I refuse to let another meeting pass us by. I couldn't wait one more day, or one more hour or minute, without telling you that I've missed you, the funny teacher I laughed with and got to know on the telephone. I need to tell you now, while I have the chance, that I had a huge crush on that beautiful girl I saw on the El, and at the apartment building, and on the jogging path."

He smiles and grazes his thumb across my cheek. "So you see, when I met you today, and the two of you merged, I had to come here tonight." His voice is husky, and he locks his gaze on mine. "Because I couldn't bear the thought of one day waking up, and finding that my train had pulled out of the station, and the woman of my dreams was left standing on the platform, waving good-bye."

I step into his arms and it feels like I'm returning to a place I've been missing my whole life. "It was you I was hoping to catch," I whisper against his chest. "Not that train."

He draws back and lifts my chin with his index finger, then lowers his head and kisses me, long and slow and teasingly delicious.

"Consider me caught," he says, smiling down at me.

With one hand clutching the flowers and the other holding Garrett's, we climb the steps to my mom's house huddled beneath his black umbrella.

As I go to close the door behind us, I look up at the sky. A crack of lightning cuts a swath through the murky heavens. If my mother were here, she'd pat my hand and tell me there would be another sky.

I'd tell her I like this one, storm clouds and all.

EPILOGUE

I stand at my dresser mirror, in the very room my mother once called hers. It's different now, with pieces of my new life scattered about, but still it smells of her, and her memory greets me each time I enter. Funny how places become people, how this house and her old iron bed still pull me in and offer comfort when I need it. But unlike those forlorn days nearly two years ago, my need for comfort is rare now.

I fasten the clasp of my pearl necklace. From the nursery down the hall — my old bedroom — I hear my daughter screech with laughter. I smile and check my face one last time. Suddenly, in the mirror's reflection, my life appears. I spin around and the gates of heaven swing open.

"Who's got my big girl?" I ask Austin.

"Dada," she says, looking delicious in her ruffled party dress and polka-dot headband.

Garrett kisses her cheek and points to me. "Look at Mommy's pretty white dress. Isn't she beautiful?"

She giggles and buries her face in his neck. Smart baby. I'd nuzzle that neck, too, clean-shaven and tan, set against a crisp white shirt and black suit.

He reaches out his hand to me. "Today's the day. Are you nervous?"

"Not at all. Just excited."

"Same here." He bends down and his lips graze my ear. "Nobody deserves to be as happy as I am. Nobody."

My body erupts in gooseflesh.

We're nearly to the car when I realize I've forgotten the programs for the ceremony. While Garrett secures Austin into her car seat, I run back inside.

The house is quiet now, none of Austin's prattle or Garrett's hearty laughter. I find the pamphlets on the coffee table, just where I'd left them. As I turn to leave, I notice my mother's photo. Her eyes twinkle, as if she's pleased with what I'm about to do. And I think she would be.

"Wish me luck, Mom," I whisper.

I lift a pink program from atop the stack and place it beside her picture.

Sunday, the Seventh of August

One o'clock in the Afternoon

Ribbon Cutting Ceremony

Sanquita House

749 Ulysses Avenue

Chicago's Newest Shelter for Women

with Children

I close the door behind me and dash to the car, where my fortune awaits — the *heart-stopping, I'd die for you* loves of my life, my husband and our baby girl.

ACKNOWLEDGMENTS

Never before have the words "thank you" felt so inadequate. But until someone coins a better phrase, the simple platitude must suffice.

Thank you to my extraordinary agent, Jenny Bent, for taking a chance on an unknown writer from the Midwest and making her dreams come true. My praise to Nicole Steen for keeping track of the business side of things. Many thanks to Carrie Hannigan and Andrea Barzvi, who also believed in *The Life List*. A huge debt of gratitude to Brandy Rivers of The Gersh Agency, along with a multitude of foreign rights agents and editors, for taking this novel to places I never imagined.

My deepest appreciation and admiration to my fantastic editor, Shauna Summers, her uber-efficient assistant, Sarah Murphy, and the entire team at the Random House Publishing Group. Their expertise is surpassed only by their kindess.

Special thanks to my first reader, my dear mother, who left me such an enthusiastic voice mail after reading the book that I refused to erase it for six months. My eternal gratitude to my dad, whose unwavering pride and steadfast belief gave me the courage to persevere. To my early and most avid reader, my aunt Jackie Moyer, for her top-notch feedback and advice.

Friedrich Nietzsche once said, "A good writer possesses not only his own spirit but also the spirit of his friends." This book embodies the spirit of my friends, and I'm especially grateful to those who offered to read my manuscript long before I was an "author." To my wonderful friend and fellow writer, Amy Bailey-Olle, who always knew the exact word or phrase to make the story better. To my fabulous friends Sherri Bryans Baker and Cindy Weatherby Tousignaut, for making me feel like I might actually have something with this book. To my dear friend and the wildly talented author, Kelly O'Connor McNees, for her generous feedback, guidance, and inspiration along this wonderful journey. To the very special Pat Coscia, whose enthusiasm was unparalleled. To Lee Vernasco, at ninety-two my oldest reader — and the most spirited. What an inspiration you are! To the lovely Nancy Schertzing, for offering up her bright and beautiful daughters as readers. Claire and Catherine, your editorial notes were some of the best I received. Thank you.

A shout-out to the gals at Salon Meridian: Joni, Carleana, and Megan in particular, for passing around the manuscript and making me feel like a writer. To Michelle Burnett, for telling Bill she had to rush home from work to continue reading my story. Love that! To the magnificent Erin Brown, whose editorial service was the best investment I ever made. To the extraordinary writing instructors in my life, Linda Peckham and Dennis Hinrichsen, without whom there would be no novel. Thank you to my writer's group, Lee Reeves and Steve Rall, whose talent far exceeds mine. And a wink to the heavens for our late member, Ed Noonan, who would have enjoyed this moment. Special thanks to Maureen Dillon and Kathy Marble, who patiently educated me on caring for a preemie and life in the NICU.

I offer my deepest gratitude to my wonderful husband, Bill. Your pride and love and support make my heart sing. This journey would mean nothing without you.

My humble thanks to the gods and goddesses, angels and saints for answering my prayers, and to each and every person who has ever shown interest in my writing. I'd list you here, but I'm afraid I'd leave someone out. You know who you are, and I love you for it. And I thank you, my dear reader, for allowing me into your life, whether for a day or a week or a month. I'm honored to share my words and world with you.

Finally, this book belongs to every girl and woman who sees the word "dream" and thinks verb, not noun.

ABOUT THE TYPE

This book was set in Minion, a 1990 Adobe Originals typeface by Robert Slimbach. Minion is inspired by classical, old-style typefaces of the late Renaissance, a period of elegant, beautiful, and highly readable type designs. Created primarily for text setting, Minion combines the aesthetic and functional qualities that make text type highly readable with the versatility of digital technology.

Learn Love in a Week

Andrew Clover

'The funniest book I've read about relationships in years' Lisa Jewell

After ten years of marriage, Polly and Arthur are at crisis point.

Polly
'Arthur is the IKEA wardrobe of husbands. He looks good in the pictures, but if you ask him to hold anything, his back pops out.'

Arthur
'I have the libido of the Giant Panda. I know what sex leads to. It leads to a small person who likes to post toast in the DVD player.'

Can they learn to love again? And if they can, will they still choose each other?

'The kind of book that draws looks from strangers as it will have you laughing so much. Also a saucy modern fable about thwarted dreams and working out what is really important' *Daily Express*

arrow books

Before I Met You

Lisa Jewell

London, 1920. Arlette works in Liberty by day, and by night is caughty up in a glamorous whirl of parties, clubs, cocktails and jazz. But when tragedy strikes she flees the city, never to return.

Over half a century later, in the grungy mid-'90s, her graddaughter Betty arrives in London.

She can't wait to begin her new life. But before she can do so, she must find the mysterious woman named in her grandmother's will.

What she doesn't know is that her search will uncover the heartbreaking secret that changed her grandmother's life, and might also change hers for ever...

'So good I practically inhaled it'
Daily Mail

'Heartbreakingly Good'
Marie Claire

arrow books

The Reunion

Amy Silver

They thought they'd be friends forever...

Jen and Conor, Andrew and Lilah, Natalie and Dan were inseparable at university until a terrible accident changed all their lives. It's been years since they were all together, but now, nearly two decades later, Jen has invited everyone to her house in the French Alps. The house where they spent one golden summer together before tragedy tore them apart.

But it's not the happy reunion Jen had hoped for, and when a snowstorm descends, they find themselves trapped and forced to confront their unresolved issues, frustrated passions and broken friendships. As relationships shift and marriages flounder, the truth about what really happened years before is slowly revealed. And Jen realises that perhaps some wounds can never be healed...

arrow books

THE POWER OF READING

Visit the Random House website and get connected with information on all our books and authors

EXTRACTS from our recently published books and selected backlist titles

COMPETITIONS AND PRIZE DRAWS Win signed books, audiobooks and more

AUTHOR EVENTS Find out which of our authors are on tour and where you can meet them

LATEST NEWS on bestsellers, awards and new publications

MINISITES with exclusive special features dedicated to our authors and their titles

READING GROUPS Reading guides, special features and all the information you need for your reading group

LISTEN to extracts from the latest audiobook publications

WATCH video clips of interviews and readings with our authors

RANDOM HOUSE INFORMATION including advice for writers, job vacancies and all your general queries answered

Come home to Random House

www.randomhouse.co.uk